PENGUIN BOOKS

The Strings of Murder

Oscar de Muriel was born in Mexico City and moved to the UK to complete his PhD. He is a violinist, translator, chemist and author who now lives in Lancashire.

The Strings of Murder

OSCAR DE MURIEL

PENGUIN BOOKS

PENGUIN BOOKS

UK | USA | Canada | Ireland | Australia
India | New Zealand | South Africa

Penguin Books is part of the Penguin Random House group of companies
whose addresses can be found at global.penguinrandomhouse.com.

Penguin
Random House
UK

First published 2015

001

Copyright © Oscar de Muriel, 2015

The moral right of the author has been asserted

Set in 12.5/14.75pt Garamond MT Std
Typeset by Jouve (UK), Milton Keynes
Printed in Great Britain by Clays Ltd, St Ives plc

A CIP catalogue record for this book is available from the British Library

ISBN: 978–0–718–17982–3

www.greenpenguin.co.uk

MIX
Paper from
responsible sources
FSC® C018179

Penguin Random House is committed to a
sustainable future for our business, our readers
and our planet. This book is made from Forest
Stewardship Council® certified paper.

The first one is for the Torcacitas

Oh, that I could find myself for one short day a partaker of the secret arts of the Gods, a God myself, in the sight and hearing of enraptured humanity; and, having learned the mystery of the lyre of Orpheus, or secured within my violin a siren, thereby benefit mortals to my own glory!

Madame Blavatsky, *Nightmare Tales*

Prologue

23 June 1883

Dr Clouston could barely keep himself on the seat. The wheels of his carriage kept cracking over humps and puddles, breaking the night's silence as they rode frantically towards Dundee.

Throughout the journey he'd been bouncing and banging his head against the carriage's roof. However, the physical discomfort was nothing compared to his state of mind; the news he'd received was too dreadful, too monstrous to sink in, and Clouston struggled to keep the faintest spark of hope.

All he had read, he told himself, was a hasty telegram sent by the servant, and old George had always been prone to overreact. He searched his breast pocket and reached for the crumpled note; only a few smudgy lines, but they included the words *berserk*, *suddenly*, *dead*, and the names of every single member of the McGray family. How could such a little piece of paper carry such a horrifying message?

Clouston shuddered again. In vain he tried to divert his mind by looking through the windows, but the sky was shrouded with thick clouds that made the road dark like an endless abyss. In the last hours of the trip, he even found it preferable to focus his thoughts on the stumbling of the carriage and the slight nausea that it gave him.

At last, when he felt like he'd been travelling for ever, he saw the broad country house emerge. The early summer dawn was already throwing its first rays over the fields, but it was still dark enough for Clouston to see the dim glow of a fire through one of the house's windows.

The carriage had barely stopped when Clouston kicked the door open himself and jumped onto the muddy ground. The horses were neighing and snorting; that and the rattle of the hooves were the only sounds he could hear.

'What a cheerful sight,' he muttered. Thomas Clouston was a sturdy middle-aged man; for ten years he had been Physician Superintendent at Edinburgh's Royal Lunatic Asylum, and the post was not for the faint hearted.

He walked briskly towards the house and almost immediately somebody slammed the front door open. Two figures came out to greet him, and he instantly recognized the only servants who joined the McGrays on their summer trips: George and Betsy, both aged and hardened by the country work.

Their faces were lit by a single candle that the hunchbacked Betsy held with a steady hand. Once he drew closer, Clouston saw the hot wax dripping on her bare fingers.

'Good heavens, use a candle holder!'

' 'Tis all right, sir,' she replied with her thick Scottish accent.

'So good ye came, sir!' George said. There were swollen bags under his eyes and his thin grey hair was a mess. 'We didn't expect ye so soon. God bless! Do come in . . .'

In fact, Clouston had not stopped at all and was already past the doorframe. 'Where are they?' he urged.

The icy, darkened hall made him think of a crypt. Only a faint light came from the adjacent parlour, which was the one lit room Clouston had seen from the road. The door was ajar.

'We're keepin' them there,' George said in a whisper, as if he were afraid of waking *them* up.

Clouston gulped as Betsy slowly pushed the squeaking door and led him in. He saw that just one log burned pathetically in the fireplace, casting trembling shadows all around . . . and then his heart skipped a beat.

Right in front of the fire, silhouetted against the weak glow, there were two wooden coffins.

'Oh, my Lord . . .' Clouston let out. He drew closer with faltering feet, a chilling fear expanding in his chest.

Only when he peered over the open coffins did he believe what George had told him. The sight was so appalling that Clouston instinctively covered his mouth, repressing a sudden retch. For a moment his mind went blank, trying desperately to take in what he was seeing.

'So – when did – did it happen?' he finally uttered. It was hard to speak with that painful lump in his throat.

'Last night,' George said, his voice almost a moan. 'The undertaker got 'em ready two, three hours ago.'

Clouston nodded and took a deep breath. That always helped him. 'Was it you who sent for the undertaker?'

'Nae. The boy Adolphus did,' George replied, swiftly wiping the tears he could not repress any more. 'Och! The poor laddie . . . Dunno where he got the strength from; he called the undertaker, sorted out all the papers . . . he even bandaged himself after –'

Then George shuddered visibly and said no more.

'He's resting now,' Betsy added, 'if ye can call it rest . . .'

'I need to see him,' Clouston said promptly, and George and Betsy led him to a nearby studio – the one that had belonged to the now deceased father, James McGray.

Slowly, George opened the door, trying not to disturb his young master, and Betsy walked in bringing the candle – she had just stuck it in a filthy saucer. Clouston snatched the light from her and walked ahead with careful steps.

His heart sank even deeper as soon as he saw the miserable young man resting on a ragged couch. The tall, brawny son of the McGrays lay there looking as though he was also dead: his cheeks were ghastly pale and the rings around his eyes were almost as red as a wound. Young Adolphus inhaled in deep, painful breaths, and his pupils stirred madly under his eyelids. Occasionally, his chin and hands would jump in small spasms. Clouston had seen that sort of troubled slumber in more patients than he could remember, but he had not even dreamt he'd ever see McGray's son, otherwise handsome and cheerful, thus broken.

'I don't think he'll manage to sleep well ever again . . .' Clouston whispered. 'I do hope I'm wrong . . .'

Adolphus's hand had another spasm and then Clouston saw the bulky bandaging around it. He drew the candle nearer to find that the material was damp and stained, a dark spot of half-dried blood spreading on one end. It looked as though Adolphus had helped to carry the coffins himself.

'You need to change his bandaging,' Clouston snapped.

'Och, I'd rather not, sir,' Betsy said quickly. 'The poor laddie's not slept since it all happened. Only when the boxes arrived he dropped here —'

'Good woman, he needs clean bandages! The last thing your chap wants now is an infected hand!'

Betsy curtsied clumsily and left the room, groping about to find her way in the darkness. Clouston turned to George and asked the question whose answer he dreaded the most:

'Where is the girl?'

The butler's face lost what little colour it had left. 'We . . . we had to lock 'er up, Doctor. She's gone completely berserk!'

Clouston patted the man's shoulder. 'Do not feel guilty. You did what you had to.'

'But, sir . . .' George began weeping miserably, this time quivering from head to toe. The wrinkles in his face looked sore from frowning. 'Miss McGray! Our Miss McGray! Our wee lass . . .'

Betsy returned, bringing clean bandages and shedding copious tears. She hurried towards Adolphus, trying to conceal her grief.

Clouston knew that he had not yet faced the worst horror of the night. He followed George upstairs, where the sun, rising but still gloomy, lit a long corridor through a cracked window. All the rooms were shut, but the last door had a key stuck in the lock.

'How did you manage to get her in there?'

'Och, sir, we didn't! 'Twas two gardeners, the constable an' me, and we couldn't pin her down! Nae, she ran into her room herself. All we could do was lock her in once she got in there. Nobody could control her; ye saw what the lass did!'

Clouston shuddered merely from thinking of the bloody bandages Betsy was changing right then. Everything was as bad as George had painted it in his telegram after all.

As soon as Clouston stretched a hand to turn the key, George leaped to seize his arm.

'Will ye just go in? Just like that? Ah'm tellin' ye, sir, the lass is –'

Had it been any other man, Clouston would have simply pushed him aside, but instead he patted George's back and gently pulled his own hand away.

'Good George, I have dealt with very sad things in my career. Believe me, I can handle this.'

For a moment George would not move, until Clouston slowly began to turn the key. The old butler instantly backed off.

Clouston opened the door just enough to pass through, and a sudden gush of icy wind hit his face. Once inside, he closed the door behind him. As soon as he heard the click of the latch, he felt strangely vulnerable. The bedroom was so silent that the buzzing in his own ears became a persistent clamour.

The east-facing window was wide open, and the dreary, dawning sky was the first thing Clouston saw. Amidst the shadows, he found the slender figure of Amy McGray.

She was sitting on the bed, hunched and slowly rocking

backwards and forwards. Her white summer dress seemed to glow in the dim sunlight, and a glance at it was enough to tell him that the poor sixteen-year-old was beyond redemption. The soft, bright fabric was stained with blood, all over Amy's chest, belly and thighs.

Clouston gasped and stepped forward, thinking her injured, but halted at once when he saw that she was holding a knife, the blade glinting in the sun.

Clouston thought it must be the cleaver that Betsy used in the kitchen to cut through bones. The girl's thin, pale finger slowly caressed the blade. Her hands were smeared with dry blood that had begun to flake off.

Clouston felt like dropping to his knees to cry. This was the girl who had played the most beautiful carols last Christmas; the girl who still smiled excitedly at whisky fudge; the girl who could snatch a smile even from her grumpy father – *God rest his soul* – with only a playful hug. Her parents and brother called her Pansy because her wide, almost black eyes, framed by thick lashes, made her slightly resemble her mother's favourite flowers.

Right then, though, she looked more like a spectre than a blossom. She was looking intently at the cleaver with a sharp yet somehow absent stare. Clouston could not help thinking of an eerie porcelain doll, and had to summon the strength that more than twenty years of practice had given him. Again he inhaled deeply and walked closer. He extended his palm and only then did he notice how much he was trembling.

'Amy . . .' he said in his kindest manner, 'give me the knife . . .' She did not reply. 'Please, will you –'

Pansy moved, but only to turn her back to him. Her glassy eyes reflected the sun and Clouston noticed that she was dehydrated; she must not have eaten or drunk at all for almost two days. She kept caressing the blade slowly . . . so gently that she did not cut her tender skin.

Clouston walked a step closer, his heart pounding. He had to gulp twice before his voice came out.

'Pansy . . .' he whispered, resorting to the family nickname. 'Give me that, please. Betsy needs it in the kitchen.'

The rocking stopped. Pansy turned around and rose up on the bed, facing Clouston. The stare was not absent any more; the eyes, dark like wells, were burning with inexplicable rage.

'You think I'm mad . . .' she hissed, and then, slowly, lifted her arm, wielding the cleaver. Her pupils trembled, frenzy taking over.

Clouston did not retreat, not even when he saw the girl tensing her calves, ready to leap forward.

'Give me that,' he insisted, kindly but firmly. No patient had ever gotten their way with him yet. 'Betsy will clean you up . . . and we'll get you something to eat . . .'

'I'm not mad!' she muttered, her chest heaving, 'What's happened to me is much worse . . .'

There was a deep silence, just the rustle of the curtains moved by the morning breeze . . . and then she laughed. It was the most poisonous noise Clouston had ever heard from a human being; an otherworldly cackle that grew louder, stabbing his ears.

'What is it?' Clouston asked, standing his ground. 'I can help you!'

Pansy inhaled deeply and uttered the last words the world would ever hear from her:

''Tis the Devil . . .'

Then Pansy let out an anguished, piercing howl, and hurled herself onto the startled doctor.

I

Perhaps the best moment to begin my telling is the evening of 9 November 1888, the day when it all started to tumble down.

I had just received an urgent message from Commissioner Sir Charles Warren, the head of Scotland Yard, asking me to meet him in the first row of pews of St Paul's Cathedral.

The message was not that surprising, for we were living through days of upheaval. London was getting ready to celebrate the investiture of a new mayor, but the festive mood would soon be tarnished: I'd heard that, on that very morning, yet another murder had been perpetrated by Jack the Ripper, or at least the latest reports suggested so. I assumed that Warren's unusual summons must be related to that – I would be only partly wrong.

My carriage took me from the Scotland Yard headquarters to St Paul's in what seemed an unduly long time; it had been a rainy day, so the streets were covered in mud and the drivers had to move at a sluggish pace.

Through the windows I saw that the roads were bustling despite the hour and the relentless rain. Countless soaked umbrellas marched up and down the road, looking like black seashells gleaming under the yellow lights of the gas lamps.

I thought bitterly that this was no longer the town

where I had loved to spend wintertime in my childhood years. I now lived in a London crowded by ill-treated workers and seamen and scavengers, blackened by the smoke from the coal-devouring factories . . . and haunted by the Ripper and a thousand lesser rascals.

The cathedral's dome rose like an unyielding guard, its once white surface now blackened by the fumes of industry, and as gloomy as the darkened sky. Soon my driver halted in front of the long atrium. I walked past the white columns and went into the temple to find it utterly silent; my swift steps on the marble floor echoed throughout the nave.

St Paul's was usually bright and airy, its imposing arches extending in perfect symmetry under the light streaming through the stained glass. That day, however, the miserable November evening made the place look dim, even sinister.

There were only two people in the cathedral: a young sacristan lighting the candlesticks, and a dark figure seated right in front of the altar – the latter was, of course, Sir Charles Warren, crouching and clenching his hat with shaky hands. Anyone who'd seen him would have thought that he was a lonely mourner.

His white, thin hair and bushy moustache contrasted with his raven black suit. I recognized the old-fashioned cut of his jacket, as conservative as the chap himself. It was no secret that Sir Charles Warren was a quaint gentleman, strongly set in his ways, and thus highly criticized. His greatest fault was exerting full control over the police force, refusing any autonomy to the assistant commissioner or the superintendents. To make matters worse, he was also unable to delegate any duty he considered vital; no wonder he wanted to see me in person.

'I never knew you were a religious man,' I said, startling him though I spoke softly.

He looked up at me and straightened his back at once, casting me a cold stare.

'You are late, Frey.'

'The roads are impossible. I do apologize.' I had to reply with the same formality, even though Sir Charles and I had been close acquaintances for the past seven years.

There was an ominous air around him, an almost tangible wall that even our old friendship could not breach.

I sat at a prudent distance. 'What can I do for you, sir?'

Warren cleared his throat. 'Two terrible murders have taken place, Frey. The first, I am sure, you have heard of . . .'

'Indeed. Mary Jane Kelly, a Whitechapel woman again.'

Sir Charles shook his head. 'This last one was different, Frey. It was brutal – I mean shockingly so. The preliminary report from Dr Bond made me sick: her entrails were strewn all about. The scene was so terrible that one of our officers vomited on the spot, and a blasted correspondent from *The Times* saw it all. As we speak, I have some agents trying to – persuade him not to publish the story.'

I nodded briefly, as I knew the persuasion methods preferred by the CID. 'Is that the reason you called me? Do you want me to lend a helping hand on the Ripper's case?'

'Why, no . . .' Warren's expression became sombre. He kneaded his eyelids as he went on. 'This has happened at the worst possible time. I knew it would happen at some point, but not so soon . . .'

'What is it?'

Warren sighed deeply. 'I told you that there have been two killings. One was that Kelly woman . . . the other was an old chap, a musician, I hear. Apparently he was murdered most viciously . . . I think in Scotland.'

I frowned. 'Excuse me, sir, but why do you say you "think"? Is the report not trustworthy?'

'I have received no report, Frey. Hearsay is all I have had access to.'

I frowned harder. 'How can that be? You are the head of the police –'

And then it struck me.

Warren gulped and shook his creased cheeks. 'I am no longer, Frey. I have been forced to submit my resignation.'

'By whom?'

Warren exhaled wearily. 'By Lord Salisbury himself.'

The Prime Minister of Great Britain. The matter must be serious indeed, and within the next few seconds of silence a torrent of images came to my head.

The mayhem caused by Jack the Ripper had reached its peak and the state of fear had lasted for an unbearably long time. The press had become so obsessed with him that everything he did was exaggerated a thousand times, and the poor Londoners could talk of nothing else – only recently the headlines had referred to a forged letter written in fake blood.

I could picture the marquess storming into Warren's office, sick of the circumstances and demanding answers, only to discover that Scotland Yard was not even close to finding the murderer. Only a handful of suspects had been traced, each one as unlikely to be the perpetrator as the others.

Then I thought of this mysterious new murderer in Scotland. If even Sir Charles Warren had no access to the reports . . .

'From the fragments of information I can gather,' Warren said, 'I believe the government is afraid of an imitator of the Ripper emerging in Scotland . . . or even many imitators, anywhere in the land . . .'

'What do you think he is planning to –'

'That is not the most pressing matter, Frey. I called you to warn you.'

'Warn me?'

'Yes. Once I am ousted, they will transform Scotland Yard in a snap.'

'Is Monro taking charge?' I pronounced the name with acrimony, for I already knew the answer.

'Most certainly.'

James Monro was Scotland Yard's assistant commissioner, outranked only by Warren himself. Lately, the two men had found it almost impossible to work together, and it soon became evident that one of them would ultimately have to leave.

'Not only will the organization of the CID change, Frey. Heads will roll soon, and yours could be among them.'

For a moment I simply nodded in silence, pondering Warren's words. His long friendship with my late mother had played a vital part in my enrolment, and his connections with my family were well known to everyone. It was only natural that if he fell, all his peers and protégés would fall as well. The papers were still talking about my success in the case of Good Mary Brown, a tiny seamstress who'd poisoned her five husbands with arsenic after buying life assurance policies in their names; however, my dedication and talents would mean nothing when politics took over.

'Do you think I should fight them?' I asked, rather daringly.

'I would strongly advise you – not to.'

I blinked in confusion. I was expecting any other reply; any except that.

'Do I hear you aright? If they decide I serve no purpose, I am to step aside like a pusillanimous imbecile? After more than seven years of service?'

He looked hard at me. 'Yes, and you must, if you know what is best for you!' Warren had raised his voice and his echo lingered. 'The situation will bring out the worst of these people, Ian . . .' he whispered. 'You will be well advised not to cross them.'

Sir Charles would seldom call me by my given name. Deep inside I knew he was right. He was giving me his best advice, with decades of loyalty to my mother's family to back him up, and I should not discount it lightly.

Still, my mind struggled. It was no easy news to swallow.

'Then I should expect Commissioner Monro to summon me and give me some bad news very soon . . .' I sighed, and then smiled mockingly. 'Part of me looks forward to it, I must confess. Confronting him will be rather amusing . . .'

Warren rose to his feet, grunting at my dry humour. 'If

they ask for your resignation you must do as they say, do you understand? Do not believe that your name or your wit will do much for you this time. Everything will change now, Frey. Remember my words.'

He cast me one last stare. I could not tell whether the man was seething or on the verge of tears. Whichever it was, he preferred to conceal it, turning away hastily and heading to the cathedral's entrance.

I left St Paul's with gloomy thoughts haunting me.

As I said, it was family connections and a good deal of chance that brought me to Scotland Yard. I began my service directly after abandoning the faculties of medicine in Oxford and then law in Cambridge. My path felt unclear and there seemed to be few ambitions to spur me on. I could have remained at home living off my family's wealth – my two grandfathers bequeathed me generous bank accounts – but my unquiet brain soon became bored. More importantly, there was an inexplicable void in that life of leisure I could not accept; the thought of passing through this world like an unnoticed breeze, of a useless existence, was sometimes so unbearable I could not sleep. As succinctly (and rather condescendingly) put by my father, I needed to 'prove my value'.

Given my uncle's connection with Commissioner Warren, I soon found a post as an assistant inspector at Scotland Yard. A rather modest position for a former Oxford student, but it did not bother me greatly, for it was intended to be a temporary diversion. My knowledge of anatomy and law, though not thorough, could prove useful for the police, and the post would give me good reason to leave the house. The latter was by no means a minor consideration; I would have died after another week of hearing my stepmother's constant gossiping or my youngest brother Elgie playing the violin at the oddest hours.

The CID, however, trapped me and would never let me go.

Before I knew it I found myself working until well past midnight each night, studying files and solving what could only be described as multifaceted puzzles. A mark on the wall, the contents of a wallet, a lock of hair from a lost love, a glove carelessly left behind . . . those tiny details of everyday life, things that the ordinary man would never normally ponder on, were our tools, and most of the time sufficient to allow us to draw a full picture of victims and aggressors. Their lives and characters, their flaws, their passions and philosophies . . . in short, their innermost, darkest secrets were at hand if one knew just how to read the world around.

How thrilling, how fascinating that game was. Finally, I'd found my place. Proved my value. My enthusiasm had surely impressed Commissioner Warren, and over the years we had become close colleagues.

A miserable rain was now pouring over London, falling from thick, black clouds, so that the only light on the streets came from the gas lamps along the road. The carriage bumped on a pothole, taking me out of my thoughts for a second. The roads in central London were in dreadful disrepair – uneven, bumpy and usually flooded – and they became worse as we moved towards the small house I rented in Suffolk Street.

It is an odd thing indeed that I should call that place

home. Like my profession, it was meant to be only a provisional arrangement. I had begun renting the house four years earlier, when cases kept me locked in my office later and later at night. Being well aware of the depravity that reigned in London, the last thing I wanted was to wander around the city at night. I thus decided to rent rooms close to Whitehall Place, so that I could spend the night there when the job kept me late at Scotland Yard.

I would also go there to meditate and ponder on my cases, for I appreciate my privacy, especially when I need to concentrate. Of course I would not dare to present myself at the headquarters wearing an unironed shirt, so I moved part of my belongings there and of course had to hire a maid. Things went on and on that way, and before I knew it the small house had become my regular residence. Modest as it was, the place sometimes felt far more homely than the family pile in Hyde Park Gate.

As I arrived I was surprised to find light coming from the kitchen window, where I found Joan, my housekeeper, helping herself to ham and bread.

Joan was a stout widow in her mid forties. With her grey hair and her ample bosom and behind, she has always brought to mind a plump, overgrown pigeon. From the moment I hired her I knew that she had a tendency to be rather too outspoken, and I later discovered that she also had a weakness for cheap sherry, but still I could not complain; Joan kept the rooms impeccable, knew exactly how I liked my clothes, and prepared the most delightful black coffee. I had consciously turned a deaf ear to her foul mouth, even when I had guests, for it ensured no other employer would ever try to steal her from me.

'Why, Joan! Are you still here? Your punctuality to leave usually compensates for your unpunctuality to arrive.'

On any other day Joan would have retorted with some earthy banter, but to my bewilderment she only remained silent.

'Joan, what is the matter?'

'Letters for you, sir,' she said in her strong Lancashire accent. I saw her pointing at two small envelopes on the table, but she did not move.

I dreaded to look down at the letters, thinking that Warren's predictions had become true much sooner than I expected; however, even before picking up the letters I recognized the hands on the envelopes.

'A note from Eugenia and one from my brother . . .' I muttered suspiciously. Had anything been wrong with them they would have sent a servant to fetch me. 'Joan, these cannot be urgent enough to keep you here until close to midnight. Tell me what is wrong.'

She took a huge bite of ham on bread as if wishing to gather courage, and once she had swallowed it, said, 'Sir, is it true? Has there been another murder?'

I let out a weary sigh as I tore the first envelope open. I knew Joan would not desist until I told her the truth. 'I am afraid so, there was an attack last night.' I was still speaking as I began reading the note. It was not at all an urgent message: it was from Eugenia, my betrothed. She was simply keeping me up to date with inconsequential daily matters, and asking for the millionth time when I would have free time to call on her. I'd been neglecting her because of my work, and should soon make up for it. The second note was from Laurence, my eldest brother, reminding me of the family dinner the following evening.

My attention went back to Joan once I had finished reading. 'You did not wait here all this time just to confirm the news, did you?'

Then she finally let it out. 'No, Mr Frey. I . . . I forgot the days are getting shorter and 'twas dark before I knew it.'

I arched an eyebrow. 'Go on.'

'I know you'll think I'm a ninny, but going home at night, you know, with everything that's happening . . . I was thinking that there's some space in the storage room, sir. I thought I might stay there when it gets too dark . . . just 'til the police catch him. You won't notice I'm 'ere, I promise.'

I could hear my father's voice as if he were in the same room – *You are too bloody soft with the servants!* – but how could I refuse the poor woman's plea? Even I, a tall, armed police inspector of thirty-one, felt unsafe when walking the streets of the city alone.

'Please, Mr Frey. I can pay you for the room!' she cried. 'You can take it off me wages and –'

She was becoming so frantic I had to stop her.

'Joan, show some composure, for the love of God! Do you not know me at all? I was not going to ask you to pay rent. And stop talking about the damn pantry; there is a maid's room you may use as you see fit.' I looked at my pocket watch. 'It is very late, though. Tonight you may sleep in the guest room – but only tonight.' Elgie was in the habit of arriving unannounced to claim it, though even he would not come so late as this.

'Oh, thank you, Mr Frey . . . I . . .'

'All right, all right,' I said soothingly and hurried upstairs before Joan abandoned herself to improper weeping. Once composed, she prepared me a light supper and I asked her to polish my very muddy shoes before breakfast.

I retired to bed thinking of Commissioner Warren's words: 'Everything will change now . . .'

Agitated though I had been, I fell asleep as soon as my head touched the pillow. That would be the last good night's rest I'd have in a long time for, the next day, everything did change.

2

London on a November morning smelled of cesspools and stale alcohol from the pubs. I wrinkled my nose at the odours as I walked hastily towards Scotland Yard, dodging the half-frozen horse dung that peppered the streets.

Stench and turds were not the only foul thoughts in my head. While having breakfast I'd received a note from Wiggins, my assistant, urging me to go to headquarters. James Monro, the new commissioner, had demanded my immediate presence. I instantly knew that my career in the London police was over.

I'd not seen much of him, but the few times Monro and I had had to collaborate had been enough to fix my opinion of him: square-minded, prejudiced, religious to the point of fanaticism . . . and to cap it all, the man was from Edin-bloody-burgh – as my father likes to call it.

It is well acknowledged that any sensible English gentleman will unreservedly abhor anything Scottish, but my father is an extreme case. As a young man some failed businesses in Aberdeenshire lost him an amount of money so obscene that, for the rest of his life, he'd never again utter the name of any Scottish city, town, village or character without inserting some blood in between its consonants.

If I was to be dismissed, at least I would spare old

Mr Frey the disgrace of knowing that one of his heirs took orders from a Scotchman.

As usual, Scotland Yard was among the busiest spots in the Westminster area. Carriages brought and took people at all times, and a constant stream of officers and constables entered and left the red-brick building. Inside, the place felt equally cluttered, with people running to and fro like frantic ants, and my small office on the second storey was no exception. Files were piled to the ceiling and more than once Wiggins had been buried under an avalanche of paper. New, larger offices were being built at the Embankment, by Westminster Bridge, and I was looking forward to moving there. As I walked into my office I found Wiggins hunched over his usual pile of paperwork.

'Morning, sir,' he said with a shaky voice. I never quite understood the source of his shyness; the young man was educated and reliable, with a promising career ahead of him if he only managed to gather some self-confidence.

'So the new commissioner wants to see me,' I said, tossing my coat aside.

'Aye, sir.'

'Should I go to *his* office or Warren's?'

'Neither, sir. He wants to see you in the main hearing room –'

'*What!*'

Wiggins dropped his dipping pen and ink pot. 'The – the commissioner called for a cabinet meeting at ten o'clock, sir,' he said, as I helped him mop up the black ink, 'but he wants to see you in private before the chief bailiffs arrive.'

'Getting rid of me first thing in the morning . . . He

won't waste a bloody minute, the old man,' I grunted, leaving the office with huge strides.

I made haste and found the hearing room looking as gloomy as a grave. The place had wide windows but was dimly lit by a half-hidden sun so that, despite the hour, it seemed as though it was late in the evening.

There was only one man in the room: James Monro, a robust man in his fifties, with a square face, a grey moustache and white mutton chops of a hideous kind. I found him comfortably seated on the master chair, at such ease as if he'd been commissioner for years.

'I believe I must congratulate you . . . sir,' I said, making my best display of hypocrisy.

'Don't be ridiculous, Frey,' he replied. 'Have a seat. I have a great deal to tell you and very little time.'

I sat down and interlaced my fingers on the long table, waiting, but Monro kept his nose on the disarray of documents in front of him. I spoke only after the lapse of time that courtesy demanded: 'Excuse me, sir. You implied there was some urgency . . .'

Monro only lifted his index finger to silence me.

How he must be enjoying it! I thought, but all I could do was to remain in my seat, gnashing my teeth and hating his bristly mutton chops, his deviated nose and his stupid, bovine little eyes.

He finally spoke, looking at me with great severity.

'I will say it simple and straight. As you are aware, your friend Sir Charles has . . . resigned. Now that I am in charge, I plan to implement substantial changes, beginning with the dismissal of any superfluous elements retained only because of Warren's sentimental disposition.'

So this is how it ends, I thought, withdrawing my hands to clench my fists freely under the table.

'It is no secret that your position is overpaid and that you find it hard to cooperate with some of your colleagues. For instance, not long ago it came to my ears that you called Berry, the photographer, a . . . what was it? *Stinking piece of rancid mutton?*'

How could I have called the man anything better? Photography was immensely expensive, only used in extraordinary cases like the Whitechapel murders, yet that ham-fisted troglodyte treated the equipment with ludicrous disregard; he constantly broke the tripods of his Gandolfi camera, and his lenses and plates were always smeared with grease from his bacon-stuffed luncheons. I'd failed to compose myself when he handed me photographs of a crime scene scattered with dry pieces of half-chewed sausage.

I cleared my throat. 'I am aware that my reaction may have been regarded as . . . severe by some people; nevertheless, I am not in the habit of mistreating –'

Monro was casting me such a killing stare that I thought it better to save my comments.

'In brief,' he said, 'I cannot keep you in service.'

Just as Sir Charles had predicted . . .

Monro clearly planned to replace all the high officials whose allegiances were with Sir Charles Warren. His 'substantial changes' were simply an exercise to surround himself with allies and secure his own authority. It was all a pathetic game of politics; one that sadly would send my career to the cesspit.

'I understand you perfectly,' I managed to utter, not a single tremor in my voice.

'If you have nothing further to say I must ask you to leave. I am expecting a very important visitor at any moment and I don't want him to find you here. God knows I have grim news to tell him.'

I stood up and could not restrain myself. 'Is it about the musician slaughtered in Scotland?'

I could almost see the blood deserting Monro's face. 'What did you . . . how do you . . . ?' And then his skin went from ghostly pale to furious red. 'Are you trying to blackmail me, you pathetic little man?'

'Absolutely not!' I said impassively. 'Blackmail would imply that I needed something from you, and there will be ice in hell before a Frey of Magdeburg seeks the aid of a dirty Lothian dweller. Good da—'

At that instant the door slammed open and a short, plump man walked in briskly, wrapped in a heavy raincoat and followed by four guards and a young assistant. The man threw his coat aside and then I saw his round belly, bald head and bushy beard. I felt a twinge in the chest as I realized that it was none other than Lord Robert Cecil, Third Marquess of Salisbury and Prime Minister of the United Kingdom.

Monro stood up automatically, almost knocking over his big chair.

'Prime Minister,' Monro said lavishly. 'Welcome to our —'

'Keep the flattery to yourself,' snapped Salisbury as he walked past me. He cast me an irate stare. 'Who is this?'

Monro seemed paralysed. He opened his mouth twice but not a sound came out.

Seeing that he could not manage to speak, I bowed respectfully. 'Inspector Ian Frey, My Lord.'

'I was just dismissing him,' Monro jumped in. 'Inspector Frey was one of Warren's inner circle. I am sorry you had to –'

'Your face is familiar,' the prime minister said, ignoring Monro entirely. 'Are you not the detective who incarcerated the arsenic black widow?'

'Good Mary Brown,' I said at once, my chest swelling like a bellows. 'I am indeed, sir.'

There was an almost imperceptible change in Lord Salisbury's expression – I would have missed it had I not been standing so close to him. He held a firm stare for a moment, slowly arching an eyebrow, studying me. I could tell that a million thoughts were teeming in his head . . . and I did not like it.

'Leave us, Mr Frey,' he ordered, but in a tone notably less harsh than his first roar.

I bowed again and left the room immediately, with the acute stare of the prime minister imprinted in my head.

I still shudder a little when I think of that moment. Had Monro simply dismissed me as 'no one', or had I left the room but a minute earlier, the rest of my life would have been decidedly different.

3

It took me only a few hours to give Inspector Swanson a full account of the cases I'd been handling. My neat filing system was of great help, and when I left the office the man was digging confidently in the piles of documents.

Wiggins, who had been my assistant for over three years, could not hide his sorrow. I could tell he enjoyed his work with the police force almost as much as I did, and it angered me that I would not be able to see how his career progressed.

As I walked out of the room Wiggins tried to compose some farewell, but only managed to swallow painfully. I patted his shoulder and winked.

'I will be back, Wiggins,' I assured him, even though I did not maintain the faintest hope. Once outside, I hailed the first cab I saw.

I realized with utter dismay that I was suddenly free to attend my parents' dinner party . . . and to tell them the grim news. My father was not going to be amused, and my brother Laurence would surely make the most of it. I looked at my pocket watch and calculated that I would have enough time to go Suffolk Street, refresh my clothing and call the barber for that shave I had skipped. An unemployed castaway I might be, but never a scruffy one.

*

The Freys' mansion in Hyde Park Gate was not far from Kensington Gardens. The elegant house had an immaculate white-plastered façade, which glowed amidst the greyness of London as the carriage drove me into the wide, pristine lane. The maples were already losing their foliage, yet the street was kept immaculate by hard-working sweepers.

The carriage stopped in front of the three-storey house, where the butler was already waiting for me and promptly took my coat, hat and gloves.

I was greeted by dark oak panelling, green velvet carpets and the mansion's characteristic scent; a mixture of rosewater and fine tobacco, which always brought the warmest childhood memories to my head.

I went through a long corridor, decorated with portraits of twelve generations of Freys, going all the way back to the Protestant banker who had fled from Magdeburg in 1583. Despite the swings of fashion, the Frey men never liked to parade facial hair; not a single portrait showed moustaches or beards or mutton chops, and my father and three brothers, like me, were always cleanly shaven.

I could have stared at those paintings for hours – even though they have been on the wall since before I can remember, they still cast a strange spell on me. I can't help feeling proud of my family's history and achievements; although they cannot be called mine, they have always made me feel part of something larger than my own short life.

Suddenly, the echoes of a violin came to my ears. It was Elgie, my youngest brother, playing in the nearest drawing room.

It was a wide, airy room with large windows and a high ceiling. An exquisite tapestry depicting the figures of a dragon, a lion and a unicorn decorated one of the walls, and the others were occupied by Italian canvases depicting Mediterranean landscapes. Mahogany chairs and settees upholstered in velvet were evenly distributed over a Persian carpet, and a merry blaze crackled in the wide fireplace.

Standing in the centre of the room, his back to me, was my eighteen-year-old sibling. Despite the age difference, Elgie had always been my favourite brother. I had always thought him too thin and narrow-shouldered, and now, with his jacket removed in order to play more freely, his slender figure was all too obvious.

Sitting before him were my father and stepmother, listening enraptured as a footman stood ready with a tray of pâté and cold meats. They were about to greet me, but I lifted a hand, so that they remained silent until Elgie finished his piece.

I cursorily inspected the room while savouring the vivacious music. Only after a moment did I notice another young man seated close to the fire: my second youngest brother, Oliver.

I honestly wish I could say more about him, but Oliver is dullness made man. I remember that even as a baby he would lie still in his cradle, not crying, not playing and not even moving; just staring at nothing with his round blue eyes. As a boy he was not fond of running or hunting or riding horses. I expected him to show a more intellectual disposition, and for a long time I presented him with books, musical instruments and art materials. Long after my father gave up on him I was still taking him to museums, theatres and operas, but he did not seem interested in anything other than sitting around nibbling at biscuits. As a result he turned into a rather chubby young man with a rounded, pale face. That evening, settled a bit too close to the fireplace, his cheeks had gone terribly red, as if marked with circular branding irons. His face showed utter discomfort, yet I knew he would never change his seat.

Compared to Elgie – who was standing, thin and lively, playing his violin vigorously – it was almost impossible to believe they were brothers.

Unlike me, Elgie and Oliver have light hair and pale blue eyes, and are of rather weak constitutions. Our different physiques are only natural, for they are my half-brothers, sons of my father and his second wife.

Elgie concluded with a vigorous trill and the whole family applauded (Oliver rather lethargically). His musician's ear instantly perceived unexpected applause behind him and he turned to welcome me.

'Ian! I thought you'd be busy elsewhere!'

I grinned and patted his shoulder. 'Well, you are usually wrong, Elgie. That piece was wonderful, though. What is it called?'

'Paganini's 24th Caprice in A minor. You should recognize it by now.'

'How progressive. I thought you only played baroque music.'

After nodding a quick greeting to Oliver, I stepped forward to kiss the hand of my stepmother, Catherine.

'What a surprise, Ian. It is so good to see you.'

'And you, Catherine,' I replied with utter politeness.

I have always managed to conceal the contempt I feel for that woman. Catherine White married my father when I was nine years old, and even then I would only twist my mouth and treat her with a pretend deference.

At thirty-eight she still looked rather well. I always thought that her long neck seemed slightly tilted backward by the weight of her extravagant plaits. That stretched neck also gave her a proud look, highlighted by her total lack of humour – she always sat with the straightest back, her hands demurely folded on her lap and her fierce eyes evaluating everything.

My father, now an old man of sixty-five (and twenty-seven years older than his second wife), saluted me with little affection. He'd always been as distant a figure as the portraits on the walls. Even though he used to be a very refined gentleman, my father had recently begun to disregard his manners as well as his health. He had been gaining weight around his waist, and I cannot recall ever seeing him without a glass of some spirit in his hand. That evening he was holding a fat balloon of cognac, the corners of his mouth peppered with breadcrumbs. I was glad he still composed himself at larger parties.

'You could have told us that you were coming,' he grunted.

'There were some unexpected issues,' I replied, hoping to appear deferential but not servile in front of the old man. 'I trust I am still welcome.'

'But of course you are!' Catherine cried, trying, as usual, to smooth the edges. 'Your father is just a little troubled that you have not come to dine with us in *such a long while*.'

Conciliatory she might appear, but Catherine emphasized the precise words that would worsen my father's mood.

'Forsaking his family and good connections for that preposterous excuse of a job,' Father grumbled in a monotone. 'Your grandfather must be turning in his grave.'

How many times we'd had that discussion I cannot tell. I looked around, trying to find any way to change the subject.

'So where is my dearest Laurence?' I asked with sarcasm.

'Your brother had the *delicacy* to send a message,' Catherine told me. 'He is detained in Chancery Lane, but he *assured* us he would be here in time for dinner.'

'Which means he should be here within the next seven minutes,' I retorted, but almost as if I'd just called him, we heard the doorbell. Elgie went to the window.

'Speak of the Devil . . .'

While my stomach twisted, Catherine spoke cheerfully. 'How delightful! We shall have a full party for the first time in *months*.'

I blew inside my cheeks as I thought, *If only etiquette allowed me to kick a woman . . .*

A moment later Laurence stepped into the drawing room with his confident gait, the most elegant attire and holding a walking cane that he had no need of at all.

People have always remarked how alike we look. Laurence and I share the dark eyes and hair of our late mother Cecilia, a lady of French descent, and our long faces with narrow jaws and high cheekbones undeniably come from the late Monsieur Plantard, our grandfather on our mother's side. Until very recently we both had the same tall, rangy figure, but my brother's more sedentary job as a lawyer was giving him a thicker waist. We have been told that we share the same acute stare, but there is a permanent hint of mockery and condescension in Laurence that I sincerely hope I lack.

'Good evening, family!' he said in his deep, loud voice.

'We thought you would be detained,' Father said, smiling for the first time that evening. 'But it is good to have you here.'

Laurence poured himself a glass of cognac. 'I almost did not come, but some incredible news forced me, Father.' The corners of his mouth were slightly tilted in a scornful smile. I could see his attack coming. 'Ian,' he said, turning to me, 'I heard from James Swanson that you have been thrown out of Scotland Yard . . . in a quite shocking manner . . . Is that true?'

Catherine gasped, but that was the only noise besides the fire crackling. I felt the colour leaving my face.

'Why do you ask if you already know the answer?' I snapped.

'Dear Lord!' Father let out, covering his brow.

'Ian, it cannot be true,' said Catherine. 'Your father will be *so disappointed*!'

'I can see he is bloody disappointed!' I cried. 'He is sitting right next to you!'

'Do not speak to your stepmother like that!' Father roared. From the corner of my eye I saw Oliver crouching in his seat and Elgie gripping his violin with shaking hands. 'What disgrace you have brought upon the Freys!'

'Indeed,' Laurence said. 'And you have not heard the best part; the bit everybody is talking about. Your dear son was dismissed in front of Lord Salisbury himself!

Not content with that, he also called James Monro a dirty Lothian dweller.'

Catherine clasped my father's hand. 'Oh, Ian, pray, pray tell us it is not true.'

'I was not dismissed *right* in front of the prime minister . . .' I said warily. 'Rather a few seconds before he entered the room, and *then* Monro had to brief him.'

'How can you even joke about it?' Laurence hissed. 'Do you believe that any respectable institution . . . or person . . . will take you on after this? You should have never joined the CID if you lacked the stomach to –'

I hurled myself towards Laurence and seized him by the collar, my eyes blazing.

'*Ian, don't!*' Catherine yelled.

'Stop it, you imbecile!' I whispered to Laurence, soft enough for only him to hear. 'You would have cracked on your first week of duty.'

'Ian, let go of your brother! *Now!*' Father ordered, and I tossed Laurence away. 'What would people say if they knew that the Frey brothers jump on each other like wild cats?'

Then we heard the butler clearing his throat. He'd come to announce dinner a while ago, and had been looking at the scene in composed amusement.

'Very well,' said my father. 'We can discuss this over dinner.'

'I am not hungry,' I replied immediately, making my way to the door.

'Oh, but you should stay,' Elgie jumped in, pulling my arm, and then whispered in my ear. 'I have some big news too!'

I sighed in resignation. Somehow I could never say no to that rogue. 'Very well, I will stay. But I will sit next to you.'

We ate in an uncomfortable silence. Elgie, trying to ease the general mood, was telling us his funniest stories from the Lyceum Theatre, where he was a resident musician.

'. . . and then Mr Sullivan said we would all be impressed by how accomplished his niece is at the harpsichord – I had to bite my lip not to say that the harpsichord sounds like two skeletons copulating on a tin roof!'

'Elgie!' cried his mother, 'I will not have such foul language at the table! Neither will your father!'

The old man, however, was laughing under his napkin. Elgie saw the perfect moment to strike.

'Talking about Mr Sullivan, he composed a fantastic score for the new *Macbeth*. Mama heard it.'

'Oh, indeed. Mr Sullivan invited me to a rehearsal; marvellous music. It only annoys me that they'll have that old trollop Ellen Terry as Lady Macbeth. Then again, one does need a vixen for that part.'

'Being "The Scottish Play",' Elgie went on, 'they want to take it on tour to Edinburgh next summer . . .' His eyes fell on me, and I knew at once where he was going. 'The Scottish Theatre Company is short of musicians, so – well, they offered me a place there.'

Catherine and my father looked at him blankly, as if they had heard an unfinished sentence. Elgie had to spell it out for them, not a trace of humour in his face.

'I want to go.'

Their stares progressed from vacant to disturbed.

37

Catherine carefully put down her cutlery. 'Elgie, my dear, you cannot be serious.'

'I am. It is a great opportunity. I will be first violin!'

Father snorted. '*First violin in Scotland!* My, oh my, what an achievement! I'd rather you played third triangle in the bloody Whitechapel parish.'

'Father!'

'Think of the practicalities,' said Laurence, as condescending as always. 'Where would you stay? We have no relatives or acquaintances up there.'

'I could rent a room,' said Elgie, making his mother gasp. 'Well, Ian does it.'

I sank in my seat.

'We are not discussing Ian,' said my father. 'You are far too young to live on your own in a different country!'

Elgie let out the expected: 'I'm not too young, Father. I'm eighteen years old!' and then threw in some salt: 'Do you want me to live here for ever and become another Oliver?'

Catherine protested at that remark, but our dear brother was too engaged with his venison to take offence.

Father's voice came out low, in that ominous tone we'd all learned to fear in our childhoods. 'You are really irritating me now, Elgie. The entire matter is out of the question and I won't hear another word. Have you heard me?'

Elgie threw his napkin on the table and rose so quickly his chair fell backwards. As he stormed away he nearly collided with a servant who was coming in.

'He is beginning to show the Freys' temper,' said Laurence as his wine glass was refilled.

Catherine glared at me. 'This is your fault! See what an

example you've set for my child, leaving our house for your flea-ridden lodgings!'

I took a deep breath, and instead of arguing I looked at the servant, who had brought a letter on a silver tray. 'Yes?'

'There is a message for you, sir.'

'Perhaps they are offering you the post back!' Catherine ventured, sarcastic to her very core.

I took the note and recognized the hand of my dear fiancée.

'It is from Eugenia,' I said. My spirits lifted even more as I tore the envelope open.

Dearest Ian,

I have just looked for you in Suffolk Street. Your maid told me that you could be found at your parents' house. May I please speak with you this evening? I must see you. It is a matter of urgency. I shall wait for you all night if I must.

E.

'Well, delightful as the evening has been, I must leave!' I said with a triumphant grin. 'Eugenia needs to see me without delay.'

'I wonder what for . . .' Laurence mumbled.

Within a few minutes I was already in a carriage, heading happily to the Ferrars' house. All of a sudden the cool, fouled air of London felt surprisingly invigorating.

4

Eugenia was waiting for me in her parlour. When I walked in she was accompanied only by a young maid serving tea.

Seeing her waiting all by herself made me feel a wave of warmth. Everything in that face was sweet and beautiful; the wide blue eyes, the snow-white skin, the childish lips and the golden curls. That evening she was wearing a pink muslin dress, perfectly fitted to her tiny waist. A white kitten was playing on her lap, meowing as she caressed its bright fur. Suddenly all my quarrels and tribulations seemed a small price to pay for being with her.

Eugenia had only turned twenty a couple of months earlier, so I liked to think of her as a young girl whom I might spoil. Her frequent whims, and the way she wrinkled her nose and stamped her feet when cross only made her sweeter.

Reginald Ferrars, her father, was a much respected barrister in Chancery Lane. The man was a business associate of my brother Laurence, and would attend Catherine's parties quite frequently. I had met Eugenia for the first time at one such occasion, and it was not long before we were engaged.

'Good evening, my love,' I said with a grin. 'Why you are all alone? Is your father not at home?'

As I sat next to her, I thought of how frequently it was remarked what a nice couple we were: she was short, sweet and demure, I tall and protective.

'He is busy,' was all she said. Then I had the chance to study her face. The warm glow of the fireplace and the gaslight partly concealed how pale her cheeks really were. A tiny frown marked her pretty face.

'Eugenia . . . is there anything wrong?'

She waved a hand to dispatch both the maid who was serving tea and the one who had announced my arrival. The women left us alone at once, but Eugenia would not speak immediately. She ran her hand over the cat's back; it was only for a second, but a quiver of her fingers told me how anxious she was.

'Pray tell me what is wrong,' I said soothingly.

She fixed her eyes on her lap, inhaled deeply, swallowed, and then spoke hastily, as if the words burned her mouth and she had to spit them out.

'Ian, I cannot marry you.'

The kitten meowed and twisted in her nervous hands before jumping onto the floor. We both fell silent.

I was expecting her to say something else . . . *anything*. Despite the torrent of bad news I had received during the day, Eugenia was the first one to make me stammer.

'Wha – wha . . . Y-you're not serious!' I laughed nervously and looked for her hand. 'Eugenia, this has not been the best of days and I am not . . .'

As soon as my fingers touched hers she drew her hand away. 'Ian, I have never been more serious in my life. I am breaking our engagement.'

Then it was Eugenia who looked for my hand, but only to push a tasteful diamond ring onto my palm.

I stared at the shining gem while she looked for her cat. The five golden tips of a tiny maple leaf enveloped the perfectly cut diamond. I had commissioned that ring from Giuliano especially for her.

'So is that it?' I asked. 'What silly matter made you change like this all of a sudden? Have you heard of my dismissal? Is that what troubles you?'

'Oh, Ian, I did hear, but it is not that . . . It's –'

Again she could speak no more. I caressed her chin tenderly. 'Whatever is wrong you can tell me. You know I will understand. I promise.'

Sobbing, she managed to speak.

'I . . . I have received another proposal . . .'

'*You have what!*'

'A-and I . . . I have accepted.'

Her blue eyes, usually angelic, were unexpectedly glowing with sheer trenchancy. I blinked, inhaled, surveyed the room and only after a moment realized that the gears in my brain had stopped turning. Once the words had fully sunk in, my mouth exploded in a torrent of injured abuse that flowed freely like spurts of acid.

'You – you sharp-clawed, treacherous, little harpy!'

'*Ian!* You promised you would understand!'

'And you promised you would marry me, dear! We are not very good at keeping our word, it seems.'

'Ian –'

'My career and my professional reputation are possibly ruined for ever – perhaps even before the eyes of Lord Salisbury himself – *and now you tell me that you have accepted another bloody man's proposal!*'

Through the window I saw passers-by turn to peer inside, for my last sentence had been an open roar. I walked around in circles like a trapped lion, trying to control my rage.

'Ian, you should leave,' she said, her lip trembling.

Very soon I'd regret my shameful display, but at that moment I could not think.

'What about your honour?' I sputtered, not listening to her. 'What do you think people will say about you when they hear what you have done?'

'They will probably praise my good sense,' she snapped. 'Have you not just said it is *you* who has little honour left?'

I could take those words from anyone else, even from my father, but coming from her they were like knives.

'Please, Ian. *Go*,' she insisted.

On any other day I would have retorted, stayed and fought her until she regained her senses. My heart, however, had never felt so heavy. The preceding hours had drained my spirit and I was tired, too tired for even one more battle.

She was right in one thing: I'd better leave before I lost what little dignity I had left.

My fingers closed around the ring as I turned to the door. Before leaving the room I cast a last glance at my former sweetheart. She was holding the kitten, her eyes staring hard through the window, as if she were no longer there.

Despite my weariness, I managed to utter one last question. 'May I at least know the name of this noble gentleman who declares his love to an already engaged woman?'

Eugenia did not reply. She simply stood still by the window, the cat in her arms.

'On second thought . . . I do not want to know,' I whispered, and then left her.

She still had another very nasty surprise reserved for me, but it would take me a while to discover it.

That very morning, oblivious of what was coming upon me, I had had a prestigious job that kept me active and passionate, and a sweetheart who made me feel like I could fly . . . Overall, I'd had a bright future to think about . . . Yet before suppertime I had lost everything but my overblown pride.

I climbed the steps to my house and swiftly produced my keys.

'Jesus . . .' I mumbled.

The door was already unlocked; ajar, actually, allowing anybody to walk inside. I swallowed painfully and instinctively felt for my pistol, only to remember that I had unloaded the weapon in the afternoon since I was no longer on duty.

From outside it appeared that all the rooms were in darkness, so I decided to draw the gun anyway. At least I would not look defenceless.

I kicked the door open as I called in a loud voice. 'Joan!'

No reply.

The street lamps cast weak rays of yellow light into the entrance hall, just enough to illuminate the way for two or three yards. With cautious steps, I made my slow progress into the shadows.

I stopped for a moment, while my eyes grew accustomed to the darkness, and then my heart stopped as I made out the crouching figures of at least five men along the corridor.

I roared. '*Don't move, or else —*'

Then a cold hand grabbed me by the shoulder and I heard the door slamming mightily. I turned around, my heart pounding, and pointed my gun firmly at the broad shadow of a man. I could see only a pair of small eyes fixed on me, maliciously, as the intruder spoke.

'Come on, Frey, I know you have no bullets.'

5

I hesitated, feeling a drop of cold sweat rolling down my temple and hearing the men around me approaching. For a moment I could not believe my ears.

'Is that . . . Salisbury?'

The man sighed and lit a match. The little flame revealed a bushy beard and the most piercing stare; he indeed was Britain's prime minister. I lowered my gun immediately, utterly puzzled.

'Yes, Frey,' he said, lighting up the nearest oil lamp with the remainder of the match. 'Although it is *Lord* Salisbury to you, my man.'

I looked around and found that the other men in the house were the guards I had seen next to him that very morning – none of them was wearing uniform.

It was bizarre beyond expression, being suddenly forced to bow low to the man who had broken into my home. 'Of course. My apologies, but Your Lordship will surely understand my astonishment –'

'Why, I am the astonished one. I did not expect a senior inspector to occupy such small lodgings . . .' My father would have had a stroke had he heard the prime minister delivering such remarks.

'And keeping only one servant, who finishes her duties in the middle of the afternoon!' said another familiar voice – the last I would have expected to hear.

Walking into the light came the plump figure of Sir Charles Warren. I had to shake my head at the picture: two of the most prominent men in Britain, whom I thought would be the fiercest of enemies, were breaking into my home in a joint enterprise! The whole situation felt like an odd dream.

'Sir Charles!'

'We do understand how untoward this is,' he said, 'but we have to deal with the most urgent matter . . . urgent enough for us to lurk in the night like common thieves. Can we speak in private?'

I quickly examined Warren's face. His gaze did seem worried, and Lord Salisbury's lips were so tense that they looked like a twisted line.

'Follow me, please,' I said, leading the way to my small study.

The prime minister nodded at the officers and all the men remained behind. A few puzzled stares fell on me, telling me that they themselves ignored what was happening.

We entered my studio, and when I lit the desk lamp I found a note from Joan. Using preposterous spelling and nearly impenetrable dialect, she told me how the dark streets scared her out of her wits, and then apologized for leaving the house early. Surely she had read the descriptions of the last Ripper's murder with too much attention.

I crumpled the piece of paper and threw it aside. 'Have a seat, gentlemen.'

Sir Charles looked outside, making sure that the men were away, and then indicated that I could close the door.

Both men sat in front of my desk; Warren rather let himself fall onto the chair, his legs apparently exhausted.

'I will go straight to the point,' Lord Salisbury began, snorting and grunting in one of my armchairs like an uncomfortable bull. 'Sir Charles has told me that you know about the situation in Scotland. Is that correct?'

'The murdered musician? Yes, My Lord.'

'This is no ordinary murder. The man . . .' Salisbury seemed more and more uncomfortable. 'Do you have brandy? I decidedly need a drink.'

I drew my best bottle from a shelf and poured three measures. The PM gulped his down and shook his bulging cheeks, looking utterly invigorated.

'At least you do keep good spirits! As I was saying, the victim was an old virtuoso in Edinburgh – Guilleum Fontaine. I understand your family is versed in music, perhaps you have heard of him.'

'I have not,' I admitted, 'but perhaps my brother has.'

'Well, there is no apparent reason for his murder,' Sir Charles intervened. 'The man was a widower leading a peaceful life. He had been teaching in Scotland for the last thirty years and from what I've heard the he was praised among his peers.'

'But . . . ?'

'He was killed most viciously; throat cut open, then they ripped apart his belly and mutilated his innards.'

Lately I had become rather used to hearing such descriptions, but they still nauseated me.

'That does sound like something the Ripper would do,' I said.

'Precisely,' Sir Charles nodded with sudden vehemence.

'It has to be some sadistic wretch that is aping the Ripper's work. Fontaine died just hours before Many Jane Kelly; it is impossible for anyone to travel from Edinburgh to London in such a short time.'

'Of course we have kept this in the utmost secrecy,' Salisbury added. 'If this case goes to the press, those fiendish journalists will feast on our flesh. Only a handful of men know the details of the murder and we cannot let it spread any further – even that damn fool Monro does not know all the particulars! As always, it takes only one man to start things before a brainless flock follows. Can you imagine what would become of the British Empire if we suddenly had a Ripper in every county? *Panic!* Bloody, sheer panic everywhere!'

I shuddered at the picture; the British Isles in an utter state of fear, with similarly ghastly murders committed every week all around us. No wonder they were so worried; the actual death of the man might not be crucial for them, but the context in which it had occurred made it dangerous in the extreme.

'And you want me to investigate,' I murmured. In fact it sounded like a very exciting assignment; one of those that can make or break a career. Unexpectedly, my heartbeat quickened in anticipation, but the thrill would not last.

'Indeed,' said the prime minister. 'I remembered your name this morning, as you probably noticed. The reports of your pursuit of that blasted black widow made most amusing reading on Sunday mornings.'

No wonder. The case of Good Mary Brown had hit the papers as one of the most spectacular arrests in recent years. The woman had lived in five counties, from Lincolnshire to Devonshire, using a different name with each new husband she decided to poison. Gathering sufficient evidence to prosecute her had cost me blood, sweat and tears.

'I need one of our best men up there,' Lord Salisbury continued, 'but with the Ripper case at its worst, the CID cannot spare any big name without causing suspicion. Monro's dislike of you provided me with the perfect alibi; nobody in London will suspect of you being transferred to Scotland in an official capacity – not after Sir Charles, your mentor and Monro's arch-enemy, has resigned.'

I noticed Sir Charles squinting at the coldness with which the end of his career was being discussed. The prime minister was undoubtedly very good at scheming.

I savoured a sip of brandy. 'I presume we will have to craft some excuse for my presence in Edinburgh.'

'We already have,' said Sir Charles. 'You will assist a new special subdivision led by Inspector McGray.'

I arched an eyebrow. 'I had not heard of new subdivisions being created.'

'This is a particular case,' said Lord Salisbury. 'Inspector McGray has championed the creation of a team devoted to investigating . . . erm . . . apparitions.'

There was an uncomfortable silence in the room.

'Apparitions,' I repeated. 'Do you mean apparitions . . . as in –?'

'Apparitions as in apparitions!' Salisbury spluttered, with a slight colouring in his cheeks. 'Ghosts, goblins, witches . . . that kind of thing. We are using McGray's new subdivision – in fact, we are *creating* it – as a smokescreen. Assigning the case to such a . . . bizarre agent will keep the eyes of the "respectable" reporters safely away.'

It took me a moment to recollect what he'd said. It sounded incredibly foolish . . . but that was precisely what would make it work.

'If that is where we stand . . .' I said, my mind swiftly analysing the circumstances, 'to the rest of the world I would just be going to Edinburgh in absolute dishonour after being downgraded by Commissioner Monro . . . Am I correct?'

Sir Charles sighed heavily and Lord Salisbury replied in a monotone. 'That is correct, Frey. Officially, we never came to see you, it was Monro alone who decided you were to go to Scotland, and you were more than willing to take on the assignment rather than being permanently dismissed.'

My chest felt like it was boiling. I had a flashing memory of my father's endless ranting against the Scots. I could almost see him, his mouth covered in crumbs, spitting pieces of buttered bread and yelling '*Edin-bloody-burgh*!'

'I hope I have been clear enough,' Salisbury said, 'and I certainly hope you understand the seriousness of the situation. I have assigned Sir Charles to monitor your progress, since he will have the free time; you will keep in constant communication with him and report any advances as the case develops. Also, I will have Monro send you all the "official" paperwork dealing with your transfer. I will leave you now to arrange the details between yourselves.' As he stood up, Sir Charles and I jumped from our seats. 'Leave the formalities for quieter days, gentlemen, I know the way out.' He opened the door, but before leaving he cast me one last stabbing stare. 'Do not disappoint us, Frey. I had a tête-à-tête with Her Majesty today and she is utterly distressed!'

He then stepped out and I could hear his group of guards swiftly leaving the house. Again I had the feeling of witnessing a dream.

'He did not even ask whether I accepted the task or not!' I said after a brief silence.

Sir Charles chuckled after a sip of brandy. 'He doesn't have to; he is the prime minister. Besides, you would be a fool not to take on the case. There is a good chance this will redeem your career: more than one Frey will be glad to know that you have been given an assignment by the PM himself and . . . who knows? If you do well, maybe that will also change the mind of a certain Miss Ferrars . . .'

The name came so unexpectedly that I blushed like a ripened tomato. '*How do you – how do you –*' I cleared my throat, realizing how high-pitched my voice had come out. 'Sir Charles, that is horribly forward. Even my father does not know yet!'

Sir Charles grinned. 'I have far-reaching ears, Frey . . . and many!'

'It only relieves me to have you on my side . . .' I gulped the rest of my brandy and sat properly behind the desk. 'I will be reinstated in London if I succeed, will I not? I would expect at least that!'

Sir Charles turned his head towards me. The gaslight accentuated the deep creases on his face; he seemed terribly tired. 'That depends solely on Lord Salisbury, Frey. Even though he asked for my help, I am afraid I have no power to help you any more. You must do as instructed and hope for the prime minister's favour.'

I cackled sardonically. 'Let me evaluate my situation: I

must go in shame to Scotchman-swarming Edinburgh, pretend to be part of a pathetic subdivision led by a hare-brained wretch that believes in fairies, break my back and brains chasing an elusive imitator of Jack the Ripper, all in utter secrecy . . . and if I succeed I may, *may* be able to come back . . . and if I am terribly lucky, resume my life at the point it had reached yesterday . . . *Barely break even!*'

A deep silence followed. Sir Charles fiddled around with his empty glass, and I could only bite my lip at the unfairness of the situation.

'It is a paradox,' he said darkly, 'that some of the most brilliant, noble people must struggle their entire lives just to keep the scum of humanity in line . . . those parasites with neither scruples nor brains that only live to suck from society like leeches. And in the end, even if our job is done at its best, the world will not have gained anything . . . only the chance to keep rolling on with its other usual troubles.'

That short speech summarized a lifetime of painful battling. Sir Charles had worked for the police for years, so he must have spoken from his very core. I could but wonder whether my own spirits were destined to end up like his. The one thing that was infuriatingly clear was that I had no choice; I had to do as I'd been told.

'I will regret this,' I whispered, dismayed as never before. 'I will go up to Scotland and will do whatever is necessary . . . although I know I will regret it.'

Sir Charles showed a weary smile and spoke in a conciliatory, rather fatherly tone. 'Perhaps . . . but look on the bright side: you will have done what is best for the greater good.'

I stretched my arm to grab the bottle and help myself to a second drink.

'A pox on the greater good . . .'

Blood! I hate blood!
And how he squealed! Like one o' those slaughtered pigs!
Thinks I'm a bug, like the rest thinks. Like those that treat
* me like a beast . . .*
They will all see . . . yes, they will all repent . . .

6

'But sir, you cannot leave!'

'And I will need more overcoats, especially the thicker ones, but those are in my wardrobes at Hyde Park Gate. Here, you can fetch them from my father's with this note.'

'I have worked for you for more than four years! You give me notice just like this? What will I do now?'

'You will see that my belongings arrive safely in Edinburgh, Joan,' I said, trying to distract her from the bleak facts. 'That shall give you some occupation for another few days, and once you deliver everything I will give you a settlement generous enough to keep you afloat for a few months.'

'Oh, but Mr Frey, what'll become of me after that? I'm a poor old widow; nobody will want to give work to these weak bones!'

I let out a cackle, doing my best to raise her spirits. 'Joan, who are you trying to deceive? You are a sturdy spud! And I will give you a fine testimonial to make sure you find employment very soon.'

'But sir –!' She sighed and dropped her arms, her shoulders hunched in misery.

I felt terribly guilty. I bemoaned losing prestige and a sweetheart, but my misfortunes were nothing compared to Joan's; she was now losing the only income that guaranteed bread on her table.

'If your situation becomes very ugly,' I said, 'you may

contact Elgie. He will let me know straightaway and we shall do everything we can to help you. Is that all right?'

Joan nodded in silence, only a little less distressed, but I could not think of any other ways to console her. She gathered the notes I'd given her and left the study.

Poor Joan had found me in a deplorable state that morning: dark rings around my eyes, my clothes creased and a pile of letters on my desk, ready to be sent. I had not slept at all in order to sort out my sudden departure for Scotland, and only when I saw her appalled expression did I realize that I had not changed my clothes either. I was still wearing the same suit that had seen me sacked from the CID, assailed by the insolence of my brother Laurence, and jilted by Eugenia, before walking home at night to have my future turned upside down yet one more time. My head felt dizzy with the realization that all this mess had occurred in just one day . . . I was oblivious of the still longer days that awaited me.

Despite my efforts, I failed to catch the day's *Scotch Express*, which would have taken me from King's Cross to Edinburgh in less than nine hours. I missed it by a matter of minutes and was left standing at the platform, irate and grunting the finest selection of vulgarities in the English language. One of the station's clerks, seeing my frustration, advised me to travel by sea; I could navigate down the Thames and reach Edinburgh's Leith Harbour the following morning.

As water transportation was slowly being relegated to moving goods, it took me some effort to find an appropriate ship. After some inquiries I found a small boat with two separate cabins for passengers. It looked pitiful, its hull corroded, but at least I would enjoy some privacy.

Stepping onto the deck was one of those moments that remain in one's memory, for ever as fresh as if it had occurred only seconds ago. I can still picture myself clambering aboard in the busy London dockland, wrapped in my thickest overcoat and carrying a heavy suitcase in each hand. I cast a last glance at London and its jungle of smoking chimneys. Ahead of me were the brown, choppy waters of the Thames, about to carry me to situations that I could never have foreseen, either in my wildest dreams or in my darkest nightmares.

I hesitated for a moment, with a foot on the gunwale, and was tempted to forget about the whole thing. I even began to turn for the safety of Hyde Park Gate. However, an invisible force would not let me. I shivered, and that sudden coldness brought me back to my senses. And then I boarded, muttering, 'From here to Hell . . .'

The journey, though short, was a torment. Not only because of the rundown steamer that kept bouncing on the waters almost like a pebble on a pond, but also because of my dreadful state of mind.

Lying on the hard bed and staring at the cracked ceiling, suddenly everything in my life seemed dull. Why should I fight for anything at all? Why even bother to travel all the way to Scotland? This second Ripper might turn out to be as evasive as the first one. What if this other rascal fooled me too? Then again, even if I succeeded, there was no guarantee I would be reinstated.

That seeming lack of purpose was a horrible, hollow feeling in my chest. I had felt like that once before, when

I left the School of Medicine in Oxford. Following on the heels of my failure to complete a law degree at Cambridge, it still aches to remember how defeated I felt. It had not been that the lessons or practices overwhelmed me; I liked learning anatomy and all its intriguing Latin names, researching diseases and their symptoms, and I particularly enjoyed the intuitive skills needed for diagnostics – even back then I could not suppress my inner detective.

Nevertheless, everything changed after the unfortunate dissection of a woman's body, snatched from a graveyard (all the bodies that we used in the faculty were obtained illegally, but both the scholars and the police turned a blind eye). Only when we cut her open did we find that she had been pregnant. It was shocking for me to find the foetus's little hand inside its mother. I will never forget the sight of those fingers, tiny yet perfectly formed, with its nails the size of grains of salt. And then the professor became crazily enthused, explaining the mechanics of the uterus and the pregnancy, before dissecting the baby to show how wonderfully formed the organs already were. It was not simply a gory or sickening image, but disturbing in a completely different way: it was heartbreaking. I knew then that I would never be a good doctor . . . or even a bad one. Perhaps I could have managed, but I am sure that the profession would have eaten me slowly. Not two months passed before I was back at home, re-immersed in my aimless existence. Then the CID saved me and gave me purpose again . . . but just as easily it had taken it all away. I had appreciated my job at Scotland Yard more than I'd thought and, as usually happens, only realized it when all was lost.

I kept rolling on the bed with those poisonous thoughts,

but there is only so much the mind can take, and I finally fell asleep. When I woke up, a few hours later, it was still dark, the boat still bouncing on fierce waves. I tried to sleep again but it was hopeless, so I decided to make good use of my time. Sir Charles had given me a thin file with a briefing on McGray and the case, and also the 'official' paperwork dealing with my transfer.

I first found a brief report on McGray's new sub-division. And I call it 'McGray's' because the county of Edinburgh and Leith had given that oaf absolute autonomy over it. The subdivision was actually called 'Commission for the Elucidation of Unsolved Cases Presumably Related to the Odd and Ghostly' – I have not enough breath to read it in one go.

Procedure stated that, should any investigation remain unsolved beyond a given period of time, Inspector McGray would have full access to all files and testimonies. He would determine whether a case was of a 'ghostly' nature and should be further investigated with an 'unorthodox' approach.

It was logical that only a handful of cases would trickle through the local CID and make it to McGray's – or our – jurisdiction. Indeed, the division had only two active cases besides my present special commission. One was a supposedly haunted house in which a woman had gone mad for no apparent reason; the other was an investigation on – I cringe just from writing it – will-o'-the-wisps reported in the Old Calton Cemetery. It looked like the subdivision had been around for a while, rather than having been suddenly created as a smokescreen for the mock Ripper. I thought that perhaps the files had been purposely miswritten to give that impression; if not, it was unbelievable that the county's funds were being spent on that nonsense. Then again, the entire thing had been conceived and managed by Scottish scoundrels.

The captain announced that we were already close to Leith so I put all the papers back in the folder. Then I noticed, clipped to the last page of the file, a note written in a hurried hand that I recognized as Sir Charles Warren's:

You will have to stay at McGray's place for the time being. 27 Moray Place. Your permanent accommodation will be arranged in no more than a fortnight.

'Wonderful . . .' I grunted.

The city was being lashed by torrential rain that turned everything into blurry splodges. The place must have been at least five degrees colder than London, for I shivered as soon as I stepped off the steamer.

Walking from the dock, I found that Leith Harbour was a din of seagulls, seamen, steamers and coaches, almost as busy as any dock on the Thames. As I enveloped my hands in leather gloves and opened my umbrella, I felt utterly out of place: a spotless black suit amidst a crowd of loaders and fishwives. From all directions came cries in that Scottish accent that rolls the R in an even more disgusting way than the Irish. Just when I thought of it, two coarse men in kilts came my way, trying to pull a stubborn ox and swearing in the foulest form of disfigured language. A gust of cold wind and rain hit us, and I only pitied them their bare, hairy legs.

A young chap approached me and offered to carry my luggage. I gave him a penny and asked him to take me to a reliable driver. With agile movements, the boy dodged the men and the ox and I lost sight of him. For one second I thought that he had stolen my suitcases, but then the men managed to move the beast and I saw that the boy had stopped a small cart for me.

I jumped onto the back seat and received my luggage. The driver, a slender man who lacked all his front teeth but one, spoke to me with a well-modulated accent. He must have been used to dealing with foreigners. 'Where to, master?'

I produced the file and searched for Warren's note. 'Erm . . . Twenty-seven Moray Place.'

He immediately showed a toothless grin. 'Nine-Nails McGray's house!'

I arched my eyebrows as the fellow set off.

We rode through a wide avenue, ascending a soft slope. Edinburgh is set on an undulating terrain, and the first summit I found ahead was Calton Hill. I looked at my left-hand side, expecting to have a view of the other hills of the city, but the weather was appalling. All I could see of Edinburgh Castle was a grey silhouette delineated against a white sky, surrounded by fog just as the jagged peak of Arthur's Seat was.

On my left-hand side I saw the entrance to the Old Calton Cemetery, and wondered whether McGray would make me go there at night to hunt will-o'-the-wisps. Descending from Calton Hill we entered a very elegant neighbourhood: grand Georgian mansions on both sides of the street, with impeccable granite and sandstone walls.

''Tis the New Town, master,' the driver told me.

After a while we turned right and went through a short

street called Forres, which led us into a wide crescent. In its centre there was a neat garden with a few benches and narrow footpaths traced geometrically on the bright grass.

The circus was flanked by magnificent Georgian houses, all of them four storeys high. I noticed a fine carriage carrying a couple away, but other than that the place was pleasantly quiet. Remarkable since we were within two hundred yards of the busy main roads.

Moray Place was, after all, very well situated in the sumptuous New Town of Edinburgh. I could only let out a sigh of relief; for a while I had thought that I would be dwelling in the overcrowded, grubby medieval lodgings of the infamous High Street.

Just when I thought that I had made it to a nice neighbourhood, the cart passed in front of a house with several windows bricked up, and not because the place was empty or abandoned. It had all started in 1696, with the introduction of the window tax. Edinburghers, unwilling to pay, went for the utterly tasteful alternative of walling up their windows. Not content with that, and to make even more of a statement against the government, people left the window frames intact, as if saying 'we *did* have windows here, but will do anything to go against your stupid taxes.' The very façades of Edinburgh had thus become an anti-English flag.

I brought a dismayed hand to my brow when I saw another granite townhouse with half its windows blocked out with the most disgraceful red brick. The tax matter was more than a century old and the tax itself had been repealed more than thirty years since – yet these people had not even attempted to restore their houses.

That could only remind me that I should not be fooled. Refined and stately as the place looked, it was far, far away from the world I was used to. This was Scotland.

My toothless coachman drove around the circus and halted in front of number twenty-seven.

'Nine-Nails McGray's residence, sir,' he announced.

It was not the grandest house in the circus, its façade only three windows wide, and right on a corner, but there was a certain charm to it (the fact that all its windows remained intact was certainly an important factor).

I climbed down from the cart and knocked on the oak door. As I waited, I had a closer look. It seemed like a well-kept place; clean windows with white frames, through which I saw green velvet curtains.

Nobody answered the door and the rain was beginning to dampen the hem of my trousers, so I had to knock again. The driver brought my suitcases. 'No one in the house?' he asked.

'There must be at least a blasted housekeeper!' I grunted, knocking much harder than before.

I was not finished banging when a coarse voice shouted: '*I'm coming, hold your bloody horses!*' A moment later an old man opened the door. 'Whit's so fuckin' urge—'

He shut his mouth as soon as he saw me. The man was rather short, with jutting cheekbones and a round nose; untidy locks of grey hair grew only on his temples. He was wearing a stained apron and clenched a greasy rag in his hand. Even though the man had a reddened face, as if he'd just come out of a steam room, the colour faded away in a second.

'I'm sorry, sir! I didn't know who was calling!'

'Save the apologies,' I replied dryly. 'My name is Ian Frey. I am looking for Inspector Adolphus McGray.'

'Oh, Mr Frey from London! O' course! We didnae expect ye so early, sir. I'm afraid Mr McGray isn't at home now.'

'I suppose I can find him at the City Chambers?'

The man shook his head. 'No, no, I'm afraid. Mr McGray must be at the lunatic asylum as we speak.'

I lifted my eyebrows in surprise. 'Oh! Well, I really cannot say that it surprises me. Do you know whether he is receiving proper care?'

Now I thank Heaven that the butler's eyes were not daggers. 'Mr McGray *doesn't* go as a patient! He's visiting someone.'

The driver let out a muffled giggle. All I could do was clear my throat and change the subject quickly. 'I understand that I am supposed to be accommodated here.'

'To whah?' The butler frowned in incomprehension.

'To be accommo – Jesus, I'll be staying here.'

'Oh! Aye sir! Do gimme yer bags. D'ye wantae wash yer face or something?'

It was tempting to bathe and change clothes, but I thought that it would be better to report my arrival to the CID as soon as possible.

'I'd like to but I cannot. Do you know whether Inspector McGray will be at the City Chambers at all during the day?'

'Aye, I think so. Mr McGray told me he needed to sort out two or three wee things for ye. Bring some papers for ye to sign, I think.'

'Fine. Perhaps I will meet him while I am there.'

Saying no more, I jumped back into the cart, followed by the driver. 'Take me to the City Chambers.'

His eyes glowed at the promise of more of my money. 'Aye, to High Street, master.'

We headed south, towards Princes Street and the main railway terminus, which effectively cut Edinburgh in two: the opulent New Town and Calton Hill to the north, and the cluttered slums of the Old Town and the castle to the south.

An offensive stench hit my nose as soon as we entered the bustling High Street. This looked more like the image of Edinburgh I'd had in mind: precarious buildings of many storeys with brown, smoked walls. Some of those lodgings had more than ten levels, cramming entire families in each room.

Such overcrowded slums make me loathe our industrial age. Manufacturing has done little else than snatch people from our countryside, locking them in claustrophobic little factories, making them breathe foul smoke and forcing them to live all hugger-mugger with less space to move than pigs in a slaughterhouse . . . all for a few more pennies a week. It strips their dignity, I believe, and I wonder what this insatiable hunger for profit will make of our world.

Projected above the tall constructions I saw the steeple of St Giles Cathedral, looking like a blackened crown, and not far from there was the Royal Exchange, the building occupied by the City Chambers.

An arcade of grey stone gave way to a small courtyard, where carriages plied to and fro throughout the day. When we arrived there were another four carriages in line, so we had to queue for a few minutes. Meanwhile, I saw that on the other side of the road, right in front of the chambers, was the ancient Mercat Cross. Centuries ago that elevated spire would have been used for public executions, where the convicts would not only be hanged, but also burned, impaled, skinned, mutilated and disembowelled in ways that would make Jack the Ripper's work look like that of a novice.

Once I managed to descend from the cart and pay the toothless driver, I inquired after Inspector McGray.

'He's not in the building,' a young officer told me, 'but he's expected today.'

'What time does he usually arrive?' I asked, and the chap whistled.

'Well, ye never know with that laddie. Some days he's here before dawn, some days he doesn't appear 'til supper time.'

I cursed inwardly and thought of leaving, but it would not be a bad idea to report my presence to the chief, whose name I had learned from Warren's file. 'Can you take me to Superintendent Campbell, then?'

'Uh, I dunno. Mr Campbell's always busy.'

'I am certain he will be willing to have a word with me,' I assured him, and gave him my name. He led me two storeys upstairs and then to the west side of the building, where Campbell's office was. The officer announced me to the superintendent's assistant, who only dared enter the office after my sharp insistence.

To the men's astonishment, Campbell bade me to enter without delay.

The office had a wide window with a privileged view of the highest towers of the castle, but the weather was so bad the room needed four oil lamps burning in order to be properly lit. Behind a wide oak desk, settled back with the tips of his fingers resting on the polished wood, was Superintendent George Campbell.

He was around sixty, or so I had heard, but for his age and rank he looked rather . . . wild. With his whitish hair fluffed up, a thick moustache and the corners of his grey eyes slightly tilted upwards, Campbell seemed very leonine to me.

'You are early,' he said in a deep voice with a very smooth accent. I could tell he had studied in the south.

'Yes. Inspector Ian Frey, at your service, sir.'

As I spoke I offered my hand to shake, but Campbell ignored it. 'I know who you are,' he replied sternly, while searching through his piles of papers.

I swiftly pulled my hand back and adopted the same stern tone. I have never been one to beg for sympathy. 'I thought it proper to report my presence to you.'

'Indeed,' Campbell muttered as he drew some sheets and scanned them with his cat-like eyes. 'I see you used to have a very good reputation . . .' He emphasized the *used to*.

I refused to reply and simply planted myself on the floor with firm feet. After reading the documents Campbell proceeded to scan me. His stare was penetrating.

'So, Mr Frey, I suppose that you know what this is *really* about. Am I correct?'

So he did not even dare to mention the matter out loud . . .

'I do,' was my dry answer.

'Good. Good.' Campbell nodded slowly, still examining me, not even blinking. 'Now, before you start, let me make something clear: I am not happy with your presence. At all. I have a list of first-class inspectors who'd already be working on the scene, had London trusted my judgement; however, they think they know better than us poor provincial folk, and sent me you – a frivolous-looking chap whose only good reference is that press-overblown frippery of Good Mary White –'

'Brown.'

'Whichever bloody colour she was! We need results and we need them soon, no excuses. And we also need someone to compensate for the unconventional nature of your new department. I will not trust you until you bring me proper results. Do you understand?'

I was grinding my teeth. 'Yes, sir. If may add –'

'You may add all the gibberish you want after you bring me the culprit. Now go, and do *not* disappoint Her Majesty's realm, Inspector Frey.'

I did not bother to say another word and walked out, my heart rapping furiously.

Before leaving I approached the officers and inquired after McGray one more time, but the man had not arrived yet.

I blew out my cheeks. There was nothing else I could do but return to Moray Place and wait for the elusive McGray there. Having to wait when such an important case lay on my shoulders! It was frustrating, but at least I would have a chance to wash and change.

I was about to seize a cab when I heard the young officer shouting at me. 'Sir! Look, sir! There's Nine-Nai – Ah . . . I mean, Inspector McGray!'

I turned quickly and saw a rider halting in the middle of the courtyard.

As he dismounted, I had my first glimpse of Adolphus 'Nine-Nails' McGray.

7

I first noticed his horse. It was a splendid animal with a chestnut coat, muscled legs and a solid back. I thought that it was either an Arabian or an Anglo-Arabian breed, for it had a long sloping neck and a deep chest. A long, strong hand patted the horse's head. That hand was missing a finger.

'Nine-Nails . . .' I whispered, remembering the words from the toothless driver and almost uttered by the officer a second ago.

Then I looked at the man himself. He was a little taller than me, so his head stuck out quite a few inches above the crowd. His shoulders were very broad, his limbs long and brawny.

'Inspector McGray!' the young officer called. 'This gentleman's been looking for ye!'

McGray approached with firm steps and I had time to study his face. His square jaw and wide blue eyes suggested that he had once been a handsome Scot, but somehow had become haggard: he had dark rings and premature wrinkles around his eyes, the most unkempt stubble and grey speckles peppering his dark hair. Despite his receding hairline he had an abundant mane, which apparently he seldom combed.

However, the most striking feature – besides his lacking a finger, of course – were his clothes. McGray wore tartan from head to toe: brown tartan trousers and green tartan waistcoat. His only garments without a pattern were his creased shirt and ragged overcoat; the latter looked as though moths had been feasting on it for years.

The man was soaking wet, his hair and clothes dripping copiously, as if he had ridden through half of Edinburgh under the heavy rain. He stretched out his right hand – the four-fingered one – in a sudden movement that spattered huge drops all over my chest. I brushed the water off my coat and took off a glove before saluting.

'Inspector Ian Frey,' I said, consciously avoiding the words 'at your service'.

He shook my hand mightily and I felt (as well as heard) a couple of phalanges cracking. Despite my best efforts, my face betrayed my discomfort.

McGray chuckled and then spoke with a rich, rough voice, as Scottish as his dreadful garments. 'Oi! They sent me a soft southern dandy!' He turned to the young officer. 'See, McNair! How long d'ye think he'll last?'

McNair looked at me awkwardly but was wise enough to remain silent.

'Tucker! Come here!' McGray yelled.

Tucker turned out to be a playful golden retriever that came running from the road. The dog was quite rangy for its kind and had an unusually bright fur of a creamy colour. The animal approached me to sniff my clothes, and all of a sudden it rose on its hind legs, trying to lick my face.

I stepped back, seeing with appalled eyes how its muddy forepaws smeared my jacket, shirt and silk tie with Scottish filth.

'Oh, Christ Jesus!' I cried, but Tucker took my screeching as an invitation to play and kept jumping up and pushing merrily at my chest.

McGray was laughing loudly, his mouth open at maximum, and within seconds everyone in the Royal Mile stared at my disgrace. McGray at last showed some compassion. 'All right, Tucker! Leave the London lassie alone!'

The dog did retreat, but so brusquely that its paws got snagged on my clothes and I heard my tie and jacket tear.

'*Bloody hell!*' I howled before having a chance to think.

Tucker paced around its master, dragging pieces of French silk that still hung from its feet. Its tongue hanging out, the animal's muzzle looked like a mocking smile to me.

I produced my handkerchief again and stoically wiped the mud off my clothes. 'I would appreciate it if you refrained from calling me a "London lassie" in the future.'

He laughed. 'Aye, yer right. Ye wouldn't last five minutes against some lassies I ken.'

'Sorry, some of the lasses you . . . ?'

'Ken.'

'Ken?'

'Ken. *Know!* Och, I forgot you Londoners cannae speak without three marbles in yer gobs. Talking of gobs, c'mon, I need to get a bite to eat. We can have a chat over a pint.'

'I did not travel all this way for *pints*,' I said, my expression stiff. 'I would rather get started on the work as soon as pos—'

He silenced me with a vigorous thump on the back that took me momentarily out of balance. 'Nae. I need some food before that. Dunno about ye, but I'm starving.'

By then he was already crossing the courtyard with huge strides. I snorted in frustration and could only follow him at a pathetic trot. Only then did I realize how hungry I felt. After all, I had not eaten anything except for a meagre breakfast while still on the boat.

'I was told that this case of the violinist is extremely urgent,' I said briskly as we walked down the road. 'I read in the preliminary report that the body is currently at the morgue. We should look at it before anything else.'

'Aye, we'll get there today.' McGray cast me a sardonic grin. 'Although promise ye'll not puke all over our Dr Reed. I've read how soft the Southrons' stomachs can be.'

'I'll have you know I began a degree in medicine, which –'

'Which ye didn't finish for bein' a squeamish brat.' McGray winked at me. 'I've also had some preliminary reports to read, y'see.'

I rolled my eyes, begging Heaven for some mercy.

I was not expecting to eat at a decent place, so I was not too surprised when McGray led me to a mucky tavern in the west end of High Street. The board hanging over the road read *Ensign Ewart*.

'What d'ye reckon?' McGray asked as we crossed the threshold.

Immediately I saw that we were entering one of those ancient public houses that have stood on their ground for centuries, and are likely to go on like that for ever.

The interior was quite dark. It could have been because it was a horrible day outside, but the small windows with diamond leading told me that the pub would be in shadows even during the brightest summer noon. Cracked, moth-eaten furniture was crammed all around, making the room look even smaller. Barrels of beer were piled by the opposite wall, right next to the bar, behind which sat enormous containers with pickled eggs and onions, and countless bottles of spirits.

'What a picturesque slum,' was all I could say. There was a group of scoundrels gathered around a long table, and as soon as I spoke, the filthiest of them jumped from his chair. It will never cease to amaze me how human beings can degrade themselves. I know I should be more compassionate, but that man would have challenged the serenity of the Virgin Mary: his hair and face looked greasy, with a repugnant beard covered in crumbs and tiny shreds of meat, and he wore the most ragged clothes. The man lurched towards us and I perceived his foul stench, a mixture of sweat and stale beer.

He grunted in the most indistinguishable dialect. 'Michty me! See who's here! Nein-Neil McGree!' The drunken men burst into laughter, one of them banging his head on the table and spilling a jug of ale.

'What an enchanting place for a meal,' I sighed.

McGray's expression did not show anger but weariness. 'Aye,' he replied, showing the man his hand and the small stump where his ring finger had been. 'See, 'tis not grown back yet. Will youse let us eat in peace?'

'Och! Won't ye fiddle a bit for us?' The men cackled so loudly that I thought the walls had shaken. Tucker growled and barked furiously, showing a set of long fangs.

'Ye must be drunk to dare teasing me.' McGray did not say that in a threatening tone, but rather matter-of-factly.

'Och, Nein-Neil McGree's gonna call his spooks and they'll drag me to Hell to Auld Nick! Abody ken he's as nuts as his lil' sist—'

McGray moved so fiercely we were all startled. In a long stride he reached the drunkard, seized him by the neck and slammed his head against the nearest table, pinning him down with one hand – the very hand they had just mocked. A splash of blood stained the old wood.

The laughter stopped immediately and the three other men stood up on wobbly legs. I dropped my umbrella, ready for a fight, as one of the drunkards hurled himself upon me. He was so intoxicated it was easy to strike him in the face with a neat punch. The man fell flat on his back, his nose bleeding.

'Oh, dear Lord . . .' I sighed, seeing that his blood had smeared my leather glove. I produced my handkerchief and wiped it off meticulously.

'Aye, yer very drunk,' McGray repeated, squeezing the man's neck with terrible strength. His voice had become a nasty, vicious hiss.

The drunkard thrashed his arms desperately, but then McGray clenched one and twisted it until I heard the joint crack. Tucker was barking madly.

'*What the hell are you doing?*' I screamed in horror, but McGray would not listen.

He leaned over the man and whispered in his ear: 'Ye ken the rules, laddie. Speak all the shite ye want about me, but don't ever, *ever* slander my kin.' The drunkard snarled in pain. 'Now, I don't think Mary likes chaps o' yer type in her pub. Ye better tell yer mates to go.'

The smallest of the men jumped forward. I thought he

was going to attack me too, but the tiny man just ran out of the tavern. The last scoundrel grabbed his fallen pal by the wrists and dragged him to the street.

'Look at that!' McGray cried, squeezing the man's neck a bit tighter. 'Ye didn't even have to tell 'em to go!' Then he lifted the man by the neck and threw him out of the pub, onto the muddy road. There was a roar of laughter from the people passing by.

'Sorry ye had to see that,' McGray said, walking back as if he'd squashed a fly on the table. The other few customers watched us for a second, but then turned and continued their chatter as if nothing had happened. McGray seemed equally unconcerned: he lounged at a large table close to the fire, wiping his bloody hand on the edge of his coat. 'I didn't expect ye'd have that in ye, Frey! That's one stout punch for a Londoner!'

I was still appalled: 'Y-y . . . you broke that man's arm!'

Nine-Nails shrugged. 'It was just a wee splinter; those dunghills heal overnight. I do feel sorry about it . . .' He could not have looked more nonchalant. 'Fancy a pint?'

An incomprehensible mumble was all I could utter.

'Och, Adolphus!' a thick voice cried. When I turned round I saw a plump young woman approaching with a mop and a bucket. She was wearing a stained apron tied up tightly around her broad waist. Her ginger hair was an explosion of orange curls that brought out the freckles all across her round face. 'Ah'm sorry about the lads. I cannae control 'em!'

McGray laughed and a spark glowed in his eyes when he spoke to the woman. The wrinkles around his mouth deepened as he smiled, yet a childish quality came afloat.

The woman began mopping the blood and the spilt ale. Then she fixed her bright green eyes on me. 'Oi! Ye brought a fetching one!'

'Och, Mary! Ye hopeless flirt! Don't tell me ye'll fall for this peelie-wally! Come on, Frey, don't stand there lookin' all stiff like a pole; have a seat.'

When I saw the greasy chairs I was about to produce my handkerchief again, but refrained from the impulse and sat down – Tucker had already ruined my suit. The dog was lying lazily right in front of the fireplace, enjoying the sudden heat; it was hard to believe that he'd been growling like a wild wolf but a moment earlier.

I was about to protest again but McGray waved his hand dismissively. 'Right, now we can eat in peace. Mary, what've ye cooked today?'

'The usual, but we got haggis today, Adolphus.'

'Bring it on, hen!' McGray was all enthusiasm. 'And a pint of ale.'

'Haggis for yer friend too?'

I resisted the urge to laugh at her. A sheep's stomach stuffed with its blood and other discarded tripe was not my idea of food.

'A plain pie, please,' I said as politely as I could.

'Ye mean a bridie?'

'I do?'

'Aye, get him a bridie,' McGray said.

One moment later Mary brought a huge, steaming bowl and served a ladleful of haggis on to McGray's plate. I must admit that the meaty smell was not that bad, but I would sooner kiss a public latrine than eat something of such foul appearance. The thing looked like a cow's ruminated cud, only soaked in fat and with a far more disgusting colour. A moment later she came with a meat pie.

'Some gravy, lad?' I saw her pulling a ladle from another bowl, a viscous brown fluid dripping from it.

'No, thank you.'

'A pint?'

'No, thank you.'

Mary looked at McGray with a puzzled face, but he only shrugged. Once I started eating the terribly dry pastry I understood.

McGray began gobbling up the hideous fried guts, chewing loudly and spilling food and ale all around him. I felt sick just from watching, but looking away did not help, for I could still hear him merrily smacking his lips.

I sighed and could not repress my contemptuous remark. 'What ever went wrong with you?'

McGray raised his head with a quizzical brow. 'Wrong how . . . ?'

'Wrong as in you live in one of the most expensive neighbourhoods in this town, you obviously have the intimidating butcher's character that can take men very high within the police, and – it pains me to admit it – there is something about you that makes me think you are not entirely stupid . . .'

McGray looked at me with firm, piercing eyes. 'And . . . ?'

'And yet you dress like the jester of Mary Queen of Scots, you have instigated the creation of the most ridiculous investigation department in the force, and apparently you like to spend your time in the filthiest pigsties on the face of the earth – No offence.'

I said the latter to the pub's landlady, who happened to be mopping right beside me. She only replied with a vague 'Eh?'

Nine-Nails chuckled before grabbing his pint and gulping a long draught. When holding the glass his absent finger became evident.

'Don't ye mock our Queen Mary. Her ghost still lurks around Scotland . . . and don't ye roll yer eyes like that whenever I speak, else I'll snap yer own arm like a piece o' liquorice! Now tell me, how much have ye heard of my subdivision?'

I was tempted to ask how he'd lost his finger but preferred to save it for later. 'I have not known about your subdivision for long. I was appointed to it only the day before yesterday.'

'All polite 'n' vague like a good Southron,' he said. 'Ye ken what we look after?'

I nodded. 'My superiors referred to them as apparitions.'

'And what d'ye think of . . . *apparitions*?'

I painfully swallowed a dry mouthful of bridie and felt it going down my throat like a tangle of rope. 'You do *not* want my honest opinion.'

'Ye think am out o' my wits, I can see. Told ye, Ah'm past caring. People mock me all the time, like ye just saw. At least ye'll use pretty words I may've not heard.'

I sighed. 'See, I cannot even be bothered to come up with an elaborate answer. Ghosts and spirits used to thrill me when I was a child and we needed a good horror around the Christmas fire, but fortunately most of us grow out of it.'

He cackled. 'Aye, yer one of those who'd whimper

"McGray, yer ruining yer career!" and shite like that; I've heard it all. And am sure yer all-michty bosses told ye I'd only be a nuisance during yer hunt for Jack the Ripper.'

That infamous name hit me like a rock. *He knew!*

I raised my head so swiftly I nearly sprained my neck. 'How on earth do you – ? You were not supposed to –'

'See, I don't only read ghostly tales. I ken they sent ye cos they think yer tripe lover has inspired some Scot to –'

'*Sshhhh!* This matter is so delicate only a handful of men in the nation know about it, yet you bark it out in detail in the middle of this filthy den!'

McGray cackled loudly and I felt fire in my stomach. 'If we Scots ever need to be inspired for depravity, the last place we'll turn to is yer glossy England, *believe me.*'

'Whether you believe it or not,' I said, 'it is a case that came at the worst of moments. So do not, *do not* expect me to jump in excitement when you decide to go hunting will-o'-the-wisps.'

McGray grinned, 'Och, ye've read about the cases we'll be working on! Aye, we'll do some research on those wee lights.'

'I do not give a damn about flames of methane produced from decaying matter. I'd much rather you finished eating that ghastly mush so we can start the work we are supposed to do.'

I pushed my dish away. Hungry as I was, I could not possibly swallow another bite.

'Ye won't eat yer bridie?'

'Absolutely not. That is the culinary equivalent of a kick in the groin.'

Fortunately McGray was a fast eater and we soon left

81

the Ensign Ewart. I swiftly put up my umbrella, picturing the contents of the tenants' chamber pots.

McGray, walking impassively under the raindrops, cast me a derisive look. 'I cannae believe that such a soft dandy caught Good Mary Brown.'

I sighed, thinking of the glory of those days. 'Well, if you'd seen her you would not have believed that she was guilty either. She was this little, wide-eyed woman with a soft voice. Her *modus operandi* was rather blatant, though; all the bodies showed obvious signs of arsenic poisoning. Which reminds me – I would like to inspect Fontaine's body as soon as possible.'

'Can do. I spoke to the laddie at the morgue this morning. He should have the post-mortem report ready by now.'

'We better go there straightaway,' I said, anxious to begin the real work. 'I still don't know whether you have got a proper morgue here; the body might well be growing maggots as we speak.'

Though meant as a joke, my words turned out to be rather premonitory.

8

For convenience, the morgue was housed in one of the basements of the City Chambers, which turned out to be uncomfortably close to our little department's office.

I felt a sudden chill as soon as the doors opened. That morgue was as depressing as its counterpart in London; its small reception only had the most essential furnishing and its tiled walls were matt after having been cleaned for years and years. Morgues always looked like that: tidy, hygienic and functional . . . yet as cold to the eye as they were to the skin.

We were received by a young man I took to be the clerk. He had plump cheeks and wide, watery eyes that made him look rather childlike. His spotless lab coat told me otherwise.

'Good day, Inspector McGray,' he said with a well-modulated, yet very noticeable, Scottish accent. 'I was not expecting you 'til a bit later.'

'My new colleague is disgustingly eager to start the job now,' McGray replied. 'Frey, this is Dr Reed, our head mortician.'

'Dr Reed!' I repeated, hardly believing my ears. I knew that good morticians were difficult to find, but I'd never seen a morgue kept by someone so young. 'Pray, how old are you?'

The young man held his chin higher. 'Twenty-three, sir.'

He saw my arched eyebrows and added proudly: 'I graduated two years early.'

'I see. How long ago?'

'Erm . . . three months – but I had a great deal of practical experience.'

'And at least he *did* graduate,' Nine-Nails intervened, making my stomach feel ablaze once more. 'Did ye finish the post-mortem, laddie?'

'Or course, Inspector. I have it right here.' Reed went to the small desk and produced a notepad with a stack of sheets clipped to it. 'I received a letter from Mr Campbell himself asking me to give priority to this. He also warned me about the confidential nature of the case.'

Reed handed me the notepad.

'Can you take us to the body?' I asked. 'I would like to see for myself.'

'Oh, I'm afraid that won't be possible, sir. I released it this morning.'

My eyes almost fell out of their sockets. 'You did *what*?'

Reed's face went white. 'We – well . . . his great nephews wanted to bury him next to his wife . . . and that's too far to keep it in here.'

I took a deep breath. The young man was surely under too much pressure and I would not gain much by bullying him. 'Well, I need to see that body myself. You will have to fetch it back.' I was expecting Reed to reply, but he just stammered. 'What is it?'

His full accent came out. 'Erm . . . it cannae be brought back.'

'What are you talking about?'

'Well . . . erm . . . they're burying him in Calais, sir.

84

That's why I released it so soon. They told me their ship would set sail by noon.'

'*What!*'

'Sir, I . . . I assure you my report is quite thorough.'

'I do not care! You do *not* get rid of bodies until you have our authorization! Do you understand?'

'Enough!' McGray barked as Reed seemed about to burst in tears. He snatched the pad from my hands, his eyes fulminating. 'We better read the damn report before ye skin 'im alive.'

I snorted. 'Well, I suppose it cannot be helped. By the time it gets to Calais the corpse's flesh will look almost as putrid as your haggis.' Reed was fiercely munching his fingernails and I could not help feeling for him. 'It is all right, boy, but never do such thing again.'

McGray read aloud. 'Gee-jum Fon-teen . . .'

'Guilleum Fontaine,' I corrected.

'Och, shut up. Let's see . . . Male; fifty-eight years of age; och, fifteen stone – not a wee chap! Erm . . . aye, here it is: throat and belly cut open; no signs o' struggle . . .'

'The man was old and overweight,' said Reed. 'He would not have been difficult to subdue.'

'One long cut in the centre o' his belly,' McGray went on. He arched his eyebrows. 'Missing organs: heart, liver 'n' half the intestines.'

'Beautiful,' I mumbled sarcastically, remembering the post-mortem report on Mary Jane Kelly, the Ripper's latest victim; her heart had been missing too, but that detail had not reached the press yet. 'Did the incision look as if it had been made by a medical man?' I asked Reed, mentally looking for more similarities.

'Erm . . . I don't understand you, sir.'

'Was it a clean, straight cut or did they . . . butcher the body?'

'The cut was rough, sir; the flesh was even torn at some points. I do mention that in the report.' The chap was obviously trying to make up for his mistake, for he promptly added: 'Also, we had photographs made at the crime scene before we brought back the body, and a few during the post-mortem.'

I could not help sighing in relief; a case like this, as important as the quest for Jack the Ripper himself, would of course have been documented by a photographer.

'Good, when do you expect those to be ready?'

'They're supposed to be sent to your offices within two or three days, but I can have a word with the photographer. He's a friend o' mine. If we're lucky you may even have them by tomorrow evening.'

'That would help us a lot, laddie,' McGray said, patting Reed's shoulder. 'Ye mind if we take this report with us?'

'Please do, sir.'

'And we better make haste, McGray,' I said. 'I would like to inspect Fontaine's house while we still have some of this pathetic daylight.'

'Easy, lassie! I don't like to be rushed all the bloody time.' Then he turned to Reed for a leisurely chat about the chap's mother and fiancée. I looked at them impatiently, tapping my foot on the floor. When we were finally stepping out, Reed ran up behind us.

'Oh! I almost forgot! Mr Campbell asked me to give you this.' He handed us a couple of bronze keys. 'These are the only keys to the room where they found Fontaine.

The odd thing is, the room was locked, but these were found *inside*.'

I took the keys, which were a matching pair. Reed bowed and went away.

McGray whispered as we walked upstairs: 'Take it easy with that laddie, Frey. I ken he's a wee bit green, but he's darn good at his job.'

'He does look capable,' I said, 'but this case may be too much to take on so early.'

McGray looked sombre. 'Aye, ye might be right in that . . .'

We decided to take a carriage to Abbey Hill, where the victim had lived and died. It would get dark very soon and, even though McGray had complained about my haste, I could tell that he was as keen as me to get on with the investigation.

The rain had ceased but the mist persisted, so the towers and chimneys of Holyrood Palace appeared slowly as we descended through the Royal Mile. When we drove around the palace I saw the roofless nave of the ancient Holyrood Abbey.

Under the dark clouds, with the jagged hills of Arthur's Seat in the background, the group of buildings looked like an engraved illustration in a gothic novel. Perhaps it was because of all the grim stories I had heard about the place when I was a child, or its gloomy baroque architecture with its pointed frontal towers, or perhaps because the eroded stones of the abbey looked as though they'd been standing there since the beginning of time.

'You Scots seem to be all about ruined and incomplete

buildings,' I said. 'Look at that derelict abbey ... it is downright depressing.'

'Well, it was the English and their wretched Protestants that pillaged it in the first bloody place!'

'I must tell you that I come from a most prominent Protestant family. My ancestors were close acquaintances of Martin Luther himself, and –'

'Och, shush! Ye sound like Queen Vicky talking about the family trees o' her hunting hounds.'

The carriage took us to the curved street of Abbey Hill, which obviously received its name from the ruins next to the palace. There was a line of fine yet narrow houses, and the driver halted in front of one near the middle.

McGray knocked on the door and almost immediately we were attended by a short, plump old woman. She had a mighty big nose and her face was all wrinkled like a prune.

Nine-Nails stepped forward. 'Evening. I'm Inspector McGray from the CID. This whiny lassie's Inspector Frey.'

'A-aye, I was told youse were to come soon.' The house-keeper let us into a small hall crammed with packed boxes. 'Excuse the mess, sirs. Mr Fontaine's landlady ordered me to empty the house right away.'

'Doesn't surprise me,' McGray said, not bothering to explain himself.

'That room where the murder took place is still untouched, I hope?' I immediately asked.

'Aye, sir. I've not even got the keys. That nasty photographer o' yours took them after they broke in.'

'Those keys found their way to us,' I replied, showing them. 'Can you show us the way?'

She led us upstairs and pointed at a locked door. 'There youse have it. I don't want to see, but I'll be downstairs if youse need anything.'

'Thanks a lot, hen,' McGray said. 'We will come down to ask ye some questions. Hope ye'll bear with us.'

The woman actually seemed excited about it, her creased eyes suddenly sparkling. 'Of course, sirs! I'll prepare some tea if youse wish.'

'That'll be great, hen!' McGray said with a wink, and we watched her leave. 'Open it up, Frey.'

I was about to ask how come he'd not called me dandy or wimp, but thought better of it; McGray would have surely asked whether I liked it.

It was hard to turn the key in the lock. 'The key seems worn,' I said. 'They locked this room very often, apparently.'

As soon as I opened the door, a faint yet nauseating smell emerged. We walked into a wide studio with a dramatic view of the palace and, especially, of the dilapidated abbey. The window was smashed and there were pieces of glass scattered at its foot. I saw a shelf filled with sheet music, and counted three violins hanging over it; there was an empty gap for a missing instrument. Right next to a narrow fireplace there was a desk, equally packed with printed scores, and a wooden music stand. At first glance, the room seemed a very comfortable place for practising music – one that my brother Elgie would envy, especially given the inspiring view.

'Look at that!' McGray cried, and he quickly kneeled down by the foot of the stand.

Only then did I notice the macabre sight.

There was a twisted symbol on the green carpet, painted hastily with blood that now looked very dark. It was a long, inverted triangle, like the point of an arrow, divided vertically by a straight line. Inside it five eyes with vertical pupils had been drawn, two in the left half and three in the right half. The tracing was crude, almost primitive, and it gave the eyes a fixed, expressionless stare that was somehow distressing . . . like the stare of a snake.

Scattered around were some small shreds of dry flesh (whoever had removed the body to the morgue had done so with great haste). I recognized the whitish colour of intestine tissue and the revolting yellow of body fat. The smell of decay suddenly seemed more evident, as if accentuated by the eerie image.

'I didn't expect this,' McGray muttered anxiously, unable to wrest his stare from the drawing. 'I was expectin' a pentagram or a goat's head or some stupidity like that . . . This is serious, Frey; *very* serious.'

'What do you mean? I have never seen this scribble before.'

McGray's eyes showed that a million thoughts were storming in his brain. 'Exactly . . . few have seen it.'

Next to the symbol there was a single, huge bloodstain of an even darker red. McGray patted it slowly.

'The man was attacked while he played,' he pointed at the empty stand; tiny drops of blood splattered on the upper corner. 'He fell and was dismembered on this spot, where most of his blood dripped . . .'

The big stain was right next to the desk, under which I saw Fontaine's missing instrument: a very fine violin half hidden in the shadows. McGray stretched his arm and lifted it carefully. The wood was varnished in a rich, reddish tone that reflected the scant light on its curved surface. It looked *really* old, like one of those violins from the seventeenth century that Elgie had sometimes borrowed.

The most striking feature, however, was that it did not have a scroll, as regular violins do at the end of the fingerboard; instead, this one had the carved head of a lion, with two blue eyes made of blown glass.

'Pretty thing,' McGray said, turning it around to examine it. The back of the violin was made of maple, the winding stripes of the wood looking almost like the skin of a tiger; it also had an unusual chinrest made of polished, pristine rosewood. The front of the instrument was dotted with thick drops of blood, only a bit darker than the reddish varnish. McGray laid it carefully on the desk.

'So they butchered Fontaine and then used him to play their little satanic act,' I summarized, as speaking out loud usually helps me think better. 'He was standing right here, with the violin . . .'

I stood in front of the stand and tried to imagine what it would have been like to be Fontaine . . . how he would have felt at that precise moment. '*Look*, what is this?' I whispered.

'What's what?'

'Of course! The stand is *empty*! Look at this.'

Then McGray saw what I had found: a small semicircle of blood, its left-hand side perfectly straight.

'Someone took his music away *after* killing him,' McGray realized immediately. 'The missin' half of that drop fell on the page and then it was taken away.'

We quickly looked for the score on the floor and among the papers on the desk, but none of those sheets was stained with blood.

'It makes no sense,' I said. 'Why take only a stack of paper when . . . can you hand me the violin? I want to look into the f-hole.'

Nine-Nails laughed childishly. 'The *f-hole*!'

I snorted, snatching the violin from his hand. 'How puerile.'

I then looked into the violin's body. The inner wood looked extremely old, yet I found a faint marking that was not hard to decipher. 'This instrument was made by one N. Amati . . . the name sounds familiar . . . in 1629! This violin must be worth hundreds if not thousands of pounds! And those hanging on the wall surely are precious too. Why not take any of them instead?'

'Well, I don't need to see the violins to know that robbery was not the goal. Ye can tell just from seeing that,' McGray pointed at the eyes drawn on the floor.

'Then why would they take the score?'

'We can always come back to speculate on that,' McGray said. 'Right now we should see how the killer got in.'

'Why, I thought that your main theory would be an evil leprechaun passing through the wall.'

McGray ignored my comment. 'I was told that Fon-teen locked himself in to practise. After the murder the housekeeper had to call the police and they had to break in through the window . . .'

'Through the window! We're two floors up! Why didn't they just break down the door?'

McGray smiled bitterly. 'Fon-teen had a mean land-lady – a right penny-pinching auld hag!'

'Oh. Do you know her?'

'Everybody in town does. She didn't want any major damage to the property, and that door is expensive oak.' I saw a hint of distaste in McGray's face. 'Anyways, the officers found both keys on this desk and they were confiscated by Campbell's request. The only other person in the house was that old woman, and she doesn't look like the sort of person to disembowel her boss.'

'I would not discard her so lightly. Remember what I told you about Good Mary Brown. Perhaps she had a third key that nobody knew about.'

'We'll interrogate the housekeeper in a moment,' McGray agreed, 'If it wasn't her, then the killer must've come in through . . .' He stepped closer to the smashed window as he spoke. 'The photographer told us this window had a padlock when the officers broke in. It could've only been locked from the inside,' he turned around and found me in deep thought. 'Are ye having a brilliant idea?'

'Unfortunately, I am thinking of another question. If nobody could get in, there is also the issue of getting *out.*'

I had McGray's full attention. 'Explain?'

'The post-mortem mentioned missing organs – intestines, heart and liver – yet, look at the carpet. There are no stains besides the main pool; no trickle of blood; nothing to show us where those organs were taken.'

'Well spotted, dandy.' McGray looked intently at the floor, and then pointed at the fireplace. 'Could they have burned them?'

'In that narrow thing? I do *not* think so.'

We both leaned over the hearth and inspected the pile of ashes. There was nothing unusual about it.

'I reckon they could have had room to burn the heart and the liver,' I said, 'but not yards of intestines – at least not without leaving a mighty mess around. No, they *must* have been taken away.'

We looked around, utterly puzzled. In my experience, the crime scene nearly always screams out the events; this was one of those extremely rare times when a first inspection in fact created more questions. I sighed, thinking this was going to be much harder than I'd expected.

'I don't think we'll achieve much standing here,' McGray said at last.

'Very well, then. Shall we go and talk to the housekeeper?'

'Sure, but before we go ...' Nine-Nails grabbed a half-burned log from the fireplace and rubbed it hard on the carpet, obscuring the five eerie eyes. He kept rubbing fervidly until there was nothing left but a wide, black stain of charcoal. He then let out a weary sigh and I locked the room again.

The kitchen was kept neat and clean, and the housekeeper served us tea so diligently that I could not help but feel a hint of sympathy. Yet I was trained to look at everyone with suspicion.

'Ah'm sorry I cannae offer youse a seat in the parlour. All the furnishings are already wrapped and piled up.'

'No problem, ma'am,' McGray said, grabbing his tea. The cup looked tiny in his thick, four-fingered hand. 'What's yer name?'

'Hill, sir. Abody calls me Goodwife Hill.' The woman was standing in front of the table, her wrinkly hands squeezing a piece of cloth.

'Do sit down,' McGray offered, but the woman shook her head.

'Thanks, sir, but it wouldn't be fitting.'

'Please,' McGray said, pulling a chair for her, and the woman obliged, visibly flattered. Rough as he seemed, McGray did know how to earn a witness's trust from the very start. 'So ye've worked for Mr Fon-teen for a long while, haven't ye, Hill?'

'Aye, sir. Since he came to Edinburgh . . . erm . . . more than twenty years ago . . . My Lord, almost thirty years, I think!'

'Was he a good master?'

'Och, the best master in the world! I never had a cross word from him. He was always so polite and so concerned about his servants. When my husband died, Mr Fontaine couldn't have done more. He took care of everything. *Everything.*' Her eyes watered and she had to use the cloth to wipe her tears. 'Ye'll excuse me. It was all too sudden . . .'

'Why did he lock himself in that room?' I said, once she seemed more composed.

'He used to lock himself in whenever he had to prac-tise. It was my fault. He would play for hours and hours without resting; without even eating. I would sneak in and leave a tray for him, even if he protested. He didn't like my interrupting and was too good to scold me, so in the end he just locked the room. He even took the spare key and never let me make a copy.'

'Did he lock himself in often?' I asked.

'Aye, he'd lock himself in several hours almost every day, especially when there were concerts comin' up.'

I nodded, remembering the worn key. She was telling the truth – it is those small, seemingly trivial details that confirm or give the lie to a person's veracity. Still, there was something that was at odds with Mr Fontaine's background.

'Was your master a good musician?'

'Of course, sir! A genius on the stage.'

I arched an eyebrow. 'Then how come he practised so much? As far as I understand, it is students and young musicians who need the long hours.'

Goodwife Hill meditated for a moment.

'Well, sir, my master needed the practice. It might've been his age, but the in last two–three years he kind of lost some o' his skill.'

'Was he getting properly bad?' McGray asked.

'Och, it isn't right for me to say so, but sometimes he played awful. There was this odd spell, a few years ago, that he sounded like he was scratchin' barbed wires again. It was then that he began to practise more and more. He slowly but surely came back to his auld standards, but he never managed to stay there without playing so much.'

I remembered my brother's comments. Elgie said that the violin was not a noble instrument at all; the tremulous, expressive sound violins are famous for can only be achieved after years and years of practice, and even short periods of idleness could take a toll on someone's skills.

'What did Mr Fontaine do earlier on the day of his death?' I said. 'Do you remember?'

'Course I remember!' She seemed upset at the mere

insinuation of a fading memory. 'In the morning he went to the music school, like any other day. He came back after visiting the luthier – he brought a fiddle the lad had been repairing. Then he had dinner and locked himself away to play.'

'Did you see or hear anything odd?'

'No, sir, and I've been trying hard to remember!' She sounded truly mortified. 'I was in the kitchen the whole time. When I went to bed Mr Fontaine was still playing.'

'So ye were asleep when . . . it happened,' McGray said.

'Aye, sir.'

'Where is your room?' I asked.

'Behind that door, sir.' She pointed at a small door at the back of the kitchen. It all made sense; a servant's room would be far from the master's study, so she would not have heard anything.

'Did anything . . . abnormal happen that day at all?'

Hill opened her mouth but no sound came out. She was definitely holding something back. I was about to say so but McGray spoke first: 'Somethin' ye don't feel like telling us?'

The old woman shook her head. 'Ye'll think I'm a crazy hag.'

McGray leaned towards her and spoke gently. 'We won't judge ye, hen. And whatever ye say may help us catch the bastard that did this. Tell us, do it for yer master's memory.'

Hill swallowed painfully, still wiping tears away. 'That night my master was playin' this . . . *horrible* tune.'

McGray frowned. 'Horrible? Like those times when ye said he was scratching wires?'

'Nae, sir. I didn't say he played badly. I wanna say . . . it was horrible music . . . made my skin crawl.'

McGray's eyes flickered in interest. 'Tell us more. What did it sound like?'

'I dunno how to explain it,' Hill scratched her grey hair. 'I could tell it was one o' those difficult pieces he liked to play . . . but it made my spine chill. It sounded like . . . like poking knives . . . and then it was as if the violin was trembling. I thought fear itself must sound like that . . .'

'Would ye recognize that piece of music if ye heard it again?' McGray asked.

'Course, sir! I cannae forget that sound! I wish I could.'

'Is that what ye were afraid to tell us?'

I could tell in her eyes that it was not all.

'Nae, sir . . . It was such a scary sound but that's not the weirdest part. I would swear it sounded like . . . like there were many violins playin' in the room, though it was just him there –'

Hill bit her lip and said no more. Her nervous eyes were waiting for our reaction.

'Ye absolutely sure?' McGray asked, patiently.

'Told ye. Now ye think I'm mad. But that's what I heard. I would've sworn there were three or four fiddlers in the room that night. And I ken what I'm saying; I've been to many ceilidhs since I was a lass.'

'Well, I believe ye,' McGray said and then gulped down the rest of the tea. 'I'm done. D'ye have any more questions, lassie?'

I hissed at the epithet before replying. 'Only one. What is the name of that luthier you mentioned?'

'Dunno. Abody calls him Joe Fiddler.'

'Can't you Scots call anyone by their given name?' I grunted.

'It's better than calling everything "Victoria",' Nine-Nails said. 'Even yer blasted cakes got the fatty's V on them!'

I ignored him. 'Do you know where he can be found?'

'Nae, sir, sorry. But ye can ask at the music school. They all send their fiddles to him for repairs.'

'Very good, that should be all.'

McGray thanked Hill for the tea and we rose to leave.

'Will ye be all right now that Mr Fon-teen is gone?' McGray asked her while she showed us out. Hill blushed a bit at the unexpected interest in her welfare.

'Aye, sir. My master's relatives are pickin' me up when they come to sort out the rent o' the house. I'll be working in one o' their houses in Dover.'

'Ah'm happy to hear so. Will that be soon?'

'Couple o' weeks, I think.'

'Fine. We'll be coming back soon to have another look at the room.'

'Can I get in to clean it up?'

'Not yet, I am afraid,' I said, putting the keys back in my pocket.

'The lass is right,' said McGray. 'We need to look at it one more time.'

As I got on the carriage I could hear Goodwife Hill whispering at McGray's ear: 'Why d'ye call 'im lassie, sir?'

'Cos he *is* a bloody lassie, Hill,' he replied out loud. 'Don't ye see him?'

Unfortunately those words coincided with me wiping mud off the edge of my shoes. The woman covered her mouth, though her sniggering was all too obvious. I preferred to ignore them as there were more important things to worry about.

I had a last view of Fontaine's house and thought of the small fireplace, the missing score, the frequently locked door and the five eyes drawn with blood. All those things showed knowledge, careful planning and, above all, some ominous, hidden purpose. There was something in that murder that felt even more sinister than the plain sadism of Jack the Ripper.

As the carriage started off I had an odd feeling. Besides the obvious questions, there had been something misplaced in that room, something that did not quite fit . . . but I could not tell what it was. I knew that I was missing some detail, and that fact may well haunt me for the rest of my days. I had not realized it yet, but there were more deaths ahead; deaths that could have been avoided, had I identified that subtle detail there and then.

Scrape off . . . scrape off . . . scrape off the slimy stuff.
Hard work, not for the squeamish!

Oh, but how beautiful it will be! How beautiful!
They will all despair . . . they will all repent and love my work . . .
  for years, endless years to come!

9

The carriage drove us back to the City Chambers at the top of High Street. I left McGray there as he had to pick up his horse and dog, and the driver then turned north, taking me back to the niceties of the New Town.

Despite the darkness, hundreds of raven-black columns of smoke could be seen hovering over the city, especially above the overcrowded Old Town. Lit from below by the yellow lights of countless windows, they almost looked like the fumes from a witch's cauldron. No wonder Edinburgh was also called Auld Reekie – the Old Smoky.

Just as we entered the beautiful crescent of Moray Place, it started to drizzle again.

'And I thought that London was bad,' I mumbled as I walked in.

McGray's butler, George, received me and took my umbrella and overcoat. 'I've prepared yer room and unpacked yer things, master. Ye'll find them in yer wardrobe. Dinner's ready too, if yer hungry.'

'Excellent. You have not cooked haggis, I hope.'

'Oh, no, sir. But I can get ye some for tomorrow.'

'Please, do *not*! Ever.'

I walked through the hall and finally had the chance to look at it properly. The place was clean yet in evident disrepair: the carpet was visibly worn out, the edges of the central table were eroded, and the oak panelling on the walls was scratched and moth-eaten in the corners.

George led me to a sort of breakfast room. It had a square table that could not seat more than four people, and I had the impression that it used to be a small parlour or study, hastily adapted for dining.

'It does not look like Inspector McGray receives many guests,' I said.

George had a bitter look. 'Nae. This is not a house the all-michty like to visit.' Then he coarsely yelled at the opposite door. 'Agnes! Fetch Mr Frey's supper!'

An even coarser voice – if possible – replied from the adjacent room. 'In a minute! Ye auld nag!'

I sat at the table, and a *very* long minute later, a scrawny, middle-aged woman appeared with a tray. Her grey hair was messy like an explosion, and with her hooked nose and malevolent expression she looked like an archetypical witch from a children's book. Agnes placed a steaming bowl of pottage and a thick slice of bread in front of me.

'There, master.'

I cast a stupefied look, my patience utterly worn out. 'For goodness' sake, fetch me a spoon and napkin, woman! Do you expect me to lick the bloody soup like a mule?'

Reluctantly, she went back into the kitchen and returned with a spoon and a stained piece of cloth.

George was looking at me intently, opening his mouth as if wishing to say something.

'What is it?' I asked.

'Sir . . . May I ask what happened to yer clothes?'

I looked at my jacket with dismay. Tucker had torn it

and stained it, and then one of the filthy scoundrels had spilt his blood on me at the pub.

'This is what comes with the job,' I sighed.

'I can mend it, master,' Agnes said, boldly rumpling the collar of my jacket. I pulled myself away.

'I doubt it.'

'I swear, master. I can stitch very well! Ye won't notice it's torn!'

'Give it a try, then. In any case, I was planning to get rid of it.'

I finally began to eat, but the thick soup had no taste, the meat and vegetables were soggy as if they'd been boiling for days, and the bread was stale. Still, having eaten only a frugal breakfast and then half the driest pie in the world, I gobbled it up in a few minutes.

I was almost done when I heard someone coming into the house through the back door. It was McGray, again wet from the rain, but not nearly as drenched as the first time I'd seen him. Tucker came in trotting happily, legs and belly all muddy.

'Och, they're feeding ye!'

'If you can call this food . . .'

Nine-Nails cackled. 'Aye, but ye survived Agnes's pottage. Now I ken ye'll live through anything.'

George came in and took McGray's damp overcoat. 'Will ye dine, sir?'

'Nae!' He even shuddered as he said that. 'I had a wee bite at the Ensign.' He and George exchanged smiles of complicity. 'But do give Rye some oats and a carrot. The auld horse's worked very hard today.'

'Right away, sir.'

'Do you have your own stable?' I asked.

'Aye. Why?'

'I would like to bring my own horse. Is it possible to keep it here too?'

McGray arched his eyebrow. 'Ye ride? I thought youse Londoners only travelled in lace-lined stagecoaches!'

'Obviously, I *do* ride.'

'There is enough room for another horse,' George said. 'And attending two animals instead of one won't be much heavier on me.'

'Are you any better at watching a horse than that woman is at cooking?'

McGray patted George's back affectionately. 'Och, yes! My George's the best with beasts, Frey. He even manages to take good care o' me!'

George blushed visibly and hurried out.

'Ye done with yer food?'

'Indeed,' I said, pushing the bowl away. Finding a proper place to eat in that blasted town would be a top priority.

'Good. I wanted to have a chat with ye.'

'Go ahead.'

'Follow me.'

McGray led me to a large room with a high ceiling that in other times must have been the actual dining hall. Its wide window offered a nice view of the crescent's garden and the neighbouring mansions, but the room itself was a mighty mess.

There were towers of books and files and old newspapers ascending to the ceiling like twisted trees (I would not want to be near when those mountains of paper lost their precarious balance). There were drawings and paintings of demons and weird beasts pinned to the walls, and also a collection of strange objects like Meso-American carved stones and voodoo dolls. A huge fire burned in a wide fireplace that had been built to warm large parties, in front of which there was a cushioned sofa and a leather armchair. Tucker snuggled up on a mat placed at a prudent distance from the hearth, which appeared to be the one free spot on the floor.

I dodged books and artefacts as I followed McGray into the room.

'Have a seat, Frey.'

I tossed aside a bundle of papers, making room to sit down. 'Do you enjoy living buried in piles of rubbish?'

'Believe it or not, I ken where everything is in this room,' he said, walking straight into a bulky mountain of books, digging for a second and immediately pulling out a very old volume. 'It's when they clean up that I cannae find my stuff.'

He sat on the armchair and laid the book on the dusty coffee table that separated us. It was a large, thick tome, bound in crumbling leather. When he opened it I saw that its yellowed pages had been filled by hand. McGray turned the sheets, searching, and I had glimpses of Nordic runes and odd sketches. I recognized a pentagram surrounded by Hebrew characters, and also wicked drawings of dissected bodies and deformed creatures.

I gulped. 'Is that a book of witchcraft?'

McGray nodded slowly. 'Aye. I've been researching the black arts for a good while. This book tells things witches don't unveil willingly.'

'Then how did you get it?'

'Ye don't want tae know.' McGray kept turning the pages indifferently.

I looked around. 'Are all these books and papers related to your "research" on the occult?'

'Aye. I have almost as many in the office, but I prefer to keep the important ones here.'

'A long research indeed,' I whispered. The only larger personal library I'd seen was my late grandfather's, but he'd had seventy years to collect it – and he always kept it neat and organized. 'This certainly shows . . . erm . . . devotion.'

I actually meant 'obsession'. I could never fully discount McGray from the ranks of the mentally disturbed.

He found the page he was looking for and turned the book round for me to see it. Drawn across two pages was the same symbol we had seen at Fontaine's study.

'So it *is* a witches' sign,' I said.

'Aye and nae. It's a symbol they created to summon the Devil. Are ye familiar with the Eye of Providence?'

'The Eye of Providence,' I echoed. 'Do you mean the symbol the Yankees use in their national seal?'

'Aye; an eye inside a triangle pointing upwards. See, the triangle emphasizes the Holy Trinity; three is a divine number. Even the pagan gods of the Celts had three faces. In this symbol the triangle is inverted to represent rebellion; the underworld.'

I brought a hand to my mouth to cover a sudden yawn. 'These satanists . . . Merely turning something upside-down is enough for them to call it the Devil's work. Inverted cross, inverted pentagram, inverted Holy

Mary . . . They should at least be a bit more inventive, do you not think so?'

McGray was now the one showing impatience. 'That's not all they did to corrupt the Eye of Providence. Ye see the five eyes?'

'Yes, and I have been meaning to ask you about that. Why five? And why are they displayed asymmetrically? Three on one side and two on the other . . .'

'These are supposed to be three pairs of eyes, or the eyes in the three faces o' Satan.'

'Wait, wait. You said three *pairs* of eyes, but I only see five.'

'Aye. In the Hebrew Apocrypha, God pierces Satan in the eye before expelling him from Heaven. That coincides with an old pagan belief: the spirits o' the underworld were mutilated or marked in some way to differentiate them from the good ones – just as they did with thieves in medieval times.'

'Are you saying that the witches created this seal to please both Christian and pagan deities?' I chuckled. 'That is the way I like to bet at Ascot!'

'Nay, nay! Ye have it all backwards! If all this stuff matches it's cos it comes from ancient knowledge, Frey. *Ancient.* This is far older than Christianity as we practise it. These hags ken what they're doin'. Ah'm telling ye; this is not a seal they use lightly. They don't even teach it to many of their kin.'

'Very good. All that is very picturesque, and I am sure I would enjoy it next to the fire on a rainy day, but let's go to the point, McGray. You know what this seal is used for, do you not?'

'Aye. When witches draw the five eyes o' the Devil with a victim's blood, they're inviting him to watch over them.'

'Do you mean . . . looking for the Devil's protection?'

'Protection, a favour, advice.'

'Typical of witches.'

'Aye, but Fon-teen doesn't look like the typical sacrifice. Witches usually offer black cats, babies, virgin lassies; not old, fat musicians. Also, I don't remember that takin' organs away was part of it.'

'Why do you think they would change the ritual this time?'

'Dunno. But I'm sure we can find some clue in my library.'

'I would prefer to inquire more about Fontaine from the people who knew him. Find out more about what happened around the time of his death.'

'Maybe, but we also need to ken what we're looking for. Tomorrow we'll spend some time researching in the office.'

'I beg to disagree,' I said firmly. 'This sort of inquiry must be done right after the murder, before people forget the details.'

'And what are ye goin' to ask them? "Hey, laddie, tell me what gravy auld Fon-teen had on his chips"?'

'And I suppose that sticking our noses into your old hags' scribbles will be more useful!'

'Perhaps not, but am in charge here. Remember that.'

I felt a rush of anger. What an idiot I had been assigned to work with! I forced a deep breath, all of a sudden noticing my clenched firsts. 'Do you mind if we discuss it in the morning? I will only end up shouting things that I must not.'

'Aye, I'll let yer head cool. It's been a long day for ye. I'll ask George to show ye yer room.' Then he yelled: '*George!*' The butler appeared within a moment. 'George, take the Archbishop of Fuss-minster to his bedroom.'

George assented, trying to hide a smirk, and led me to the corridor. I gave McGray a last look and found him turning the crumpled pages of his old book with one hand, the other stretched to pat the dog's head.

'Does he not sleep?' I asked George, suddenly realizing how tired I was.

'Nay, sir. My poor master has not slept well for years. He goes to bed only in the small hours.'

I nodded slowly. 'Obsessive behaviour and sleeping disorders . . .' I mumbled.

'Beg pardon, sir?'

'Nothing,' I said promptly. 'Just a thought.'

George took me to a reasonably large bedroom. It was neat and clean, with an old canopy over the bed and a small window looking over the back yard. The first thing that caught my eye was the terribly narrow wardrobe; the ancient thing could not take more than ten garments. When I opened it I saw that it was half full with the meagre luggage I had carried with me. I could only hope that Commissioner Monro found me better lodgings before Joan arrived with the rest of my possessions.

Worn out as I was, I decided to pick my clothes for the next day. It had become an old habit, as it invariably helped me release my mind from the pressures of work. There was no better way to forget about horrid crimes than matching jackets, shirts and ties.

However, something kept tossing and turning in my head. There *had* been something odd in Fontaine's study, but I could still not pinpoint what. Everything in that room – the symbol, the stain of blood and the red splattering on the shiny violin, the missing score, Hill's words about a spine-chilling melody . . . It all flashed over and over in my head. Something I'd seen had definitely been . . . incongruent . . . out of place.

The door's worn lock came to mind; the fact that both the keys to the room had been inside; the window also locked from within. Whoever had attacked Fontaine had managed to go in and out cleanly, without breaking bolts or leaving the slightest trace – not even a trickle of blood, despite the butchery practised on the corpse. My brain almost ached trying to think how.

I would have dwelled on those thoughts a long while, but something distracted me: After picking a navy suit, I looked for the tiny chest where I kept my cufflinks. When I opened it, the first items that I saw were a couple of very pretty ivory cuffs, shaped as minuscule roses mounted on gold.

I felt a pang in my chest. Eugenia had given me those for my last birthday, but I did not remember putting them in my luggage – unsurprisingly, since I had packed frantically, throwing in whichever clean clothes and other items I found at hand.

I cursed myself for not setting my eyes on those little white roses previously. Perhaps I would have discarded them out of bitterness, or perhaps I would have taken them with me as tokens of my lost love. Either would have been better than that unpleasant surprise; Eugenia's fierce eyes, her coldness when I said goodbye, my own furious speech . . . all those images caught me off guard, surging past my eyes as vividly as if they'd just happened.

My pride still injured and the wounds still fresh, I tried to lock myself away from any feeling. I tried to convince myself that I had never truly loved *her*, that I'd merely fancied the idea of having a wife, a home and a family, and that Eugenia was but a compulsory piece in that picture.

However, looking at it objectively, it really was a regrettable loss. Had my life continued in London, Eugenia would have been the most perfect match for me. We would have complemented each other with our imperfect tempers, our haughty characters and our social pretences . . . perhaps to the world we would not have been the most affable of couples, but indeed we would have made each other happy.

Things would have been so different . . . for both of us.

I remember going to bed in the most exhausted state of mind and, as I laid my head on the pillow, tossing the cufflinks aside.

I never knew what happened to them. Perhaps Agnes took them and sold them for a few shillings . . .

10

My jaw hit the floor when McGray showed me our 'office', which turned out to be a dingy storeroom in one of the basements. There were narrow barred windows right below the ceiling, through which I could see people's feet and horses' hooves moving about the courtyard.

McGray lit an oil lamp and the room's mess fully hit my eyes. There were as many books and bizarre artefacts as in his personal library, but also countless formaldehyde bottles preserving things that were too ghastly to keep at home.

'I'm a bit scruffy,' McGray said, 'but that'll change now that yer here. That'll be yer desk, by the way.'

He pointed at a small writing table in the corner, half hidden among the debris. I stared perplexedly at the miserable piece of furniture and the old wooden chair behind it, a thick blanket of dust covering both.

'Do you truly expect me to clean up this hole?' I cried. 'I am an inspector, not your bloody maid.'

'Someone's got to clean this up and it ain't gonna be me.' McGray threw a thin file at me. 'Oh, and take yer transfer paperwork to the archive.' Constable McNair came in as I said that, followed by a little old man in a grey suit.

'Inspector McGray, this man wants to talk to ye.'

McGray, who was already looking at some old witch-craft book, lifted his eyes slowly. 'Who? And what for?'

The little man stepped forward. 'I'm Charles Downs, the late Mr Fontaine's solicitor. I was told I should talk to you regarding his will.'

'I'll take care of it, McNair.' The officer left and McGray invited Downs to have a seat. 'What can we do for ye?'

Downs was already producing a bundle of documents from his briefcase. 'I have recently been to my client's residence and was told the police had restricted all access. I am Monsieur Fontaine's executor, you see.'

'I see.'

'Monsieur Fontaine left almost all his possessions to his nephews and his housekeeper – everything but four objects . . .'

The man paused dramatically and McGray lost his temper. 'Stop yer theatre shite and speak!'

Downs startled and reddened visibly. 'Well, Monsieur Fontaine wanted his collection of violins to be distributed among his students and colleagues in the Edinburgh Conservatoire of Music.' He handed the will for McGray to read. 'As you can see, the late Monsieur Fontaine explicitly wanted those violins to be delivered as soon as possible. He assigned each specific violin to a given recipient.'

McGray read and then nodded. 'And I guess ye want us to give ye those fiddles.'

'That's correct, Inspector. I was told by the house-keeper that you locked the room where they are kept and took possession of all the keys to it.'

'We are investigating that room, Mr Downs,' I

intervened. 'We cannot release any objects until we have completed our inquiries.'

'I do understand, but my client's last wish was . . .'

'With all due respect,' I interrupted, 'anybody's wish, whether last or first, is utterly irrelevant at the moment. We are investigating a murder, Mr Downs, not hosting a garden party.'

McGray sat back, stroking his stubble. He looked at me. 'Ye wanted to get out, didn't ye, Frey?' I gave a grouchy nod. 'Ah'm thinking we can get round this nicely: ye can go with Mr Downs to Fon-teen's house, check the room again if ye want and get the fiddles for him, then he'll show ye the way to the Conservatoire, where ye can do the questionings yer all mad about. In the meantime I'll do more research here.'

'Excellent. Sounds like you are not completely devoid of sense, Nine-Nails.'

I feared he'd punch me for calling him that, but he simply raised an eyebrow. 'Och, I got yer approval. Now my life's complete!' He looked at his pocket watch. 'Lunchtime already! Fancy goin' to the Ensign?'

I could not possibly eat there again, neither could I keep on punishing my stomach like that – a few days eating like the day before and I would starve. Fortunately, Mr Downs misunderstood McGray, thinking that the invitation was extended to him too, and he refused first.

'You're very kind, Inspector, but I prefer to eat at the New Club. I can come back at any time you request.'

McGray asked him to return that afternoon and Downs set off. I frantically jumped to my feet: *'Pray, wait! Where did you say you prefer to eat?'*

*

116

The New Club proved to be a proper gentlemen's establishment with edible food, fine whiskies and decent cigars. Its best asset, however, was its location at the very centre of Princes Street, within a relatively short walk from the City Chambers. Regarding food, it would be my salvation.

Since it was a private club, Mr Downs signed me in as his personal guest (the gesture almost made me feel guilty for treating him so harshly but a few minutes earlier). Once inside I was told that I could join for a very reasonable fee – I was so hungry I would have happily paid three times the price.

It was quite hard to keep my manners while eating that huge, juicy, well-seasoned piece of sirloin and a glass of French wine.

Invigorated by the food, I thought I could use the time to find out some more about Fontaine's character.

'A very quiet man,' Downs told me, munching on a steak even larger than mine, 'very quiet indeed.'

'How long had you represented him?'

Downs looked up, counting in a mumble. 'Thirteen, four– no, wait, fifteen years! Lord, time flies!'

'Oh, so I presume you knew him well?'

'Not at all, Inspector. As I said, he had a quiet life, which gave me very little work; some conveyancing, a couple of insurance policies, and now his –'

There was a sudden commotion in the club. We heard the slightly high-pitched protests of the head waiter, and I had to cover my face when I saw him chasing the towering figure of McGray. His absurd clothes were like a beacon amidst the black suits and white tablecloths, and for some reason he was carrying a bull's-eye lantern.

To make matters worse, next to him was a short, slender boy, who could be nothing other than a chimneysweep. He appeared to be around twelve, but he could have been older; those ill-fated children rarely get enough food to grow properly. I thought he had dark hair, but as he drew closer I saw that he was actually blond, his head utterly blackened by soot. He was wiping his face with a handkerchief so stained that he only made himself blacker.

'Sir, *please*, I must ask you to leave. Our dress code –'

'Laddie,' Nine-Nails grasped the waiter by the collar, 'Ah told ye Ah'm CID, so shut that hole in yer face or I'll break yer twiggy arms right here.'

'I am afraid he is not joking,' I said, and the poor man was wise enough to step back. 'What is it, McGray?'

He leaned down to whisper. 'Change o' plans. I ken how they broke into Fon-teen's study.'

11

'The fireplace, McGray?' I asked in the privacy of the coach, as it drove us back to Abbey Hill. 'Are you serious?'

'Can ye think of another way?'

'Well, no, but you saw that narrow thing! Besides, Fontaine died at night. A November night, so the fire must have been lit. Had some wretch tried to sneak in through the chimney, they would have roasted their feet! Not to mention all the smoke coming up.'

'Can ye think of another way?' I tried hard to find another explanation but, to my dismay, McGray was right. The chimney was the only feasible explanation and it was our duty to investigate it further.

'I also have my doubts,' McGray said, 'but if there's anything up there we'll find out with the boy.'

Sooner than I expected we were by Holyrood Palace once more – fortunately, for the temperature had been dropping quickly. When we got out of the carriage, an icy breeze was blowing.

The boy hopped off from the driver's seat.

'This is Larry,' McGray told me. 'He's been cleanin' my chimneys for the past two years, haven't ye?'

'Aye, sir.'

'But today I got a more exciting job for ye. Ye'll help us solve a murder!'

The boy smiled, but the poor creature was so skinny

I thought a bowl of stew would have excited him much more. I thought I'd give him a handsome tip once we were done.

Mr Downs, who had followed us in his own carriage, arrived a few minutes later.

Goodwife Hill received us as attentively as before, yet she was a little surprised to see us again so soon. McGray, Larry and I were going upstairs with Mr Downs following us closely. McGray raised his hand to stop him.

'I'm sorry, Mr Downs, it's police business.'

Downs groaned in a most exasperating way. 'But that is my client's property and it's my duty to –'

'*Can you please stay downstairs?*' I snapped. 'For the love of God!'

Downs cast me a filthy glare and spoke bitterly. 'We'll see who shows you where to eat next time!'

Hill addressed him with an appeasing voice. 'Would ye like a cup of tea, sir?'

McGray winked at her as she took the man away.

'You may not like what you will see,' I told Larry in a concerned tone. 'A man was murdered here.'

Under normal circumstances I would never expose a child to such a ghastly sight. However, far from being frightened, Larry's eyes widened in excitement, and Mc-Gray's smile told me that he was expecting that very reaction. I realized that the boy had, probably on a regular basis, seen tragedies as bad as anything I'd seen on the job.

We stepped inside and found the room exactly as we'd left it. The one difference was that the foul smell had diminished a bit.

Larry walked in, his blue eyes flickering all around the

room, but his sight finally fixed on the huge stain of blood on the carpet. 'Woooooow!'

I also looked around, but far from excitedly. I had been trying to pinpoint what had been out of place in that room, but being there again just puzzled me more. I had not missed any detail: there was the stain of blood, the black mark where the Devil's symbol had been, the stained violin and the splattered stand. I shrugged, thinking that probably I was being paranoid, trying to find clues where there were none. After all, the case was very important for my career.

McGray patted Larry's bony shoulder. 'Laddie, we need ye to look up into that chimney 'n' tell us exactly what ye find there.' He set the bull's-eye on, a white beam lighting the dull afternoon, and handed it to the boy. 'Up ye go.'

The lantern had leather bands that Larry passed around his shoulders – he was so skinny that he had to turn the straps twice around his torso. As he went into the fireplace I thought that he looked filthier than the very chimneys he was supposed to clean.

I expected McGray to kneel down and peer up into the flue, all excitement, but he simply stood still while stroking his stubble. 'What ye see, Larry?'

Larry's voice reverberated across the hearth. 'Erm . . . I see bricks, master . . . 'n' a Hell of a lot of ashes!'

'*Really!*' I whispered in my most barefaced sarcasm.

Nine-Nails elbowed me in the ribs. 'Looks like it's not been cleaned in ages, ye think, laddie?'

'Ermmm, aye and nae.'

'What d'ye mean?'

'Looks like someone scraped it, master.'

'Aha! Ye recognize anythin' like . . .'

'I see finger marks, sir.'

'Great. They clear, laddie?'

'Aye, very clear!'

'Splendid. Can ye climb to the top? Tell us if ye find something odd?'

'Aye!'

I peered inside the chimney and saw the shining of the bull's-eye moving as Larry ascended. He was almost at the top when he yelled: 'There's somethin' here, master! A piece o' paper!'

McGray gasped. 'Can ye bring it doun?'

'Aye! But it's all wet 'n – yuk!'

'What is it?'

'It's got blood on it!'

'Then we definitely need it, laddie.'

'All right, all right.'

After a louder 'yuk', Larry began to descend. As I saw the lantern's light coming closer I moved back.

'Right, Ah'm comin' out!' As soon as he jumped down, Larry let out a sudden squeal of pain, so sudden that I started. McGray leaped forward and caught the skinny boy just before he fell onto the floor.

'*My foot!*' he yelled, his eyes watering.

McGray carried the boy and tenderly sat him on the desk. Then he gently lifted Larry's foot. He spoke sounding deeply concerned, almost fatherly: 'There, there, laddie. Ye landed on a shard o' glass . . .'

I drew closer and saw it: a piece of dark glass had pierced straight through Larry's sole and plunged into his foot. No wonder; the boy was wearing the oldest, most worn-out shoes.

I pulled a handkerchief out of my pocket. 'Larry, this is going to hurt, but it shall be quick. I want you to bite this.'

The boy did so, his teary eyes trembling. McGray patted his head and then, with a swift movement, I pulled the glass out. Larry groaned in pain, fiercely biting the cloth, but then sighed with relief. I took the shoe off and then wrapped the foot tightly with the same handkerchief. 'There, there. You will be all right.'

'We'll take ye to a doctor, laddie. Don't worry.'

'Ah'm fine, master,' he retorted stubbornly. I saw that he was clenching his right fist. 'I found this.'

He opened his hand to show us a crumpled piece of wet paper: the corner of a page, most of it soaked in dark blood. I took it and carefully tried to smooth it. Immediately I recognized a page number, an unintelligible scribble stamped in blue ink, and the very corner of a group of quaver notes.

'This is part of a music score,' I gasped. 'It must be the one Fontaine was playing.'

Larry frowned. 'The blood still feels fresh, master.'

I shook my head. 'The weather has been quite wet, that is why it has not dried. We had better keep this.' I folded it carefully and wrapped it in another handkerchief.

'Mighty chip ye stepped on!' McGray said, examining the piece of glass. Pointy and sharp, it looked like a shark's tooth to me. McGray narrowed his eyes. 'This has dry blood on it.'

I looked closer and noticed tiny yellow speckles along the dark green glass. It looked as though it was part of a very expensive, artfully crafted vase. There was a coagulated stain next to the boy's fresh blood.

'I think we have our murder weapon, Frey . . .'

'Do you think they killed and disembowelled Fontaine using glass?' I asked out loud.

'Aye, but this looks like part of a bigger piece.'

'Do you think they broke some ornament and used the shards?' I asked, but even as I said it I realized it could not be.

'Nay. There's no other pieces o' glass in the room, and ye wouldn't stop to sweep up a broken vase after killing a man. Whoever did this must've brought the glass with him, then broken it while climbing up, and torn the score too.'

McGray was reasoning well. He handed me the shard. 'Ye keep this too, lass. I ken someone who can examine it.'

'Oh, do you know a glass-blower in the city?'

'Nae. A clairvoyant.'

'What!'

'Hey, don't pull that shite-sniffin' face! Ye've not even met the wifie. Madame Katerina is the best gypsy in the business . . . at least in Auld Reekie.'

'This is getting more and more ridiculous,' I muttered, wrapping the piece of glass together with the paper.

McGray made me call Mr Downs, who by then was utterly relaxed eating buttered teacakes in the kitchen. He had asked Goodwife Hill to fetch Fontaine's violin cases and she had lined them next to the study's door.

Before letting Downs in, McGray asked Hill to bring a large bed sheet, which we used to cover the stains on the floor. The true circumstances of the death were still of the utmost secrecy. Downs passed inside, looking at the cloth with piercing eyes. He could not have been more curious had he seen the actual blood. Then he saw Larry seated on the desk.

'What happened to the boy?'

'Tripped on my feet,' Larry replied immediately, the clever chap.

Downs produced his stack of documents and carefully took each of the violins from the shelf. 'Let's see . . . we have the Guadagnini . . . the dark Galiano . . . Oh, the pride of Fontaine's collection; the Stradivarius . . .'

As he picked them up he ticked a list, made some notes and then put the instruments in their cases. The tiny man was taking his time.

'Care to stir yoursel'?' McGray finally snapped. 'We need to take the boy to a doctor.'

'Oh, yes, yes, Inspector. It's just that one violin is missing . . .'

'That's on the desk, behind the laddie,' McGray said. Larry was about to hand the violin to Downs, but the attorney almost jumped on him.

'*I* will handle this, boy.' He lifted the violin as carefully as if carrying a newborn, and looked into the f-hole. (Thanks to Nine-Nails I shall never be able to even write that at ease . . .) 'Oh, yes, the Amati Maledetto! Fontaine liked this little one very much.'

That phrase made me frown and McGray noticed. 'What?'

I hesitated. I did not want to feed his delusions. 'Maledetto . . . I recognize the Latin root . . . maledictio . . . It means . . .'

'The Cursed Amati,' Downs said, placing the instrument in the last velvet-lined case.

McGray's face went red with excitement: 'Cursed!'

'Aye, Inspector. They call this violin the Cursed Amati. You know, musicians like to have their legends.'

'Do ye ken why they call it that?'

'Jesus Christ,' I muttered, exasperated. 'You said that we had to take Larry to the doctor, did you not?'

'Hush! I wanna hear too!' the boy cried, suddenly oblivious to any pain.

'Aye, shut it, lassie!'

Downs shook his head. 'Unfortunately I do not know the story. But I am sure that someone at the Conservatoire will be able to tell you.'

McGray grinned like a child. 'Well, I was gonna take Larry to the doctor and let ye do the boring questioning in the music hall, but now I have a good reason to join ye . . .'

12

'Before you even utter a word, let me see if I can be a clairvoyant myself . . . I predict you are about to say that Fontaine was a victim of that violin's morbid curse.'

'Pish! Ye don't even ken if it's morbid or not.'

'Well, those things always are! There is always the bloody bride hunting all the virgins who dare move into her ancient manor, or the murdered child that appears at midnight with a bloody dagger. In this case, I would expect at least an impaled Renaissance violinist who will drag to Hell all those who dare play his beloved instrument.'

'Good. Yer startin' to think like me.'

The cold was bitter and the fog kept shrouding the city. I could see it being dragged down the Royal Mile as the carriage took us back to the City Chambers. McGray had decided to take Larry to Dr Reed, for the boy might not be accepted at the Royal Infirmary – he simply looked too filthy. Young Reed was all too happy to attend the boy, and I seized the opportunity to ask him about the photographs.

'Oh, I'm afraid those aren't ready yet, Mr Frey,' he apologized as he cleaned Larry's foot with a piece of cotton soaked in alcohol. The boy was groaning but held on bravely. 'Some chemicals ran out,' Reed said. 'I did manage to pull things forward; the photographer assured me that the pictures will be on Inspector McGray's desk by tomorrow afternoon.'

'Great job, laddie,' McGray said. 'Larry, ye mind if we leave ye with Dr Reed? We still need to catch these folks in the school o' music.'

'That's all right, master.'

'Good,' I said. 'Here, have something good for dinner.' I tossed a silver shilling to the boy, who caught it in the air with swift reflexes.

'And come to the house and ask George to give ye some milk and flour,' McGray added. 'We got tons o' that stuff.'

Larry could not have been more grateful. After that we set off.

Downs had preferred to wait outside with the violins, and apparently the cold was getting to his bones, for he was embracing himself tightly.

The carriage took us north. We passed right next to the white columns of Scotland's National Gallery as we crossed the gardens of Princes Street, and then entered the New Town again.

We went up along some elegant streets until we reached a curved avenue called Royal Crescent, where I saw a white, round building and I had to point at it. 'Mr Downs, is that a gymnasium?'

'Indeed, Inspector, and a grand one. Not that I frequent it, though.'

'Do you know whether they practise fencing there?'

'Yes, they do, Inspector. A few of my clients have told me about it.'

'Good. I must join, then. I am glad I asked my maid to fetch my fencing equipment after all.'

'Ye like doing that girly thing?' McGray asked, his face wincing in disgust.

'Girly? Fencing is a man's sport, McGray.'

'Oh, aye! A bunch o' delicate laddies dressed up in white cotton nappies, pokin' each other with long sticks! Sounds *really* rough!'

As we reached the gymnasium we turned west and very soon we were in front of an old, baronial building behind a long lawn. Its walls were built with dark, smoked stones, and it had a couple of spiky turrets and many chimneys pointing up to the grey sky. The place had certainly been a grand tower house when it was built, centuries earlier.

'The Conservatoire, gentlemen!' the driver announced.

'Will you give me a hand with these?' Downs asked us, having trouble carrying all the violin cases. The man was very short indeed.

As we walked inside, the gloomy building seemed forbidding, although the darkened sky might have had something to do with that.

Downs inquired after one Alistair Ardglass and McGray jumped.

'Ardglass!'

He immediately cleared his throat, and I stared in wonder, for it was the first time I had seen him discomfited.

'Indeed,' Downs said. 'I suppose you are familiar with his aunt, Lady Anne Ardglass.'

'Aye, I am,' McGray grunted. 'The old bitch lives on and on and on.'

Downs's face paled after McGray's remark, and then we could only walk in an uncomfortable silence.

As we went deeper into a long corridor, we heard the muffled music of countless instruments. Apparently there were many students practising in the upper storeys, and even though they all were playing different pieces, the overall sound was rather soothing, even pleasant.

We approached a wide oak staircase, where a fat, middle-aged man received us.

He had all the looks of a mad musician: half bald, with messy grey hair on the back and sides of his head; his eyebrows were thick and projected upwards like pointy brushes; his uneven whiskers were a loud statement of bad taste, just like his jacket, which was a couple of sizes too small for his round waist.

'Mr Downs! What a surprise.'

Downs introduced us immediately as CID inspectors investigating the death of Guilleum Fontaine. The fat man, of course, was Alistair Ardglass, dean of Edinburgh's Conservatoire of Music.

As soon as he saw McGray his eyes widened. 'Oh, but it is none other than Nine – Mr Adolphus McGray! Pray, tell me, how is your family?'

McGray cast him the most hateful stare. For a moment I feared he would explode as he'd done in the tavern. Fortunately he only hissed: 'As you'd expect. And Lady Glass?'

Mr Ardglass cleared his throat noisily and Downs's face reddened like a ripe cherry.

'Inspector Ian Frey, at your service,' I said neutrally,

trying to break the tension. 'We would like to ask you a few questions about Guilleum Fontaine.'

'In the meantime, I can give these violins to their new owners. You see, Mr Ardglass, my client bequeathed his instruments to his most distinguished students and colleagues.'

Mr Ardglass could not hide a greedy spark in his eyes. '*Did he?*'

'Ye'll have to wait,' McGray prompted. 'I want to interrogate all the legatees, and to be present when they receive the fiddles.'

I saw McGray looking at me, eyebrows arched. I understood what he was looking for: a suspicious inheritor.

'As you wish, Inspector,' said Downs. 'In fact, the first instrument I was intending to deliver is for Mr Ardglass.'

Ardglass pressed his chest in the most unconvincing gesture of surprise. 'Oh, good, *good* Guilleum! *To think of me!*'

'Please, don't soil yerself,' Nine-Nails muttered.

Ardglass looked annoyed, but then Downs said something that would upset him even more: 'Actually, the violin is not for you personally. It is for the Conservatoire.'

'Pa-pa – pardon?'

'Monsieur Fontaine wanted the instrument to be in your custody, but he stated very clearly that the violin will legally belong to the institution, and it is to be lent only to its most gifted students and professors.'

Ardglass's smile vanished in an instant. 'Typical Guilleum,' he grunted. 'Well, which instrument am I supposed to have in my "custody"?'

'The most precious, of course. My client's Stradivarius.'

That was like salt in a wound and Ardglass received the violin case with utmost acrimony. I could see the avarice in his face, the injured pride.

He hastily signed the appropriate documents and then McGray went on to his questioning.

'D'ye ken much about Mr Fon-teen? His career . . . personal life . . . ?'

'I know the necessary. The man was half French and half Scot. He studied music in Paris, got married, then lost his wife and never managed to recover. That is why he settled in Edinburgh, I believe. Very quiet old man, he was; his life was divided between teaching here, playing at home, and sometimes joining us for the receptions we hold after important recitals.'

'Did he have problems or quarrels of any kind?' I asked.

'No, no. As I told you, he was very quiet . . . even dull, if you do not mind my saying so.'

McGray was nodding, stroking his stubble. 'Did youse two get along?'

There was tension in Ardglass's voice. 'I cannot say we were actual friends; our connection was purely professional. He was my second in rank. The best maestro we've had in years.'

'And I understand that he'd been working here for a good while, right?'

'Yes. Around erm . . . well, twenty-odd years, I think.'

I looked at Ardglass with interest. 'Are you not sure?'

'Well . . . he arrived here before I did.'

McGray arched his eyebrows. 'So the auld man got here before ye, yet he was second in rank? How come?'

Ardglass instantly became defensive. 'He was offered the position and he refused. Fontaine never was a man of authority!' He noticed his tone and took a deep breath. Then he looked at me and spoke in a whisper. 'You must forgive me . . . We have been told nothing as to how he died. Even his maid does not know! And now we have people from the CID coming here to investigate . . . It was something grisly, wasn't it?'

I pulled my most neutral expression. 'We are not allowed to divulge any details just yet. But believe me, there's no reason to be alarmed.'

I studied Ardglass's reaction most carefully. He *was* alarmed, but he also seemed confused.

'One more thing,' I said. 'We would like to question Mr Fontaine's luthier. We were told that you could provide us with his address.'

'Oh, but of course. Let me write it down for you.'

Ardglass came back with a note. When I first read it I thought it was a joke: 'Joe Fiddler? Do you call him that too?'

'Yes, we all call him that. Nobody knows his actual name. He is a very eccentric fellow I must say, but very good at his craft; people from all over Scotland come to him to repair their instruments.'

'Will those be all your questions, Inspectors?' Downs asked, once again going through his crumpled papers, and McGray and I nodded. He looked at his documents. 'Mr Ardglass, you may help me find the second heir. Is Miss Caroline at the Conservatoire?'

Ardglass's face was perplexed. 'Miss Caroline? Do you mean my niece?'

'Indeed.'

'*What?* The spoiled child only plays beginners' waltzes and horrid folk reels and she gets a violin!' He had to clear his throat. 'Unfortunately she is in London at the moment. She should be back in a few days.'

'Ye better keep that instrument 'til the lassie arrives,' McGray told him. 'And tell us before ye deliver it.'

Begrudgingly, Downs agreed. He then saw that Ardglass was meaning to say something, but could not manage to utter the words.

'Yes, Mr Ardglass?'

'May I ask . . .' he was almost whispering, 'which instrument is she inheriting?'

'She is to have the Guadagnini.'

Ardglass twisted his face as if sucking a lemon. 'Oh, the one with the sweetest tone!'

'If Miss Caroline is not present,' Downs went on, 'then I will deliver the Galiano violin to . . . Signor Danilo Caroli.'

'*What?* That blasted Italian gets the –'

'Oh, shut up, ye smarmy leech!' McGray cried. 'Just tell the man where to go!'

After gnashing his teeth, Ardglass told us that Caroli was teaching and asked a student to show us the way.

As we walked to the classroom, I whispered in McGray's ear. 'Is there a history between you and the Ardglass family?'

McGray chuckled with bitterness. 'Och, ye noticed! Aye, we loathe each other's bones . . . but that's not what upset me. Their name is appearing too often in this case.'

'What do you mean by too often? This is the first time I have heard their name.'

'I'll tell ye later, Frey.'

We arrived at the door of a small classroom, where a student was playing a very fast fugue. Louder than the frantic notes, we heard the hearty yells of a man who sounded Italian to the bone:

'You 'ave to stroke with feeling, man! 'Arder! *Come on, you won't break the violin!*'

McGray had to knock hard on the door to make his presence known.

'All right, you can rest now.' Then the door opened and a lean man in his thirties almost jumped out of the classroom. He looked as Mediterranean as he sounded: olive skin, wavy black hair and wide dark eyes. I could picture a good deal of ginger 'lassies' sighing for him. 'Can I 'elp you? Oh, Mr Downs, so good to see you!'

He shook Downs's hand so effusively that the entire body of the little man jerked.

Again, Downs introduced us as inspectors from the CID and explained we had urgent matters to discuss with him.

Caroli nodded. 'Very well. Let me dismiss this boy and I'll be right back.'

One moment later a chubby student left the classroom and Caroli invited us to walk in. I saw that the small room was an utter mess: broken bows and instruments in need of repair in one corner, crumpled sheets on the floor and piles of old scores spread all around. There was barely enough free space at the centre of the room for one student to play in front of an old music stand. Caroli tossed aside a pile of paper, revealing two chairs underneath. 'Please, sit down.'

Downs and I sat, but McGray preferred to remain standing. Caroli moved a decrepit violin out of the way to sit on the desk. 'This is regarding Guilleum, isn't it?'

Once more, Downs told him about the instrument he was to inherit and showed him a dark brown violin. 'Fontaine wanted you to have his Galiano.'

Unlike Ardglass, Caroli's surprise seemed genuine. 'Oh, good old Guilleum, 'e shouldn't 'ave!'

Caroli quickly signed the relevant documents and then received the violin case. Throughout the rest of our meeting he kept it on his lap. I saw his eyes glittering on it, obviously impatient to have his first play.

When we asked him about Fontaine, Caroli's affection for the old man also became evident. He spoke with candour as he mentioned all his virtues, yet he could not tell us anything new about his character. Fontaine had been indeed very quiet, in love with his profession, much respected and without enemies or quarrels.

'I truly envied 'is technique,' Caroli confessed. 'Fontaine was trained in France and Italy by the best European masters, including Paganini, I believe.'

'Paganini?' McGray asked.

'A very famous violinist,' I said.

'I ken that!' And then he smacked the back of my head.

I turned around slowly and looked at him with wrath. 'Do that again and I shall make you eat every single square of your clown's tartan.' When I turned back to Caroli, the

Italian wretch was grinning in utter amusement. I cleared my throat. 'From what you say, Mr Caroli, I would assume that you were close acquaintances.'

'Oh, yes! We were very good friends for years. Guilleum was the first one to befriend me and my wife when we moved 'ere. We dined together at least once a week. My Lorena enjoyed the old man's company, and Guilleum *loved* 'er cooking. She makes some pasta you wouldn't believe. The secret is in the tomatoes. She roasts 'em with some sea salt and ba–'

'We get the general idea,' I interrupted. 'Now tell me, did you see Mr Fontaine on the day of his death?'

'Yes, at work, as usual.'

'And since you were very close to him, I assume he would have told you about anything unusual that might have happened to him?'

'Yes, but everything went as normal that day. We 'ad the usual chit-chat, Guilleum taught the students . . . I think the only unusual thing 'e did was leaving early to see the Joe Fiddler.'

'We know about that,' I said. 'Well, if you recall anything, no matter how insignificant, please let us know.'

'I will. Rest assured.'

'Mr Caroli, you seem a reliable man,' said McGray just when I was about to stand up. 'Can we show ye something 'n' ask ye a question in the strictest confidence?'

I looked at McGray in puzzlement.

'Yes, yes,' said Caroli. 'If there's anything I can do!'

After asking Downs to leave us for a moment, McGray turned to me. 'Frey, show him the paper.'

'I thought that you were saving that for your gypsy hag.'

As I spoke I produced my handkerchief. I tried to pull the paper out so that the shard of glass did not show.

Caroli gasped when he saw the paper stained in red. His olive skin turned yellowish. 'So it's true! Guilleum was murd—'

McGray seized his shoulder and looked at him intently. 'Mr Caroli, I ken it's hard for ye, but we need ye to focus right now. All right?'

Caroli gulped and nodded just once.

'Could ye possibly tell where this piece of paper came from?' McGray pointed at the little notes visible on the paper. 'Can ye tell which composition?'

Caroli shook his head. 'Of course not! There's 'ardly three notes there. But . . . erm . . . that stamp there, it looks like the stamps from our library. Guilleum was always borrowing scores to practise at 'ome.'

'Good, we might be able to tell which score he was playing. Do you have access to the library records?'

'I don't, I'm afraid, but I know the librarian; he'll let me look at the logs if I ask him.'

'Great. Could ye go and tell us which books were on loan to Mr Fon-teen?'

'Of course, but right now the librarian is ill. A damn drunkard, 'e is. But I can ask 'im for the keys to the records as soon as 'e comes back.'

'We will appreciate your help,' McGray concluded. 'And if ye don't mind, could ye keep whatever ye find between us?'

Once again Caroli nodded, and I wrapped the little paper with my handkerchief again. We then told Downs he could come back in.

'There is only one more violin to deliver,' he said, 'but I am afraid it may be too late now. Mr Caroli, do you know if this chap, Theodore Wood, is still around?'

Caroli chuckled. 'That boy would live in the classroom if we let 'im bring a bed.' As Caroli led us along another corridor, he spoke softly: 'Theodore . . . erm . . . doesn't 'ave a natural talent for music – you must forgive my saying so – but 'e practises like a madman. Day and night! Sometimes the chap doesn't sleep or forgets to eat. I couldn't be that diligent.'

'You seem to know him very well,' I said.

'Oh, yes. We're comrades. You'll see that Theodore is quite – well, let's say *eccentric*. People tend to avoid 'im, but my wife and I 'ave become 'is closest friends.'

The Conservatoire had fallen silent and the sun had already set. We passed in front of a window and I saw a parade of students and maestros going home, most of them carrying instrument cases. Only one violin could be heard in the old building, its echoes bouncing in the now darkened corridors. Even though there were three other men walking next to me, the place suddenly felt desolate.

Caroli knocked on the door of one of the furthermost practice rooms. We heard a muffled voice crying 'Not now!'

'Let me go in,' Caroli said when he saw my exasperated face. 'I'm one of the few who can reason with 'im.' Caroli walked inside and we heard him muttering for a moment, then his hearty laugh, and then he came out. 'The chap will see you. Now, if you'll excuse me, I must leave. My wife must be waiting for me. She is expecting our first child, you see.'

We saw him leave and then entered the practice room

to meet the last beneficiary we would see that day . . . and this one would turn out to be the strangest of all. He was playing in semi-darkness, illumined only by the dim light from a narrow window and the orange flames of a small fireplace, sharp shadows projected on his face.

Theodore Wood was a skinny man but he had a swollen belly, so his body looked like a small pear with long sticks for arms and legs. He had a funny crooked nose, sunken cheeks and wore his long ginger hair in a twisted ponytail. Nevertheless, his most striking feature was the dark bruise on the left-hand side of his neck.

It is common for violinists to exhibit a reddish mark a the chin and neck. They have to hold the instrument solely with their shoulders and jaw, leaving their left hand free to press the strings, so the violin is constantly abrading their skin. When I looked closer I saw that Theodore's case was particularly severe: he did not only have a mark, but a cluster of calloused lumps. My brother Elgie had told me that some musicians even developed allergies to the varnish of their violins. My stepmother was very concerned about this, so she forced him to practise protecting his neck with a silk cloth, which he dropped only when playing in public.

McGray also saw Theodore's neck, and whispered his elegant remark into my ear: 'What a nasty fiddler's hickey!'

For the third time Downs explained Fontaine's will, and Wood listened to him with a rather . . . eerie expression. The man did not even blink, and when Downs showed him the violin case he looked at it as though it was the Ark of the Covenant.

'Fontaine wanted me to have this?' he asked, as if in trance.

'Yes, he did. He left you his Amati.'

'*I don't believe it!*' he hissed. His eyes almost fell out of their sockets as he received the case with shaky hands.

'He's gonna wet himself,' McGray whispered again, and for the first time I agreed with him. Downs was telling Wood about the documents he needed to sign, but the man ignored him. He was already opening the case, and basking in the sight of the ruddy violin with the wooden lion head. It was still stained with blood, but Wood did not seem to notice.

'I don't deserve this . . .' he said, and immediately lifted the violin, felt its weight, then tried it on his neck and plucked the strings. 'I have to tune it.'

'Mr Wood, I must insist on the paperwork!'

Wood finally obliged, but signed so hastily that his name was an unintelligible scribble. Then he kneeled by the fireplace and began to adjust the strings' tuning pegs.

McGray leaned next to him. He, too, was looking at the violin with fascinated eyes. 'Theodore, can ye tell me why this fiddle's so special?'

At first I thought that Theodore would ignore him as he had Downs, but being asked about music only impelled his crazed enthusiasm. His awkward voice even turned bright.

'Oh, there is so much to this little devil! This is one of the oldest instruments known. It belonged to Antonio Stradivari; he used it as one of the models for his violins, when he was perfecting his craft. You may say that this is the father of the Stradivarius violins!' Wood was literally smacking his lips when he said that. 'Then it belonged to Paganini; the most virtuoso violin player in history! Of him you've heard, I assume.'

'Aye,' McGray said, looking at me in mockery. 'O' him I've heard.'

'When Paganini went bankrupt and he had to auction all his instruments, he only kept his most precious violins: this one and his very famous Canon Guarnerius. That violin gave an explosive sound during his concerts, but apparently he only played this Amati in private.'

McGray frowned. 'Why was that? D'ye ken?'

Theodore shrugged. 'No, nobody knows. Some say it's because it has a very dark, kind of breathy sound. Look carefully; the waist is slightly wider than that of a normal instrument, so it does sound a bit graver – up to this day that sort of sound has never been in fashion. Others say that Paganini was so in love with its tone that he reserved it for himself . . . *Now I'll want to believe the latter!'*

His long, bony fingers plucked the strings as he spoke. Each time the violin trilled Wood would inhale deeply, as if the sounds were the dashes of an exquisite fragrance.

Poor Theodore is mad, I thought as I saw him crouched by the fireplace, his eyes staring at the instrument with an intensity that was almost sickly.

'Well, my job here is done,' Downs sighed, visibly tired and quite bored of Wood's chatter. 'Inspectors, do you mind if I leave?'

'Not at all,' I answered, and Downs shoved the signed documents into his briefcase.

I turned to him. 'Mr Downs, do remember we would like you to let us know before you give the violin to Miss Ardglass. We need to be pre–'

Then we heard a sharp plucking sound and Theodore letting out a piercing shriek.

I turned around swiftly and found him on his knees, covering his face with his right hand. Trickles of blood ran between his fingers, and a red splash had stained the fireplace. He'd dropped the violin and I saw it lying on the carpet, one of its strings broken and bloody.

'Dear Lord!'

I kneeled down and gently tried to pull Theodore's hand from his wounded face. The poor man was shaking and moaning.

'The-the . . . the string snapped,' he stammered.

'Easy, easy,' I said in a soothing tone, but I knew I looked as appalled as McGray and Downs.

Finally, Theodore lowered his hand. I retched when I saw his left eye tightly closed: the skin of his eyelid was soaked in red.

'Did it hit the eye?' Downs gasped.

'Dear Lord!' Theodore cried again. 'It burns!'

'Easy, easy,' I insisted, looking closer. Theodore's skin had two straight rips; apparently the string had missed his eye socket – barely. 'It looks like it just hit you in the cheek and eyebrow. I need you to open your eye to check.'

'*No, no!* It burns!' he kept yelling. '*It burns!*'

'You have blood in your eye,' I said, 'that is why it burns.'

I was not so sure about that, but we had to know whether he needed proper medical care or just to wash his wound. I thought I could carefully open the eyelid, but Theodore jumped as soon as my fingertips came in contact with his skin. Then he crawled, whimpering, towards a corner, where he curled up like a foetus.

Nine-Nails leaped forward, and nearly stamped on the

violin as he tried to reach Theodore. He grabbed him by the arms and lifted him effortlessly.

'Laddie, we're trying to help. I ken yer in pain, but . . .'

Theodore would not calm down, so McGray simply pressed him against the wall with one arm and held his head with his free hand.

'Do what ye have to do, Frey.'

In other circumstances I would have been appalled, but that was no time to hesitate. As gently as possible, I pulled the skin of the cheekbone and eyebrow.

'It bu– it burns . . .' Theodore moaned.

I faltered for a moment, but finally managed to open his eye. I saw the white of the eyeball, and for a horrible instant I expected the worst.

Theodore blinked a couple of times, still panting and horrified, but then his pupils began to move all around.

'I . . . I-I can see.'

We all let out a sigh of relief.

'That's great, laddie,' McGray told him, letting go of him. 'Sorry about that, but we had to check.'

Theodore nodded nervously. The skin around the cuts was already swelling.

'You should wash your face,' I said. 'Your eye is fine, but we still have those wounds to attend. Mr Downs, can you help him?'

'But of course!' Downs said immediately, offering his handkerchief to Theodore. 'Come on, lad. We'll give you a good rinse.'

I was going to follow but Downs shook his head. 'It's all right, Inspector. I have seen many a wound,' he said as he helped Theodore out of the room.

As soon as they were gone, McGray kneeled down by the violin, looking fascinated. 'Who would've thought the strings were so bloody tense?'

'I think they have to be,' I said, 'to give the right tones.'

'How . . . interesting.'

'You already think that the bloody thing is cursed, do you not?'

McGray arched his eyebrows, the wrinkles above his forehead deepening. 'Perhaps . . . but I cannae prove it. Not yet.'

He picked up the violin with extreme care. Anyone would have said that he was touching gunpowder. The glass of the carved lion's eyes reflected the flames in the fireplace, and for a moment it looked as if the wooden head was blinking.

'Now . . . whatever angered ye, lil' boy?'

'Do not – do *not* talk to the violin.'

'Why not? It may have interesting things to tell us.'

For a moment he seemed all seriousness, but then he grinned sardonically and I lost my temper. 'Oh, give me that!'

Just as I snatched the violin from his hands, a second string snapped.

It must be in place by now . . . together with my little present.
   Placed so well!

And yet it feels so long, so painfully long, waiting here, squatting
   like the dogs do.

Soon . . . soon . . . soon . . .

13

'Agnes! *Agnes!*'

'Aye, master?'

'*What the hell is this?*'

'Yer suit, master. I mended it.'

'You said that nobody would notice it was torn!'

'Aye, and 'tis not torn no-more. Don't ye see the stitches?'

'*I bloody see them, woman!* It looks as though you were stitching a stuffed ham!'

'But master . . .'

'Oh, shut up! And take the damn thing out of my sight.'

'Don't ye want it? Can I keep it for my husband?'

'Keep it, burn it, use it as a mop, but do *not* touch my clothes ever again! Understood?'

'Aye master.' Then Agnes grabbed the suit with greedy hands. I would also need to find a proper launderer. I could not believe that I was missing Joan more than I did my own father.

That morning Campbell summoned me to his office. I had been working on the case for two full days – which in fact had felt like two weeks – so it was about time to deliver my first report.

Campbell interlaced his fingers and looked at me as quizzically as on the first day. 'Well, Frey? What news can you tell me?'

'The main thing, sir, is that this is definitely not the work of an imitator.'

'Oh, are you certain?'

'Indeed. I can tell that the person we are after is definitely not trying to emulate. The modus operandi is totally different; so is the victim. Jack's killings came out of pure sadistic pleasure, and an imitator's work would have the same taint. There is no such thing in this case; it is clear that the murderer acted with some purpose, as a kind of ritual. We are seeking somebody well versed in the occult.'

'Good, good. What else can you tell about the killer?'

'There are a few things we know for certain. We are looking for a slender, agile person; one able to access the room through the chimney. That immediately discounts Fontaine's maid.'

'Good. I had my doubts about her too.' The man's jaw seemed only a little less tense when he said that. That probably was the way he showed his approval. 'Even if this was not an imitator, you must be as careful as before. This must not leak to the press. You know that these journalists do not look for the truth; they build a saleable story and then just try to find ways to support their twisted tales.'

'I understand, sir.'

'Good, good. I shall leave you to it. Do you think it is possible that we shall see more deaths like this?'

'That I cannot tell . . . We are not certain of the actual nature of the ritual; it might as easily be an isolated event. Whichever the case, I assure you I will make my best efforts to find the murderer as soon as . . . as soon as McGray's eccentricities allow.'

Campbell's eyes opened a little wider. 'Oh! Is he being an obstacle?'

I could only think of the whole morning wasted reading pathetic witchcraft books.

'I will be entirely honest, sir. Things could move a lot faster without having him in the way. Today, for instance, he has scheduled a meeting with a gypsy clairvoyant.'

Campbell meditated, and for a moment I was innocent enough to believe that he would support me. 'Unfortunately, things must stay the way they are, Frey. McGray could not be a better smokescreen.'

'I do understand that, sir, but if at least I could move with autonomy rather than being tied under his authority –'

'Is this really about the case, Frey? Or is it merely your inability to act as a subordinate?' I hesitated one instant, which was enough for Campbell. 'Things seem to be moving at a good pace, so I see no reason to change this arrangement.'

'Sir, with all due respect . . .'

'You mentioned that the murderer appears to be an expert in the occult, did you not?'

'Yes, but . . .'

'Then McGray will be of some help. I doubt you have that sort of knowledge.'

I bit my lip in frustration. 'I suppose that is true, but I cannot see how –'

'I shall not discuss that with you, Frey. Is there any other issue you wish to mention?'

I could not repress a frustrated grunt, but then remembered that I did have something else to complain about.

'Well, I also wanted comment about this chap in the morgue . . .'

'Dr Reed?'

'Indeed. I would strongly recommend you to hire another forensic doctor; a man of more experience. Reed is far too young to be running the town's morgue.'

Campbell nodded. 'I know that. We had to appoint him after Dr Carter retired. Reed is one of the most distinguished graduates in town. In fact, you are the first to complain about him.'

'I am not complaining, sir. I simply think that this case in particular might be too much for him. I am not asking for his dismissal; simply for a more experienced person to be sent.'

'Frey, I have a very busy agenda today. You will have to make do with Reed, and that is not up for discussion. A more experienced forensic would cost us money and we are not in a position to squander our budget. You would do well to remember that this is not your wealthy London.'

I blew inside my cheeks. 'Sir, Commissioner Monro sent me because he trusts my judgement. Frankly, I do not see the point of my presence if all my suggestions are dismissed by you and Inspector McGray.'

'Would that be all, Frey?'

I grunted. 'Yes, sir.'

'Good. Then you may go.'

Once more, I could only leave the office with tied hands. However, Campbell did not know that I was sending another report to Sir Charles Warren, and that my comments were likely to reach the prime minister's ears.

While the accounts of my progress would not differ much from what I had just said, I spared no adjectives to condemn McGray's foolish authority.

I went downstairs to that pigsty of an office, which I had privately christened 'The Dumping Ground', and found McGray with his feet on the desk again. He lifted a file.

'Pictures, Frey. The photographer finally brought them. D'ye want to have a wee look?'

I went through the glossy photographs, meticulously scanning every inch and feature. I was happy to see that the scene had indeed not been altered at all. The first few images showed Fontaine's eviscerated body before it had been removed from the study's floor, then there was a close shot of the bloodstained violin, which lay close to the body, half hidden under the desk as we'd found it. There were also a couple of pictures of the satanic symbol and of the empty music stand, where I recognized the dark specks of blood.

The stack ended with some photographs taken during the post-mortem, which showed the half-emptied belly of the old man in detail. I felt glad I'd only had coffee that morning, for I had to pay particular attention to those pictures. I could corroborate that Fontaine had been attacked most viciously – the cut on his throat was a clean, straight slash, but the work on his abdomen was as savage as Reed had reported it.

'Can ye tell anything from those?'

I shook my head. 'They did a good job at documenting the scene and the post-mortem, but to be honest I cannot deduce anything new from these.'

'Neither can I. File them, anyway.'

I threw the file into one of the empty drawers of my desk, not knowing then how useful those images would eventually prove to be.

'What now?' I asked wearily. 'Gypsy clairvoyant? I would be keener to talk to the luthier.'

'Aye, we have to see that lad some time soon, but today we go to Madame Katerina's. Also, I think we should have a wee talk with the Ardglass clan.'

'Oh, yes.' I remembered McGray's tension when we'd met Alistair Ardglass. 'What was all that about?'

McGray sighed, toying with a wooden amulet of some sort. He passed it through his fingers, and it surprised me how skilled the remaining phalange of his lost finger actually was. 'I probably shouldn't tell ye this, and I will only cos I don't want ye to whine if I treat them like the scum they are.' A deeper sigh followed, as though McGray was gathering patience. 'It all began when my father bought our house in Moray Place, nine . . . God, almost ten years ago! That Lady Glass bitch defamed us as much as she could. We were new money and she didn't like that. For a good while we weren't well received in society . . . Of course, it all changed when the rascals found out how much the McGrays were worth in gold – we had some nice wee times then. It didn't last long, though. When –' McGray suddenly stopped, his jaw tense and hatred in his eyes. He dropped the amulet onto the desk. 'When my folks died Lady Glass struck again, gossiping and planting her poison against this household. That's why I cannae even get a decent bloody cook!'

'Why do you call her Lady Glass?' I asked.

He cackled, a joyful glow in his eyes. 'It's not only me. Abody calls her that for her drinking . . . She claims to come from noble lineage, all the way back to the War o' the Roses, just marrying commoners from time to time to avoid harelip. Well, she may be as grand as she wants, but she still cannae spend more than three days without getting blootered.'

'Getting what?'

'Blootered! Drunk! Unable to put her glass doun! Anyways, the hag owns about a third of Edinburgh and makes a fortune every year from letting her properties.'

'Oh! So she was Fontaine's landlady?'

'Aye. Fontaine's maid called the police and Lady Glass when she couldn't open the door and Fontaine didn't reply. Lady Glass was the one who wouldn't let the police break the door cos a window would be cheaper to replace. The stingy hag . . .'

I nodded, pondering the information. 'There could be a connection, yes. And there is something I do not quite like about that Alistair. Then again, if that woman owns so many properties, it might be just a coincidence. Whichever the case, it would not harm us to ask them a few questions. After we visit your charlatan witch, perhaps?'

'We'll play it by ear. And don't call her a witch. Yer gonna love Madame Katerina.'

I knew that McGray would not change his plans, but I whined throughout the ride nonetheless – through the Old Town, along the avenues around the castle, and then to one of the filthiest spots in Edinburgh: the Cattle Market.

'I presume you have consulted this bloody clairvoyant in the past?'

'Aye.'

'What does she do? Does she read tea leaves? A crystal ball? Or does she keep guessing until she gets one fact right after a few hours?'

McGray mistook my mockery for actual interest. 'Actually she's got this gift that she calls her "inner eyes". She can see things whenever she touches somethin' with enough . . . she calls them imprints – energy we leave behind.'

I could not believe how stupid all that sounded. And McGray's throaty accent made it all sound far more stupid.

'Actually . . .' I said, producing my pocket watch and wrapping it in the handkerchief with the other items, 'it will be most interesting to gauge your beloved witch's accuracy.' I winked. 'You know, for the sake of scientific curiosity. I shall give her my timepiece, pretending that it is part of the evidence. Let us call it . . . our "control sample", as biologists like to do.'

McGray looked at me most intently. 'Do what ye want, but ye might not like what she'll say.'

The gypsy lived in one of the dreadful shacks that surrounded the wide esplanade of the Cattle Market, only a few blocks south of Castle Rock. Fortunately for me, it was not a market day; otherwise the place would have been packed with smelly cows and oxen from all around Scotland, and the air would have roared with the yelling of sellers and bidders, as well as the bellowing of their beasts. The square did stink of animal, though, and the bare soil, pressed by the hooves of countless cattle over the years, was peppered with their droppings.

We found some posts to tie the horses to and walked towards one of the dilapidated buildings. Only too late I felt my foot plunging into a soft mass of faeces.

'Oh, for Christ's sake!'

Nine-Nails cackled when he saw my otherwise shining shoe covered in dung. He headed to what looked like the filthiest, most crooked beer stall in town, set in the windows of a lodging house. It reminded me of the slums I had seen in London's East End; murky spots where the poorest workers gathered to drink and alleviate a little the misery of their existence.

'I thought we were going to see your crazy witch, not for a drink. Although this does strike me as a place sophisticated enough for you.'

'Madame Katerina keeps the brewery as a side business.'

I whistled. 'Beer seller *and* fortune teller! Why, she gets the clients drunk and then reads their hands! What a bright businesswoman.'

McGray talked to the fat chap who was serving beer to a couple of builders. 'Mornin', laddie. Can we see yer boss?'

'Course, Mr McGray. Ye ken she always welcomes ye.'

The man took some coins from the already half-drunk workers and then led us in. We followed him through a darkened, damp storage room crammed with barrels of beer, and then up a creaking staircase. We passed into an equally dark room, lit only by the orange glow of a small fireplace. The room did have a window, but it was covered with thick curtains.

'Madame Katerina won't be long,' the chap said and then walked away.

I looked around in discomfort. 'Oh, McGray! Where have you brought me now?'

The weariness in my voice was well justified. Out of all the dubious places I'd seen in the previous days, this one was the strangest: the walls were completely covered with faded, moth-eaten tapestries (most likely second or third hand), there were shelves displaying stuffed birds and snakes, skeletons, crystal balls of all sizes, and many other artefacts whose use I preferred not to question. It resembled the mess in McGray's office, only ten times odder.

As I looked around a heavy drowsiness began to hit me, partly because of the intense smell of incense mixed with other odorous herbs, but also because the fire kept the room much warmer than required. The tapestries on the walls helped to keep that uncomfortable heat inside . . . and to retain the herbal reek.

I sat at the round table in the middle of the room, took off my overcoat and produced my clean handkerchief. I pressed it against my nose for a moment and then carefully wiped beads of sweat off my temples.

Nine-Nails cast me a mocking look. 'Och, next time we'll bring ye a lavender posy and a Flemish lace fan!'

I was about to retort but was interrupted by the loud, coarse voice of a woman: 'Oh, Adolphus! I knew ye were coming! I dreamt about ye last night!'

Turning round, I saw a medium-built woman emerging from behind the hanging tapestries. The wretched gypsy was so unbelievably weird I still do not know where to start . . . She was all wrapped in colourful cloaks and veils, over which lay countless chains, pendants, bracelets and charms, so she jingled with every move she made. She had a chiselled, angular face; her aquiline nose, thick eyebrows and rather pointy ears were all pierced with either a drop or a pendant.

Among her total extravagance there were a couple of things literally standing out, for she had the widest, largest bosom I have ever beheld. And she wore an indecent, plunging neckline, and walked with her back arched in a shameless, most vulgar way.

I chuckled, still not believing that I was actually there. 'Did you hear that, McGray? She *knew* that you were coming! Why, she must have seen your hairy face in her tea . . . oh, sorry, you said that she uses her *inner eyes*!'

She looked at me with bitterness and, again, spoke with her loud voice and the strangest Eastern European accent I had heard. 'Oh my! And you brought Inspector Frey! The greatest let-down of the English police!' She drew closer and winked maliciously at me. 'And I didn't need to use my inner eyes to see *that*.'

I pulled my face away, for her breath stank of stale beer. Her green eyes, despite the abnormally long eyelashes agglomerated in excessive mascara, were fierce and alert. I could tell that I was in front of a clever, yet ruthless person.

'Lassie, this is Madame Katerina,' McGray said . . . needlessly.

She sat in front of me, stretching her arms on the table, as if to reaffirm that she fancied herself in charge, and drummed her *very* long fingernails on the red tablecloth – painted in black, they looked like vicious claws. Her bosom was so offensively wide that it was hard to keep one's eyes off it. 'Well, Adolphus, what brings you here today?'

I mumbled: 'Oh, so when you foresaw that McGray was coming, you could not see what for.'

'Shut up and give her the stuff,' McGray snapped, sitting next to me. 'We found these things in —'

'Shush!' she cried, 'remember you mustn't contaminate my vision! Give me that and *I* will talk.'

She extended her hand towards me and I could see that the sides of her fingers were tattooed with the shapes of thorny roses.

I first produced the piece of paper and Katerina snatched it, twisting and stretching her neck as if preparing for a tough physical chore. Her eyes were closed tightly when she began to run her fingers across the little paper . . . and then she groaned.

The woman spent several minutes in that attitude and I felt like an utter idiot simply for looking at her. However, whenever I was about to speak or tried to take the piece of notation from her, McGray would invariably elbow me in the ribs.

Finally, after a seemingly endless trance, she spoke hesitantly. 'I-I . . . see a dark tunnel . . . black, very black. And then . . . some weak light in the end . . .'

I arched an eyebrow, for once as baffled as McGray. Could that mean that she was seeing . . . ?

Katerina let out a growl of frustration and opened her eyes. 'I'm sorry, that's all I can see . . . this paper doesn't have enough imprints for me to see more.'

'What a surprise,' I mumbled.

Katerina banged her palm on the table and snapped: 'Would you be able to see if I turned all the lights off, you insufferable know-all? I wasn't finished! There isn't enough energy imprints in this . . . but I do feel that . . .' She seemed confused, looking for words. 'I feel that there is more to it than it seems. As if I'd been looking through a window and someone had drawn the curtains.'

I shrugged and replied carelessly. 'That is one *imaginative* argument. You may be luckier with this one,' and I gave her my very own pocket watch. McGray's eyes were fixed on her, even more expectant than when she'd held the fragment of notation.

As soon as her fingertips touched it the woman started: 'My goodness, *so much noise*! So much noise in this man's head! It all comes in a torrent. Pernickety . . . cantankerous . . . conceited . . .'

'*What!*'

'Sounds about right to me!' Nine-Nails declared, grinning.

'But there is something else. Something subtle, sort of whispering underneath all that noise. Yes. A very conscious sorrow; a feeling of – of . . . what does he call it? *Lack of purpose . . . of not belonging.*' Then she dropped it on the table. 'Other than that, this belongs to a quite harmless boy.'

I took the watch again, seeing with the corner of my eye that McGray was grinning mordantly. 'We have one last item. You should be careful, it is sharp.'

I laid the piece of glass on the table and, from the moment she saw it, Katerina's mood changed. She stared at it for a moment, examining it warily.

With a hesitant hand, Katerina picked it up and for a moment nothing happened. She closed her eyes and tilted her head, as if she were trying to make out a very faint sound, and waited.

All of a sudden Katerina gasped and changed colour, as if hit by a sudden nausea. For a moment I thought that she was about to vomit. She was quivering, her face distorted in a horrified expression, as she gripped the glass so tightly that I feared she would pierce her palm.

She opened her mouth and tried to speak but another voice came out; a vile, coarse whisper that chilled my spine.

'I see ... thin, long shadows on a filthy floor ... It's a cage, the bars of a cage! And there's something there; something nasty, crouching, lurking – Oh, it's a strong presence; turbulent ... tormented. An encaged, deranged ... *genius*!' Her entire body shuddered then. 'Bloodthirsty! Bloodthirsty and desperate to prove its value to the world!'

And then she threw the glass onto the table. I could see the outline of the shard printed on her skin, yet no wounds. She lounged back, panting as if she'd run a mile, her face distorted.

'Are ye all right?' McGray asked.

'I thought you would be used to her theatricals,' I said, but McGray seemed genuinely concerned. He moved closer to the woman and talked softly.

'I've never seen ye quite like this, hen. Can we bring ye some water or something?'

I shook my head, still not believing her act. Katerina was taking deep, troubled breaths.

'I think I've seen the Devil,' she muttered at last. All fierceness had abandoned her eyes. She was totally frightened, and there also was a great confusion in her face. Then she grasped McGray's hand. 'Oh, Adolphus, you must catch this one! This is a monster, a monster I tell ye!'

McGray assented. 'Now that ye've seen that, I can tell ye that we found those wee things in a crime scene. Mr Fon-teen –'

'Fontaine.'

'Shut up! A musician, he was, Cut throat and all butchered.' I was going to protest, for McGray was giving away confidential information, but he extended his four-fingered hand, asking me to hold back. 'Katerina, there was a mark painted with his blood . . . the five eyes.'

Katerina gasped. 'Doesn't surprise me, not now that I've looked into this wretch's heart . . .'

'Can ye see anything else?'

Katerina shook her head, visibly annoyed. 'Nae, nae, Adolphus. Let me try again.'

She lifted the shard, held it for a while, mumbled and grunted, but that first, explosive reaction would not happen again.

'I'm sorry,' she moaned, her face all dejection. 'It's spent all its energy . . . But I did feel a weaker presence. I can't quite describe it; it's a gentle one – old. Doesn't make sense to me.'

McGray assented, as I began to wonder whether she referred to Fontaine. I cast those silly thoughts out of my head.

She gave me back the shard and then took the piece of score one more time. 'What a shame I can't see more from this. It feels like there is more to this wee paper.' She was looking at it with piercing eyes. 'Oh yes. There is more to it, Adolphus, *believe me*. Find more about it, as much as you can. I'm sure this paper will lead your way.'

14

McGray left Madame Katerina's brewery in an exhilarated state. 'Told ye, dandy! She's one in a million – and I almost met a million seers before findin' her.'

'I still do not believe what she said.'

'Oh! Then how can ye explain what she said about ye?'

'A lucky coincidence for her,' I retorted, munching my bad temper.

'Aye, yer *always* right! Also, she missed a mighty important bit about ye: she didn't mention what a whiny bitch ye are! Anyways, I'm glad that chap Caroli's looking for the name o' that tune. My gut told me I had to ask him.'

'There, there. Next you will tell me that you have inner eyes too. Shall we go and question that bloody Joe Fiddler now?'

'Nae. 'Tis past noon. I need lunch.'

I sighed wearily, for I was beginning to learn that protesting against McGray was a total waste of energy. He innocently invited me to eat with him at the Ensign Ewart, and I could only laugh. '*Eat there again?* I'd as soon rub my tongue with a culture of bubonic plague.'

Nine-Nails replied with an unintelligible splutter in his most impenetrable Scottish and then went away. I saw him ride towards Castle Rock followed by Tucker, while I turned north heading to the New Club. That day they served the most succulent platter of fish and mussels, and as I savoured it I reflected on our visit to that bloody gypsy.

She was one disgusting person; undoubtedly one of those cold-blooded rogues who know exactly how to squeeze the paupers' pockets. Nevertheless – and it pains me to even write this – the wretched woman had simply talked with sense! Her accuracy when describing my character was most remarkable ... disturbing even: I still doubted that my efforts to redeem myself professionally were worth the doing, and felt utterly out of place in this town and in the stupid subdivision I had been assigned to ... and Katerina managed to mention those sentiments with astonishing precision. She even divined my 'lack of purpose', which were the very words that haunted me throughout my dreadful journey to Edinburgh. Could such coincidences come to be? It was very unlikely, but not impossible.

And what if the information she'd given us regarding the case was similarly accurate? Her description of something that could have well been the interior of a chimney also puzzled me, and her further words – those that I could not verify from my previous knowledge – were intriguing, especially regarding the cage: 'an encaged genius ... bloodthirsty and desperate to prove its value to the world'. It was a chilling statement, and I could not forget that humbled, petrified look in her eyes, as if fear had displaced all her shrewdness.

So absorbed was I in these thoughts that I did not hear the voice of a man calling my name. He had to clear his throat loudly for me to notice, and looking up I found none other than Alistair Ardglass, with his jutting belly, standing next to my table.

'Why, Mr Ardglass!'

'Inspector Frey, what a delight to find you here! I did not know that you held a membership.'

'I only acquired it recently.'

'Would you mind if I joined you for a few minutes?'

'By all means. Have a seat.' Ardglass did so, and immediately the waiter cleared my table and served us some strong coffee. 'I must tell you that I cannot be detained for long. I need to go back to my duties.'

'I understand, Inspector. I shall not entertain you more than a little while. You see, last night I happened to have dinner with my good aunt Lady Anne Ardglass, have you heard about her?'

McGray's sneering description of 'Lady Glass' was impossible to forget. 'Her name has been mentioned once or twice since I arrived.'

My answer appeared to mortify rather than please him. Lady Glass must have her reputation after all.

'While conversing with her, your name inevitably came up,' he continued, 'and my dear aunt was intrigued. She wishes to know whether you are related to the Freys of Magdeburg, connected to Chancery Lane.'

I arched my eyebrows in surprise. 'Indeed I am. I did not know that our name would be acknowledged this far from London.'

'Oh, believe me, some distinguished few do know about you. You see, my aunt had some thorny conveyancing business settled by a very good attorney; Mr William Frey. Do you know him?'

'You might say so. He is my father.'

'Your father! Oh, how delightful. My aunt will be so pleased to know that. She told me how troublesome that case was, and that your good father took care of everything quickly and neatly. She said that she hardly had to lift a finger once he was involved.'

I nodded. 'Yes, my father is still well known in Chancery Lane. He is retired now though.'

'A well deserved rest, I am sure. Inspector, I must tell you that my aunt would be very happy if you paid her a visit at your earliest convenience.'

I instantly remembered what McGray had said about Lady Glass being Fontaine's landlady. Paying her a visit might help us a good deal, but the fact that she herself had requested the appointment inevitably raised my suspicions.

'I am afraid that may take a while,' I said, for I did not want to appear too keen. 'The case of Mr Fontaine is top priority for the CID.'

'Of course, we understand that. You have a very serious profession. But do, *do* feel welcome to call on her whenever you have some time to spare. I shall give you her card . . .' He produced a card written on expensive cotton paper. 'Are there any means to contact you?'

'Well, I am staying at 27 Moray Place; you can send any correspondence there.' I checked my pocket watch. 'You will excuse me, I must go now.' I was not in a terrible rush, but I have never liked to become too close to the people involved in my investigations. I took the card and kept it safe in my breast pocket.

'Oh, Inspector Frey!' Ardglass called before I left, and

then came and whispered at my ear. 'Do not believe everything that Nine-Nails tells you, please. People say that mad blood runs in the veins of the McGrays; *mad blood*. I know that we are civilized gentlemen, not to believe in such tales, but one cannot deny it when a family happens to be that . . . odd.'

I could not help but wrinkle my nose. Every time Ardglass opened his mouth I liked him a little less.

15

'*What the hell is this, Frey?*'

I had not passed through the doorway when McGray's thunderous yell pierced my ears.

The main hall was full of trunks and packages of all shapes and sizes, so many that there were hardly any free spots on the floor. Sticking up between the mess there were two high piles of boxes, between which I found the plump, round figure of old Joan. The woman was wearing a mighty frown, her irreverence more evident than ever, and the dark bags around her eyes told me how tired and sick she was. Nevertheless, seeing her familiar face brought me a warm feeling I did not quite expect.

'Master!' George cried, trying desperately to find a way through the crammed hall. 'This auld woman came in as if she owned the house and got the place all jam-packed! The witch won't listen to me!'

'*Who're ya calling witch?*' Joan howled. I had to put a hand on her shoulder to keep her from screaming out all the slander I know her capable of.

'McGray, this is Joan, my personal servant. I asked her to bring my essentials from London.'

'*Yer essentials!*'

'She even got a dammed mare and pushed it in the stable with yer horse, master!' George snapped.

'Why, you brought Philippa!' I exclaimed, grinning like a child on Christmas Day. Then my eyes met McGray's furious face and I had to clear my throat. 'Joan, I gave you a very concise list of the things you were supposed to fetch! Why did you bring all these bundles?'

'I only brought what you asked me, sir,' Joan retorted, handing me the two-page list that I had written myself. I scanned it swiftly and checked the piles of stuff around me. I was sure there was a mistake, but very soon it became clear that I had slightly underestimated the size of my requirements.

'Dear Lord . . .' I sighed. 'I never thought this list would turn out to be so voluminous.'

'Sir, the one thing I brought that's not in the list is your mare, but Mr Elgie insisted. He said that you would not be happy without a proper mount.'

I nodded and slowly turned back to McGray. 'Is there any, ehem, problem if I keep these things here?'

McGray shook his head. 'I imagine I have no choice.'

Joan sighed in relief and extended a hand, waiting for the settlement that I had promised, but then a brilliant idea hit me.

'Actually . . . McGray, I suppose I should be entitled to have a personal servant. Am I not? I would prefer to have Joan staying here.'

'Impossible! We only have rooms for two servants!' George cried, and McGray had to restrain him just as I had restrained Joan.

'We shan't be here for too long,' I added promptly, recalling the poor suit that Agnes had patched and the nasty, lumpy porridge she served in the mornings. 'After all, Commissioner Monro is supposed to arrange my permanent accommodation in less than a fortnight . . .'

'And I hope he does,' Joan spat in a monotone. 'This place is a whiffy hole!'

I cast an infuriated look at her. *You are not helping!* I mouthed.

McGray shook his head again; I could tell how sick of me he was. 'How can ye call all this twaddle yer essentials?' He walked around and picked one of the boxes. 'Earl Grey tea! Cos we wild Scots don't have tea, I suppose! And now ye want to be served by an Englishwoman! That's typical. Wherever youse English go, there youse take yer teas, yer jams, yer nauseating cucumber sandwiches!' He looked at Joan. 'And yer hogbeasts too!'

Joan's eyes almost popped out of her face. 'Hogbeast your mother, you nine-nailed prick!'

Joan had been in Edinburgh but a few hours, yet she already knew the infamous nickname! McGray blinked for a second and I covered my face. Then I heard what I least expected: McGray exploding in laughter.

'I like this one, Frey! She stays!'

Immediately we heard George's frantic howl: '*What?* Master, ye cannae be serious!'

'I'm sorry, George. Agnes's pottage makes me gag, and she's not kept her promise of not drinking when she's lighting the fireplaces. Besides, this one looks like she can cook properly.'

George went on complaining but McGray had made up his mind. As they kept arguing Joan approached me. 'Mr Frey, I have two letters for you.'

'Letters?'

'Yes. One's from your father and one's from Mr Elgie.'

I took the messages. 'Well, I can imagine what my father has got to tell me, but Elgie?'

First I saw a thick pack of paper sealed in wax. My father never liked envelopes; he always preferred to fold the letters on themselves as in the times of my grandfather. I opened the seal to find that the old Mr Frey had rambled on and on for eighteen sheets – front and back. His compact, elegant hand covered the paper in neverending paragraphs containing all sorts of reprimands, which soon invited me to toss the letter aside.

I crumpled it up and gave it back to Joan, then opened the other envelope. It was a very short note, undoubtedly by the hasty pen of my youngest brother:

Hello Ian,

How are the Scots treating you? I would tell you how shocking it was to hear about your departure, but I am sure Father must have covered that already in lengthy prose. He has been grumpier than usual – the vein in his temple has never looked bluer.

Nevertheless, one very good thing has come out of your calamitous situation – as father refers to it. It took some convincing, but he has finally let me join Sullivan's orchestra in the Lyceum Theatre. His main concern was my not having connections in Edinburgh, but since you are there now, he cannot object.

I must warn you that he has asked me to give him a full account of your circumstances, but I suppose we can concoct some credible lies together.

You must excuse the short letter, but I must start packing presently.

I shall take the next suitable train and meet you very soon.

Your favourite and very excited brother, Elgie

'What the hell! Joan, did you know that Elgie was planning to come?'

'No, sir, but he did tell me he had a surprise for you.'

'What a surprise!' I grumbled. 'Joan, I need you to send a telegram first thing tomorrow morning.'

As I spoke I ran to my room to get some ink and paper. In the telegram I told Elgie in the firmest of ways that I did *not* want him in Scotland. While chasing a Ripper with McGray leading the charge, the last thing I needed was my little brother jumping around and asking me to walk him across town.

The next morning Agnes simmered her last ghastly porridge. McGray gave her a generous settlement and the woman left the house with a wide grin.

George, on the other hand, did not take things so calmly. The old man was furious, casting bitter glances at Joan and me, and mumbling unintelligibly whenever we entered a room. He exploded that very morning: as McGray and I stepped out of the house, we heard him yelling at Joan.

'Now take all that shite out o' the way, ye auld nag!'

Joan's retort was such a display of roaring vulgarity that even the sturdy McGray seemed to squint a bit.

Since we both had horses now, McGray preferred to ride to the City Chambers instead of taking a coach. The morning air was damp with a fine drizzle but, wrapped up in one of the thick overcoats that Joan had brought, I could hardly feel it. I was happy to mount Philippa, my lively white mare, but could not help feeling uneasy while we went along the streets of Old Town; being showered with the contents of some chamber pot was a constant threat.

'Nice beast ye have,' McGray said.

'Oh, I am proud of her,' I replied, patting Philippa's neck. 'A Bavarian Warmblood, she is.'

'Nae, I meant yer maid. That woman's got a sharp tongue!'

I could only laugh. 'Well, now that you mention it, you have a good mount yourself. Is it an Anglo-Arab?'

'Aye, it is.'

'Yes, I recognized the deep chest and the sloping shoulders. Good animals; strong as the English thoroughbreds, yet without the temperament. What is his name?'

'Rye,' McGray said proudly.

'*Rye!* What kind of name is Rye? You might as well call it *oatmeal* . . . or *wheat* . . .'

'I'm sorry it's not as all-michty-arsey as ye'd like. What d'ye call yer mare? Queen Margot?'

'Philippa, actually,' I replied. I preferred not mention that I had named her after Philippa of Hainault, the wife of Edward III.

Nine-Nails chuckled. 'And ye still wonder why I call ye names . . .'

I sighed. 'Anyhow, what is your plan for today? Again, I would suggest we question the luthier.'

'Aye, we need to see that laddie. Did ye bring the piece o' paper?'

'Yes, it is in my pocket. Do you think that the luthier will recognize it?'

'We're not going to the luthier just yet. I wanna show that score to someone else.'

I remembered immediately. 'Do you mean Caroli?'

'Aye. The laddie sent me a note. He found the name o' the tune and is asking us to visit him.'

'Why didn't he tell you in the note?' I protested with a deep frown.

'Dunno, and it really intrigues me.' McGray looked ahead with impatience. 'If he wants to see us in person, he must have something very important – or very delicate – to say.'

16

Danilo Caroli owned a fine house on Hill Street, actually not too far from Moray Place.

To my surprise, it was Caroli himself who opened the door for us, and before I could do anything he received me with a rib-cracking hug and a resounding kiss on each cheek. I simply stood stiff and waited for him to draw his hands off me.

'Mediterraneans . . .' I whispered while he gave McGray the same inappropriate welcome. 'Disgustingly forward.'

'Come in, Inspectors! My wife 'as prepared some antipasti.'

'Mr Caroli, we do not have time for –'

'Haud yer wheesht!' McGray whispered at me.

I whispered too. 'Sorry, could you repeat that? Erm, in English?'

'Och, shut up and get in!' Then he told Tucker to wait outside.

'Oh, let the dog in,' Caroli said. 'My Lorena loves animals. She's got three large dogs 'erself!' Despite being less than four feet away from McGray, Caroli shouted those words from the bottom of his stomach (and the rest of the conversation would proceed at that volume).

Patting our backs with excessive enthusiasm, Caroli led us to a small parlour furnished with Moorish benches crammed with cushions. These were arranged around a cedar-wood chest, richly engraved, that the Carolis used as a coffee table. My eye was caught by the wooden carving in its centre; it was a Venetian gondola complete with its gondolier, and crafted in the most exquisite way. The folds in the man's clothes, the muscles in his arms and even the veins in his clenched hands were all perfect.

'Oh, 'ere is my wife, Lorena!' Caroli pushed us forward when the young lady entered the room.

Mrs Caroli, almost as tall as her husband, was a ravishingly beautiful woman with full red lips and eyes as black as charcoal. Her hair was a cascade of dark curls, framing the white, smooth skin of her cheeks, and she had the most welcoming smile. She wore a mourning dress as black as her eyes, which not only highlighted her white skin, but also her round belly, for she was in the last stages of pregnancy. I saw her hands swathed in black lace mittens, gripping a rosary against her lap. There was something odd in the way she clasped the beads, as if her hands were incongruously tense underneath her pleasant countenance. I would soon learn why.

'Welcome, Inspectors. Please, have a seat.' Unlike her husband, her voice was soft and had a pleasant southern English accent; only occasionally would an open vowel or a rolling R escape from her lips.

The three dogs Caroli had just mentioned were in fact hounds that came trotting around her: huge, dark and drooling. Tucker did not look too keen to approach them, and simply remained crouching in a corner, whimpering from time to time. The golden retriever would not move from that spot throughout our visit.

McGray and I sat down as Caroli called his servants with animated yelling. Two girls and a boy came in immediately, carrying bowls of olives, crusty bread, cold meats, a jug of wine and a cruet set with vinegar and olive oil.

'Mr Caroli, this is not a social visit . . .' I began, but Caroli was shouting commands in fast Italian, and the girls were already pouring wine for us in fat glasses. As if Caroli's voice were not enough noise, the dogs started to bark madly around his wife. She had some difficulty to let go of the beads, and then used her knuckle to push a few pieces of bread off the plates for the dogs to eat from the floor. I had a glimpse of her fingers, which were stiff and knotty, before she quickly gripped the beads again.

It did not take a genius to tell that she suffered severe arthritis. What did surprise me was to see such a serious case in such a young woman; arthritis is mostly an ailment of the elderly. Unless it is triggered by another condition.

Unfortunately, Mrs Caroli noticed my staring. She caught my eye and I believe I even winced.

'I shall take the dogs back to their shack,' she said, visibly uncomfortable. 'You gentlemen have important matters to discuss.'

Caroli jumped off his feet. 'Do you need to do that now? Let me 'elp you.'

'No, you need to attend the inspectors.' Caroli's face would not relax, but Lorena was already pushing the dogs away with her ever clenched hands. 'Don't worry, Danilo. I'll be *very* careful. And don't imply I am clumsy; I do know how to lock the shack.' Then she leaned over the nearest dog and patted its back with affection, 'No bad boy will escape today, will you?'

She smiled at her husband and, reluctantly, Caroli let her go.

'I'm sorry,' he told us. 'She's expecting our first child, as you can see, but all the same she jumps and dances and takes care of the animals . . . It makes me uneasy, especially with 'er condition –'

'We understand,' I said promptly. I felt too embarrassed to let him go on talking about his wife's infirmities.

Mr Caroli then almost forced us to partake of his bread and olives and wine. McGray seemed quite happy; he tried to tempt Tucker with a slice of ham, now that the huge hounds were gone, but the dog refused to leave the safety of his corner. I, as usual, was impatient to get started with the inquiries.

'So ye've found the score,' McGray finally said.

As if she had read his mind, Mrs Caroli came back with one of her maids, who brought a bundle of paper. 'Danilo, I think this is what you wanted the inspectors to see.'

'Oh, yes. I found Fontaine's last loan in the registry, but I thought you might like to see the book itself, so I borrowed this – we keep two copies of all scores in the library.'

The maid handed me the papers, which were very old and rudimentarily sewn together in a soft leather cover. I opened it in the middle and needed but a glance to tell that it was a very difficult piece to play; dotted with quavers, semiquavers, ligatures and very long trills all the way through. I turned to the first page to see the title. What a surprise it turned out to be!

'*Il trillo del diavolo!*' I read, and McGray jumped on his seat.

'The what?'

'Fontaine was playing the Devil's Trill Sonata. How fitting!' I arched my eyebrows. 'In fact ... it is a bit *too* fitting.'

'Tartini's sonata?' McGray asked, before even having a chance to look at the score. I looked at the front page, and the composer was indeed Giuseppe Tartini.

'Do you know about him?' I asked in bewilderment. 'I thought you would only listen to tunes with names like "Toss the Feathers" or "Tripping down the Stairs".'

'Nae, ye halfwit!' McGray exclaimed, looking revolted. 'Those are Irish! Actually I ken the story of that Tartini chap very well.'

'So you know the legend be'ind the Devil's Trill?' Caroli asked.

'I do not,' I declared. 'My brother might have mentioned it to me at some point – he is a proficient violinist, you see – but I do not recall it just now.'

'Mr Caroli, can ye please tell the story to Inspector Frey? I think he'll give it more credit if he hears it from anyone but me.'

'By all means, Inspector. I like telling that story.' Caroli cheerfully bit into a slice of bread soaked in olive oil before beginning the tale. 'Well, Giuseppe Tartini was one of the chief composers of the baroque period. Early eighteenth century, I'm talking about. The man was gifted, but, at least in my opinion, far from being the best of 'is time; 'e began to play the violin at a late age, at about twenty, or so I read, and then spent several years without being very successful. This sonata changed it all, not only because of the music, which is extraordinary by itself, but also because of the way 'e came to compose it. One night Tartini dreamt that the Devil appeared to 'im and took up 'is violin to play. According to 'im, it was the most intelligent, most beautiful music ever 'eard. When Tartini woke up 'e tried to write it down and then composed the sonata from those notes. Until the day of 'is death Tartini claimed that what 'e wrote is not even a shadow of what the Devil played in 'is dream.'

McGray spoke before I could even scoff at that last remark. 'But there are other versions of that story, ain't there?'

'Oh, yes. The grim one. Some people say that it was not a dream; that Tartini in fact sold 'is soul to the Devil in exchange for the best violin piece ever written. It's also said that the Devil put a curse in the music itself.'

'A curse?' I repeated. 'What sort of curse?'

'It's a curse on anyone attempting to play it. And there is some basis for that belief: the last movement is fiendishly difficult to play, even for the maestros . . . And also, there are some passages – the Trills – that can give you cramps in the wrist after playing them for a long while. I've 'eard of violinists who even damaged the nerves of their 'ands from playing this sonata – and never played again!'

I pondered for a moment. Under any other circumstances I would have thought it an old wives' tale, but it actually gave some shape to all the tangle of evidence – a morbid shape, in fact. 'What is your . . . opinion of those tales, Mr Caroli?'

He started by saying what I was already thinking. 'Well, you can always believe that Tartini made it all up to give some distinction to 'is music, or that the Devil's dream came from a drunken night or terrible indigestion ...' then he showed a hint of a smile. 'Still, I sometimes want to believe it's true. The story does 'ave its charm.'

'Charm!'

'Yes, Inspector. Well, at least for us violinists. The Devil's Trill Sonata was the first truly virtuoso piece written for an instrument. See, instrumentation was nothing but an accompaniment for singers before that; very simple and very dull to play. The Devil's sonata drew attention to the beauty of abstract sounds instead of the words and the voice. Personally, I think it's exciting to believe that all the rich instrumental music that we 'ave today was triggered by a gift from the Devil.'

McGray and I exchanged puzzled looks. For a moment his eyes flickered, giving away how troubled his thoughts were.

Mrs Caroli noticed it as well and rolled her eyes. 'You must excuse my husband. All musicians have their share of insanity; it comes with the profession.'

'Ey!' Caroli protested, playfully patting his wife's cheek. By the way they looked at each other I could tell how much he cared for her.

McGray put down his glass of wine. 'Erm ... Mr Caroli, would ye do us another favour? Can ye play a wee bit o' the piece for us?'

'Oh, I can't play the complicated passages without practice; this is one of the most difficult pieces ever composed. But I can try some bars of the first movement, the Larghetto. Let me bring my violin.'

Caroli left the room and Lorena attentively offered us more wine, which I refused.

'How do you find Edinburgh, Inspector Frey?' she asked then. Some small talk to show she did not mind my peeping, I supposed.

'Tolerably well, Mrs Caroli,' I lied, 'thank you. Have you been living here for long?'

'Danilo indeed has – almost seven years now – but not me. My father is a Venetian trader so he splits his time between London and Italy. My sister and I were both born in Venice, but received most of our education in London. I only moved to Scotland after marrying Danilo, a little more than three years ago.'

'That explains the perfect English that you speak,' I said.

'I appreciate it, but I would be a stupid woman if I could not speak properly, after being educated here since I was eleven.'

I winked at McGray. 'Do you see? Perhaps if we take you to London *now*, in about ten years' time you will be able to imitate something that resembles actual English.'

'And maybe if I start kicking yer crotch *now*, I'll take the dandy jabber outta yer mouth by Christmas time.'

Caroli came back bringing his violin and a music stand on which McGray placed the score. After quickly fine-tuning the instrument, Caroli inhaled deeply and began playing.

After listening for a moment I wondered how anyone could relate that music to the Devil. It was the sweetest melody. Written in a six-eight tempo, it almost felt like a waltz – one-two-three, one-two-three. Beautiful notes moving rhythmically like the gentlest swell, I thought they were exactly what the weeping of a fallen angel must sound like.

'I'm afraid that's all I can play.'

McGray assented. 'That's all right. Can we borrow the sheets for a wee while?'

'By all means, if you think they might help you.'

Caroli offered us yet more wine and food, but this time both McGray and I refused. We could have stayed chatting in that house well into the night, such was the Carolis' hospitality, but the streets were getting dark already, so McGray politely refused.

Before we made our way to the entrance, Mrs Caroli set one of her stiff hands on McGray's arm. She had an apprehensive look.

'Aye, Mrs Caroli?'

Lorena bit her lip, but then inhaled deeply and spoke. 'Inspector, I wanted to . . . plead with you to do all you can to find the person responsible for Guilleum's death.'

'What –'

'Nobody has told us anything, but everybody knows by now that poor Guilleum was . . . murdered. Why else would you be questioning people? I am sorry I am so forward, but . . . oh, he was the most extraordinary man, and I do not say it because of his talents – genius seldom does people any good – but because he was so, so compassionate. He befriended my husband and me . . . I think he was our only true friend in town; he understood perfectly what it was like to be a foreigner . . . an outsider . . . to be different.' Her eyes were tainted with sorrow, and she looked down. 'He was an old friend of my father; in fact he was the one who introduced me to Danilo. Oh, poor Guilleum did so much for our families . . . More than I can say. He did not deserve such an end. Please, bring him justice.'

McGray kindly pressed her hand and gave her a long, reassuring look. 'We'll do everything we can, be sure o' that.' He smiled at her and then tried to ease the mood. 'So when do ye expect to deliver?'

I frowned, for in London it is considered terribly inappropriate to ask such questions of a lady. Nevertheless, Mrs Caroli was happy to reply.

'It could happen any moment now. I am looking forward. This is our first child.'

'Merry, merry! D'ye have names in mind?'

'If it is a boy, I was thinking I could call him Giacomo.'

Just as he heard that, Caroli choked and almost spat out the olives he was eating. '*Giacomo!* Ma *sei pazza, Lorena?*'

Mrs Caroli blushed visibly, but then went on as if her husband had not spoken. 'And if it is a girl I would like to call her Lucía, like my late sister.'

Caroli only shook his head. Apparently neither name pleased him much.

Finally they saw us out, and Tucker ran out of the house as one of the servants opened the door. The poor retriever looked relieved as soon as its paws were on the muddy streets.

Caroli said goodbye with another inappropriate hug and then yelled deafening farewells.

'How annoying these Italians are,' I spluttered as soon as we were out of their hearing range. 'They think they can throttle with hugs and suffocate with kisses everyone they stumble across. And do they have to be so unbelievably loud?'

McGray chuckled. 'Aye, for youse English the Frenchman is a stinky clown, the Scotsman's a wild dog, the Spaniard's a mighty fool, the Italian's a bandit . . . Aye, only Englishmen are the pinnacle o' perfection!'

'But of course! Why else would God let the English rule an Empire upon which the sun never sets?'

Nine-Nails chuckled with pleasure. 'Cos even God himself cannae trust leaving an Englishman in the dark.' McGray looked at his pocket watch. 'It's too late to see that Fiddler laddie.' He shrugged. 'Nah, we'll do that tomorrow afternoon.'

'Afternoon? Do we have something scheduled in the morning?'

To my surprise, McGray did not reply, but simply rode on, pulling his horse a little further away from mine. I would have pressed for an answer, but there was something strange in his sudden silence; he was frowning, with his shoulders slightly hunched and an evident discomfort in his stare. It was as though he had wrapped himself in a bubble I should not even attempt to burst.

17

McGray's foul mood would take a while to vanish.

The next morning he refused breakfast, even though Joan's bacon had filled the house with delicious smells. I could not eat much either, for Nine-Nails soon came to rush me. I nearly choked when I saw him: he was wearing a clean shirt (well, cleaner than his usual one) and an overcoat that could almost be described as decent.

'Get ready, lass,' he said instead of good morning. 'It's late.'

He was carrying some items I would have never associated with him: lavender soaps wrapped in ribbons, a package of whisky fudge and a small bouquet of white roses.

'Are you taking that for an investigation? And *I* am the lass!'

'Oh, shut up and move yer royal arse! The coach I called is already waiting.'

'Coach?' I asked. 'The weather is not that bad yet.'

'Aye, but I don't fancy riding today. Not to where we're heading.'

'Are you at least going to tell me where that is?'

'Ye'll see.'

'*The case of the haunted house!*' I roared as the coach took us down south across Lothian Road. 'I cannot believe you! We are in the middle of a case that —'

'Oh, shut up, ye've been whining all the way! I'm sick o' yer accent! Why do youse Southrons talk as if youse got a piece o' hot spud in yer mouths?'

I grunted. 'Do *not* get me started on irritating accents, please!' I banged my fist on the carriage's door. 'I cannot believe your attitude. We have no clear trails on Fontaine's case so far, yet you decide to wander about Edinburgh. What is there so important in this other case?'

'A man named Brewster died in that house. He was frightened to death one day in his own cellar, or so the post-mortem suggested. And his wife went mad without explanation, but a few weeks later, in the same room. Nobody in the CID cared about their case. Who would care about an elderly man who died without leaving much wealth? Or his lunatic widow? But those people deserve a proper investigation as much as Fon-teen does.'

Had my entire career not been depending on the success of Fontaine's case, I perhaps could have agreed with McGray . . . but not right then.

'So where is this "haunted house" we are going to?'

'Up north, just off the Botanical Gardens, but we're not going there today. We're going to the Royal Lunatic Asylum, to find out more about Mrs Brewster's condition.'

'And I suppose you are taking flowers for the mad lady . . .' I said bitterly, glaring at the bouquet and box of sweets McGray was carrying. He went silent in the same odd way he'd done the day before, which made our way all the more uncomfortable.

The ride took us a good while, for the Royal Lunatic Asylum was at the southernmost edge of Edinburgh. We crossed Castle Rock, the Old Town, a huge green area imaginatively called The Moors, and kept going south until the neighbourhood of Morningside. For the rest of the ride I remained silent, arms crossed and frowning, hating every minute I wasted with such nonsense.

Finally, when my bad temper was reaching its peak, the carriage descended beside a bright green lawn towards the asylum, which turned out to be the complete opposite of what I expected.

Most asylums I'd had the chance to see (because of my profession) were filthy gutters; museums of madness. Basically, places to dump the lunatics somewhere to keep them out of sight. Edinburgh's asylum, in contrast, was a wide, very pretty building with brown sandstone walls and many chimneys. The driver took us around it and I saw nothing but lawns: very well-kept gardens with some pine trees and oaks and birches, and a good number of benches evenly distributed. A few patients were pacing about while some male nurses looked after them.

The carriage stopped by the main entrance and when the horses' hoof beats died out, the most peaceful silence came to my ears; only the soft wind, birds twittering and the very occasional voice of a lunatic or a nurse. Even to me, that garden felt like a nice place to have a pleasant read.

A thin, middle-aged man came out to greet us. Dressed in a spotless black suit and walking in a gentlemanly manner, he looked more like the kind of experienced, confident doctor I would have wanted to find in the morgue. His skull was as bald and smooth as a peach, except for dark, neatly combed hair on his temples, and a long, yet very well-trimmed beard.

'Good day, Mr McGray! I was expecting you.' He looked down at McGray's flowers and effeminate gifts. 'Why, I see you'll seize the day and pay a visit to Miss McGray too!'

I blinked in puzzlement. Who on earth was Miss McGray?

'Aye, but we'll see Mrs Brewster first. Ye ken ... business is business. This is Inspector Frey, freshly arrived from London to assist me.'

'Thomas Clouston, the asylum's superintendent, at your service,' he said with a firm handshake. 'Please, follow me.'

He took us along the asylum's spacious corridors towards one of the rooms in the West House, which apparently was the side of the building reserved for working-class and pauper patients. Mrs Brewster's room was on the second level, and when we got there a nurse was leaving with an empty tray.

'Did she eat well, Cas?' Dr Clouston asked.

'Aye, Doctor. But I had to force her a bit. She wouldn't have the stock. Thank God she's resting now.'

'Good work, lass.'

We walked into a small, austere-looking room with just the essentials: a narrow bed, a ewer and a basin, and the smallest cupboard and night table. A bony, elderly woman was sleeping on the bed, her grey hair carefully tied back. Far from being relaxed, her lined face wore a deep frown and she breathed in sharp inhalations. She almost looked as if she were on her deathbed.

McGray leaned over her. 'Is she unwell?'

'No, she is sleeping,' Dr Clouston replied. 'She sleeps a lot these days, but apparently it is helping her. She still is deeply unsettled, but her physical health has definitely improved.'

'How long has she been here?' I asked.

'Next week it will be three months, Mr Frey.'

'Not a terribly long time,' I said. 'Considering how long a lunatic can be stranded in these places.' I noted uncomfortable looks from McGray and Clouston.

'The symptoms remain the same?' McGray asked.

'Yes, Mr McGray. As I told you in my last letter, she is a typical case of general breakdown, although the symptoms have diminished to an extent. During her first weeks she was in a state of constant anxiety; the nurses would find her utterly distressed in the mornings, gazing upwards and clenching the rail of the bed. She manages to sleep now, but as you can see, it is an unquiet slumber.'

'So . . . her case is similar to . . .'

'Yes, Mr McGray.'

'Similar to what?' I asked, but McGray just shrugged.

'She hasn't spoken yet?'

'Unfortunately, not a word yet, Mr McGray.'

I paced around the bed while Dr Clouston continued describing Mrs Brewster's condition in detail. He was indeed a very professional man.

'So what is your theory, McGray?' I asked at the first chance. 'The woogyman in the cellar? What is there so incredible about an elderly widow collapsing?'

'There's nothing in her medical history to hint she'd lose her wits like this,' McGray said.

Dr Clouston nodded. 'That is right. Nothing I can trace from her way of life. Her husband was retired, and even though they had little wealth, Mr Brewster had saved enough to maintain himself and his wife without any privations. I could, however, attribute her state to the strain of losing her husband.'

I lifted my eyebrows. 'I think we have our answer, McGray.'

He shook his head. 'Nae, it's not that simple. She lost her only son many years ago. The laddie was an army cadet in India, only nineteen. Then she lost her parents and three sisters over the years. I think she was prepared to deal with losing a loved one. Besides, that house has a dark history; tragic deaths, one after the other . . .'

'It is not the same as facing tragedies when one is young and strong. If, as you said, she had lost all her loved ones, it is not hard to imagine her dismay when her husband, her very last companion, left her.'

'And how d'ye explain her losing her mind in the exact same room where her husband died?'

'Why, I do not know! Anything sounds more likely than some ghost scaring this woman's husband to death . . . and her to insanity. Shall we go now?'

McGray looked at me with just as much impatience. 'Is that how youse Southrons work out all yer cases? No wonder Jack the Ripper is still as free as a bird!' He turned to the doctor. 'I think there's not much we can do right now. Dr Clouston, if she ever speaks send someone to fetch me, no matter what time or day.'

'I will, Mr McGray.'

'Can ye give her files to Frey? I'd like to have a closer look. Ye ken, when nobody's rushing.'

'By all means, I shall fetch them. Will you please wait for me?'

'Frey can go with ye. In the meantime, I can see Pansy.'

'Very well, then. Do you want me to walk you to –'

'Nae, don't ye worry, I ken the way.'

McGray pulled a couple of roses from the bouquet and laid them on the woman's night table. Then he left the room quickly.

As Dr Clouston led the way to his office, curiosity finally betrayed me.

'Doctor, may I ask who is this . . . Miss McGray?'

He cast me a perplexed look. 'Has he not told you?'

'Well, we have not had many chances to chat.'

Dr Clouston took off his spectacles. 'He is visiting his sister. Miss Amy McGray. He calls her Pansy, like their late parents used to.'

My mouth must have been a perfect O. Until then I had not realized how little I knew about McGray.

'Well, erm . . . What is her condition?'

Clouston's eyes became sombre. 'General breakdown, like Mrs Brewster, and equally unjustified. One day, without any apparent reason, her mind simply snapped. The one difference is that Miss McGray also had paroxysms of rage.' He sighed. 'Poor girl . . . she has been here for five years.'

'Five years!' No wonder McGray had cast me scornful glares when I mocked his flowers and when I remarked how long-lasting mind disorders can be. I cannot express how guilty and embarrassed I felt; I can only say that my cheeks became suddenly hot.

'Are you well, Inspector?' Clouston said. To his eyes I had simply blushed without reason.

I shook my head dismissively. 'Yes, yes. You said five years. Without any improvement at all?'

'Oh no, she improved tremendously during the first few months. She never had violent fits again, and she doesn't tap her head against the windows any more. After six months or so she even began to show some occasional lapses into sanity'

'Oh, really?'

'Yes – well, petty things to the untrained eye. We have a suicidal lord among our patients, and I encouraged him to read aloud to her. Sometimes she seemed to understand and follow the plots: I once saw her biting her fingernails at the climax of a Wilkie Collins, but I am afraid that is all we will ever get from her.'

Something in Clouston's manner had changed. The man had talked about Mrs Brewster's symptoms in a neutral, merely scientific approach, yet he seemed deeply, personally concerned for Miss McGray's state. He was trying to hide it, but that slight tension in his eyes and jaw simply betrayed him. Years of questioning witnesses and suspects had given me the knack of telling when someone was holding something back, yet at that time I preferred not to question him any further.

Once we arrived at his neat office he gave me a thin file. I went through it quickly and saw that it was a typed copy. 'I see McGray had already asked you to have a copy ready for him.'

'Indeed; as soon as he knew about the case. My clerk now keeps track of any new developments and types them with carbon paper so Inspector McGray can have a look too. We used to do the same for his sister up until last year, I think.'

'Oh, why did you stop?'

Clouston shrugged. 'There had been nothing new to report for two whole years, so McGray himself decided to put an end to it.'

Two years reading his sister's medical files without seeing any change . . . the very thought made me shiver. I walked out of Clouston's office in a sombre mood, wondering whether my grip on reason would hold if something like this were to befall Elgie . . .

'Would you like me to show you the way to Miss McGray's room? You can wait for your colleague.'

I nodded without paying much attention . . . All too soon I would regret that.

We were walking silently through the wide corridors of the west wing, when suddenly a horrendous howl echoed behind us. It sounded like the desperate groaning of a gagged man. Clouston turned faster than me, and he was already pulling me aside before I'd even looked.

There was a deranged inmate running along the hall, wearing only a torn nightgown and snarling like a wild animal. He ran past us and I had a glance of appalling, bloodshot eyes, and pieces of torn cloth jutting out of his mouth.

Behind him came three male orderlies screaming frantically. They managed to catch him only a few yards away from us. The man twisted madly and roared so savagely that even I felt disturbed.

As the orderlies dragged him back to his room, one of them pulled repulsive strips of cloth from the man's mouth.

'Poor Johnnie,' said Dr Clouston after a sigh. 'He suffers from an extreme case of delusion. He believes that there are foul vapours in the air, which, in his very words, "waste his insides". He stuffs his nose and mouth with rags or paper to "protect" himself – actually, once he even stuffed his . . . well, I should not tell you such revolting things. You must excuse me; I become passionate about my job.'

'You must indeed,' was all I could say amidst the enraged roaring.

'Fascinating phenomena, delusions,' Clouston went on, his enraptured eyes on the patient. 'I have always wondered how fervently these people must fear or yearn for something . . . how *desperately*, for their minds to simply crack under the strain.'

'Let us hope we never find out ourselves,' I replied.

Just when I was beginning to feel philosophical, the madman got himself loose and ran towards us, charging like a wild buffalo.

The orderlies chased him but caught him one second too late, for the man had gotten close enough to let out a spurt of vomited rags that fell straight onto my trousers.

I do not wish to even recall how repugnant that was for the eyes and the nose. A nurse immediately gave me a clean towel to wipe my suit, and Dr Clouston apologized in every imaginable way. Despite their attentions, my face remained distorted in indignation until we finally arrived at Miss McGray's bedroom.

'Well, this is the room, Inspector,' Clouston told me, still slightly flushed. 'I must leave you now, but thank you for enduring my chatter.'

'Not at all, Doctor. I'll always welcome a civilized conversation.'

Dr Clouston smiled and walked away. I then noticed

that the door to the room was ajar, so I could hear McGray's voice talking cheerfully. I could not quite make out what he was saying though, for he was displaying his thickest Dundee accent.

I could not help myself and, slowly, stepped towards the door and peeped inside.

The first thing I saw was the bouquet of white roses, now in a crystal vase on a small mahogany table. McGray was seated nearby, on an armchair, his arm stretched beyond my field of vision. I tilted a little and managed to see a second armchair . . . and a slender girl facing McGray.

Seemingly in her early twenties, she was a *very* pretty sight.

Everything in that face was delicate and demure: the soft line of her jaw, her pointy nose, the smooth skin and the thin lips like those painted on dolls. Her dark hair was held in a neat braid and adorned with tiny white flowers, wavy locks framing her small ears. Wearing a white muslin dress with lace and embroidered trimmings, she did not look like a lunatic at all.

I recognized in her the wide eyes of McGray, with the same shape and thick eyelashes, but instead of blue hers were of the darkest brown, almost black. She was staring hard at nothing, her expression vacant as her pupils scanned the room around her, seeing but not seeing. Still, there was a certain . . . intensity about her.

Her eyes stopped at some point on the floor and then, in a sharp movement, she lifted her face.

She was looking straight into my eyes . . . And I found myself unable to look away.

She watched me with a firm, arresting stare and I simply could not take my eyes off hers. Those were not the eyes of a demure girl, but of a turbulent, distressed woman.

She opened her eyes a little more, and I could almost tell that she was about to blush. That hint of a coy face lasted less than a second, for she immediately looked away, turning her head towards the window as unexpectedly as before.

McGray caressed her hands. 'What is it, Pan?'

He turned around and saw me, and in a blink his face turned red with rage. All sensible words deserted me as I thought McGray was about to strike me down.

'I-I am sorry!' I spluttered. 'I was about to knock but –'

McGray jumped to his feet and slammed the door in my face.

18

It was one of the most fraught silences I have ever endured. McGray was simply looking out of the coach window, breathing heavily and munching the end of a thick cigar; I could almost see the hatred radiating from him.

After the incident, I had decided to wait for McGray by the carriage, where I stood for more than half an hour until he finally emerged. He simply jumped up to his seat without saying a word, and even though I tried to apologize again, he would not reply. The old phrase 'an atmosphere you could cut with a knife' acquired full meaning for me as the carriage took us back to Moray Place.

I soon understood more apologies would not help. I had clearly touched McGray's most delicate nerve, like that drunkard at the pub. I should be grateful all my bones were still intact.

We had postponed our visit to the luthier so many times that I felt quite weary when we finally reached Saint Julia's Close, where he lived and worked.

It was one of those very narrow closes, as old as Hell, that descend from the north side of the Royal Mile towards Princes Street Gardens. The close ran along steep, irregular stone steps delimited by those horrid tall buildings – only a thin stripe of white sky could be seen, some fifteen yards above our heads.

There were piles of rubbish all around and the street stank of piss. I could only imagine what a frightful experience it must be to walk down there at night.

'How can those violinists choose to bring their instruments to a man who dwells in this sort of place?' I wondered out loud, especially thinking of Alistair Ardglass and his very fake airs of superiority.

'The lad must be terribly good at his trade,' McGray said when we made it to Joe's address. There was a wooden sign hanging from the wall, eroded and cracked after many years of rain, which showed the carved silhouette of a violin.

The door to the workshop was open, so McGray and I simply walked in. Our steps lifted small clouds of sawdust, for the small room was an utter muddle: tools, violins in repair, crumpled diagrams of violins, blocks of half-carved ebony and maple, and timber shavings scattered all over the floor. The place smelled of freshly cut wood and oily varnish . . . and also as if the man had been breaking wind in the room throughout the day.

Nine-Nails whistled and then cried as he fanned his nose: 'Pheff! This laddie farts worse than Tucker!'

I could only agree. 'I even prefer your weird gypsy's brews.'

There was a line of freshly varnished violins hanging to dry. I had a close look at them and noticed that their backs were all signed with a winding character. Carved in the wood so that the varnish formed a dark pool, the symbol was the amalgamation of a J and an F.

'Joe Fiddler,' I said in a whisper.

'*Who's that?*' a rough voice demanded, and then we saw the luthier himself coming from some back room.

Joe Fiddler was a very short man and seemed to be just skin and bone. He did not strike me as too old but rather battered, for not a single spot on his face was free of wrinkles. He had a twisted nose, lacked his two frontal teeth, and his hair and beard were grey bushes of knotted hair, speckled with sawdust.

Over his mucky clothes he wore a leather apron stained with varnish. 'What d'ye want?' he cried again in the coarsest tone.

'I'm Inspector McGray, from the CID. This is my colleague, Inspector Frey. We came to ask ye a few questions about Mr Fon-teen.'

As soon as he mentioned the name his hostile countenance disappeared. 'Aye, I've been expectin' youse folks to come and ask questions.' Walking with a limp, he pulled some wooden boxes across and wiped away the thick layer of sawdust that coated them. 'Siddoun.'

McGray sat but I preferred to remain standing. I had ruined enough suits already.

'Ye aware o' Mr Fon-teen's passing, ain't ye?'

'Aye.'

'D'ye ken ye were the last man he spoke to before he died?'

'I ken now. I kinda thought so, from what his housekeeper told me.'

'So ye ken Goodwife Hill?'

'Aye.'

McGray nodded. 'Can ye tell us about that day? Why did Mr Fon-teen come here?'

'Aye. To pick up his fiddle.'

'Ye were repairing it, weren't ye?'

'Aye' – His monotonous way to utter those 'ayes' was soon getting on my nerves.

'Did ye notice anything weird with Fon-teen?'

Then a surprise: 'Aye.'

McGray and I exchanged a triumphant, yet discreet look. Joe Fiddler was the first person actually reporting something abnormal around Fontaine. Suddenly his foul vernacular sounded like Heaven.

'Tell us,' McGray asked him, his full attention on scruffy Fiddler.

'Well, Guilleum had been worried about his fiddle for a while. He wouldn't tell anyone else but me.'

'So he had a good deal of confidence in you,' I said.

'Aye. I've been repairin' his fiddles even before he moved into town. The last ten years he'd have me for dinner now and then.'

McGray nodded. 'Very well. So ye saying that Fon-teen was concerned about his fiddle. Are ye talking about his Amati?'

I studied carefully the man's reaction and noticed McGray doing the same. His mentioning the right instrument did surprise the luthier, who wrinkled his nose as if suddenly aware of the room's odour.

'Aye. How'd ye ken?'

'We ken a good deal, lad,' McGray said. 'So, what was Mr Fontaine's fear? He afraid someone would steal the Amati?'

Joe Fiddler opened his mouth but then hesitated. 'Errrrr . . . Nae . . . well – maybe.'

'Can you elaborate on that, please?' I said.

'Can I ela– what?'

'Tell us more about it,' McGray jumped in.

'Well, it all began early last year . . . I think. The fiddle had been givin' up – 'Tis a very old piece. But both Guilleum and me were surprised the neck and the scroll were givin' way: he'd been playin' it for decades, but all of a sudden the thing cracked.'

McGray intervened. 'Sorry, Joe, I'm not too learned about fiddles. Can ye explain me to exactly how it cracked?'

Joe Fiddler grabbed one of the half-finished instruments and pointed at the pieces as he spoke. His fingers were long and knotted. 'The neck is this long piece o' wood, almost always maple wood, holding the ebony fingerboard. The scroll is . . . well, the scroll: this curly carved piece at the tip of the neck, where ye have the tuning pegs. The only piece o' the fiddle that's there for decoration.'

Just like Theodore Wood, Joe Fiddler was spurred to talk when one asked him about his craft.

'The neck looks glued on very firmly,' McGray observed. 'Yet ye said it cracked. How come?'

'Playing it very tensely for hours and hours. It does happen, Inspector. One can tell a lot o' the fiddler by lookin' at the fiddle. This guy Ardglass, d'youse ken him?'

'Aye we do.'

'He plays like a damn beast; I have to adjust his fiddles every few months cos he wears them out. He grips the neck with his harsh, fat fingers and breaks the bridges with his mad bowing. Old Guilleum was very gentle with his instruments; only brought them to me for maintenance, and even then more often than needed. Aye, he treated his fiddles like they were his children. That's why I was so dazed when the Amati started to get all worn and torn. I would repair it and adjust it at least once a month for a while, until the poor wee fiddle finally gave up. Old Guilleum was appalled when he brought the pieces, but I did a good job, Ah'm tellin' youse. Adjusted the neck, got a new fingerboard cos the auld one was all scratched . . . and I also added a pretty lion head instead o' the scroll.'

'Really?' I interrupted. 'Why was that?'

'Guilleum's request.'

'I see. Did you carve that yourself?'

'Och, nae! That was very fine work; even I cannae do that kind o' detail. Nae, Guilleum told me he got that from some good friend and he wanted it on the Amati.'

'That sounds like a very special request,' McGray said. 'Did he ever mention who gave 'im that?'

'Aye. He said it was this Italian laddie. Mr Caroli.'

'How strange Signor Caroli would not mention that,' I muttered, remembering the very fine carvings we'd seen at his house. It made sense. I took a mental note before moving on to my next question. 'Did Mr Fontaine ever explain the sudden change in his playing?'

'Never. He always claimed to be playin' too much himself, but I could tell he was lying. He kept playin' his other fiddles and those were normal. I just had to give them the usual maintenance.'

'So . . . what d'ye reckon was happening?'

'I can tell, almost assure youse, that someone else was playin' that Amati. And for a good while, I tell youse. There's no way Guilleum wouldn't notice who.'

There was a moment of silence while McGray and I recollected the whole story.

'That is very . . . interesting,' I muttered, and McGray nodded.

'That last day he came, Guilleum looked a wee bit nervous to take the fiddle back. In the middle of our talk he said somethin' 'bout someone wanting to get hold of it – I cannae remember the exact words. I found that weird, but he wouldn't say no more. It looked kinda like he was sorry to have mentioned the matter at all.'

McGray drew a bit closer. 'Why would anyone be particularly interested in that fiddle? Fon-teen owned a Stradivarius, far more valuable and far more appreciated by musicians.'

Joe Fiddler clicked his tongue. 'That wee fiddle's an Amati and it's got a lot o' history. It belonged to Paganini, which abody ken, but only a few ken that before that it belonged to Stradivari, and even fewer ken that between Stradivari and Paganini it belonged briefly to this chap . . . what's his name? Tartini.'

McGray almost fell off the box he was sitting on. '*Tartini!*'

'Aye. Ye ken about him, I see. Some people like to think that it was the fiddle he used to write his Auld Nick's sonata.'

'Old Nick?' I repeated.

'That's what we call the Devil, Frey,' McGray said, suddenly very serious.

Joe Fiddler nodded.

'So that instrument is supposed to be the very violin that, according to Tartini's mad tale, was played by the Devil,' I concluded.

'Aye. That's why people call it the Maledetto, the cursed one, and say that it'll only bring disgrace to its owners. Some even blame Paganini's demise on that fiddle. The man lost all his money in gambles and died in misery. Even I have more wealth than him in his last years. It is a famous anecdote, too, how he lost it: someone actually stole it from his home right before he died and his household was in commotion. Apparently they were after his famous Guarnerius, but the idiots took the wrong one!'

'What happened then?' McGray asked, enthralled.

'The fiddle's history gets blurry after that. It must've passed from hand to hand in the black market for more than twenty years. In the end Guilleum bought it from a wretched French merchant that was dying of tuberculosis. Youse can see the fiddle deserves its reputation.'

Just like when we questioned the Carolis, McGray's eyes flickered, his mind apparently working at full speed. He jumped up from his seat.

'I think this is all we need to ask ye for now. Unless the stuck-up dandy wants to ask ye somethin' else.'

I was not sure I should ask what I was about to, but I'd rather speak than remain in doubt.

'Mr Fiddler, I could not help but notice that you walk with a slight limp. Is your leg injured?'

Joe Fiddler chuckled bitterly. 'That's a way to put it . . .'

Then, saying no more, he pulled up his baggy trousers. He had a wooden leg.

19

'D'ye really believe Joe Fiddler could've done it?' Nine-Nails spluttered as we returned to Moray Place.

'Not strongly,' I said, 'but I find it best to suspect everybody.'

'Even with the lad's pirate leg? And ye say *I'm* mad!'

As soon as I stepped out of the carriage I wrapped up in my overcoat, for it was already dark and the temperature was dropping. We were well into November and the days were speedily getting shorter.

Before we made our way to the entrance George stormed out through the backdoor, his cheeks red with rage.

'Master! C'min! See what that mad hag's done with the house!'

I covered my face in utter frustration and we walked into, well, some place that looked nothing like the house we'd left in the morning.

The mountain of boxes was gone from the main hall; the rug had been washed to reveal that, underneath its former layer of dust, it bore a Persian pattern; the furnishings and the wood panelling on the walls had been polished, and the chandelier lighted it all up with an entire new set of candles.

Joan, in fact, looked as if she'd absorbed all the scruffiness of the place; her apron stained and greasy, her hem torn in a few spots, her hair a mess and her reddened face peppered with beads of sweat. Still, she was grinning with pride when she saw us come in.

'D'you like it, master?'

'To say the least!' I said, trying to contain my true and utter delight. 'Did you do all this on your own?'

'Nae! She brought an army o' tatty brats to help her,' George yelled.

'You didn't expect me to clean years and years of filth all by myself, did you? Oh, and I also spent some money on new pots. I wasn't gonna cook my master's dinner in one of those old spittoons you had here!'

'Dinner!' McGray cried, stepping into the breakfast room, where a steaming beef stew was waiting for us. My mouth watered as soon as I smelled it – after a whole day riding in the frosty streets, the hot, meaty stew was precisely what we needed.

McGray attacked the food with utter pleasure (I guessed he had not eaten a decent homemade meal for years). Minutes later he was smacking his lips and letting out a delighted belch.

'Frey, I'm not gonna miss ye when the case is done; I'm gonna miss yer maid.'

George grunted and McGray patted his back with affection. 'Come on, George, don't be jealous! If anything, this woman's givin' ye more free time.'

Nine-Nails burped again, his belch half mixed into his following words: 'Come on, lassie, we've got a good deal to discuss.'

We left Joan and George to clear the table. As they did so, the pair argued in angry hisses, among which I could made out 'ye fat cow' and 'you ancient wreckage'.

I joined McGray by the big fireplace in his messy library. He was already leaning over his small table, where Caroli's open score still lay. Tucker was sleeping peacefully next to him.

'Gimme the piece o' sheet.'

'Pardon me?'

'The piece o' music sheet!'

'Oh, I see!'

I gave him the now dry paper and he went through the score, holding the reddened piece over it as he turned the pages.

'What are you doing?' I asked.

'I wanna make sure 'tis the tune we're looking for. I didn't want to show the bloody piece o' paper in front o' the pregnant lady. It's a very auld copy, copied by hand, so this particular bit may not be on the same spot.'

McGray scanned over the pages for another minute, his three long fingers and stump running through the stave lines.

'Och, there it is!' he exclaimed.

He held the torn corner over the handwritten notes. It was a short passage, but it was clear that every single note matched.

McGray rubbed his face heavily, the golden glow of the fire casting shadows on his lined face. His frown was deeper than usual. 'Looks like my suspicions were true . . .'

'What suspicions?'

'Ever since Campbell told me about this case I've had this theory in my head, but I didn't want to tell ye until there was enough evidence. Now, lassie, I need ye to do what I brought ye for.'

'And that would be . . . ?'

'To hear my theory and then judge it with an unclouded head.'

I lounged on the armchair in front of McGray and lit one of the Cuban cigars that Joan had brought me. 'Tell me everything. This should be entertaining.'

'I confess, Frey, that when ye said that I would only dance to folksy tunes, ye weren't entirely wrong. I dunno anything about those almighty composers and players, except for Tartini and Paganini. And I ken about them only cos they've one thing in common: they are believed to have had dealings with the Devil.'

'And the Devil appears to be your area of expertise.'

'Thanks! Even if ye said it mockingly. Ye heard the tales o' Tartini and his sonata composed by the Devil . . .'

'*Allegedly* composed by the Devil,' I remarked.

'Whatever! Now ye also need to hear Paganini's legends.'

'I know that Paganini is believed to be the best violin player in history.'

'Indeed. So darn good that some folks thought him . . . twisted.'

McGray stood up, plunged his hand in a pile of books and pulled one out swiftly. The ease with which he found his way was most impressive; he'd probably be able to find a specific sheet of paper in that room even with his eyes covered.

'Hear what some people thought about him,' he said, turning the pages of the thin volume and then reading aloud. '"The excitement that he caused was so unusual, the magic that he practised upon the fantasy of his hearers so powerful, that they could not satisfy themselves with a natural explanation. Old tales of witches and ghosts came into their minds. They tried to explain the wonder of his playing, to fathom the magic of his genius by invoking the supernatural. They even suggested that he'd dedicated his soul to the Devil! There is in his appearance something so demonic that one looks for a glimpse of a cloven hoof."'

'You said it yourself; that is nothing but ignorant people trying to explain something they did not understand.'

'Aye, but even the wildest legends have their share o' truth. Paganini, among other oddities, had abnormally long fingers.'

He showed me an engraved page which depicted a very bony, rather handsome violinist in the centre of an astounded crowd. His hands, casually holding the violin, looked terribly long and sturdy. I calculated that, if that portrait was accurate, those fingers would have easily spanned more than two-thirds of the violin's fingerboard.

McGray pulled out a piece of paper that was inserted in the book. The sheet was crammed with handwriting. 'Here are the notes I scribed when I met a very auld chap who'd seen Paganini playing. He told me that his fingers looked like long claws; his hand could go all the way to the highest notes with no trouble. And everybody agreed that when he played there was something unnatural, eerie about him.'

I let out a puff of fragrant smoke. 'And that was enough for people to say that he had dealings with the Devil?'

'That, and the stories about his dead mistresses, and that throughout his career he refused to play with metallic strings. He only used catgut.'

I raised my head slowly once I heard that. Things indeed were beginning to take shape. 'Tell me.'

'Ye ken that catgut is not made from cats . . .'

'But from goats. Yes, I know.'

'Well, there was word that Paganini didn't use strings made from goat bowels . . . but from humans . . .' My mind whirled with those words, and somehow the crackling of the fire appeared louder to my ears. 'And he didn't use guts from mere strangers,' McGray added, 'but from his mistresses.'

I felt a sudden chill, recalling the ghastly photographs showing Fontaine's open carcass and also the report from Dr Reed: Fontaine's body was missing several feet of intestines.

'Paganini had many, *many* lassies, and several women around him died in mysterious circumstances through the years. The tale became famous; the tale o' Paganini murdering his women, trapping their souls into his fiddle, and then using their guts to make strings.'

'I see now,' I muttered, 'but you look desperate to tell me the whole thing, so go ahead.'

McGray sat again, his blue eyes glowing next to the fire. 'The murderer is *not* trying to imitate Jack the Ripper, but Giuseppe Tartini; someone wants to use the same fiddle the Devil played – the one that Paganini used to encage the souls o' his lovers – and to play it with human catgut. This bastard is a clever one too; he's not using just any guts, but the guts of a virtuoso, and he's used the symbol – the five eyes – to tell Auld Nick what he's up to; to invite him to appear and play his violin once his set o' strings is ready. Most likely he wants the Devil to compose another sonata.'

McGray then sat back, as if those words had drained all his energy. 'So?' he sighed. 'Makes any sense to yer scientific mind?'

I savoured the tobacco for a little while as I thought. It was a great deal of information to digest.

'In my opinion,' I finally said, 'those tales about Paganini are utter rubbish, and Tartini's dream of the Devil sounds awfully like a frustrated man appealing to superstition in order to draw some attention to his work . . .' I raised a hand as I saw that McGray was about to protest. '*Nevertheless*, stories do not need to be true to poison the minds of disturbed people. Now, Nine-Nails, do not, *do not* get used to hearing me say this, but . . .' I had to gather strength to utter the next words. 'What you say does make sense. Even more, I doubt that all these things – Tartini's violin, the score, the symbol, the missing intestines – can be explained simultaneously by any other theory.'

McGray grinned. 'Good, Frey. We finally are on the same ground!'

'Indeed.' I nodded. 'And your theory narrows down the number of suspects quite a bit: We are definitely looking for a violinist; someone young and slender enough to climb and crawl through a chimney. And, according to Joe Fiddler, Fontaine was worried about someone seizing his violin.'

'Yet the fiddle wasn't taken after his murder.'

'Exactly. That immediately makes me think of . . . inheritance.'

McGray's eyes widened. 'Do ye suspect that scrawny Theodore Wood?'

'Indeed.'

He stroked his stubble for a moment, his blue eyes fixed on the fire. 'Well, the laddie does look skinny enough to get himself through a chimney, and now that I think about it, we found those pieces o' score and glass. Remember ye said the killer couldn't be very skilled?'

'Yes. I can definitely imagine Wood clenching things clumsily while climbing up the chimney. Besides, he got disgustingly thrilled when we gave him the violin; he almost made me shudder.'

McGray nodded slowly. 'Indeedy. Now we need to bring the Devil's mark and the missing guts into the picture.'

'Do you think that Wood could be involved in satanic rituals?'

'Ah'm not sure. He doesn't look like someone into witchcraft to me. We can find out easily if we search his house, though. I ken exactly what we should be looking for.'

I savoured the last bit of my cigar while walking out of the library. 'Excellent. I will get a search warrant signed tomorrow morning so that we can investigate immediately. Finally, it seems like we are getting somewhere.'

It is time . . . yes, it is time.
But one needs to be sure.
Just a quick trip to check on him. Just a little jaunt to see.

He is rotting . . .

20

The following morning I rose more than an hour before it was time to go. Knowing that I could not possibly sleep again, I got myself ready and took extra time to give myself a perfect shave. I missed going to a proper barber, though.

'You're up early, master,' Joan said when she saw me coming down the stairs. 'You want some breakfast already?'

'Yes. Is McGray not up yet?'

'No. I heard him snoring like a bear when I walked by his room.'

Joan served me a cup of strong coffee and I thought I'd use the spare time to sit back and relax with the newspaper. At least that was my intention, but I'd not had three sips when someone knocked on the door. Joan went to the entrance but George ran frantically to overtake her.

'I'll get that, ye stupid cow!'

Once more Joan burst into vulgar yelling, so loud this time that I utterly lost my temper. I tossed the paper onto the table and followed them, intending to scold the pair as never before. Nevertheless, I had no chance to say a word. George opened the door and I saw the very last person I could have ever expected:

My youngest brother, Elgie. Wrapped up in a thick overcoat that made him look terribly slender and childish, he was smiling at me as if it were Christmas morning. He carried a trunk and his violin case – God, how sick I was of violins!

'*What the heck are you doing here?*'

His smile would not give way. 'Is that any means of talking to your favourite brother?'

'*My favourite brother!*' I squeaked. 'After this, you have switched places with bloody Oliver!'

'At least you did not say Laurence!'

'*Oh, shush! I am not bloody joking!* Did you not receive my telegram? *Joan!* Did you not send the damn telegram? I told you that it was urgent!'

'But I did, sir! I swear I did.'

'Why, do not scold the poor woman,' Elgie intervened. 'It must have reached home when I was already on my way. I caught this marvellous train a couple of days ago. I would have arrived sooner, but I had to stop overnight at Beattock Summit. I did not know that the Scottish landscape was so inspiring: those mountains I saw on the rail . . . and that castle and the hills in this town! Brother, you and I are going to have a lot of fun.'

I covered my exasperated face with both hands. '*Fun!* Do you think that I am on a holiday? I am far too busy, and attending to your whims is the last thing I need! You will catch the next train back home, do you hear me?'

I did not realize how strident my shouting was until McGray came downstairs, his still sleepy face quite put out.

'*Blast!* The *one* day I manage to sleep like a log! What's going on here, Frey? Don't ye think it's enough with these folks' clatter –' he then saw my brother. 'Who the heck's that laddie?'

Before I had the chance to speak, Elgie walked forward, extended his hand and greeted McGray with a foolish grin. 'Mr Elgie Frey, sir. Inspector Frey's youngest brother.'

Not only did Nine-Nails not shake his hand, but he cast him a killer look as he yelled at me. '*Whaaat!* For God's sake! Am I goin' to receive all the bloody Freys in the country? Weren't ye happy bringing yer old hag and yer mare and yer mountains o' useless shite, ye pretentious London lassie?'

Elgie blinked and looked at me in confusion. 'Pardon me, brother. Why did this gentleman just call you a London lass—'

'*Enough!*' I roared. 'McGray, save your smelly breath; he is not staying.'

'But, brother —'

'You are *not* staying! Joan, send him to London on the first train, steamer, horse or mule that you find. If I see him here when I return, I will kick *you* out; I swear I will.'

I had my overcoat and hat fetched and was about to leave the house, but then Elgie planted himself firmly in front of me.

'I am not leaving, Ian. I cannot believe that you, of all people, are asking me to go home. How it is right for you to come all this way for your career, yet you expect me to stay home and ignore mine? First violin in an Arthur Sullivan debut! How can you ask me to let that pass me by?'

I massaged my temples. I could hear Catherine shouting what a terrible influence I'd been on her little boy. Right then, however, I did not have time to argue.

'Very well, stay a few days if you must. We shall talk whenever I have some time to spare.' Then I turned to

McGray. 'I will send him to the New Club. They shall find him some lodgings, so do not worry about having more of my kin in this derelict pigsty of yours.'

I walked out before Elgie could say another word. I knew that his presence would only mean trouble.

As we mounted our horses McGray said, 'I wouldn't have minded the laddie staying here. Honest.'

I arched an eyebrow, intrigued by McGray's change of attitude. 'Why, are you feeling guilty now?'

'Nae. Don't be such a cod's head! But the laddie seems much nicer than ye. He definitely has some guts.'

'Thanks, but I would rather have him as far from my work as possible.'

We rode to the City Chambers in silence, and on our way a poignant thought came to me; that Nine-Nails surely missed the company of a sibling.

Campbell's eyes kept moving from left to right, scanning the still unsigned search warrant that lay on his desk.

'That is one bold theory, Frey.'

'It may sound like such, sir, but the evidence speaks for itself.'

'Did you say that McGray suspected this all along? Why did he not mention it before?'

'He told me that he lacked enough evidence. To be quite frank, I believe that McGray *wanted* this theory to be true, which turned him cautious. You must know how obsessed he is with anything related to the Devil.'

'Only too well! Did he also suspect this Wood chap?'

'No, sir. That was my natural conclusion.'

Campbell arched his thick eyebrows. 'Good, good.

Together, you two make *one* fair inspector.' He signed the warrant and handed it to me. 'Search as much as you please, Frey. I do hope you are on the right track. You are not in a position to make any mistakes.'

After that pleasant warning I joined McGray at the front yard of the City Chambers, where our horses were waiting, and we headed to the Conservatoire.

'What did the old fox have to tell ye?'

I shrugged with a grumpy face. 'He wanted to moan, basically. Dear Campbell is as sweet as a kick in the crotch. He signed the warrant; that is all that matters.'

We went north and made it to the Conservatoire precisely as the dark clouds broke in a relentless rain. McGray and I dismounted our horses and walked hastily to the entrance, our faces lashed by the cold raindrops. Fortuitously, Mr Ardglass happened to be talking to a couple of students in the main hall, so it was not necessary to announce us.

'Why, Inspector Frey!' he said to me with a smile, which faded when he turned to McGray. His hideous whiskers seemed to stand on end. 'What can I do for you? Do you need to question anyone else?'

'Aye,' McGray replied harshly. 'We need to see Wood. Can ye call him?'

'I have not seen Mr Wood this morning, I'm afraid. I think he is ill.'

'Ill?' I asked. 'Was it anything to do with his injury?'

Ardglass grimaced. 'Oh, what a terrible sight that was; he told me how it happened. He'll have a nasty scar. But no, the last thing he said was that he was feeling queasy. That was yesterday, right after luncheon, I believe. I assumed he'd eaten a rotten fruit or something, so I let him go, but you can find him at his home. I can give you the address.'

Ardglass scribbled the address hastily, obviously not wishing to spend too much time with McGray, and again we left the Conservatoire. The rain had turned into a mighty storm and we rode miserably under the appalling weather. My hat and overcoat protected me rather well, but McGray's black hair became soaked within minutes. His countenance, however, remained immutable.

Wood happened to live at the eastern end of the Royal Mile, in fact only a couple of streets from Fontaine's rented property.

'What a convenient location,' I said as we approached the large guest house, for Wood did not live by himself. 'Close enough to his victim.'

'We're not sure yet, lass.'

There was a large black carriage parked in front of the main entrance, another small cart and a couple of horses waiting for their riders; they were all gathered in front of the wide door, looking rather agitated.

'Busy place,' McGray said. We had not yet dismounted when a familiar face came out of the house: Charles Downs, Fontaine's lawyer.

The little man's eyes fell on McGray and me, attracted like magnets. 'Inspectors! What a surprise! Are you here to investigate the case of Mr Wood as well?'

McGray had to dismount to address him, for Downs was so short that his face had been level with McGray's calf. 'Wood's case? What d'ye mean?'

'Oh, I supposed that you knew . . . Well . . . Mr Wood, also my client, sadly passed away yesterday.'

21

I almost fell off Philippa's back when I heard that. 'He what?'

'He passed away,' Downs repeated, somewhat perplexed by our ignorance. 'Yesterday afternoon, I was told.'

'What happened?'

'The housekeeper told me that he got very sick; vomiting all over the place. Poor Mr Wood always was of a sickly constitution, I'm afraid.'

Then we saw two men coming out of the house, carrying a very big chest. Two violin cases lay on its top.

'Ye want this in the cart, master?' they asked.

'Where are ye taking that?' McGray snapped before Downs could say anything. 'Is that Wood's property?'

'Indeed,' Downs said. 'As his lawyer it is my duty to deliver his belongings according to his will.'

'I'm afraid ye cannae take anything out o' this house. Not right now, at least.'

'What do you mean?'

'We've got a search warrant. Show him, Frey.'

I did so and Downs snatched the sheet from my hand; his little eyes ran madly over the text. 'Why, this is no longer valid! You were granted the right to search Mr Wood's dwellings and possessions. Since he has passed away, legally these things belong to somebody else now, and a new order is in d–'

McGray stepped towards Downs in an imposing move. 'Mr Downs, ye can use all yer legal shite against us, but we'll eventually find our way and look at those things. Besides, given the nature o' the case, yer blocking our work will only give us reasons to suspect yer involvement in these men's deaths. Both Wood and Fon-teen.'

He said those last words in a threatening whisper, so that only Downs and I could hear him. The lawyer's boldness immediately faded away; he turned pale and gave me the order back. 'As you wish, Inspector. But you must let me know once you are done with your search.'

'In fact, you should stay,' I said, seeing that Downs was turning to his carriage. 'We may need to ask you a few questions too.'

He cast me a bitter look, but could only swallow and assent.

'Laddies, get that stuff back in,' McGray said. 'I want youse to put every single thing *exactly* where it was.'

The men carried the chest back and we followed them into an airy hall with high ceilings. As they climbed the stairs a rather young woman appeared. 'Oh, I thought youse were takin' those away!'

'Ye the housekeeper?' McGray asked.

'Aye. Youse are?'

McGray introduced us (fortunately he did not call me lassie) and asked me to show the search warrant, but the woman did not take it.

'I cannae read very well. I take yer word. Youse can look as much as youse need.'

'Thanks, hen. Can ye show us the way? We need to ask ye a few wee questions too.'

We walked into Wood's room as the men were leaving. I needed but a quick glance to analyse it all: an old bed, a desk covered with nothing but sheet music, a jug and an almost empty wardrobe.

'Doesn't look like we're gonna search a lot,' McGray said.

I nodded, still not completely recovered from the initial surprise. The place in fact reminded me of the abodes of the Ripper's victims, not because it was shabby, but because of its total lack of personality: no pictures on the walls, no letters, no portraits of relatives; just the starkness of one who lets his life pass by without caring. I felt a light chill in my spine.

A maid was mopping the floor fervently, but the room still gave off a strong stench of vomit. I had to produce my handkerchief to cover my nose.

'Were ye here when it happened?' McGray said.

'Aye,' the maid and the housekeeper replied at the same time, their faces marked by repulsion.

'Tell us what happened,' McGray asked. I saw the housekeeper's face going paler as she spoke.

'Well . . . It was about half past noon when Mr Wood came back from his job. He was feeling very ill, he said, and he had an appalling face; all yellow.'

'Had he been ill recently?' McGray asked.

'Nae, but he wasn't a very stout lad. He never ate properly and fell ill with a sick gut every now and then. That's why we weren't too worried when we saw him. We only thought it had hit him a wee bit harder than usual.'

'He locked himself in here and played for a bit,' the maid said. 'But then we heard him choking and grunting.

We had to break in and found him all . . . soaked in sick.'
The poor woman covered her mouth; thinking of the
sight made her retch again. 'He passed out and never
woke up again.'

'What did youse do then?'

'I sent one o' the maids to fetch the doctor and another
girl to fetch the Italian gentleman, Mr Caroli.'

'Mr Caroli? Why him?'

'Mr Wood didnae have any family and Mr Caroli was
his only friend; the only man who'd ever come to visit
him. It was a good thing we sent for him. He took care of
everything; he called the undertaker's, the lawyer . . . he is
even holding the wake at his house.'

'Where is the body now? At the undertaker's?'

'Aye, I think so, sir. They must be gettin' him ready.'

McGray nodded and paced around as he pondered on
the answers. I could tell that he was as staggered as I.

'Did you notice anything unusual during the last few
days?' I said, rather mechanically.

'Well, just that he played all the time! He always did, but
not like this, not until the small hours without a single
break. He wouldn't even come down for dinner. I brought
him trays but he left them untouched.'

'Some of the other guests complained,' the housekeeper added. 'I was going to call my mistress if that went
on one more might.'

'Who owns this house?' McGray asked. The answer
was shocking, yet not surprising.

'Lady Anne Ardglass, sir.'

We both nodded at each other.

'And how many people live here?' McGray asked again.

'Seven other guests sir, also three maids, including Mary here, a cook, a handyman and myself.'

'Can ye fetch as many o' them as ye can right now? We'd like to question them all. In the meantime Inspector Frey and I will search the room. In private.'

'Aye, sir.'

The housekeeper left, asking the maid to follow, and then McGray and I began the search.

'It is a shame they cleaned,' I said, looking at the polished floor. 'They might have removed evidence.'

'Aye, but this room wasn't a potential crime scene 'til we arrived.' McGray stood in the centre of the room and looked around for a moment. 'What dy'e see, Frey?'

'Not much. An affordable room. Second floor . . .'

'No fireplace,' McGray remarked, pointing at a very small log burner. 'There's no room to hide anything here.'

He looked at the chest he'd told the workers to bring back. From the marks on the floor I could tell that they had placed it but a couple of inches off its original position.

The chest had no lock, and when McGray opened it we found it half empty: there was an expensive black suit (which Wood probably only wore to concerts), his legal documents (nothing but the regular birth and school certificates and so on), loose accessories for his violin (pegs, bridges, rosin, etc.), and a small ebony box with a violin beautifully carved on the lid.

McGray grabbed it. 'Let's see what we've got here . . .' He opened it and we found a bundle of violin strings, snugly rolled between velvet lining. 'My, my! A fancy box to keep his strings, don't ye think?'

'Indeed. At odds with everything else in this room.'

'What can ye tell about 'em?'

I took one and inspected it closely. 'It is definitely not metal. It could be catgut, but I cannot be sure.'

There was a glow in McGray's eyes. 'I've only just met someone who could tell us a lot about fiddle strings.'

'Oh, really? Who?'

McGray raised his eyebrows.

'What, Elgie? No, absolutely not. I do *not* want him involved in this.'

'There's no one better to give us unclouded information.'

'Why, there must be. We have Caroli, or that Ardglass man, or someone else at the Conservatoire.'

'Aye, and any o' them could be involved.' I was shaking my head. 'Come on, Frey, yer brother doesn't even have to ken details o' the case.'

'Does he not? I suppose you will simply show him these strings, ask him whether they are made out of human gut, and then expect him to ask no questions.'

'We'll think o' something,' he concluded, carelessly tossing the wooden box into my hands. 'We better take them with us.'

I could not protest any further, for McGray was already going through the contents of the chest again and again. He also looked carefully at the walls, tapped the floorboards and inspected every possible nook and cranny.

'There is nothing more to see here,' I said, looking at the clean, bare walls. 'My feeling is that Wood was a violinist and – quite literally – nothing else.'

McGray inhaled deeply, sitting on the bed. 'There are two possibilities: either Wood *was* the murderer, but he happened to snuff it too soon after his crime . . . Or some-one got rid o' him to get hold o' the fiddle.'

'I am inclined to believe the latter.'

'D'ye always have to talk like that?'

'McGray, will you focus, please?'

'Right, right. Aye, I agree with ye. Wood died at a very strange moment.'

I tapped the little wooden box, thinking. 'Do not ask me how, but the story strikes me as one of poisoning.'

'Ye think so?'

'Aye – I mean *yes*! It should be easy to find traces of poison in Wood's stomach, but we need to take his body to the morgue immediately.'

'Aye, but we also need to question all these folks very soon, while they still have it all fresh in their heads. I think we should split up. Ye question all the people here – I ken ye love doin' that – and in the meantime I'll take the body to the morgue.'

'You will need an official order for that.'

'Mnah! Gimme the search warrant we already have. I'll get *persuasive*.'

'Please, do *not* do anything stupid like cracking the mor-tician's arms . . .'

'Cannae promise anything, laddie,' he said as he walked away.

I went downstairs and found that the housekeeper had gathered all the people present in the house – Downs was sitting among them with a mighty frown. I decided to question him first, since a moody state of mind is most likely to contaminate a person's declarations. I told the housekeeper that I would prefer to question everyone in private, so she led us to a small, secluded parlour.

Downs's version of the story agreed with the housekeeper's: he had received a message from Mr Caroli telling him about Wood's death; he then looked for the man's will in his files, and immediately set off to do all the paperwork and distribute the goods ... which were not many, nor too valuable.

'His only valuable possessions were his two violins ... and perhaps the mahogany chest you saw,' Downs was saying, sipping a cup of tea which appeared to have relaxed his temper. The man did like his teas. 'As you remember, he only received the second instrument a few days ago.'

'Can you tell me who is to inherit Mr Wood's possessions?'

'Well, he had no family, as you probably know by now, and although he had quite a few acquaintances he wasn't close to many. He simply left everything to Mr Caroli.'

'Very interesting . . .' I muttered. 'All right, Mr Downs, you are free to go now. I am sorry we had to detain you for this long. Unfortunately, I will not release the goods just yet. I hope that you understand.'

Downs was going to rise but he faltered. He opened his mouth but it was hard for him to make any sound.

'Mr Downs, is there anything else you would wish to tell me?'

'Erm . . . Well, yes, yes, Inspector. You see, I am not stupid. I can tell that you and Inspector McGray are following the trace of Monsieur Fontaine's violin, and that my hands have been on it too much for my own good.'

I only nodded. I did not want to give away any information as to my theories. The truth was that, until the moment he mentioned it, I had not considered him more suspicious than any of the other people involved.

'You'll surely understand that it is simply because of my profession!' he said. 'I have been the lawyer of those musicians for decades; they recommend me among themselves; it is only natural that I would take care of all their legal matters, including their wills! Mr Wood was not a very practical fellow; he only hired me because Mr Ardglass strongly advised him to. Ardglass and Monsieur Fontaine were two of my first clients.'

Downs's insistence on clearing his name was in fact having the opposite effect. He had beads of sweat on his temples and his voice trembled at certain points.

I simply nodded again and told him he could leave, but he walked away with hesitant steps. Could it simply be that McGray's words had scared the man . . . or was he worried by something else? Whatever it was I would have to decide later; I still had many people to summon. I interviewed them one by one, jotting down their entirely predictable replies in my notebook.

The young housekeeper: 'Ye'll excuse me, sir, but Mr Wood gave me the creeps sometimes. No sweetheart, no friends other than those few musicians he had to deal with . . . And so weird-looking! When I saw that ghastly cut on his face I almost ran the other way.'

The scruffy-looking, sweat-smelling handyman: 'No, not much, boss; he rarely spoke to anyone, but I tell ye, if a bad oyster killed 'im it wouldn't surprise me; the laddie was very flimsy. I usually had to open his jam jars.'

The very young maid: 'Horrible, horrible stuff, and I had to mop it all on an empty stomach! Although it looked more like bile, sir, like Mr Wood hadn't eaten anything for a while. I know 'cause that's what my late dad's puke looked like when he came home from the pub.'

The bony spinster who lived in the room underneath Wood's: 'Very strange lad. Very strange, but living at a guest house I've seen worse, I suppose. I can't say his music usually annoyed me, but last night I was tempted to knock at his door and ask him to stop. He was playing a mighty awful song. Well, not even a full song, He was playing the same passage, over and over and over. It gave me nightmares.'

My eyes had been closing, but those words brought me back from my stupor.

'Nightmares? May I ask why?'

The woman perked up, utterly flattered by my sudden attention. 'Well, it wasn't something pleasant to hear, like a sweet melody or a waltz. It was more like . . . like the violin was trembling.'

My last witness was the chubby man who lived across the corridor. 'And it suddenly stopped. It just stopped, and then I heard the poor lad choke and the maids making a fuss. They asked me to help them crack the door open, and . . . well, you know the rest.'

Once I was done with the inquests I confiscated all the keys to Wood's bedroom and went upstairs to lock it myself. Before doing so I had one last glance round the room, just to make sure that everything was still in place, which was the case. When I saw the two violin cases, now lying on the bed, I took a mad decision: I would take the Amati Maledetto with me. I opened the cases to make sure I was taking the right one; it was easy to recognize it because of the wooden lion head.

That decision still haunts me at night . . . taking the violin . . . Only God knows where the case would have ended up if I'd left it there.

It was still raining hard when I went back to the City Chambers. I found Constable McNair by the entrance and he told me that he had seen McGray coming back a couple of hours earlier. I went to the morgue and found him there, waiting patiently at the entrance.

'Did you manage to fetch the body?'

'Aye. Reed is looking at it now.'

I was glad McGray had decided to go to the undertaker straightaway, otherwise we would have wasted precious hours locked in that guesthouse. While we waited for Reed to finish the post-mortem I told him what little I had found out from Wood's neighbours, and the strange speech Downs had made.

'D'ye think he could've been involved?' McGray asked. 'I only threatened him cos I didn't want to ask Campbell for another bloody order and lose more time – Ye screech like a knife on a bottle when we lose time!'

'I do not imagine someone like him climbing chimneys, even if he is tiny enough! But he did seem too keen to exonerate himself; I daresay his conscience is not completely clear.'

McGray was going to say something but right then Reed emerged from the small examination room, his apron still smeared in red.

'Inspectors, you may come in now.'

We followed him in and found the corpse covered in a bloodstained sheet. Only Wood's pasty face was exposed; the long scar where the string had lashed him looked almost black in comparison.

'It is a clear case of cholera,' Reed said, looking down at the body. 'I found nothing odd in his stomach . . . well, nothing at all, actually; he spewed it empty before expiring.'

'One of the maids mentioned that he didn't seem to vomit food,' I said.

'That wouldn't surprise me,' answered Reed. 'And it's likely he didn't drink anything either. There are clear signs of dehydration; look at his sunken eyes.'

'Didn't ye find any injuries, laddie?' McGray asked.

'Not at all, sir. No traces of injury or trauma of any kind. If I may say so, disease is the most logical explanation, given the state of the man's body. He was a tragedy waiting to happen: brittle bones and teeth, undernourished, apparently he had frequent infections in the digestive tract, skin conditions . . .' He pointed at Wood's fiddler's hickey and the nasty boils around it. 'It looks like he simply didn't take care of himself. Didn't eat properly, didn't attend his diseases . . .'

'He just fiddled,' McGray said.

'Whatever he did, his body was in no state to endure a sudden attack.'

I looked at the still face, my mind struggling to come to terms with what Reed was saying.

'Many poisons cause symptoms that can be mistaken for cholera,' I finally said.

'D'ye still think he was poisoned?' McGray asked.

'I do not know . . . There is something here that does

not feel right, McGray. Yes, this man could have died of any sudden malady . . . but, as you said, why *precisely* now? It is not impossible, but it is a bit difficult to swallow. I will not be at peace unless I have him fully tested.'

Reed assented. 'Yes, sir. I can take samples of his digestive tract and run tests for all the poisons you want.'

'Can you take blood samples as well?' I asked.

'Aye, sir. It will take several days, but I will let you know as soon as I find something unusual.'

'Perfect,' McGray said. 'Can ye take all the samples ye need right now and keep 'em cool? I'd like to return this chap to the undertaker as soon as we can.'

'Of course, sir.'

'Why the rush?' I asked McGray.

'I'll tell ye in a bit. Let's go to the office.'

'Should we tell Caroli that Wood is going to be buried without his stomach?' Reed asked McGray as we left the morgue.

'Nae, laddie. The less they know the better.'

Back in our basement office I found Tucker napping under McGray's desk. That dog was always napping; it reminded me of my brother Oliver.

I laid the Amati Maledetto on the desk and let out a weary sigh. 'What now?'

'I'm not sure,' McGray answered, dropping himself on his chair. 'But I'm glad ye brought the fiddle. I have an idea . . . but it's risky.'

'Tell me.'

'I think we should use the fiddle as . . . bait.'

'Bait? What do you mean?'

'Even if we prove that Wood was poisoned, that may not

give us many more clues about the actual killer. It would probably not be a bad idea to let the events . . . unfold.'

I remained silent for a moment. 'That is very risky indeed, McGray. If someone is trying to make their way to this violin, letting things *unfold* is precisely what we want to avoid.'

'Don't think I'm careless, Frey. I wouldn't leave the fiddle around for someone to slaughter its owners at will. I'm thinking we should try and foresee its path and then follow it.'

'Foresee its path?'

'Aye. And that worm Downs will surely help us – if only to save his own skin.'

Downs's office seemed custom-built for him: it was one of the smallest workspaces I'd been to, and it was utterly packed with file cases and towers of paperwork. The desks and chairs were so cluttered that there was hardly any space to move. Then again, such a small man would not need lots of room.

McGray and I sat in front of the desk as the attorney consulted his archive. My knees were almost at the level of my chest – so little space we had.

'I have it here . . .' Downs said, climbing down a small ladder and bringing a file from one of the top shelves. 'Signor Danilo Bartolomeo Caroli.' He sat at his desk and looked into the papers. 'Oh, yes, just as I remembered: he leaves all his possessions to his wife, Signora Lorena Caroli. If something was to happen to her it would all go to his second cousin, some chap in Rome called Fausto Larpi; a distant branch of his family. I think I remember him saying that they had not met since they were children.'

'Going back to Mrs Caroli,' McGray said, 'does she have a will of her own?'

'Oh, yes, in fact she changed it only a couple of months ago . . . Let me have a look.' This time he looked among a pile of documents right next to his desk, from where he produced a much thinner file. 'Yes, yes. Like I told you, she changed her will in July. Before then all her properties and savings were to pass to Mr Caroli and, in his absence, to be split among several churches and charities. Now she has split her will between her husband and her child. Do you know that she is expecting?'

'We know,' I said. 'What do you reckon, McGray?'

He was stroking his stubble in deep thought. 'Those are very normal wills . . . and both take us to dead ends.' He seemed half absent as he muttered, but then came back to his senses. 'Mr Downs, would ye mind if *we* give Caroli some o' the possessions that Mr Wood left for him?'

'Not at all, Inspector. I would only ask you to tell me, if possible, which possessions you are talking about, so that I can cross them off the list of goods that I must deliver.'

McGray's eyes were fixed on Downs's as he spoke. 'Not much. Just the cursed fiddle . . . and some strings.'

Both McGray and I looked at him intently, waiting for the slightest hint of a reaction. However, Downs simply nodded and jotted down the items on a piece of paper, his face devoid of emotion.

'That *must* remain confidential, Mr Downs,' McGray said.

'But of course, Inspector,' he replied, his expression as blank as before.

22

Elgie was finding his way in Edinburgh as if he'd spent half his life there. We inquired for him at the New Club, only to be told that he was already rehearsing at the Royal Lyceum Theatre. The imposing white building was very close, almost at the foot of Castle Rock, so our horses took us there in less than fifteen minutes.

I was pleasantly surprised as we walked in. Though not large, the main hall was of impeccable taste: the domed ceiling was richly decorated with gilded plaster surrounding a wide, sumptuous chandelier. Equally impressive plasterwork embellished the balustrades of three levels of balconies, and the rows of velvety red seats faced a wide, deep stage. I could picture my father and Catherine twisting their mouths in begrudging approval.

We found Elgie at the orchestra pit, and were lucky to arrive just as the very grumpy director allowed them a rest. Elgie recognized my graveness and led us to one of the highest balconies that overlooked the stage, where we could talk in privacy.

'It is a very nice place,' he said, grinning. 'Do you not think so?'

'Too glittering for my taste,' said Nine-Nails. The cushioned seat appeared to be giving him a rash.

'I thought Sullivan would be conducting,' I said.

'Not right now. *Macbeth* premiers in London on New

Year's Eve, so he is busy with that, but he will come when they bring the play here next year. I hope he is not as cantankerous as this one; the man is wearing us out!'

I noticed that Elgie's neck was quite reddened. 'Indeed, I can see it from your skin. Are you not using that cloth?'

'I left it in my room this morning, but I will definitely bring it tomorrow.'

I gave him my own handkerchief. 'Use this in the meantime. I have seen how nasty those, er, "fiddler's hickeys" can become, and I do not want Catherine telling me how bad I –'

'Och, save the clishmaclaver for later, Frey,' McGray urged. 'Laddie, we need some information from ye.'

Elgie's eyes opened in excitement. 'Oh, do you? Will I help you convict another Jack the Ripper?'

I almost shuddered at his enthusiasm.

'No. It is rather trivial,' I lied, producing the small ebony box. 'What can you tell us about this and its contents?'

Elgie examined the box, running his fingers on the violin carving. 'It looks like an expensive little thing, and the violin is perfect.'

'Perfect?' McGray repeated.

'Yes. Perfect proportions and every part where it should be. I've seen preposterous paintings of violins with six strings or no bridge. To me it is like painting a man with three arms. Whoever carved this was either very observant or had an exceptional knowledge of violins.'

McGray nodded, recording every word in his memory.

Elgie opened the box. 'Violin strings. Again, expensive ones.'

'How d'ye ken?'

'They're catgut, and of very good making. Most likely Italian.'

McGray looked up. 'Italian?'

'Yes. The best strings come from Italy. Some people say that making catgut is almost an art. It takes years of practice to perfect the method.'

I pondered. 'Do you know how they are made?'

'Well, the basics of it. First they soak the guts in brine for a day or two so they don't rot. Then they scrape off the fat, and treat them with lye until the gut becomes translucent. That takes about a week of constant work. Then they cut them into thin ribbons and twist them like rope, before leaving them to dry. That can take another week. Finally, they sand them and polish them with a mixture of grass and olive oil.'

'Very long-winded,' I said. 'I assume the guts have to be fresh?'

'Yes. You can imagine that intestines are not the cleanest of organs, so the brine bath has to be done as soon as possible.'

'And it is not a craft you could hide easily.'

'Why, no! You need a large workshop to stretch the strings, and I understand that the guts in lye give off a horrible smell.'

I assented, already thinking of the possibilities. 'I think that is all we needed. McGray?'

He leaned towards Elgie and lifted one of the strings. 'Strings are made out o' goat, aren't they?'

'Mostly goat or lamb, yes, but also horse or hog. Some musicians say that cow gut is the absolute best.'

I could see where McGray was going, but could not stop him.

'Laddie, can ye tell if this is made o' goat or – something else?'

Elgie must have sensed something in McGray's tone, and immediately put the string down, looking slightly revolted.

'No, I could not. If you saw a drop of blood you could not tell whether it is man or beast.' He closed the box. 'The sound does differ, which could give you some guidance, but my ear is not trained enough. One of the maestros at the Conservatoire might be able to help you.'

McGray mumbled so that only I could hear him. 'Perhaps Fon-teen would have known.'

'I'm glad we talked to the laddie,' McGray said as we left the theatre. 'If it takes more than two weeks to make strings, the murderer must be working on Fon-teen's guts as we speak. That gives us another trail to follow.' He noticed my deep frown. 'What is it now? Ye didn't like the questions I asked him?'

I shook my head. 'No, he will be fine. It is looking for foul, corroded intestines that worries me. I see this case becoming increasingly messy.'

Nine-Nails cackled. 'Och, we've not even started, Frey, so ye better prepare yer puny stomach. A cat in mittens won't catch any mice.'

23

'I thought ya didn't like black, master,' said Joan as she passed me the only black jacket I'd asked her to bring.

'Indeed. I avoid it whenever I can. This time, however, I cannot. I am attending a wake.'

'Oh my! I hope it wasn't one of your friends!'

'No, no. This is work. I only saw the man once in my life, but I still must show some respect. The hosts will be two Italians, and I suspect they are very religious people. The wake will be in their old Catholic ways; open coffin and all, the burial itself tomorrow morning. Why they like to stare at their deceased ones all night, I cannot fathom.'

'Italians! You must be talking about Mr and Mrs Caroli.'

I dropped my tiepin in surprise. 'How do know about them?'

'Oh, well, I was in the market this morning and met this very chatty girl that works for them. The poor thing was carrying a mountain of baskets with onions, and carrots, and parsnips, and the most dreadful little tomatoes I've ever –'

'Joan, unless you have a point, I do not care how many bloody turnips she was carrying.'

'Well, I know 'cause the girl tripped and dropped all her baskets. Mighty scene, vegetables rolling all over the place! And can you believe that I was the only person who helped her? We had to chase her onions across the road!

We chatted a good deal while I caught my breath, and she told me people here don't like her household at all. Not the masters, not the servants. I felt so sorry for her.'

I arched an eyebrow. 'Why, you *are* good at gossip!'

'Oh, sorry, master. I know you don't like all this chatter. I'll leave you to –'

'No-no-no, wait! Why do people dislike them? Did she tell you?'

Joan started giggling like a mischievous teenager. 'Oh, I've stirred your curiosity now, haven't I?

'*Joan!*'

'Oh, well, she wasn't very clear. She said that people are afraid of her mistress – that they call her "witch-fingers" and children run away from her when she's in town. They say it's some curse running through her family. Some people even say they've seen demons lurking around their home at night.'

I shook my head. 'Jesus! How can people be so bloody cruel? That poor woman is ill, not cursed!'

Then I understood why their social circle was so reduced. I had found it strange, given their loud hospitality. McGray and I were strangers to them, yet they had smothered us with attention. They surely were desperate to find some company. I also understood Mrs Caroli's affectionate speech about losing Fontaine, the only person who befriended them despite her illness, and why they had befriended Wood despite his peculiar character.

I decided not to tell the story to McGray, whose alienated and tragic situation – and fingers – were awkwardly similar . . .

*

A thick, heavy fog fell over Edinburgh during the evening, and when we rode to the Carolis' household McGray and I could hardly see each other. The almost-full moon shone above us like a blurry lamp, and under its light the fog looked like silvery streams of smoke dragged by the wind.

I was happy to see the house emerging from the mist, for the night air was icy and damp, and the yellow lights coming from the windows spoke of warmth. The door was decorated with a wide wreath of yew and laurel tied with black ribbons.

Our knock was answered by a young maid (probably the one Joan had helped in the street), who took our coats and offered to hold the violin case that I carried, wrapped in an old cloth.

'That won't be necessary,' I said. 'Can you announce us to your master?'

The girl nodded and then led us among a sea of people clad in black.

This was no moment for fashion: the men wore lacklustre jackets, and the only fabric allowed for the ladies was that dreadful crêpe, which has a flat, lifeless quality. The only specks of colour were the white handkerchiefs of the weepers, but etiquette demanded that even those were edged in black. The funeral was better attended than I expected, given the taciturn nature of poor Wood. We were surrounded mostly by musicians, but there were also a few people from the guesthouse and a couple of neighbours. The whisky coffees passed around as they all chattered about the deceased, his life, his talents and his doings; Wood's colleagues were taking turns to play his favourite pieces by the coffin, and as we entered, a violinist and a cellist were improvising on one of Mozart's masses. It is at moments like this when I get perplexed by how intricate the web of life is. Even the seemingly dullest, most inconsequential person can gather a little crowd at his funeral. In my experience, lonely funerals speak of even more complex stories. Good Mary Brown, for instance, did not have a single mourner.

The undertaker had certainly made an effort, for the parlour looked like a wilderness with white flowers and green foliage. All the mirrors had been covered with drapery, for people still believe that the departed soul can become trapped in the glass. There were so many candles spread all about the room that there was no need to light the candelabra, and the house was so full of people that setting the fire would have only smothered us.

One of the drooling hounds was pacing carelessly in between the guests, and right behind it I saw Mrs Caroli. She was all dressed in mourning black, like the last time we'd seen her, and like the last time she tried to conceal her arthritis, her hands in black mittens and clasping a Bible close to her stomach. I saw more than a few morbid eyes trying to catch a glance at her knotted fingers.

'Inspectors!' she said, a hint of a grunt in her voice. 'Good evening. What can we do for you?'

She sounded polite enough, but her slight frown gave away how uncomfortable she really felt.

'First of all, we want to express our sympathy,' McGray said. 'We learned how close youse were to this laddie.'

Mrs Caroli looked down for one moment, and her expression was enough for me to realize the full extent of their sorrow – within days they'd lost their two best friends in town. I felt for them more than I thought I would.

'Also, we wanna talk to you and yer husband,' McGray went on, and Caroli approached us right then.

'Good evening, Inspectors. More questions about Fontaine?' he asked.

'Not quite,' McGray said. 'May we speak in private? It's very important.'

Caroli led us into a small study adjacent to the main parlour, his wife following us. We were but a few steps from the door when a heavy hand pressed upon my shoulder.

'Inspector Frey!'

I turned around to find that it was Alistair Ardglass.

'Oh Lord!' was my rather sickened reaction. I could not help wrinkling my nose as if smelling dung, but the man smiled stupidly all the same.

'Inspector Frey, it is so good to see you. I must deliver a message from my dear aunt –'

'Not now, Mr Ardglass,' I replied curtly. McGray and the Carolis had already stepped into the study, so I followed them and promptly shut the door behind me.

'What can we do for you?' Mrs Caroli asked again, leaving her Bible on a desk. I had a quick glance round the darkened room: it was a rather small, cosy study with a homely fireplace, its walls lined with bookcases utterly crammed with volumes of all sizes and subjects. I recognized titles on astronomy, chemistry, history and mathematics. It was what McGray's library might have looked like, were it tidy. Some of the furniture had been crammed there to make room for the coffin; I recognized the finely carved wooden gondola.

'Your carvings are excellent, Mr Caroli' I said.

Caroli blinked. 'I beg your pardon?'

I pointed at the gondola. 'Those carvings. You never told us you made those yourself.'

Caroli took a step towards the piece and touched it gently. 'So . . . 'ow did you know I made them?'

'Your luthier, that Mr Fiddler. He fixed a lion head to the Amati violin. He told us that you gave it to the late Mr Fontaine as a gift.'

'My husband likes to give his carvings to friends,' Mrs Caroli intervened. 'Not long ago he also gave Wood a little trinket box.'

I nodded, remembering that box. Elgie had indeed said that whoever had carved it must have had a good knowledge of violins.

'That lion head seems like a very personal present,' I remarked.

'Oh, yes,' she said. 'Guilleum was very dear to us. He was dejected when he told us that his violin had broken, so Danilo made that lion head to cheer him up. I don't know why, but I believe it was his favourite instrument.'

'Which is precisely what we came to talk about,' McGray said, lifting the case and tossing the cloth aside. 'This is the Amati fiddle. Mr Wood wanted youse to have it.'

There was a gasp. For a moment they all stood so still that I thought I could be looking at a photograph: McGray holding the worn-out, bloodstained violin case with his spoiled hand, Caroli and his wife as stiff as posts, their faces utterly distressed.

Caroli extended a hand, but right before his fingers touched the case he faltered.

'I'm not sure I want this,' he muttered. His wife stepped closer to him and whispered something in Italian.

Their perplexed eyes left no room for doubt: they had never wanted the violin.

'Why not?' McGray asked. 'It's legally yers.'

Caroli shook his head, almost absent minded. 'Guilleum first . . . and then Theodore . . .' he mumbled.

McGray leaned towards him and spoke softly. 'D'ye believe in the violin's curse? D'ye believe that the Devil touched this?' He was not done talking when Mrs Caroli jumped in front of her husband and grabbed the violin case. I am sorry to admit I wished she'd kept her fingers on the Bible, for as soon as she let go of the book I caught an eerie glimpse of protruding knuckles and misshapen phalanxes through her black gloves. We could even hear her crunching bones when she grasped the case handle.

'Excuse me, Inspector! This is not a time to talk about curses and fiends – our good friend's body is still in this house! If you need any information with urgency we will of course answer your questions, but if you came only to discuss who inherits this instrument, I believe that can wait.'

'Do ye believe in the curse?' McGray reiterated. His stare only softened when Mrs Caroli pressed her belly with a shaking hand.

Mr and Mrs Caroli stared hard at each other for an instant. Neither uttered a word. Their nervous silence, however, could not have been more eloquent. They did believe in the curse, and were thus reluctant to accept the violin.

'I'm sorry if I disturbed youse,' McGray said at last. 'Do ye mind if we pay our respects to Mr Wood?'

Mrs Caroli simply looked at her husband.

'Of course you can,' Caroli said, taking the case from his wife's hands and placing it on the desk. 'Follow us, please.'

He opened the door and gently pressed a hand on Mrs Caroli's shoulder, pushing her ahead of us.

'Please excuse my wife,' he whispered, so that only McGray and I could hear. 'She's been under a lot of strain; you know . . . these deaths and our first baby . . . also . . .'

'We understand,' McGray said, patting his back. I thought that Caroli was going to lead our way, but he simply melded into the crowd.

'I am not sure where you were trying to go with that,' I muttered.

'It never hurts ye to know where people's beliefs stand.'

We walked slowly towards the coffin. More than paying our respects to the wretched man, our real motivation was to simply observe the scene.

'How long do you reckon we should stay?' I asked.

'Not long. I doubt we'll find much more here.'

As we walked to the open coffin I heard someone calling my name, and had to lower my gaze to find Downs coming hastily towards us. Alistair Ardglass came behind him, apparently in the middle of an inner struggle: eager to talk to me, yet terribly unnerved by McGray's presence.

'Inspector Frey!' he said at last. 'Pray, are you free to talk now? I shall only steal a few minutes of your precious time.'

'Take all ye need,' McGray said, rapidly stepping away.

Ardglass cleared his throat. 'Oh, that Nine-Nails McGray . . . time after time he proves he is as rude a drunk as a —'

'You said that you'd only steal a few minutes,' I interrupted.

'Oh, but of course. I only need to tell you that my niece is coming back to town.'

'Why should that be of any interest to me?'

Downs jumped in. 'You asked me to keep you well informed about all the violins of Monsieur Fontaine. Do you remember that the last instrument, the Guadagnini, is still in my possession? Miss Ardglass is to inherit it, but I recall you wished to be present when she received it.'

I had completely forgotten that last violin. There was a hint of bitterness in the face of Ardglass, which also reminded me of his frustration at not having been included in Fontaine's will. He tried in vain to conceal this bitterness as he spoke.

'Coincidentally, tomorrow night my aunt is throwing a ball to welcome her, and she — as well as my dear niece — would be most delighted to have you there. It would be a most proper chance for her to receive her — inheritance.'

'How appropriate,' I muttered. I could judge the reactions of Fontaine's last heiress and also have a word with the infamous Lady Ardglass, all during one party. 'Well, I . . .'

'Yes, I know this is a very rushed invitation,' Ardglass said hurriedly, 'but her arrival was totally unexpected. Of course, you are welcome to bring your brother if you wish.'

I arched my eyebrows. 'How did you know that my brother is in town?'

'Oh, Edinburgh is not as big as London, Inspector;

news travels fast here, especially to so well-connected a family as mine. It would be excellent for the boy to be introduced to Edinburgh's good society.'

I blew inside my cheeks. That pretentious, provincial bourgeois trying to give me lessons on good society!

'Evidently,' was my composed answer.

'So . . . may I confirm your presence to Lady Anne?'

I simply nodded and Ardglass gave me another of his cards with the address and time. Both he and Downs made an exaggerated reverence and walked away.

'How pathetically servile,' I muttered. As soon as they left, McGray joined me.

'It looked as if you ran away from the arrogant oaf . . .' I said. McGray responded with an extremely vulgar remark – which I would rather not transcribe – and then I told him about the invitation.

'Och! Ye'll have a mighty good time in that nest o' serpents!'

'I think it will be a good time to ask Lady Glass about her dealings with the victims too.'

As we finally reached the coffin, McGray stroked his stubble. I suddenly became aware of how out of place he looked; his tartan waistcoat and trousers amidst a crowd of mourners in black.

'Aye, I think ye should go. But I won't go with ye.'

'Why not?'

'What? Will ye miss my company?'

'Surely; as much as I would miss a thorn in my nether regions. I simply think that you should not let your personal quarrels with this family get in the way of your professional –'

'Oh, shush it, lassie! I'm sending ye on yer own cos I think yer pompous ways will work far better to get some information out o' them.'

'Well . . . I must concede that. Your vulgarity can make any well-mannered people uneasy . . .'

'Besides, I can use that free time to go to Old Calton Cemetery.'

'I beg your pardon?'

'Old Calton Cemetery. Don't ye remember I'm also doing research on the will'-o-the-wisps?'

I let out the loudest, most scornful 'HA!', and everyone around turned their baffled eyes towards me.

'How can you possibly think of such nonsense at this moment?' I said in a low hiss. 'We have two dead men in this case and yet not the slightest lead to the killer!'

'It will all clear up in time,' McGray said with such calmness, such unfounded certainty, that I even felt my hand raising, ready to slap some sense into him.

On the other hand, being able to conduct myself without McGray's interference struck me as a great advantage. He would not be there to upset people with stupid questions about curses – as he had just done to Mrs Caroli – or wasting my time in pointless interviews with the likes of Madame Katerina.

'I shall do as you wish,' I concluded, this time feigning a discontented expression. 'Can we go now?'

'Aye. Just let me look at this chap again . . .'

Following McGray, I looked over the coffin to have a last glance at Wood. Despite the talent displayed by the flower arrangements, the undertaker had not done a good job on the actual corpse: the man looked ashen, the only colour coming from his bruised fiddler's neck and from the long wound on his face. His lashed cheek and eyebrow reminded me of that dreadful moment when I thought that the string had torn his eye.

He could not have foreseen then what was coming upon him . . . even if that accident with the violin had been taken as a dark omen, as McGray had thought.

In a moment of indulgence I let myself get carried away by McGray's odd and superstitious ideas. What if that violin was truly cursed? What if Satan had really held it and his fingers had played hellish music with it? What if he had cursed not only the sonata but the instrument too?

All those were foolish thoughts, I know . . . but *what if?*

Suddenly, as if my gloomy meditations had summoned real ghouls, a chilling shriek came from the other side of the room.

Everyone turned towards the sound and I saw that Mrs Caroli was leaning over a chair, one hand on her belly, and slowly sinking to the floor.

Caroli ran like a gust of wind and supported her just as the woman let out another scream.

'Move aside!' I yelled. 'I have medical training!'

'But ye never graduat–'

'Oh, shut up!'

When I was nearer I saw a dark stain spreading swiftly on Mrs Caroli's dress. Her waters had broken.

'*For Christ's sake!* How long have you been in labour?'

Her face was pale and distorted. She muttered something that sounded like 'a few hours'. No wonder she'd been hostile to us.

'Why on earth would you not tell anybody?' I cried.

255

'One – one doesn't speak of such things,' she said with a panting voice.

Caroli spluttered something in Italian. He was going to fetch the doctor, or so I understood from my rudimentary Latin.

'May you please see that she gets to 'er room?' He said to me in an imploring tone and I could not refuse. Caroli then kissed his wife's forehead and gave her the most affectionate, most caring look. Then he stormed out of the house, leaving an utterly confused crowd behind.

McGray and two maids came to help me lead Mrs Caroli to the stairs.

'I must lock up the dogs!' she cried. 'There'll be no one to lock them if I don't –'

A contraction came and the poor woman almost fell on her knees. McGray held her with his thick hands and spoke firmly.

'Mrs Caroli, with all due respect, how can ye be worried about the dogs when yer about to give birth to yer own child?'

Mrs Caroli inhaled deeply and assented. I could tell she would have retorted had she not been in such pain. She walked to the staircase obediently, but turned to me as soon as she climbed the first step.

'May you please bring my Bible? I believe I left it in the study . . .'

'Go, Frey, I have her,' McGray said.

While he helped her upstairs I ran to the study. The Bible was still on the desk, in the exact spot where Mrs Caroli had left it when she first received us. I grabbed it carelessly and turned around, but then the corner of my eye caught something odd in the room. I lifted my face and then my heart jumped.

The violin case was gone.

24

I stormed out of the study, still clutching the Bible, and my eyes combed the hall. One of the maids was handing coats to some people at the door, and I noticed that most of the attendants were preparing to leave. I let out a guttural howl from the bottom of my stomach: '*Nobody will leave this house!*'

Everyone halted at once as if their feet had been put in irons; all their heads turned towards me. Among the crowd I recognized the shocked eyes of Ardglass and Downs.

I held my credentials up high so everyone could see them and headed to the door in long strides. '*I am in the service of Her Majesty's CID. Anyone who refuses to follow my orders shall be prosecuted and will be under suspicion of robbery and murder.*'

There was a general gasp and many an indignant frown, but not a single person remonstrated. The only movement in the hall was McGray, who came briskly down the stairs.

'What happened, Frey?'

I whispered in his ear. 'Somebody took the Amati.'

McGray went white and his frown was the deepest in the house. 'Ye ken what that means, don't ye?'

'Indeed. As we speak, that violin is in the hands of whoever murdered Fontaine and – possibly – Wood as well. We *must* act quickly; the bastard may still be near.'

Ardglass then approached us with a timid, almost blushing countenance.

'Erm, Inspector, with all due respect, may I ask how long will it take to –'

'As long as bloody necessary!' McGray shouted, and so began one of the longest nights in my career.

We summoned all the officers that the police could spare and deployed them to search every corner of the surrounding streets. Constable McNair was among the first to arrive, and very keen to be doing something other than guard the entrance to the City Chambers.

McGray decided to lead the search of the neighbourhood; in the meantime I would stay at Caroli's house, questioning every single person before letting them go.

After placing two armed guards by the main door, I turned back to a scene that was bizarre to say the least: mourning men standing still and casting me nervous stares, a few of the ladies fussing around smelling salts or being fanned by their relatives, the housemaids running about like chickens. The wax candles still burned around the coffin, but somehow it seemed as if the house had become darker. To sink the mood even further, we could hear the screams of Mrs Caroli, who was going through labour but a few rooms away.

I saw a maid still pouring whisky into the coffee of a grinning old man, and I swiftly snatched the drink. '*Do not serve any more spirits!* I need these people's statements. Is there a quiet place, other than the study?'

The girl was shaking, and mumbled something while pointing at the kitchen door.

'That will have to do.' I turned to the guests. 'Ladies and gentlemen, the easier you make this for me, the sooner you can all go home.'

As the maid led me to the kitchen I saw shaking heads, heard whispers and whimpering. I knew that such a large crowd would not keep quiet; as soon as I let them leave, the news would travel through the city like fire. The faces of Campbell, Sir Charles and Lord Salisbury himself came to my head, aghast at the situation, but there was nothing else McGray or I could do.

I decided to worry about one thing at a time, and installed myself at the kitchen table, where a police clerk would help me take the name and address of every witness. The room was anything but peaceful: the servants kept running to and fro, boiling water and fetching cloths, and I could not bid them keep quiet, for they were attending Mrs Caroli. Her screams came and went, only slightly muffled by the walls and ceiling.

One of the hounds was lying on the floor, turning its head nervously as it watched the maids dashing.

'I know how you must feel,' I told the animal.

I dispatched the people as swiftly as possible, but it still took me long hours to go through them all.

The half-intoxicated neighbour who scratched his privates throughout the questioning: 'D'ye know who I've got to kill to get another o' those coffees?'

The youngest maid: 'No one could have come in without us noticing, sir.'

The bony spinster (again), who had inhaled enough salts to deplete the Dead Sea: 'What a ghastly, ghastly night, sir! I'm so shocked I can't remember . . .'

The not so young maid: 'There's another door in the back yard, but only my lady and me have the keys.'

Alistair Ardglass: 'Oh, Inspector, I hope this incident doesn't give you a bad impression of Edinburgh, or keep you from joining us for the ball on –'

Each useless statement eroded my patience a little more. The coffin, which I could see clearly every time the maids or the witnesses in turn opened the door, was a constant reminder of how vital my assignment was.

I thought it would be all in vain, but then came the declaration of a very old, yet lucid enough gentleman who claimed to have been seated by the door to the study almost the entire evening. The only people he'd seen passing through that door had been the Carolis, McGray and myself. Senile as he seemed, he described accurately how Ardglass had tried to intercept me and how I'd slammed the door in his face.

'Did you move from that seat after you saw us come out?'

'Nae, sir. I stayed there all the time until Mrs Caroli screamed, and you went back into the room, I remember, and it was then when you came out shouting.'

I let out a weary sigh and let the man go. Right then I heard yelling in the main hall: another hound was at large, and it had pulled away the black cloth that had been covering a large mirror. I had to step out to restore order, but the oldest lady would not cease yelling until the glass was concealed again. Everyone considered that a terrible omen.

There were a dozen people left to question, but none gave me useful information. Once they were all gone the clerk and I went through the list of names and his notes, and then I had more liberty to inspect the house without curious eyes around.

The first place I looked over was the study.

A quick scan was enough to tell me that, if nobody had entered the room after us through the door, there was only one other way.

'The fireplace!' I remember saying out loud. I instantly knelt by the hearth and felt the ashes with my finger-tips. They were quite cool, reminding me that the fires had not been burning since before McGray and I arrived. The ashes were freshly disturbed, but I could not make out any clear footprints; on the other hand, two small stains in the fireside stones immediately caught my eye. I bent over until my nose almost touched the bricks. Undoubtedly, those were two marks of fingers, smeared in a hasty movement . . . coming from inside the chimney.

I cannot remember how many times my eyes went from the marks to the narrow fireplace, for their conjunction was utterly impossible; that flue was incredibly narrow, only a little wider than the head of a grown man. Larry the chimneysweep would have fitted in there, but only just.

I grabbed the first oil lamp I found and made haste to the back yard, which I found dark and silent like a grave. Looking up, I saw that the study's chimney ascended with other shafts on the back wall of the house. The roofs of the neighbouring houses were too far for anyone to jump to, and I felt a chill when I realized this, for it meant that the only way to leave the house was by descending to the very yard where I was standing.

I unholstered my gun at once. I was not expecting the robber to be still about, but decided to inspect the entire place all the same.

The Carolis owned only one old horse, and the somnolent beast barely moved when I threw some light into the stable. As I expected, there was nobody hiding there, only a very thin layer of hay scattered on the floor.

Next to the stable, and almost as large, was the hounds' shed, with its door ajar and a soft snoring coming from within. I kicked the door open and found that the third hound was there, dribbling and sleeping at leisure.

The animal lay on a neat pile of straw, covered with some ragged blankets that gave off the distinctive stench of dog. I thought wryly that many East London beggars would envy the hounds' lodgings.

I poked the improvised bed, looked under the blankets and through the straw, even though I already knew there was nobody hiding there. My fingers did touch something smooth though; a small glass bead. I pulled out what proved to be a rosary. I could not look at it properly under the dim light of the oil lamp, but I saw enough to know that the beads were made of colourful Murano glass. I assumed that Mrs Caroli kept it there to 'protect' her dogs, so I left it where it was and went back into the house. I had nothing left to do but help McGray and the officers outside.

I dragged my feet towards the door, my back aching, and heard Mrs Caroli letting out further piercing yells. Her voice, together with the hounds now lurking around the lonely coffin, made one morbid scene.

A young maid was coming downstairs, carrying a

basket with bloodstained towels. The girl's hands were trembling – her entire body, in fact, like an old woman balancing on strained legs.

'How is she doing?'

'She's holding up well. It should all be over soon . . .' She inhaled deeply, her eyes darkened with tiredness.

'Is she having a difficult labour?' I asked and the girl stuttered, her cheeks blushing. 'It is all right, you can speak freely. I have some medical experience.'

I saw her gulping painfully, repressing tears. 'Babies in this family never do well, my mama told me . . . and now I know what she meant.' I was about to ask for details, but then the girl said something that shocked me: 'This would have been difficult enough with a proper doctor to help us, but we had to fetch the first midwife we could find and I'm afraid we hurt more than we helped.'

'Why, a midwife! Mr Caroli could not find the doctor?'

The girl grimaced and cast me a sombre look. 'Mr Caroli hasn't come back, sir.'

She curtsied and hurried back into the kitchen, leaving me standing by the staircase, flabbergasted.

I left the two officers guarding the door and instructed them to keep a record of anyone coming in and out. I specifically asked them to inform me as soon as Caroli returned. I did not like his sudden disappearance at all.

The air outside was damp and frosty, and even though the fog had cleared a little, the world still looked as if painted only in hues of white and grey. I saw a couple of our officers patrolling the street and asked them where McGray could be found. One of them led me to a neighbouring road, where McGray was questioning a young watchman. Once he was done I told him about the finger marks in the fireplace. He was thrilled to hear that, but when I told him about Caroli not returning home, his jaw almost fell to the pavement.

'I cannae believe it!' he murmured, 'with the wife givin' birth and all! Something must have happened to him.'

'That is my same thought; this feels very wrong. Caroli seems to adore his wife.'

McGray pondered for a second. 'I'll ask the lads to look for him too. Ye can check with the men from Hill Street to the east and I'll look on the west side. My home's that way so I ken the area; that might help.'

We walked in opposite directions and went on searching for a couple of hours.

While trotting about the darkened streets of Edinburgh, surrounded by officers, yelling commands and almost passing out from exhaustion, it seemed almost as if we were not after a person, but a handful of that very fog around us.

A horrendous feeling of hopelessness invaded me. The case was doomed; McGray and I were meant to fail . . . I felt it in my guts with cruel certainty. We would find nothing in that blasted mist, then we would go on interrogating useless witnesses and making ludicrous assumptions, while Campbell and Monro would keep pressing ever harder for results, and my career would be in ruins even sooner than I had predicted in my most pessimistic predictions. As I dwelled on those thoughts my feet felt heavy, as if the Scottish mist had turned into shackles.

Just when my frustration was about to become unbearable, a grey figure emerged from the fog. I recognized Constable McNair, running towards me as he yelled.

'Inspector Frey! We found something!'

'The violin?'

McNair bit his lip. 'Not . . . quite, sir.'

Trotting ahead, he led me to a narrow close between two large Georgian mansions. The first thing I saw was McGray's tall figure, black against the beams of five bull's-eye lanterns, all directed at the cobbled street.

'What is it?' I asked as I approached, but McGray only pointed at the spot that the officers were lighting. A wave of nausea invaded me when I looked down. I saw a pool of freshly spilt blood, a black mess that turned out to be a charred human hand . . . and a familiar twisted symbol roughly drawn in red.

Nine-Nails took one step ahead.

'Ye had a good look at this, Frey?'

I nodded, speechless, and then, before I could even open my mouth to protest, McGray swept away the five-eyed scribble with his shoe.

'*Why did you do that?*' I howled. 'That was evidence, you idiot! It should have been properly documented! Photographed!'

'We can document the rest as much as ye please, but that's a damning symbol, Frey,' McGray retorted, reminding me of the superstitious lady screaming at the uncovered mirror. 'It invites the Devil to watch. I don't want more people to see it.'

I snorted, my face reddened with indignation. Infuriated as I was, there was nothing I could do but resume my work. Dawn was approaching and we did not want to attract curious stares, so some of the officers managed to find a dirty canvas to keep the scene from public view.

Once the site was properly covered, McGray and I kneeled down by the charred hand to look at it in detail. The smell of burned flesh made my stomach churn. We found that it was a rather long hand, undoubtedly of an adult man. Half hidden in the ashes I saw the golden spark of a wedding ring.

'That ring may have an inscription,' I told McGray. 'But I would prefer to have the whole scene photographed before moving anything else.'

We ordered McNair to fetch the photographer and the young man made haste to his horse. Less than half an hour had passed when he came back, followed by a small cart loaded with the bulky camera and a box of plaques. I did not see it at first because of the fog, but behind them came a large, luxurious coach. The driver halted and hurried to open the door, and I immediately recognized the silhouette of Superintendent Campbell.

The officers bowed before him as the man approached. Campbell had a slight limp and walked aided with a cane. Only then I realized I had never seen him standing, for he'd always been sitting at his desk during our meetings.

He came towards the scene in utter silence, but that made his presence all the more intimidating. He peered over the pool of blood and stared at the burned hand for a moment. Then he clicked his tongue in a reproving manner.

'Another death . . . Connected to this violin, I suppose?'

'Ye would think so,' McGray replied, his chin up high.

Campbell shook his head. 'When will you two begin your actual work? One would think that you are waiting for the murderer to knock on your front door.'

'Sir, we mobilized as many agents as we could, and interrogated –'

'Oh, but of course!' Campbell interrupted me with a mocking scowl. 'You interrogated *everyone* at that funeral, kept people waiting around for hours, and now you have kept half of New Town awake with your search.'

'Sir –'

'Does your pompous brain not understand that we want this matter dealt with quietly?' He spat those words in a cruel hiss, giving me a killing stare. Then he looked at McGray. 'You should be aware of that too, McGray. Do not forget that you are supposed to be in charge here.'

For a moment neither McGray nor I said a word, but as soon as I opened my mouth Campbell interrupted again.

'One more death,' he said. '*One more death*, Inspectors, and your careers are over. Did you hear? O-V-E-R. I hope that is clear enough even for your sluggish brains to grasp.'

Before we could say anything he was already walking back to his coach.

I was red with anger and my mood would not improve for a good while, but McGray only had to spit a couple of coarse remarks to be back to normal. He had a way of following his own road, no matter who objected.

We had the whole area photographed and then thoroughly cleaned. McGray himself picked up the ghastly hand with meticulous care and placed it in a leather bag. By the time we were done it was already mid morning. I did not realize it was quite so late until we saw a funeral cortège on our way to the City Chambers. It was, of course, Wood's, and they were carrying his body down south to Grange Cemetery.

There were thick clouds in the sky, and another thundering storm began before we arrived at the City Chambers courtyard.

We went straight to the morgue and showed the hand to Reed. The young doctor was appalled by the sight, but carried out a thorough examination nonetheless.

'I can't tell you much more than you probably deduced yourselves. The hand belonged to an adult man; the bones look rather young to me, but it is so badly burned I can't place the time when it was cut – or *how* it was cut.'

'Can ye show us the ring?'

'Of course. I will try to pull it off.'

Reed removed the golden ring with tweezers. As he did so, the burned flesh tore, some of it stuck to the gold.

'Like burned bacon in the pan,' McGray remarked.

Reed had to use a scalpel to scrape the shreds of charred skin off the metal before handing it to us. McGray took it without the slightest hesitation and even scraped the inner side with his nail.

'Ye were right, Frey. There's an inscription, but –'

He said no more.

Slowly, he handed the ring to me. I borrowed Reed's tweezers to hold it, and had no difficulty in reading the inscription, for black ashes had encrusted into the fine engraving.

My heart leaped when I saw that the words were not English, and even though I managed to decipher the meaning, one did not need to understand it to know who the ring had belonged to.

Con questo ricevi il mio cuore, mio amato Danilo.

I took a deep breath before translating the line out loud:

'"With this receive my heart . . . my beloved Daniel".'

25

'Caroli is dead! This is his hand!'

'Poor Mrs Caroli,' McGray murmured. 'Her husband dead the very night she gives birth to their child.'

I kept shaking my head. 'I did not expect another murder . . .'

'*We were so stupid!*' McGray cried as he kicked a chair, smashing it against the wall. His eyes were bloodshot.

I cleared my throat loudly, for I did not want Reed to hear the most morbid details of our investigation; the young man looked anxious enough. 'McGray, we should discuss this in the office.'

We thanked Reed for his services, and before we left he handed me a file.

'Here, Inspector. This is the first batch of analyses I've done on Mr Wood's stomach.'

'Can you summarize it?' I asked him; my eyes were too tired to read anything.

'The stomach was empty, as I told you, and I found none of the most common poisons: I looked for mercury, arsenic, cyanide, the usual agents. I will search for more obscure substances if you think it necessary. Also, I shall test his blood samples.'

'So up to now you would say that the man died of natural causes.'

'Indeed, sir.'

'Good work. Send us word immediately if you find anything.'

'Yes, sir.'

When we got back to the filthy office I sank onto my hard wooden chair and gave in to the widest yawn in the history of mankind.

'There's something that doesn't quite fit here,' McGray snapped, pacing around the room like a caged lion. 'There's something we're not seeing.'

'You are a master of the obvious, Nine-Nails,' I said, all drowsiness.

McGray was too euphoric to mind my sarcasm. 'Caroli was taken by the same person that killed Fon-teen, *that's* obvious. Everything was the same: The same mark, the pool o' blood . . .'

'Everything but one thing,' I said. 'The burned hand. There were no burned pieces of Fontaine in the previous scene.'

'D'ye still have those photographs?'

'I do.' I opened the nearest drawer and produced them. 'Here, but I do not think a piece of human flesh could have . . .'

'It was burned,' McGray interrupted me, although he'd only seen two photographs. He showed me an image and I understood immediately.

'The fireplace.'

'Aye. Remember Reed's report: Fontaine was missing not only a good chunk of intestines, but also his heart and liver.' McGray ran to a bookshelf and pulled out a tattered volume. He found a page and scanned it within seconds.

'Everything fits: murder yer victim, draw the symbol to summon Satan, then burn an offering to make 'im happy.' He ran his finger along the lines. 'Any flesh from a victim'll do, but the most precious organs are heart, liver, eyes.'

I nodded. 'Very well, but how does that fit in the puzzle? I do not see how that gives us any new information.'

'It confirms that the killer did not just want the fiddle, but the intestines too. Caroli *must* have gone the same way as Fon-teen, but the killer didn't have time to do the whole ritual in the middle o' the street; he simply murdered him, made the offering (a hand would be much easier to chop off than some organ) and then took the body somewhere else to work in peace.'

'But where? We made a thorough search.'

McGray shook his head. 'It's not hard to guess, but leave that to me, Frey. What really intrigues me now is that the bastard decided to kill again even though he already had Fontaine's guts . . . how many more murders has he got in mind?'

I groaned. 'There doesn't need to be a number. He might be planning to keep doing it again and again . . .' I kneaded my temples with frustration: 'God! As if things were not bad enough already!'

'Don't get so whiny. Things can *always* get worse; but we've still got some trails to follow. I'll take another look at that street where Caroli died.'

'A waste of time, I must say.'

'Perhaps. But I think I can get a better idea now in the daylight.'

'If this sickly, murky Scottish gleam can be called daylight . . .'

273

'Och! Look who's talking! Yer London's skies are smokier now than right after the 1666 Great Fire.'

'Oh, shush! You are right; we should follow whichever trail we . . . h – ha –' I yawned again, my mouth open so widely I could have swallowed McGray. I was so tired my eyes were itching.

'Ye look as battered as a canary caught in a cockfight. We better go home and get that maid o' yers to make us something to eat. Then I want ye to rest; I need ye to go to the ball o' that bitch Lady Ardglass. Ye better have yer beauty sleep before that.'

My exhaustion was turning into apathy, so I did not even bother to contradict McGray. I simply followed him when he had our horses fetched.

Even though the worst of the storm had passed, the shower was still persistent as we rode back to Moray Place. I saw murky rivers of rain flowing down the slopes of Princes Street Gardens. The city's main railway ran along the deepest point of the indented lawns, where huge storm drains kept the endless Scottish rain from flooding the rails.

Joan had not been expecting us to return so soon but she quickly improvised a wholesome meal: fried eggs with thick slices of crispy bacon, fresh bread, black coffee for me and thin ale for McGray – I could not help noticing that she served him the thickest rashers of bacon.

We dug in happily – it still surprises me how much a good, fatty serving of meat can do for the mood.

'Och, there's something else I must do!' McGray said, the corners of his mouth peppered with breadcrumbs and egg yolk. 'I must tell Mrs Caroli about her husband.'

He shook his head, a sombre look on his face. 'That isn't going to be easy.'

I decorously wiped my mouth with the napkin. 'In fact, I would like to be there as well; the prospect is gloomy to say the least, but it is a matter of honour.'

George was coming in to pick up our dishes: 'An honourable Englishman! I thought I'd never get to see one!'

Sadly, Joan was standing right behind him. '*Don't talk to my master like that, ya creased sack of spuds!*'

McGray and I exchanged tired looks and left the breakfast room before our servants' rants turned into carnage.

Just as McGray was opening the back door to the stable, Joan ran towards him carrying a freshly pressed overcoat. 'Master McGray, take this! 'Tis freezing out there!'

I could not tell whose eyes were more bewildered, mine or McGray's.

We made swift progress to Hill Street to see Mrs Caroli, and as soon as one of the servants opened the door we heard the newborn crying – or rather roaring – in the most desperate manner.

'Are they doing well?' McGray asked, while the servant led us to the stairs.

'Our lady's fine . . . well, as good as she could be after all that's happened. But the poor baby is ill; feverish. The doctor came and told us to keep the boy cool . . . but there's nothing else he can do.'

'So it was a boy,' McGray said.

'Aye, sir. It was a boy . . . Just like master Caroli wanted.'

Before going upstairs I had a glimpse of the main

parlour, where the youngest maid, the one who'd talked to me the night before, was beginning to remove the flowers from the funeral. The half-withered petals hung languidly from the bent stems, as if to announce that death had truly arrived in that house.

'I told you babies don't do well in this family,' she murmured as she worked.

I grimaced as soon as we walked into the upstairs bedroom, for it had the characteristic reek of illness, and then I almost shivered when I saw the poor woman lying on the bed.

Her face was simply ghastly: her skin as pale and dry as parchment, her dark hair utterly dishevelled, and her eyes, bordered by dark rings, were misery itself. It was as though giving birth had drained half her life. When she saw us she frowned in the most awful sorrow; she understood that our presence meant harrowing news.

McGray kneeled by the side of the bed and carefully held one of her hands. The contrast between her stiff, twisted fingers and his thick, strong hand could not have been greater. 'Mrs Caroli, we hope yer not goin' through a lot o' pain.'

'I can get through this,' she said, with a firm voice which did not match her fatigued looks. 'There is just one thing I need to know. Pray tell me; where is my husband?'

'I mustn't lie to ye . . .' Tenderly, McGray turned her hand and laid the golden ring in her palm. 'In the early hours we found yer husband's ha– . . . We found evidence to indicate that . . .' McGray inhaled deeply, 'he's been murdered.'

There was a horrible silence. It must have been a matter

of seconds but it felt like painful hours. Then, putting her elbows together, Mrs Caroli covered her face with her clenching hands and began to shudder until the bed shook. From between her hands came a low, desolate wail, and soon her fingers were soaked with tears.

'We are so, so sorry,' was all I could say, but any words would sound hollow at a moment like this.

'I wanna ask ye a few wee questions,' McGray murmured, resting a comforting hand on her shoulder. 'But I'll do so only when ye feel fit for it.' Mrs Caroli did not reply; she shook her head in assent, and then mumbled something that vaguely sounded like 'leave me alone'.

McGray patted her shoulder again and then we left. We told the maids where we could be found, whenever Mrs Caroli felt like talking to us.

As we were mounting our horses, I saw that McGray was wearing the tightest frown.

'I fear it was we who brought this upon the Carolis,' he said, his eyes fixed on the ground and burning with guilt.

'Because we brought the violin to them, do you mean?'

'Aye. Think about it, Frey: everyone who's owned the fiddle is dead! I feel like finding the damn thing just to give it to ye and see what happens . . .'

I would have responded, but McGray seemed so regretful I felt sorry for him.

'Go home, dandy,' he said. 'Have a rest and then go to yer snooty ball.'

'Are you sure that you do not want me to help you?'

'Aye. I can tell yer exhausted; yer face looks far more shite-sniffing than usual. Besides, I'm planning to bring

Madame Katerina to help me and she'll work much better without ye bitching about everything she says.'

I tilted my head. 'That, I must grant you. I can hardly imagine an encounter that could be more injurious to the soul.'

'And also, I need ye to question Lady Glass tonight. The old viper was Fontaine's and Wood's landlady. I don't like her being so connected to the case. I'm sure she'll chatter more freely if ye meet her alone.'

Saying no more, we went our different ways.

Once at Moray Place I thought that Elgie would certainly enjoy some distraction, and there was little that could go awry at such a social gathering, so I sent a note telling him about the ball. He sent the same messenger back with his reply, stating that he was 'decidedly elated' by the prospect.

After telling Joan to have my finery ready for the evening, I spent most of the day sleeping. I am glad I did so, for that night would again turn out to be . . . rather bloody.

26

'Joan! *Joan!*'

'Yes, master?'

'What the hell is this?'

'Your brown suit, sir. I pressed it today.'

'I see it is my brown suit, woman! I asked you to press the black one! *The black one!* This is a very formal party and I need the black one!'

'I was going to press the black one, sir, but I don't know what you did at that funeral to get those poor clothes in such a shocking state! Mud and ashes all over, and they stank of dog so much I had to soak 'em in milk!'

I groaned in frustration as I hysterically rummaged through the wardrobe.

'There's no use, sir,' Joan said. 'You asked me to bring only one black suit. But there's the navy one you like so much. Nobody'll notice you're wearing navy if the ball's by candlelight.'

A gentleman in London would never wear a navy suit to a formal ball. *Never!* I was appalled to find that Joan was right; I had no suitable attire and there was no time to do anything about it.

'Very well, then. Give me that navy one.' I cannot tell how much it pained me to say that – I was about to break one of the most basic rules of etiquette.

While I changed behind the folding screen Joan went

on rambling about how much she hated George and the 'snooty fishwives' who worked in the neighbouring houses.

'Mr McGray came back when you were sleeping, sir,' she said at some point. 'He was in just for a second and said he needed to check something in the city library . . . or the registry or something. Oh, the poor man looked wasted, but he got on his horse as if all fresh. Not long ago he came back carrying these mighty rolls of paper and he's been reading in his study ever since!'

'You seem to have taken a lot of interest in Nine-Nails,' I said, recalling how attentively she'd served him lunch and fetched his coat earlier. 'I thought that you hated the man.'

'Oh, master, even *you* would be kinder to him if you knew his misfortunes.'

'Misfortunes?'

'Yes. Haven't you wondered how the poor man lost his finger? Or why nobody visits this house?'

I remembered McGray mentioning that he kept that silly Agnes because nobody else would work for him, and then saying that Lady Glass had spread scandalous rumours about his family, but he had always spared me the details. 'Well . . . yes, I have wondered, but I cannot say the intrigue keeps me from sleeping.'

Joan's eyes almost swelled in the excitement of telling the tale. 'Oh, sir, 'tis such a dreadful story . . .'

I sighed in resignation. 'It is too late now to keep you from talking. Go ahead, but be quick. And hand me the cuffs and the tiepin.'

'Yes, sir. Well, it all happened five years ago, when the McGrays were well placed here in Edinburgh. The late Mr McGray had many properties; farms and ships and also I think a distillery of fine Scotch, nearby the –'

'He was wealthy, I follow the general idea.'

'Oh, yes, sir, very wealthy. George got all enthused when he told me all these stories about his late master. The late Mr McGray made himself, you know; all the way from a clerk in a filthy pub in Dundee – wherever that is. Of course the very high peoples around here didn't like such a family, without exalted ancestors and all that. That Ardglass hag you're calling on today especially devoted herself to –'

'Joan, you are beginning to ramble.'

'Oh, yes. Sorry, sir. Well, five years ago, like I told you, the family went to spend the summer in one of their houses near Dundee. They liked their horses and the hunting and the country life, you see. Every year they spent something like a month in their country properties, taking only a couple of servants; a maid, of course, and a man to bring the charcoal to the fireplaces and all those things us women cannot –'

'Joan, are you getting any closer to the point? Actually I will wear a navy tie, too.'

'Here it is, sir. I was telling you that they took only one or two servants . . . and *that* would be the last trip of the family . . . Everybody's got a different version of what happened that day, but George told me to believe none . . .'

'There, there; you are getting in the bloodcurdling mood.'

'Well, sir, it *is* bloodcurdling! What would you do if one of your own kin went all berserk and attacked you? That happened to poor Mr McGray!'

I frowned. 'What do you mean?'

'Oh, sir, I would like to have finer words to say this . . . but his sister butchered her parents!'

So abrupt was her statement that I bit my own tongue. '*She did what?*'

'Butchered . . . killed 'em horribly! Oh, master, I can hardly repeat that! The girl pierced her mother with a fire poker and stabbed her father in the heart with a kitchen knife! One maid was there but she told everyone she saw nothing, only heard Miss McGray shrieking like a monster. That woman ran to fetch our Mr McGray, who happened to be out right then . . . And when he got back to the house he found his poor sister all covered in blood, still with the knife in her hands and completely out of her wits. Poor, poor girl.'

'And then . . . ?'

'Mr McGray tried to calm her down, but his sister attacked him, and would've probably killed him too, but thank God she only –'

Joan could not say more, frightened by her own story. It took me a moment to notice that I too had fallen still, staring at her reflection in the mirror, my motionless hands unable to finish the knot of my tie.

'McGray's *own sister* chopped his finger off!' I cried at last.

Joan assented and the eyes of Miss McGray came back to my head like a flash. I had been right; those were not the eyes of an ordinary girl, but I would have never thought that such a stare belonged to a demented parricide.

'And I suppose she has been in the asylum ever since.'

'Yes, sir. Poor Miss McGray never spoke again. The last person who heard her uttering a word was some Dr Clouston; the girl was yelling something about being possessed by the Devil.'

'*Possessed?*'

'Aye. I know you don't believe these things, but nobody's come up with a better explanation. Even the doctor in the madhouse can't tell what's wrong with her.'

In that she was right. I remembered my brief chat with Dr Clouston.

'So George told you all these things?'

'Yes, but sir, everybody knows the story! For months and months after it happened people in this town would talk of nothing else at their parties. Now people even tell the story of the McGrays around the fire, just as they tell stories of witches and spirits on Christmas Day. I'm astonished you don't know any of this. Haven't you spoken to anybody since you got here?'

'Why, I have been fiendishly busy since I arrived! The last thing I would want to do is to hunt gossip in the fish market.'

One moment later someone knocked on the door and Joan ran to look through the window. ''Tis your brother, master!'

I checked my pocket watch as I adjusted the chain to my waistcoat. 'Lord, he was supposed to be here twenty minutes ago!'

Joan gave me my thickest coat and I went downstairs, my mind still dwelling on McGray's turbulent past.

The door to the library was ajar and I caught a brief sight of him, leaning over the table where a gigantic blueprint lay. He was utterly focused on the document, his nose almost touching the yellowed paper and his four-fingered hand running meticulously over the intricate plans.

Suddenly everything made sense: his premature wrinkles, the bags under his eyes, his utter disregard for appearances and good society . . .

Most importantly, that morbid story explained McGray's obsession with ghost stories and all his superstition. Each book in that library, each twisted artefact he kept, each sleepless night researching witches and goblins and demonic rituals, each day struggling to get his subdivision approved – all those efforts were spurred by a family tragedy. I recalled how tenderly he'd touched his sister's hand while visiting her at the asylum, and how infuriated he'd been when he caught me peering into the room.

Could he, in the back of his mind, still maintain a desperate hope of bringing his sister back? After five long years sitting in front of that girl's empty face and enduring the mockery of the entire town, how could he possibly keep himself standing? I could only imagine how much he still loved the girl – and surely how much he had loved his parents – to completely devote his life to such a hopeless quest. It is hard to admit, but at that moment I truly pitied the man.

I was going to tell him that I was about leave, but preferred not to. It is awkward when one learns something very personal about someone; one no longer knows quite how to address them.

Joan's tale left me in a grim state of mind, and as I walked out of the house the evening climate lowered my mood even more: the air was frosty and the rain had turned into a thick sleet that fell almost horizontally.

Fortunately, I did not need to walk far. Elgie had arranged for a coach to pick him up at the New Club, which would take us from Moray Place to the Ardglass estate. I was glad to see that he had chosen a splendid brougham carriage.

'Lord, how can you be so bloody unpunctual?' I snapped as soon as I got into the carriage.

'Oh, brother, do not make such a fuss. We are but a few minutes late.'

'A few minutes late! You are so late Joan had enough time to tell me the entire life and tribulations of McGray.'

Elgie's eyes glowed. 'Oh, did she tell you all about his crazed sister?'

'Why, you already know it!'

'Well, I have been chatting with people at the New Club. I mentioned your job and McGray's name naturally came up.'

'I will appreciate it if you stop mentioning my job to any stranger you stumble across on the street.'

Elgie went on as if I'd not spoken. 'Oh, my brother, that story of the mad sister is simply astounding; worthy of being written down in a book! This good man told me that they even tried to exorcize her with the priest and the holy water and the whole thing! Can you believe that?'

I found myself frowning hard. 'Would it be so amusing if it were me or Oliver?'

Elgie went silent, his cheeks as red as cherries. His blond hair looked almost white in comparison.

'I . . . I thought you did not like the man.'

'I do *not* like him, but there are things you should not joke about.'

I am still surprised that such words came out of my mouth: I, of all people, was defending Nine-Nails McGray!

Elgie sighed as he always does when he wants to change the subject.

'Ian, is the CID giving you a hard time? You look rather – haggard.'

I smiled wearily. 'You are better not knowing. Let us talk about you. What have you been doing with your time?'

'My word, it has been so boring! I am either rehearsing at the theatre or locked in my room playing the violin. This weather here is dreadful! Who would imagine that even London can be beaten in that respect?'

'But of course, Elgie! You are surely the only person mad enough to willingly travel to Scotland in the last days of November.'

'Although I must confess that, in a way, I like it.'

'*Do you?*'

'Yes. Every time I look at the castle all wrapped in fog it feels as though I am reading a gothic novel. I almost expect to hear the howling wolves and to see the shades of beheaded monks!'

I could only smile at my brother's nonsense; his dreamy

excitement and his sense of wonder. I lost those qualities a long time ago.

'In fact, I do have some news to tell you,' Elgie said in a sterner tone. 'I received a lengthy telegram from my mother.'

'*Have you!* What does Catherine have to say?'

'She is concerned about Father. Apparently your not replying to his letter has affected him more than he would admit.'

'Of course I did not reply! He sent me an entire treatise on how damning my conduct is!'

'Well, Mama told me that he is really suffering, and –'

'Did she ask you to try and persuade me to write back?'

Elgie tilted his head. 'Erm, certainly not. She asked me to persuade you to *return* as soon as possible – which I must confess, would be no bad thing.'

I let out a loud, wry laugh. 'Lord, this is not to be borne! Elgie, do not go on! I would hate to speak ill of your mother in front of you!'

That was a tactic typical of Catherine; manipulative and scheming as always. Elgie's very presence had most likely been championed by her: she knew that Elgie was the only one with a chance of persuading me, so she had washed his brain and sent him all the way to Scotland to bring me back. And then, as usual, she'd end up being a heroine in the eyes of my foolish father.

Elgie resorted to childish pleading. 'Ian, I know that you and Papa do not always agree but, quite frankly, I do understand his concern. *I myself* do not comprehend why you insist on staying here like a stubborn child. This position is eating you. Look at yourself: tired, poorly shaven and wearing a navy lounge suit to a formal ball! Do you want to prove something to Father?'

'Elgie, do not be ridiculous.'

'Then . . . do you want to get back at Laurence for the things he has said?'

'Dammit, no!'

'Then what is it?'

I shook my head. 'Forget it. You would never understand . . .'

'*Well, how could I, if you will not bloody explain yourself?*'

Elgie had never snapped at me before. Had it been anybody else I would not have bothered to reply, but with him I felt obliged.

I had to meditate for an instant, for even I was not entirely sure about my real motives. I remembered the instant, standing before the steamer that would take me to Scotland, hesitating, about to give it all up and go back to the safety of my family home. Yet something had pushed me forward, and up to then I'd not had time to truly reflect upon it.

In fact, the answer was not that intricate.

'First, I tried law school, where all we did was read endless Acts only to find a way to bend them. Then off I went to study medicine and found that I lacked the character for it . . . And then I even tried staying at home like Oliver, but nothing ever felt right. Finally, in the CID I thought I'd found my place; my job there was something I was fit for doing and that I utterly enjoyed. I finally felt like I was something more than hollow-headed gentry; I was doing something meaningful! And then all this whirl of rubbish happened and it all went to the cesspit again. I will not go back home defeated. Not again.'

'Is it worth the fight?'

'Proving to myself that I am not a total failure? Of course it is bloody worth it!'

27

I was not fully aware of how illustrious the Ardglass clan was until I saw their splendid mansion in Dublin Street, one of the most sumptuous roads in New Town. The mansion's gardens were adjacent to Queen Street Gardens, a long strip of grass and oaks amidst the grey stones of the Georgian neighbourhood. Moray Place and Dublin Street were actually on the opposite ends of those gardens and we could have easily walked there; however, it would have been terribly improper to arrive on foot. We had not crossed half the lawn when we joined the long line of carriages queuing into Duke Street; the rain had ceased only a while ago and the streets were still muddy and slippery, so the drivers had become cautious.

When we finally reached the entrance to the Ardglass mansion, we saw a small crowd of very smart ladies and gentlemen, all dressed up in the most elegant furs and hats. It was hard to believe that someone like McGray lived so close to such refined gentry, yet it made me understand why his name was loathed so much.

A familiar voice came from amidst the small group of people ascending the granite steps to the entrance: 'Inspector Frey!'

As before, I could not see the short figure of Downs until he stepped right in front of me. He was carrying the violin case as agreed.

'Good evening,' I said, and then introduced him to my brother. 'So this is the last violin you need to deliver to complete the will of the late Mr Fontaine.'

'That is correct, Inspector. And I'll be relieved once this is taken off me, I must confess. It is not that I am a superstitious one, but these instruments do seem to be . . . rather macabre.'

'Macabre?' Elgie asked before Downs had finished the word. 'It sounds like a story that you *must* tell me, Brother.'

'Not tonight, most certainly.'

We advanced to the entrance and found Alistair Ardglass saluting the incoming guests. He was kissing the hand of a very elegant lady, but almost pushed her aside when he saw us. His eyes immediately fell on the violin case, like peas rolling to the bottom of a bowl.

'Why, Inspector Frey! How good of you to come! Is that for my niece?'

On close examination I found him rather pale and haggard, his temples shiny with perspiration and his whiskers rather messy. His grin was sickly servile and I could only nod with contempt. 'Indeed, this is her violin. This is my bro—'

'Oh, your good brother! We have already met; at the New Club.'

I arched my eyebrows. 'I see now. So Mr Ardglass is the one who told you about the exorcisms with holy water . . .'

'One of them,' Elgie added.

'Please, do come in. I shall join you in a second; as soon as I fetch my aunt. She will be delighted to finally meet you!' He seemed so excited he could have pushed us all the way into the ballroom.

A stiff butler received our overcoats and then showed

us to a huge parlour. As we walked in I looked at the high ceilings and saw three enormous chandeliers ablaze with candles. The place was already packed from end to end, the dancing couples spinning tirelessly like a sea of waving silk and muslin. The crowd made the room so warm it was hard to believe that icy rain and sleet had lashed Edinburgh throughout the day.

As the dancers flashed before us I caught blurry glances of a grand orchestra playing at the opposite side of the ballroom.

'Good musicians?' I asked Elgie, for his ear was the only one I trusted.

'They are excellent, to be honest. They even make *me* want to waltz . . . Oh, we should have a bite!'

Elgie was about to make his way towards the imposing mountains of food on display: crystallized chestnuts, vol-au-vents stuffed with salmon and scallops, Dutch asparagus, pickled guinea-fowl eggs, ice-cream on strawberries soaked in Porto wine . . .

Discreetly, I seized my brother's arm. 'Wait a bloody minute! You do not want everyone around to believe that you are a starving pauper!'

Elgie unwillingly composed himself. Fortunately he did not have much time to sulk, for Ardglass returned sooner than we expected.

I saw two women following him, one very old and the other in her mid twenties – clearly 'Lady Glass' and her granddaughter, Caroline Ardglass. Alistair introduced them accordingly and my eyes flickered from one to the other, not knowing on whom to concentrate.

Lady Anne Ardglass was in her seventies but she still

walked with a very straight spine, her shoulders pulled backwards, her chin high, giving her a powerful demeanour. She was thin and rather tall for a woman, and wore an impressive headdress of white plumes that made her appear even grander. Nevertheless, her face did reflect the passage of time, her cheeks gnarled like the bark of a tree. She had dark, veined bags under her eyes, no doubt from her drinking, which had probably begun when she was still young. As she walked towards us I noticed a slight sway, possibly from the drink she'd already had.

Caroline, on the contrary, had an arresting face: a soft jaw, pointed chin and nose, and a small mouth of scarlet, parted lips. Her eyes were very dark and glistened with a cunning, firm stare. I could tell that she was evaluating me, though I did not know – yet – to what end. Even though her manners seemed elegant and refined, there was a certain air of wildness in her general attitude.

'We are pleased to finally make your acquaintance, Mr Frey,' Lady Anne said. Her voice was deep and well modulated, her accent quite concealing her Scottish origins. 'You will surely have a pleasant evening.'

'Thank you, Lady Anne. However, this is not entirely a social visit. First of all, we are to deliver an inheritance to Miss Ardglass.'

I looked at Downs, who immediately extended the violin case to the girl.

'Miss Ardglass, the late Monsieur Fontaine stated explicitly that he wanted you to have this instrument: a violin by Guadagnini, dated 1754.'

She did not seem particularly impressed, and simply received the case and curtsied.

'This violin has one of the sweetest tones I've ever heard,' her uncle said, a hint of bitterness in his voice. 'You are luckier than you think, Caroline.'

'That is marvellous, Uncle,' she replied, still showing no emotion. In fact she seemed rather bored.

Lady Anne had to intervene: 'Say thank you to Inspector Frey, Caroline. He has gone to a lot of trouble to bring you this.'

Caroline looked at me, showing the wryest of smiles. '*Thank you*, Inspector Frey. I do realize that delivering a violin might have caused you hardships that few humans could bear.'

I felt my gut burning at her insolence. How some women take advantage of the fact that one cannot punch them! And my brother could not keep himself quiet . . .

'Indeed,' he said, before I could stop him, 'but any hardship will be nothing when suffered for such a *fine*, *charming* lady.'

The rogue has certainly learned from his mother how to emphasize *just* the right words. He left the rest of us terribly uncomfortable, and I had to break the awkward silence.

'Lady Anne, there is another reason for my visit; some questions I need to ask you, rather urgently.'

'Oh, odious business matters! Why do gentlemen like to work themselves to death? You should first have some distraction. Pray, dance with my Caroline. She will be delighted.'

Caroline cast a stabbing look at her instead.

'Charming as the prospect is, I must decline, Lady Anne. As I told you, this cannot wait any longer.' I saw

Elgie looking earnestly at the canapés. 'Besides, my brother will also be delighted to dance with your granddaughter.'

I could not tell who was the most infuriated; both Elgie and Caroline looked at me with more anger than many deranged murderers I have interrogated.

A vein had popped out in Lady Anne's temple. 'Very well, then. We can talk in my parlour.'

She cast her nephew a dismissive nod and I saw Elgie walking away with Miss Ardglass, apparently whispering malevolent things at her. I followed Lady Anne across the room, the crowd instantly parting for her as though we were in Windsor Castle and she was the Queen of England. I heard a plump woman murmuring to her daughter: 'Remember to tell yer brother that the latest fashion in London is navy!' My eyes simply rolled.

As soon as we were in the corridor, Lady Anne snapped her fingers and a butler appeared with a gas lamp. He led us to a small, rather cosy drawing room whose windows looked out on the main road.

Crammed with ledgers and piles of letters and documents, the place looked nothing like a lady's parlour, but more like a businessman's study. A piece of on-going embroidery and a set of flowery china were the only traces of a feminine presence. The walls must have been thick, for once the butler closed the door the echoes of the party were completely muffled. A few gas lamps lit the room, casting sharp shadows on the wrinkled face of Lady Anne, and the yellowish light bounced on the big pearls of her many necklaces, making them gleam like a myriad eyes. As I noticed that her lips were stained with red wine, I felt as if I were sitting in front of one of Shakespeare's weird sisters.

'What is it that you wish to know, Mr Frey?'

'Lady Anne, I regret to tell you that during our investigations into Mr Fontaine's death your name has been mentioned . . . rather more frequently than one would expect.'

The woman looked at me with a raised brow, but there was hardly any other motion in her face. 'Continue,' she said.

'Mr Fontaine's testament, as you know, indicated that his most valuable violins should be delivered to his closest colleagues and students – your granddaughter included, as you know now. One of the violins went to Theodore Wood, who happened to die but a few days ago, and the violin in question is now missing.'

'And what is my role in all that, pray?'

'Both Guilleum Fontaine and Theodore Wood lived in properties owned by you, ma'am.'

Her eyebrow now looked like an inverted U. 'Do you need any information from me? Something about their characters or their finances?'

'Oh, no. Inspector McGray and I have collected enough information as to the victims. Right now I am interested in finding more about *your* involvement, ma'am. Your closeness to two sequential deaths is rather puzzling.'

Again, not a movement in her face: 'I do not understand. Are you implying that I –'

'I do not like to imply; that is why I am questioning you. It all may be an unfortunate coincidence, in which case your answers should prove it instantly.'

'A coincidence it is, of course!' She stood up and went to a nearby shelf, looking for a volume. 'Guilleum, as I recall, moved into my property in 1865 – mid spring, to be precise – I like to keep detailed records.' She handed me a thick ledger and pointed at the appropriate entry; then she went back to the shelf. 'Theodore, that poor creature, came to town in 1883. Before that he made his living playing at some godforsaken parish in Glasgow, until his last relative died. He told me he had no connections of any kind, so he decided to try his luck in Edinburgh. It was Mr Fontaine who first heard him play and invited him to join the Conservatoire; he also suggested him as a tenant for one of my properties. Musicians live in a very compact circle, Mr Frey; it is only natural that they share landladies . . . and solicitors. Fontaine even used to go to the same barber as my nephew!'

'The tenancy is not the only issue that prompted me to come. There is the matter of the broken window.'

Lady Anne clicked her tongue in exasperation. 'Dear Lord, that blasted window! Had I known it would cause me so many troubles I would have smashed the door with my bare hands!'

'Can you elaborate on that?'

She sat again. 'I was asked for permission to tear apart the door to Fontaine's study. I refused, as you know, and suggested they should climb and break the window instead.'

'On the basis of . . . a window being cheaper to replace than a fine oak door . . .'

'I am a businesswoman, Mr Frey, and I treat my investments with the most critical eye. My family did not come this far by squandering capital. Ultimately, it is my property we are talking about.'

'To be utterly honest, ma'am, asking for your permission was a courtesy I would not have offered. Under such circumstances I would have broken in first and given explanations later. Do you realize that your decision delayed the tasks of the police, when every second could have meant Mr Fontaine's life or death?'

'That is nonsense. When they came to me, Guilleum had been locked in that room for hours and hours. He could not have possibly been alive by the time they asked for my permission to break in.'

'How can you say that? You did *not* know what had happened to him . . . or . . .' I leaned a bit closer, 'did you?'

'Of course I didnae!' she cried at once, her Scottish inflection coming to the fore. 'I am utterly offended by your mere insinuation! Why should I plot anything against a respectable gentleman who'd been my faithful tenant for twenty-three years? And what does it have to do with Theodore's death? My nephew told me that he died of cholera.'

I nodded slowly. 'A puzzling situation, indeed. In other circumstances I would take your word and attribute it all to coincidence, but there is one more thing.'

'Another thing?'

'Indeed. Your nephew insisted, in a truly annoying manner, on making my acquaintance and then inviting me to this ball . . . apparently obeying your wishes.'

'And does that instantly make me a murder suspect?'

'As I told you, ma'am, if it is coincidence, it will immediately shine through. You need but speak the truth.'

'I refuse to dignify your ridiculous accusations with a reply!'

'Lady Anne, unless you want the CID to carry out a deeper investigation, which, surely, would not be good at all for the reputation of so well known a family, you shall provide me with a good explanation as to why you were so determined that I should be here tonight. If your answer satisfies me, I shall quit this room and forget whatever you say.'

Lady Anne shook her head, her frown deeper than ever. I could see the guilt in her manner, the anxiety . . . even a hint of embarrassment. The corners of my lips insisted on pulling into a triumphant smile, but I did my best to maintain a neutral expression. The woman stretched an arm to one of the cabinets and produced a silver hipflask. She gulped a good sip and then, finally, spoke. A strong scent of whisky filled the room.

'It is a pity that you force me to reveal this, especially this early. And it will be most detrimental . . . particularly for you.'

I frowned. 'Pray, explain.'

She gulped a second draught, deeper than the first one. 'Ever since I knew of your being in town it has been my intention to introduce you to my granddaughter . . . since she is of marriageable age.'

I blew inside my cheeks and kneaded my temples. 'Oh, goodness!'

'As I told you, it is a pity that you force me to have this conversation today of all days. I am a sensible woman and I would not have introduced this matter until you and my Caroline were more closely acquainted.'

I did not bother to hide my laughter as I stood up. 'Lady Anne, I understand it all now. You are free of all suspicion. I must leave.'

'Mr Frey!' she insisted. 'You must not dismiss her so lightly. Caroline is an enviable match: beautiful, vivacious, accomplished in languages and music ... but most importantly, she is to inherit all my possessions as well as my title. A most advantageous union; it would bring together the nobility of the Ardglass with the gentility for which the Freys have been admired for generations. None of your kin has ever risen to nobility, while my late husband came from a most distinguished lineage.'

I opened the door, feeling almost bilious. 'Lady Anne, pray, *pray* say no more! I could refute each and every one of those arguments, but I would prefer we remained on respectful terms.'

'Mr Frey, won't ye —'

I had to raise my voice for she would not give up otherwise. '*A Lady should know how to preserve her dignity!*'

She stood still and cast me the foulest stare. Again she looked like an old witch about to toss a toad into her cauldron. She inhaled deeply and grabbed her little flask. 'Make yourself at home, Mr Frey,' she hissed as she quit the room. 'I hope you enjoy the rest of the ball.'

The ballroom was in turmoil. The music and the dancing had stopped, yet all the attendants were gathered around the small orchestra.

I found Downs at the very end of the crowd, standing on tiptoes and stretching his neck, trying to get at least a glimpse.

'What is going on?' I asked him.

'Something really exciting: a violin duel!'

'A violin duel?'

'Yes, between Mr Ardglass and your young brother.'

I felt my jaw falling all the way to the hardwood flooring. 'What the heck has that little brat gotten himself into?' I grunted as I elbowed my fellow guests aside, making my way towards the musicians.

Indeed, I found Elgie there, smiling in front of the crowd, and Alistair Ardglass standing next to him. By then the older man was soaked in sweat as he fine-tuned the strings of his violin. He also seemed paler, his yellowish hands contrasting against the dark-coloured violin.

I pulled Elgie's arm and hissed, my face burning with anger. '*What on earth do you think you are doing?*'

His smile made me want to slap him. 'I want to shut him up! He believes he knows it all when it comes to music theory. He is the most insufferable, arrogant old man.'

'*And you are ten times more arrogant!* I will not let you flaunt like a bloody chorus girl! Do you hear me?'

Ardglass approached us. 'It is too late, Inspector. Your brother has made such a fuss that our guests are looking forward to it.'

I snorted and let go of Elgie's arm. 'Very well. If you insist on making yourself ridiculous I shan't get in the way.' And so I left him by the orchestra and went straight to the wine table. I thought that I could not feel more aggravated, but then Miss Caroline approached me . . .

'You have the most disgusting brother, Mr Frey.'

'I wish you had met my eldest one.' I chuckled bitterly

and then indulged myself with a very long sip of wine. How strengthening that was; at least part of my brain could now take care of the social niceties. 'I must apologize if Elgie was in any way insolent.'

'I can deal with boys like him,' she said. 'There is something much more delicate that made me come to you. I must beg you to answer something.'

I saw danger coming – not of murder or injury, but from the far more horrifying and baffling realms of the female character. However, my manners did not allow me to send her away. 'Then pray ask, miss.'

'Mr Frey, I am so sorry to put you in such an awkward situation but –' she took a deep breath, '– has my grandmother asked you any . . . *improper* questions?'

I inhaled, trying to think of a courteous way to tell her the truth. She read my expression before I could say anything.

'*Dear Lord!*' she squealed. 'Has she offered you my hand already? She must be utterly desperate to do so on the very night she met you! Mr Frey, I must make something very clear immediately.'

'Miss . . .'

'My grandmother might have sold herself to a bankrupted lord, but that does not mean that I will follow her steps. I shall not be paraded like a calf in the cattle market. Do you understand?'

'Miss . . .'

'It is disgusting enough to hear her talk about lineage and bloodlines as if she were breeding mules . . .'

Her speech was becoming so impertinent I had to forget all decorum and place two fingers on her forearm.

'Miss Ardglass, before you get carried away, rest assured that I never, *never* had the slightest desire or intention of accepting your hand.' Too late I realized how appalling the words had sounded. 'Oh . . . forgive me. I did not mean . . . that is to say, in other circumstances – well, a fine lady like yourself would be –' I was now dangerously close to offering an actual proposal. I cleared my throat. 'Miss Ardglass, this is not a conversation to be had with a twenty-minute acquaintance. Kindly excuse me.'

I bowed and walked away swiftly, feeling both sorry for the young woman and shamed by my stuttering. She seemed a spirited, smart girl, and perfectly able to fend for herself. Still, I wondered how much Lady Anne's efforts to secure her future were actually driving suitors away.

I moved to a table on the other side of the hall, away from the crowd, feeling my guts writhing in the worst state of frustration. I could not remember having been at a more disastrous party . . . and yet the worst was still to come.

Alistair had just finished tuning his violin and then, with the most ridiculous attempt at an eloquent voice, he introduced the violin duel. They would try to outperform each other until one of them admitted defeat, or until the crowd decided that one of them was clearly the better.

'Ladies and gentlemen,' he said at last, 'as a good host I will cede to my challenger the privilege of playing the first piece. I give you *Mr Elgie Frey*.'

There was some sporadic applause as Elgie received the violin. He covered the chinrest with a handkerchief; it was the one I'd given him at the theatre, and I could not help feeling a little flattered. After carefully protecting his neck, Elgie got the instrument in position, tried a couple of notes and trills, and finally took a deep breath.

Elgie only had to play two or three bars before we all recognized the main theme of 'The Hunt', from Vivaldi's 'Autumn'. I had to give him credit; he'd chosen a well-known, friendly piece to begin with, and soon I saw ladies swaying from side to side, following the catchy melody. Close to the ending, his violin exploded in a frenetic passage that utterly surprised the crowd – almost as much as if a real fox and a pack of hounds had suddenly appeared in the middle of the hall. The ovation was great, and it cheered me to see that Caroline and her grandmother were grimacing.

Alistair took the violin, reflected for a few moments, and then smiled maliciously as he pressed the instrument against his chin.

From the very beginning, his bow stroked the lowest string at full speed. It was the dark, prestissimo movement of 'Summer', also by Vivaldi, and Ardglass played it even faster than the piece was supposed to be. Not content with that, Ardglass also enriched it with embellishments that were not in the original score. The music sounded like a ravaging storm.

In the end, the roaring applause came from admiration rather than pleasure. By choosing a more difficult movement of the same composition, Alistair was trying to make the superiority of his skills crystal clear. Elgie would find it difficult now; nevertheless, his reaction could not have been more suitable.

'I did not know that we were confining ourselves to the

Four Seasons!' he said. 'If you raise no objection, I shall try to be a little more imaginative.'

Ardglass gave him a filthy look as he handed over the violin, and my brother grinned as if fed by the man's resentment.

Even though Elgie was beginning to foresee his defeat, he welcomed the instrument once more. His second piece was definitely not as quick as Alistair's frantic 'Summer', but his perfect rhythm and the bright notes, melded with his happy, childish attitude, gave us the most vivacious, uplifting piece of music. From time to time I could see him glancing at the crowd, rejoicing in their appreciation, and then I understood what he was attempting; while Ardglass was focused on showing off his virtuosity, my brother wanted people to *like* his music. A brilliant move, for even if Ardglass beat him on the technical side, Elgie would win people's hearts.

Suddenly I realized that I had heard him playing that piece before . . . and not just on any day. That was the piece he'd been playing on the very day I had lost my position in London; that dreadful day after I had faced the prime minister at Scotland Yard. It was Paganini's 24th Caprice, the same theme. Nevertheless it sounded somehow . . . different. I had to listen carefully for a moment, enraptured by my brother's skill and enthusiastic movements. I had to transport myself back to that awful day and remember every image, every step, every word and every smell . . . And then it all came clear; the sound *was* different because Elgie was playing a different violin. The resonance from the strings was not quite as bright;

the echoes of the low notes were louder and deeper, and the higher notes sounded pleasantly muffled, almost dark.

'Could it be that . . . ?' I did not realize that I'd muttered those last words out loud until Downs spoke to me.

'I beg your pardon, Inspector?'

I shook my head. 'Nothing. Just a thought . . .'

When Elgie finished, there was a second of bewildered silence, and then a thunderous applause resounded across the room. I could hardly imagine that the ovations could get any louder and, apparently, Ardglass was thinking the same, for he received the violin with faltering hands. For a moment he held the instrument and stared at it with his confused little eyes. Slowly, he raised his head and gave Elgie a scornful stare. Everyone noticed his sombre mood and a tense, sepulchral silence fell on the room.

Alistair then lifted the violin and placed it against his already reddened neck. The silence was so deep that every scrape and scratch against the violin's wood seemed amplified. He inhaled and exhaled deeply and noisily, and then brought the bow to the strings, as meticulously as a surgeon about to press a scalpel against a patient's flesh.

Sharp, acute notes came, which immediately brought to my head the shrilling sound of a sword being sharpened. They began slowly and softly, but Alistair gradually increased both speed and volume, like an eerie chuckle rising to become a piercing, cruel cackle.

He played some extravagant passages, and then, twisting his fingers at abnormal angles, he played two different themes on two strings simultaneously; something I can only describe as spine-chilling.

One string quivered like the broken voice of a terrified

soul, while the other provided a low, anguished accompaniment that brought to mind Mrs Caroli's desperate wails. Altogether, the strings produced unimaginable echoes and harmonics – had I not seen it with my naked eyes, I would have sworn we were listening to an entire string quartet brought from Hell.

The soft voice of an old woman came to my memory: 'It was horrible music . . . like poking knives . . . fear itself must sound like that . . .'

Alistair concluded with a roaring chord, literally banging the strings with the bow.

The echoes took a moment to fade and then there was no clapping, but an eerie silence that could not have been more expressive. We were all open-mouthed; it was as though we'd seen Alistair go into a momentary fit of madness, which started and ended with that fiendish melody.

I remembered McGray reading that old book of his; the things that people said about Paganini and his 'demonic deportment'.

And then it hit me!

I thrust myself towards Ardglass, frantically pushing and elbowing people. Elgie told me later that I was panting and snorting, though I did not even notice. I snatched the violin from his hands so swiftly that one of his fingers was cut by the strings.

'Hey! I was win–'

'*Shut up!*' I howled. I lifted the violin and looked into the case through the f-hole.

Amati, 1629.

Those were the very characters that I was expecting to find. I immediately turned to Ardglass. His face was as red as if it had been scalded, the most frightened sparkle in his eyes.

'Alistair Ardglass,' I said firmly, so that everybody could hear, 'you are under arrest for the murders of Guilleum Fontaine and Danilo Caroli, and possibly also of Theodore Wood.'

A general gasp filled the ballroom and the coarse voice of Lady Anne travelled all the way from the farthest corner: '*This is outrageous!*'

Ardglass pulled the most miserable face. 'I-I . . . can explain! It's not what it seems!'

'You *will* explain,' I said. 'You shall have plenty of time in the questioning room.'

'No, no!' he babbled, cowering and stepping backwards until he tripped on the music stands of the orchestra. How pathetic he looked.

'Do not make me force you out!' I hissed. I did not feel like running after him and dragging him away as if he were a child in a tantrum. Fortunately he did come back to his senses and, very slowly, started to make his way to the entrance. I followed him closely, for I am used to unpleasant surprises when arresting people, but Ardglass simply kept saying once and again that he could explain it all. When we reached the main hall it was almost surreal to have the butlers help us put on our overcoats. One of the old men patted his master on the shoulder and Alistair could not hold back his tears.

Finally, we walked out of the house to find that Duke Street was unusually busy, given the time. While we waited for the carriage I looked at the violin, still in my hands. The instrument had a normal scroll instead of the instantly recognizable lion head. Looking closely, new fittings over the original wood were pretty obvious.

'What did you do with the carved lion?' I asked. 'Did you truly believe that nobody would notice?'

'I found it in my office, Inspector!' he whimpered. 'I swear. I *swear!*'

I chuckled. 'How convenient! Especially hard to swallow, though, given that you *were* present when it was stolen from the Carolis.'

He grabbed me by the shoulder. 'I want to talk to Mr McGray. He will believe me.'

I laughed. '*Will he?* I do not think that McGray will be too keen to defend your case.'

'He will believe *this!* He's seen these things.'

'Seen what things?'

Then Ardglass shuddered visibly, pressing his stomach with both hands, his face even redder than before. At first I thought that the tension was making him sick.

'The Devil.'

It was as though the words ripped him. Alistair's face turned into all the wrong colours and then, exploding like a breaking dam, he threw up the most disgusting spurt of wine and half-digested canapés. He fell onto the pavement, his hands and knees splashing on the pool of vomit, and then he yelled with his mouth still dripping: '*The Devil came to me! Gave me the fiddle. Talked to me!*'

I leaned over him. 'Ardglass, do not speak, we'll take you to a doctor . . .'

Ardglass did not seem to hear; his crazed eyes flickered about while he kept mumbling and spitting. I turned for a second, looking for someone to help me lift him up, but that second was enough for him to leap to his feet and sprint towards the road.

He was a gruesome thing to behold: howling like a demented wretch, his arms flailing madly and his feet sliding on the mud.

Just as I started towards him, Ardglass ran across the path of a dray cart loaded with barrels. The two horses pulling it neighed loudly and the driver roared as he pulled the reins, but the road was so slippery that they could not stop. In an instant the beasts ran directly over poor Alistair: I had a full view of their hooves stomping on his chest and torso, and then the front wheel of the cart rolling over his legs. He did not even have time to scream.

As soon as the cart halted I ran towards Ardglass, not even aware of the small crowd of screaming people gathering around us. I had to crawl under the cart, where he lay in an awkward position, only to find what I already knew.

Alistair Ardglass was dead.

I want to tear my heart to rags; spoon my eyes out!
It is doomed, my perfect plan! All falls apart!
Pox on my bad luck! Pox on my cursed life!

These thoughts are venom. Venom! The mind poisons itself . . .

I must not despair, not despair. I must act quickly. I can still fix it
quickly!

28

McGray stormed into the questioning room in his ever imposing manner. He took off his overcoat and tousled his soaked hair heartily, splattering tiny drops of water all over my face.

'Who's snuffed it now?'

I produced my handkerchief and wiped my face carefully before replying.

'Oh, come on, Frey! The one moment I need ye to talk!'

'Alistair Ardglass.'

'*What!*' McGray looked at the cart driver I had detained. The chap was not yet twenty, and was so scruffy one could easily scrape filth flakes off his face. Trickles of sweat were running on his temples, and just like Ardglass barely an hour earlier, he looked as though he was about to wet himself.

'Did this laddie kill him?' McGray asked, arching an eyebrow.

I told him briefly how things had occurred, including Ardglass going mad and mentioning the Devil, and showed him the Amati violin, which lay on the room's dusty table.

''Twasn't my fault, sir!' the chap moaned amidst tears. 'The man ran into the street right in front of me! Ye were there! Ye saw him!'

'Ye did say that Ardglass was goin' all mad . . .' McGray murmured, his eyes fixed on the violin.

'I did, and I did see Ardglass running across the road out of control. However, I have found that this man has some interesting connections.'

'Connections?'

'Indeed. He happens to be employed by none other than your –'

Someone slammed the door open and the first thing to enter was the large, protruding breasts of Madame Katerina.

'*Where the Hell's my lad?*' she roared, her fake eyelashes framing an infuriated stare.

'Your "lad",' I snapped back, 'has run over one of our main suspects!'

McNair came panting behind her. 'I'm so sorry, sirs! I told her to wait but she pushed me and –'

''Tis all right,' McGray said. 'The lady here's got some questions to ask.' He looked at me. 'By *the lady* I meant *ye*, Frey!'

I pointed at the driver, whose tears could not be distinguished among his copious sweating. 'Since Mr . . .'

'McCloud,' Katerina said.

'Since Mr McCloud is unable to put two sensible sentences together, I must ask *you* to answer my queries.'

'Go ahead,' she answered challengingly.

'What was this man doing on Dublin Street at such a late hour? He was not on a business errand, was he?'

'Well, he was! On his way to Leith Harbour to deliver some barrels of ale that were s'posed to sail off tonight!

Thanks to you my clients in Dunbar won't be getting' their booze and I'll lose –'

'*I do not give a damn about your business!*' I roared.

McGray had to stand between us; Katerina's abnormally long nails were getting too close to my face.

'All right, ye've said enough. McNair, take these two outside. I need to talk to Frey.'

McNair led Katerina and her drayman out of the questioning room. The woman kept glaring at me, but a second before crossing the threshold there was a shift in her eyes. She gasped and halted, and then staggered as if stricken by a sudden nausea. McNair was going to help her but Katerina refused; she walked towards me slowly, waving her claw-like hands mysteriously. A strange glow in her eyes made it impossible for me to look away.

'Oh God . . . *oh God* . . .' she sighed as if the words were a physical pain. 'You're about to lose your most beloved one!'

We all looked at her in puzzlement. There was a moment of eerie silence . . . and then . . .

'*Oh, get her blazing arse out of here!*' I yelled.

Once they were gone McGray sat on the table and examined the violin. 'So ye think Madame Katerina's involved? I thought ye smarter than that!'

'It is too much of a coincidence,' I said. 'Besides, I remember you giving away confidential information when we first met her, and God knows what you told her today when she was helping you make a fool of yourself all around the New Town!'

Nine-Nails gnashed his teeth, a hellish fire in his blue

eyes. 'I ken ye believe I'm an idiot and I can live with that, but don't keep messin' with the people I trust.'

'*The people you trust!*' My voice came out piercingly high-pitched, and McGray took one step forward, as if about to punch the life out of me. He restrained himself and took a deep breath.

'Believe it or not,' he said, 'she helped me get very useful information. Come on, I'll tell ye in the library. Ye need to see what we found.'

Right before we left the City Chambers, Katerina approached McGray and gave him a thick leather bag, claiming that she'd almost forgotten.

'What is that?' I asked, and McGray looked slightly embarrassed.

'Erm ... Caroli's hand. Forgot I gotta give it back to Reed.'

'You should do it right now. That is not something you want to take home.'

'Och, is Reed around? At this hour?'

'Yes. I had him fetched to perform a post-mortem on Ardglass. He must be working on it as we speak.'

We found Reed at the entrance to the morgue, filling out some paperwork. He looked up at us with sleepy eyes. 'Inspectors!'

McGray tossed the bag onto his desk. 'Here ye go, laddie. Can ye put this with the rest o' Caroli?'

I turned to him swiftly. 'Why! Did you find the body?'

'Aye. While ye were sleeping and getting yer petticoats and tiaras ready. I'll tell ye when we get home.'

Reed came back and I noticed how clean his lab coat was.

'Have you not begun with the post-mortem yet?' I asked.

The young man crouched. 'N-no, sir. I was forced t-to . . . release the body . . .'

McGray held me back and spoke before I could let out another indignant roar.

'What happened, laddie?'

'It was Superintendent Campbell. He came here not twenty minutes ago and asked me to release the body. Some undertakers carried it away.'

'What the Hell!' I cried.

'He came with an elderly lady. You may still find him at his office; he was offering her a cup o' tea to calm her down.'

McGray and I instantly stormed towards Campbell's office, where, indeed, we found him giving Lady Anne a double whisky.

'*How dare you!*' Campbell yelled when McGray slammed the door open.

'Sir,' I said, 'I must insist, most emphatically, that –'

'Insist on what, Frey?' he yelled back. 'On doing a post-mortem on a man whose accidental death was witnessed by *you*?'

Lady Anne covered her face and pretended to cry – though I'd never seen a drier pair of eyes.

'I do not want my poor Alistair to be all cut up,' she whimpered. 'There is no need, *no need at all*! The entire street saw what happened! Mr Campbell, these men are out of their wits! I do not know what they want from me. One would think they take delight in my grief!'

McGray took a step towards Campbell. 'Mr Ardglass is

our primary suspect, sir, and this old hag trying to take the body away looks damn suspicious.'

Lady Anne grunted. 'You would love that to be true, wouldn't you?' She rose, gulping down the whisky like the professional drinker she was. 'You would *love* to see my kin going down! Well, you're almost done now! It's only my granddaughter and me left! I only pray to God for my heirs to outlive the filthy McGrays!'

'Lady Anne,' Campbell said soothingly, 'pray calm yourself . . .'

'How can I be calm when justice itself is in the hands of such swine?'

McGray's eyes glowed with the most furious hatred, but he would not move a muscle. I expected him to explode, to turn over the furnishings and to throw Lady Glass through the window. Instead, he murmured sombrely, 'No matter what ye do, ye ken I always find the way, ye bitch.'

Then he turned and left the room briskly. I had no choice but to follow him.

'Commissioner Monro will hear of your interference,' I said before we left.

'Is that a threat, Frey?'

I shrugged. 'No, it is a plain statement.'

As he closed the door I caught a glance of Lady Anne, grinning scornfully.

'Shit!' I cried as soon as I walked into McGray's library. 'Shit-shit-shit!'

'At last yer speaking clearly.'

'What is wrong with that woman? Your families are like

the Montagues and Capulets – considerably more vulgar, of course.'

'Never mind,' McGray said. 'We have lots of more important things to work on. First of all, I gotta tell you what I found with Madame Katerina.'

McGray grabbed a huge rolled blueprint and extended it on the table. Tucker tried to sniff the ancient paper but McGray pushed him away. 'Not now, laddie. Go to George.' He snapped his fingers and the golden retriever immediately left the room.

'Blueprints of the city's sewage system . . .' I said, looking at the intricate schematic. 'Does that mean what I am thinking?'

'If yer thinking that Caroli's corpse was dragged to the sewers, then yes.'

'That is something I do *not* want to tell his poor widow . . . How did you come to that conclusion? Was it your bosomy gypsy?'

'Aye. She had a vision from holding Caroli's hand. The laddie was murdered here . . .' McGray pointed at some spot around the New Town. 'Whoever killed Caroli chose the street carefully: it's a lonely spot in between Danilo's house and the house o' the doctor.'

'So the murderer most likely knew where Caroli was going?'

'Aye.'

'But how? The only people who knew that Mrs Caroli was giving birth were inside the house, and we did not let anybody out!'

'Ardglass was there . . . and he didn't look fit enough to climb through a chimney.'

'So you suggest that he had an accomplice.'

'Aye.'

'I am glad you say that. He swore you'd believe his story about the Devil.'

'Nae. There are things even I cannae swallow. Someone got into Fontaine's place for him; someone stole the violin and then followed Caroli down the street, and then . . .' McGray pointed at a marking in the blueprints. 'The bastard did his duty and took the body away; this again tells me that they'd studied the neighbourhood thoroughly: There is a wide manhole at this point, not twenty yards from the crime scene, and it's just wide enough to take a slim body like Caroli's . . . perhaps yours too, but it definitely won't take me.'

'How can you be so certain?'

'Cos I tried to get in! Katerina told me there was definitely something in there. We had to call McNair; he's skin and bone! In he got, and –'

'Wait-wait-wait. Did that Katerina actually tell you where to find the body?'

'Aye.'

'From, I suppose, touching Caroli's hand?'

'Aye. So what? That's what she does.'

I blew inside my cheeks. 'And then her minion ran over Alistair, and then you – Lord, we shall deal with that shifty gypsy later. Now go on. McNair found Caroli's body, then what?'

'I wanted McNair to inspect the sewerage properly, but the laddie almost lost his dinner after two minutes walking in the shite!'

'He could not have found much,' I said. 'The sewage stream would have dragged away any evidence.'

'Aye, but I wasn't looking for evidence. I was looking for an escape route. Only so many ducts are wide enough to let a person through. If we follow those, we could work out where the bastard went. I wouldn't want McNair – or even ye! – to wander through those sewers, so I thought I'd look at the blueprints instead.'

'From the city library I assume?'

'Aye.'

'I thought we needed a formal request to borrow engineering documents. How did you get hold of these so quickly?'

'Ye ken how persuasive I can be.'

I rolled my eyes. 'Unfortunately I do. Have you found anything?'

'Nay, these are useless; the sewer system for the New Town is all nice and pretty, but for the rest o' the place is a scrambled mess o' crap, especially for the Old Town. We could spend months down there and still get nowhere.'

Indeed, the schematics for the north side of Edinburgh were almost a perfect grid of ducts and pipelines, which gradually branched out to become a chaos of winding dotted scribbles in the centre and south. Apparently, the sewage system of the Old Town relied mostly on natural caverns and underground streams, all of which discharged their flows into the North Sea.

'The Scots don't have clear blueprints of their own capital city!' I arched my eyebrows. 'What a surprise!'

'Och, shut up! Again, this takes us to a dead end.'

'*Really?*' I sank on to the armchair, kneading my temples again.

'On the bright side, after all the bloodshed I can see a faint pattern emerging.'

I raised my face. 'A pattern?'

'Font-teen died, then Wood, then Danilo, then Alistair . . . God's wounds! It all sounds worse when ye list 'em up!'

'Will you get to the point?'

'Fon-teen and Caroli got their guts cut out . . . while Wood died of some disease, possibly cholera, and Alistair had that terrible accident.'

'Exactly! Where do Wood and Ardglass fit in the equation? Their deaths are not connected in any way to Caroli's and Fontaine's.'

'Maybe not. But maybe . . . they are connected to each other.'

I squinted. 'Pray, explain that.'

'Theodore died after fits o' puking, and Ardglass . . .'

'Was vomiting right before being run over!' I added.

'Right! And I think there must be something in common in those two bodies; something that maybe we saw in Theodore, but which by itself seemed innocuous.'

I nodded. 'Nine Nails, I am astounded . . . both by your sudden display of good sense . . . and by the fact that you actually know the word *innocuous*.'

'Oh, sod off!'

'I said your reasoning is right. We *must* see that body! I must telegram Monro, get an order from him to do a post-mortem . . .'

'Aye, ye could, but I ken that wily Lady Glass; she'll pull all the strings she can to slow us down. By the time we get

322

access to the body, Ardglass will be worm's manure. And I ken Campbell only answers to the highest bidder.'

'How can you be so certain?'

McGray sighed wryly. 'Cos I've bribed him myself! He only allowed me to start our subdivision for the odd and ghostly after I paid him handsomely.'

I shook my head in disbelief. This case had been nothing but dead ends. 'Can you think of another way?'

McGray arched an eyebrow. 'Course I can! Come on, Frey, ye went to medical school. Don't tell me ye never used the services of a body-snatcher!'

29

The death of Alistair Ardglass resounded throughout Edinburgh, and this time Lady Anne's vanity worked in our favour: the woman made sure that the burial appeared on a prominent page of *The Scotsman*. The column boasted that Alistair Ardglass would rest in Calton Hill's Old Cemetery, which was reserved for 'Scotland's most exceptional citizens'.

The morning of the interment McGray called Larry, the chimneysweep who'd helped us search Fontaine's study. We asked him to pose as a beggar – since he already looked like one – so that he could follow the funeral procession for Ardglass. Larry did a good job; not only did he come back telling us the exact spot where Alistair had been buried, but he also played the begging part exceptionally well, or so we could tell by the good deal of coins tinkling in his pockets when he left.

McGray then arranged the whole thing: he contacted a body-snatcher through Madame Katerina's connections (the woman scared me sometimes . . .) and then sent a message to Reed, asking him to meet us for a late supper.

The temperature dropped swiftly during the evening, and I was surprised to look at the window and find the pavement covered in white.

'Why, it's snowing!'

'Even better!' McGray said, not taking his eyes off the

book he'd been reading since lunchtime. 'Ardglass will be less rotten . . .'

Reed arrived punctually. The young surgeon was wrapped up in a thick coat, his cheekbones and nose reddened by the bitter cold, which made him look even more like a silly child. He asked why we'd called him but McGray did not tell the truth immediately. First of all he let him enjoy the hearty supper that Joan had prepared: thick pottage, tasty mutton and buttered bread. We all would need extra energy that night. McGray offered him some of his single malt whisky and once Reed was done drinking we told him what we expected from him. I shall never forget the expression of the poor chap; Reed watched us with dumbfounded eyes.

'*Are you crazy!* You want to desecrate a grave! On top of that, you want me to do a post-mortem on the spot!'

McGray and I remained silent, neither of us able to hide a hint of shame.

'How can you be willing to do this?'

'Ye ken why I do it,' McGray retorted immediately and Reed fixed his eyes on the floor. I thought of McGray's sister and the story about her sudden breakdown. Reed must know that McGray did all this for her, despite his lost finger and his dear parents . . . I was beginning to feel sympathy towards his cause, but McGray cancelled it out with his following words: 'Frey here only does it because he's bloody desperate to redeem his stupid career.'

I frowned. 'You should be grateful my situation suits you; I do not intend to remain this desperate for much longer.'

McGray poured another whisky for Reed. 'Come on,

laddie, we need ye! We trust in yer skills and yer discretion. Besides, there's a chance there's nothing wrong with the body. In that case there's no need for everyone to ken what we've been up to!'

Reed shook his head. 'When do you plan to do this?'

McGray cleared his throat. 'Tonight . . .'

'*Tonight!*'

'Yes, Reed,' I said. 'It must be done as soon as possible. Checking on a putrid body would be of little use.'

Reed hesitated a good while. For a moment he even made as if to stand up and leave. Then, after a frustrated groan he simply said: 'Sophie's going kill me; I was supposed to meet her parents for breakfast tomorrow!'

The wait felt like an eternity, particularly since Reed kept pacing as if waiting to be hanged, and peering through the kitchen window for the body-snatcher, who was supposed to enter the house through the back yard.

We had sent Joan and George to their rooms, telling them that it would be best for their own sake not to know what we were up to. Something told me that Joan would not be so obedient, but warning her was all I could do.

While we waited, McGray went back to his reading and from time to time he'd scratch Tucker's ears. I envied the dog's careless slumber.

Finally, a few minutes after twelve, Reed pressed his nose against the window. 'Is that your man?'

Before either of us could move, someone was knocking on the door.

'That answers my question . . .'

Reed opened the door and we saw the filthiest,

scruffiest of men leaning on the doorframe. His bony, lined face was half-hidden behind the most disgusting, uneven stubble, and under a crushed top hat. He wore an overcoat riddled with holes, so discoloured that McGray's looked like silken finery next to it.

The man smiled, showing off two gold teeth. 'Michty me! 'Tis Nine-Nails McGray!' He sounded coarse and slightly drunk; I could not tell whether he was tipsy or he simply spoke in such a manner. 'I'm happy to serve youse, masters! Youse can call me Billy.'

Reed gasped and I saw his face go from white to yellow to green.

'What is the ma–'

'Good Lord, but it's Reed!' Billy jumped forward to pat the shoulders of the staggered chap. 'Oh, look at yerself; a grown-up doctor o' the CID and rubbin' shoulders with the michty inspectors!'

McGray arched an eyebrow. 'Ye ken this man?'

The green cheeks turned red in a blink. 'Erm . . . well . . .'

'Ken! This laddie worked for me! Och, the good auld times!'

Reed cleared his throat so loudly I thought he was about to choke. 'Well, you know . . . I'm not from a wealthy family . . . I couldn't afford my studies without undertaking . . . alternative employment . . .'

I chuckled. 'And you were the one showing scruples when we told you about tonight!' Reed was turning abnormally red by human standards so I stopped teasing him. 'Well, I suppose it will be even better to have not one but two men with experience in this trade. Let's away.'

Billy was already crossing the threshold.

'Hang on!' McGray said. 'Yer not carrying any tools?'

Again, the gold teeth shone in a mischievous grin. Billy opened up his overcoat and, ingeniously attached to the inner lining, we saw a shovel and a small pick, their handles cut to less than a foot long.

'Youse asked for the best in the trade, didn't ye?'

The snow had ceased while we waited and the clouds had vanished, leaving behind nothing but the moonlit sky. Still, the chilled air made our breath steam as we walked, painfully, to the top of Calton Hill.

'Good auld trade, body-snatching,' Billy was saying. 'I could tell you so many stories about us . . .'

'That won't be necessary,' I said.

'My favourite is William Burke's,' Billy went on as if I'd not spoken. '"The Resurrectionist", they called him! But the man was no body-snatcher as such; he took the trade a wee bit further. He murdered people according to what the medical school needed, and then sold the bodies to them.'

'Was he ever caught?' Reed asked.

'Och, yes! Caught, tried and hanged! Not content with that, the police gave his remains to the same medical school that bought corpses from him. The boys like yerself had a field day dissecting the bastard. I've never been to the museum, but my folks tell me that his skeleton's still there on display . . . och, and that next to the bones there's a wallet that the students made from the skin o' Burke's neck!'

'Are we there yet?' I grunted.

'Aww, are ye gettin' frightened, lassie?' McGray said.

I did not need to reply; we had already made it to the tall stone walls of Old Calton Cemetery. Above the treetops I saw the castle-like tower of Calton Jail, black against the moon's silver glow.

'All clear as usual,' Billy said, pointing out how deserted the road was. 'Not a single peeler patrolling; just the way I like it.'

He led us to the barred gate, produced a bundle of picklocks of all lengths and widths and began working on the thick chains and padlocks. I was astounded by the quietness of his work; not once did the picklocks or the chains rattle.

At least he is worth what we are paying him, I thought bitterly.

Reed was rubbing his hands together, his eyes about to pop out of their sockets. One would think that stories about human-skin wallets did not amuse him – although I must say that those are not the sort of things one wishes to hear at midnight . . . especially if one is about to break into an old graveyard.

Billy opened the gate and stepped slowly into the cemetery, as silent as a lurking cat. The three of us followed him, trying not to make any noise. I was about to light up our bull's-eye lantern but McGray pulled my hand.

'Open up yer eyes for will-o'-the-wisps!' he muttered.

'Will you please focus, McGray?'

We were about to go into another argument, but then Billy waved a nervous hand in front of us.

'Shh! Listen.'

We stood motionless, straining our ears, but heard

nothing. Billy waved again, asking us to follow. I heard him sniffing the air like a bloodhound.

In front of us I saw wide stone steps, all covered in snow, ascending still further. Those steps ran down the middle of a smooth slope, dark tombstones laid all across the place and projecting their shadows on the white lawn.

Reed was walking a bit too close to me, quivering and looking around in the most anxious manner. Even I began to feel agitated.

Billy ascended to the top of the hill as he looked around . . . and then he halted, his steamy breath stopping all of a sudden.

There *was* someone else there.

I almost said something but McGray patted my arm to keep me silent, and as he climbed the few steps that separated us from the snatcher, Billy started panting.

The wretched man walked backwards and almost tripped on McGray, then started off in a frantic race towards the gate. In a trice, he'd vanished!

McGray and I exchanged bewildered looks. Reed's face was contorted in a terrified grimace.

Nine-Nails and I unholstered our guns and climbed the steps. I saw that the grandest funeral vaults were on the other side of the hill; great stone niches that looked like small churches. Behind them there was a panoramic view of Edinburgh, the tall building blocks of the Royal Mile and the silhouette of its ancient castle. I had but a glance of them before McGray poked my shoulder again. Now even *he* was breathing in distress.

He pointed his gun down the hill, somewhere in

between two lines of tall chambers, but I could see nothing amidst their shadows.

Slowly, McGray stepped ahead, every movement a struggle against anxiety, and I followed. Each step took me closer to that dreadful, thick darkness; despite the frosty air I could feel beads of sweat running down my temples.

And then I saw it.

Among the shadows there was a figure of deeper blackness; a dark lump jerking eerily next to Ardglass's grave. I instantly thought of a human-sized vulture scavenging on rotting flesh, as the icy wind brought to my ears the sound of the most repulsive splattering.

McGray halted immediately and waved his hand slowly. Only then did I notice that Reed had followed us closely, and McGray was asking him to stay away. Then, moving as carefully and silently as we could, we headed towards the grave. The snow muffled our careful steps, so we managed to approach and enjoy a better view of what was happening.

The grave had been opened; a pile of muddy soil lay next to the hole in the ground, over which that black figure was leaning.

I wanted to believe that it was human, for I could see the outline of shoulders and head beneath a black cape, but there was something primitive . . . unearthly about it. Squatted by the edge of the grave, it reached for the open coffin with what surely were abnormally long arms, contorting as I thought nobody could, trying to draw something to the surface with spasmodic tugs.

I had to make a tremendous effort to keep breathing quietly. There were only a couple of yards between the beast and me, so that the stench of the desecrated body reached my nostrils – together with a smell I had unfortunately become acquainted with of late. Burning flesh.

My heart raced, yet I did not make a sound. McGray gestured at me, asking me to point my gun, and simultaneously we prepared to shoot. The triggers clicked at the exact same time, and immediately the beast went still.

We all remained static for a moment, for we were not completely sure what was happening. Neither, presumably, was the beast.

'*Don't move!*' McGray shouted at last. 'Get yer hands out o' there! Put 'em where I can see them!'

He walked slowly as he spoke, describing a circle as he drew closer to the bloody grave.

The beast did not move.

McGray inhaled to let out the most tearing bellow. '*Do as I –*'

With the speed of lightning, the beast tossed a handful of bloody guts in my face.

I fired aimlessly as I felt it hitting me, the wet mass sliding down my cheeks. Blood got into my eyes, but I still managed a fleeting glimpse of the creature, crawling away with the agility of the quickest spider.

I wiped the blood off my face and saw that McGray was already running like the wind, jumping over sepulchres and tombstones after the black shadow.

A white light suddenly filled the graveyard and the blood on the snow shone like a scarlet rose. I saw the five-eyed symbol drawn hastily on the white field, a black mass of some charred organ, and the ghastly tip of an intestine jutting out from the grave's edge.

The light came from Reed's lantern. I snatched it as I started off. 'Stay here!'

'But sir –'

'*Watch the damned body!*'

By then I was already jumping down the frozen steps, my feet slipping dangerously on the stones. I crossed the open gate and lighted both sides of the road, the lantern blinding in the nocturnal darkness. I caught a glimpse of McGray's overcoat flailing in the distance, running west, and before I'd fully realized it I was chasing him at full speed.

I saw him turn left and enter a narrow alley; following him I entered a two-yard gap that separated the cemetery's wall from the adjacent building. I saw McGray's tall figure cut against the starry sky. He was standing, motionless, at the very edge of a cliff. The jagged hill descended steeply towards the cluster of railways that separated the two towns.

'Did you lose it?' I asked, panting.

'Aye, but it mustn't be far. It was carrying –'

There was a crack.

I sensed movement right over my head and turned just in time; the black hooded figure was jumping over me, a shiny blue blade catching the light. I howled as McGray pulled me aside, the blood-dripping knife waving but inches from my face.

I felt a blow that knocked the lantern from my hand; as the beam spun in the air it lit the inside of the creature's hood and I caught a glance of a ghastly face. Amidst sickly yellowish skin, the light bounced over five glazed eyes, each one gleaming in a different colour. It was like seeing the Devil's sign in the flesh.

It was such a brief moment that I only realized what I'd seen when the light was already gone, the bull's-eye lantern rolling down the hill, and just as soon the black figure was running behind it.

McGray roared like an animal and leaped recklessly after the creature. Under the moonlight I saw them both rolling and hopping wildly towards the railways.

'*McGray!*' I yelled, and then heard him fire his gun twice. Without thinking, I took off my overcoat and set off in pursuit.

I was lashed by the branches of half-frozen bushes and bruised by jagged stones as I tried, helplessly, to control my descent.

The last few yards were but a blurry mess of pain, until I landed on all fours at the foot of Calton Hill. It took me a few seconds to rise and regain control of myself, and another few to recollect where I was.

The railway ran in front of me, the snow turned into dark slush by the trains, and far beyond I saw the yellow lights of the Old Town buildings. It was an anguished moment before I saw the two running figures; they were so far away that I could barely make out McGray's silhouette, sprinting heedlessly across the rails. I jumped onto the ballast, my feet slipping on the slush. I suddenly had the feeling of being inside a bustling factory: there were carriages, wagons and locomotives roaring along many parallel railways, their steam whistles piercing the night.

The cars dashed constantly in front of me, blocking both my path and my view, and each time they did I feared I'd lost McGray's track for good. The stench of burned coal filled my lungs and the ashes stung my eyes. I ran desperately until my legs burned, but gained enough ground to see McGray getting closer and closer to the creature. Finally, he thrust himself over the hooded figure and knocked it down.

He had it!

I ran on and was but one rail from them when I heard the deafening whistle of a train. I turned around and my heart jumped; an engine was approaching at full speed, so close that I could even see the expression of its driver as he blew the whistle frantically. I hesitated one blasted moment and then it was too late; the train cut across my way to McGray.

'*Pox!*' I howled as the wagons powered right in front of my nose, one after the other.

Over the train's rattle I could hear McGray's feral screaming and also the most unnerving squeal. It was as though he were fighting a wild boar. I dropped to my knees and looked through the passing wheels: I saw fleeting glimpses of McGray's muddy boots and the edge of a black cloak embroiled in a savage wrestling match. Lying on the earth there was a bulky sack, its bottom soaked with blood.

I saw McGray falling onto the ground, his head but a few inches from the wagons' wheels, and then the cloaked figure pinning him down, one of its long arms pressing McGray's throat. I tried to make out the five eyes again but it was too dark.

McGray struggled fiercely, his four-fingered hand trying to push the gleaming knife away from him, but despite the roaring train I could hear him choking.

I let out a tearing shriek. There was nothing I could do to help!

The glass blade was descending slowly towards McGray's face and he was not strong enough to stop it. I wanted to shoot but I could only do it blindly, and the bullet could easily ricochet on the train's wheels and hit me or McGray.

The knife flashed under the train lights, unyielding, approaching McGray until I heard him howling in pain. I howled too; I was going to witness McGray's death while standing but a few feet from him!

At that moment the last wagon passed us and I instantly shot. I missed by some distance, but it was enough to scare the beast away.

I saw its black form grabbing the bloody sack and running away. I kneeled by McGray and saw his neck bleeding with the mark of the thin blade.

He pushed me away. 'I'm fine, ye go catch it!'

'You need –'

'*Fuck, catch it!*'

His roaring voice was like a push in the back and I simply ran and ran towards the tall, ancient buildings of the Old Town.

I saw the black cloak entering a narrow close whose ascending steps led to High Street. I shall never forget that frantic race; advancing with all my strength, cursing and panting. My knees burned as I ascended, the pain growing swiftly and steadily. Suddenly there was nothing in front of me but stone steps that seemed to go on for ever. No sign of the beast! I had lost our murderer . . .

My legs burned like the fires of Hell, but then I saw a faint light at the end of the close. The sight gave me second wind, and as I climbed up and the pain grew, I let out a rising growl that ended up as the loudest scream I have ever unleashed.

Like a gust of air I reached the last step and stormed into the Royal Mile, looking desperately in all directions. We were so close to the City Chambers!

'*What a bold bastard!*' I cried out loud.

I finally saw it again as it flashed across my vision, running towards Holyrood, though at a much slower pace, in a clumsy loping gait.

'I've got you now!' I said, gathering what little strength I had left and resuming the chase. The creature, whatever it might be, was not an infallible demon; it was tired after the frantic race, its movements becoming erratic. That gave me hope.

But that moment taught me that I should never be too optimistic: as I cheered my success, my boots slipped on the iced flagstones and I fell backwards, the back of my head hitting the pavement. I did not even feel the impact; the world simply twirled around me and all my senses but my sight deserted me.

Then, a black figure appeared before me, obscuring the street lanterns and then the sky. For a second I thought I was looking at its multiple eyes . . . but I could not tell how many.

And that was the last thing I saw.

30

Blood.

The air reeked of it, as if a soaked sponge were being held in front of my nose. But there was no sponge . . . The stench came from my chest! *From my face!*

'*God!*' I howled, sitting up in despair.

Then I had a vision of whiteness: white walls, white sheets and white bandages . . . but the smell of blood was no dream.

I panted for a moment, my head still spinning, and very slowly the world around me took shape. I was in Moray Place, lying on my bed in my nightclothes, with a tight bandage around my head. I felt my brain beating and all my joints ached. I pressed a hand on my pained forehead and in a blink all the events of the previous night came back to me. That stench of blood was simply the remnant of what that beast had thrown at my face.

The door opened and I was surprised to see Larry, the young chimneysweep, coming in with a breakfast tray. I nearly gasped when I saw how brutally bruised his left eye was.

'Mornin', master. Ye hungry?'

'Good lord! What happened to your eye?'

Larry laid the tray on the bed. I saw that half his eyeball was bright red; a blood vessel in his eye had burst.

'It was my dad. He got drunk with the money I begged yesterday . . .'

I felt a pang of guilt in my chest, thinking how detached I was from that poor boy's world. How charitable I'd always felt, tossing shillings and farthings around, not knowing that perhaps they did more harm than good.

'I see . . . McGray is letting you stay, I suppose?'

'Aye.'

I was going to tousle the boy's hair, but the poor soul was startled when he saw my hand rising. I shook my head indignantly.

'Does your father know where you are?'

Larry looked away. 'N-no, no, master, I left when he was sleeping. But please don't send me back to him!'

I nearly laughed. 'Send you back! Why, on the contrary.'

I pondered my situation. If my permanent lodgings in Edinburgh were indeed to be arranged soon, I would probably need a second servant to give Joan a hand – she'd always hated to set the fires and, quite frankly, she was not getting any younger.

'If McGray already let you stay,' I said, 'I do not think he will mind me employing you. How would you like to become my footman? You would also have to help my maid with some domestic chores.'

Tears pooled in the boy's eyes, and he turned swiftly to run towards the door. Just as I thought I'd offended him I heard his proud voice even through the walls: '*He says I can stay!*'

I also heard a loud '*shhhhhh*', undoubtedly uttered by Joan. She'd surely thought that sending the boy to serve my breakfast would touch my heart. A part of me felt somewhat manipulated, but the sight of the boy's face would have shaken the toughest of men.

I then dug into the breakfast tray with particular gusto, suddenly realizing how hungry I was. As I chewed buttered toast my mind went back to the case and all the questions I urgently needed to ask – I did not even know how I'd ended up back in my own bed . . . or what had ultimately happened to that thing we'd chased.

Half an hour later Larry came back to pick up the tray. His wide smile now contrasted with his ugly bruise. 'Ye need anything else, master?'

'Oh, yes, fetch McGray. I need him to tell me what happened last night.'

'Och, Master McGray left early. He got a summons from some grand man asking him to go to the City Chambers.'

'Oh, Lord!' I muttered. 'Was the message from a man called Campbell?'

'Erm . . . Aye, I think so.'

'*Oh Lord!*' I jumped out of the bed. 'Did you hear anything of what happened last night?'

'No, sir. But master McGray jumped up just like ye when he read the note . . . also when he saw the newspaper . . .'

'*Oh Lord!*' I shrieked again. 'Did you know what was in the headlines?'

'Nae, I cannae read, sir.'

'I need Joan. Either she or George must have squeezed every last bit of information out of McGray. Joan! *Joan!*'

'I've not seen her since I brought yer tray, sir.'

'Typical. When one needs that bloody pair, they vanish!'

My only choice was to go to the City Chambers myself. I went through the room looking for clean clothes, and found a filthy bundle by the foot of my bed. It turned out to be the suit I'd worn the night before: bloody, soiled and torn beyond redemption.

'Good grief! This is the fifth fine suit that has been ruined since the Mary Jane Kelly case!'

I would have to wear the infamous navy suit I'd worn to Lady Ardglass's ball – creased and muddy as it was.

I looked at the mirror and found myself decidedly appalling: stubble, pale cheeks, messy hair sprouting from under the bandages, and dark bags under my eyes.

'Elgie was right,' I sighed. 'This place is eating me alive.'

I told Larry to throw away the ruined suit and then made my way to the entrance. The house appeared to be deserted so I had to go to the cloakroom and grab my own overcoat. When I hastily opened the wardrobe my eyes almost ached from what I found.

George and Joan!

Locked in a tight embrace and kissing wildly!

Joan's hair was an utter mess and one of her chubby legs was bare and stuck up in the air.

My voice came out weary rather than anything else: '*Ohhh!* Just when I though my eyes could behold nothing more gruesome!'

'*But sir –!*'

'I've no time for this, woman!'

I pushed George aside, grabbed the nearest coat and quickly shut the wardrobe again.

*

On my way to the City Chambers I saw a newspaper boy crying out the day's headlines on Princes Street. I could not make out a word over the road's bustle, so I simply tossed him a sixpence and snatched a copy from his hand without even slowing down my mount.

The enormous headline was like a drill poking into my eyes:

THE RIPPER IS IN LOTHIAN!!!!

I yelled, groaned and thrashed about, abandoning myself to the most enraged fit and receiving the dazed stares of everyone around me. I crumpled the filthy paper and hurled it in front of me, ensuring that Philippa's hooves trampled on it. I thought that I could not possibly feel angrier, little knowing that the worst was about to come.

When I made it to the City Chambers I saw a gaggle of reporters crowding the courtyard. As soon as I dismounted, a man emerged from the crowd and approached me.

'*Inspector Frey!*' he babbled. 'Was it you who discovered the desecrated grave? Did you really fall on the ice while chasing the Ripper?'

I felt like punching his nose and kicking his crotch, but that would only give him more scandal to publish.

'Get out of my way, you rancid piece of dung!' I said, elbowing the reporters aside as I made my way in.

McGray was not in the basement, but I found him waiting by the door to Campbell's office. He was gripping a copy of the newspaper and I could tell that he'd been crumpling it for a while.

'Och, there ye are! I thought ye'd be knocked out 'til next week! Ye all right, yer highness? Ye look awful.'

'I know . . . but it is not from the fall. Believe me.'

He showed me the dreadful front page. 'Och, so ye've read the papers, have ye? What d'ye think o' this?'

'Four exclamation marks are overexerting. Pray tell me what happened last night.'

'The scandalmonger Joan didn't tell ye?'

'No. She was . . . otherwise engaged.'

'Well, I laid there on the rails for a wee while before goin' after ye, but I still lost yer track. Ye ran like the wind, Frey! When I didn't see ye I thought I'd better go to the City Chambers to get reinforcements, but when I made it to the Royal Mile there was already a commotion there; some peelers found ye lying on this huge frozen puddle. I cannae believe ye didn't see that on yer way!'

'Oh, do excuse me! I was busy trying to catch that bloody thing that nearly slashed your jugular!'

'Anyways, some peelers and me took ye to the house and I asked George to fetch a doctor for ye. Then we went back to Calton Hill and found poor Reed still lookin' after the grave. He couldn't avoid some children seeing the bloody mess, and when we were bringing the body here for a proper post-mortem, a damn bunch o' reporters caught us.'

'Damn it . . .'

'I also had a few peelers looking around the area where we found ye. There was a trail o' blood from where ye lay; they followed it for a couple o' streets but then it just disappeared. Can ye guess where it ended?'

That was not difficult. 'By a sewer?'

'Indeedy. Another bloody sewer. I sent one o' the laddies to fetch the blueprints and we were trying to plot a track 'til the small hours but we never found' – his face darkened – 'that *thing*.'

I drew a bit closer so that I could whisper as softly as possible. 'Then you do not know yet what that . . . *thing* was, do you?'

McGray allowed himself a bitter smile. 'Ye tell me. Ye saw it too.'

'I do not know what I saw . . .'

'Och, don't gimme that crap, ye sissy sod! Ye saw the five eyes didn't ye? When it kicked the lantern off yer hand? I had a better view when it was tryin' to butcher me.'

I could not deny it. That image was imprinted in my memory. 'I . . . I have never beheld anything like that.'

McGray sighed and lowered his eyes; he was looking at the void where his fourth finger should have been.

'I have,' he said, after a painful gulp. 'Once.'

He said no more. I wanted to ask what he meant, but Campbell's assistant came out of the office right then. 'The superintendent is waiting for you.'

'This is not going to be easy . . .' McGray grunted.

More than ever, Campbell looked like an angry lion waiting for us in his lair: silent, drumming his fingers on the pristine newspaper that lay on his desk. We walked in, bowed, took our seats, and I believe it took him another full minute to finally utter his most despicable words: 'I *must* congratulate you, gentlemen; both of you!'

'Congra–?'

'You are the most infamous people in Scotland, and by this time tomorrow, will be the most infamous in the entire British Empire!'

I clenched my fists. That brute could be the best of friends with my brother Laurence!

'It is unreasonable to ascribe the desecration of Ardglass's grave to Jack the Ripper!' I said. 'Ardglass was a completely different sort of victim; the crime took place under completely different circums–'

'Do not try to preach to me, Frey! I know that journalists are but a bunch of brainless arses that can barely spell, but so are their readers! And now, thanks to you, I must liaise with the filthy cattle we have shouting in the courtyard.'

'I can talk to them, if ye . . .'

'I will deal with the press myself, McGray. The last thing we need now is your outlandish face on show.'

'Sir,' I intervened, 'I believe I can handle –'

'Frey, you can't handle a teapot without a cosy!'

'Sir, if I may –'

'No, you may not! I want results and I want them *now*, before the bloody papers inflate this to uncontrollable proportions. I expect you to bring me an identified, charged culprit by this time tomorrow. Understood?'

'*What!*' McGray howled, 'Ye cannae possibly expect –'

'You have spent enough time working on this case, have you not?'

'Indeed,' I said, 'but you have read my reports: meagre evidence, unconnected deaths . . . until Ardglass died there was not a clear trail to follow –'

'Excuse me, Frey, all I hear is *blah-blah-blah, we are a pair of blithering idiots.*'

'Sir –'

Campbell shrieked even louder than McGray: '*Tomorrow, Frey!* Or you two will be dismissed permanently. I shan't take more chances for the sake of redeeming your pathetic career, and I am sure Sir Charles and the prime minister will agree. And McGray, whatever arrangement we had regarding your special subsection, consider it ended. I am sure your idiotic theories have done no good to the case, and I will not risk my own reputation to help you in your dim-witted obsession with your lunatic, murderous sister.'

For an instant, McGray remained still like a statue, but then, in a startling move, he thrust an enraged fist straight into Campbell's nose. I saw the splash of blood, and as Campbell's head bounced backwards, McGray stood up, quick as a wolf, to seize him by the throat.

'McGray!' I gasped.

Campbell was dazed. It took him a second to fully realize that he'd just been hit and that McGray was throttling him with both hands.

'They say lunacy runs in the blood,' McGray whispered, and then squeezed Campbell's neck a little harder with each word. 'Ye only need a wee – something – to – trigger it.'

Campbell was choking. 'H-help . . . Frey . . . ! *Help!*'

Aghast as I was, I could not restrain my sarcastic self. 'I would be most compelled to help you . . . but I am only a blithering idiot . . .'

Out of pure self-indulgence, I sat back and let him

346

suffer for a moment. Then I patted McGray's shoulder. 'Come on, Nine-Nails, there is no time to play! You heard the superintendent: we have one day to solve this mess.'

McGray let go and Campbell fell onto his desk like a bundle of clothes. The blood from his nose artistically splattered the newspaper's headline.

McGray roared madly as he stormed into the basement office.

'What a fucking pig! Blasted, goddamn-goddamn pile o' shite! I could nail his fucking balls to the spire o' Mercat Cross and have him pulled by two oxen!'

'I could not have expressed myself more eloquently,' I sighed, sinking on the hard wooden chair. I offered my handkerchief and McGray wiped Campbell's blood off his knuckles. 'I doubt we will manage to keep our jobs after that little scene . . . yet, I feel strangely . . . elated.'

McGray lounged on his chair, raised his legs and put his boots on the desk. 'I'm truly sorry things didn't work out well for ye, Frey. I really am.'

'Well, we still have to –'

He clicked his tongue. 'That's how life works, ain't it? Ye work and work like a bloody mule and when ye finally think ye've got something in yer hands, it all goes to Hell . . .'

'I was going to say that we should act quickly, now that –'

'Ye can leave if ye want, Frey,' McGray added, his mind utterly adrift. 'I need to fight my own battles . . . and I ken there's nothing here for ye. Let's face it; ye hate the sight o' me and this place. If I'm to sink, I should sink on my –'

I had to stand up and smack him on the side of his head. 'Oh, will you let me bloody finish, you nine-fingered perch of moth clusters!'

McGray almost fell backwards, suddenly returning to reality. 'Ye better have something absolutely crucial to tell me, lass; else I'll do to ye what I just said I'd do to Campbell . . . And Mercat Cross is just across the road!'

'Do you not see it? We are in the most advantageous position we have ever been.'

McGray raised an eyebrow. 'Are ye all right, laddie? I think ye hit yer head harder than we thought.'

'Think about it,' I insisted, looking fervently at him.

Then, very slowly, McGray's wrinkles deepened as his roguish smile came back. Somehow it was only then that I realized how young he actually was; perhaps a couple of years *younger* than me. 'We've got the fiddle and we've got what's left of Alistair's body; the two things we needed the most.'

'Indeed!' McGray jumped on his feet, life running through his veins again. 'All right laddie, let's give it one last try . . .'

It was late afternoon when Reed came into the office with a report in his hands. His eyes were red-rimmed and he looked as though he could faint at any moment – quite understandably, for he had not slept at all since our chase in the graveyard.

'Here it is, Inspectors,' he said, handing us the documents.

'Was it a thorough post-mortem?' I asked, and to my surprise Reed's reply lacked his usual deference.

'I checked every single inch of his big, fat body, and, by God, I swear my salary is not worth this!' The poor chap shuddered. 'I will demand a pay raise and Campbell can't refuse.'

'Right, but don't talk to him today, laddie,' McGray said. 'Something tells me he won't be in a good mood.'

We gave the papers a swift scan.

'Missing intestines . . .' I read aloud.

'Yes, almost seven feet missing, sir. They hardly left any . . .' and then Reed gave into the widest yawn.

'Ye saw that sack the beast was carrying?' McGray asked, but he did not need me to answer.

'The beast?' Reed whispered.

'Never mind,' I told him. Then I went back to the report and, among the hurried scribbles, a short phrase caught my eyes.

'You mention hyperpigmentation in the neck . . .'

'Yes, sir, concentrated on the left-hand side of the neck. A fair bit in the chin too, and to a lesser extent in the fingertips of his right hand.'

His words immediately evoked my most glorious days in the CID and once more I felt that rush of adrenaline that only came when I hit upon the right answer.

'May I see the body?' I asked immediately.

'But of course, sir.'

Reed took a deep breath and drew the white sheet away. A nauseating whiff arose and even McGray squinted, for the corpse looked simply appalling: the flesh was beginning to swell and to turn a sickening greyish colour. Only then did I understand Reed's indignation.

'Very well, show me,' I said. 'I do not want to stare at this for too long.'

Reed slightly tilted Alistair's head, for the flap of his double chin was obscuring most of the mark. 'There you have it, Inspector.'

It was a mighty stain: dark brown, almost blackened at the edges, and that spot of flesh, compared to the rest of the decaying body, remained rather firm and elastic, as if no parasite dared to corrupt it.

'Show me his fingers,' I prompted, although I was already pulling the dead hand myself. Only the very tips bore a similar tint.

'What is it, Frey?' Nine-Nails asked. 'Yer grinning like a constipated hag that's just discovered prunes.'

'I have seen this pigmentation before,' I murmured.

'Have ye, Frey?' McGray asked, peering over my shoulder.

'Yes! And more than once.' I went from the neck to the fingertips several times, the epiphany taking full shape in my mind. Those were the glorious instants that had made me a slave to my profession. I turned back to Reed: 'Do you have equipment to perform the Marsh test?'

Reed looked blankly at me for a moment, but then his eyes widened with amazement. 'Do you mean that . . . ?'

'I do.'

It took him another moment to process my words, but then he hurled himself forward and leaned over the body: 'Of course! *Of course!* I should have thought so! I saw a few cases like this at university.'

'It was not entirely obvious,' I said. If possible, my

smile grew wider. 'Not until now, at least. Do you have the equipment?'

'Yes, I do, sir. That's what I used to analyse Wood's stomach.'

'Well, now you know why you found nothing in his tripe.'

'Indeed I do.'

'Good. Prepare the apparatus and test this man's skin. If you still have samples from Wood's body, test them too. There is another sample that I need you to analyse. We will fetch it and come back within the hour.'

I walked out of the morgue with McGray behind me. He had to pull me by the arm

'Ye better tell me now what's goin' on, Frey!'

'Have you not worked it out yet? Wood and Ardglass indeed died of the same cause.'

'Which would be . . . ?'

'Poisoning by cutaneous transmission.'

McGray frowned. 'Through the skin? Transmitted from whe–?' He did not have to finish the sentence. He understood. 'Come on, let's get that sample!'

The Marsh apparatus was quite simple, yet it looked like the convoluted glass devices that one would expect to find in a chemistry lab: A U-shaped tube filled with a white powder, one end of the U connected to a round flask – containing scrapings of the sample – and the other end connected to a longer, thinner tube heated by a Bunsen burner. Reed held a white porcelain dish close to the open end of that thin tube, and as soon as he did so, the pristine ceramic turned silvery black.

'Lord!' he cried. 'I have never seen a result like this!'

He took the dish with a pair of tweezers and placed it next to a collection of coloured films that went from the palest grey to raven-black. The stain on the dish was darker than any of them.

''Tis off the chart!' McGray cried. 'This could kill an elephant!'

'Indeed,' I said. 'And now we know who did it all.'

31

I tossed the rosewood chinrest onto Joe Fiddler's working table. His workshop still smelled of confined flatulence.

McGray stood next to me and displayed the photographs from Fontaine's study; all the ones that showed the Amati Maledetto. 'How clever ye are, laddie!' he cried in true admiration. 'Ye managed to deceive us all!'

Joe Fiddler was casting us an astounded look, his eyes almost popping out. 'How can youse think I killed Guilleum?'

'And Theodore Wood, and Danilo Caroli, and Alistair Ard—'

'*Nonsense!*' Joe yelled, jerking a hammer about. 'Youse are talking shite!'

McNair stepped in behind us. 'Ye want me to look for the stuff?'

'Yes,' I replied. 'You can begin in Mr Fiddler's personal rooms.'

Joe blocked McNair's way. The poor man looked pathetic trying to stop the tall, young officer.

'It will be wisest to let us do our job,' I said.

McGray approached him and gently pulled him aside. 'Come on, laddie, we need ye to come with us for questioning.'

'Not if youse don't tell me first why!'

He seemed so frail, so broken, that even I could not help feeling a smidgen of compassion.

'Very well,' McGray said. 'Have a seat and Frey will explain it all to ye.'

Joe Fiddler sat on a wooden box, his face all confusion. Whether it was genuine or fake, I could not tell right then.

'You made this chinrest, did you not?' I said while pacing around the workshop. I grabbed an unfinished violin and laid it next to the chinrest. 'It has your mark on it.' I pointed at the symbol I'd seen before: a winding character that formed both a J and an F. 'Also, you were the last person to see Fontaine before he died, and you delivered a violin you had been repairing for a while; the same violin he was playing when it all happened.'

Joe confronted us with a firm face. 'Aye, I made this piece and I repaired Guilleum's fiddles. That doesn't make me a damn murderer!'

'You gave a rather special treatment to this piece,' I continued. 'You soaked this piece of wood in a concentrated solution of arsenic . . .'

Just as if he'd been called, McNair walked back into the room. 'Found it, bosses!'

He was holding a large bottle of amber glass. I grabbed it and read the label. 'Bed-bug killer, and the label tells me this comes from a very good chemist. You know that this is basically arsenic dissolved in soap, of course? Wash away the soap and you are left with pure arsenic.'

'Ye cannae –'

'Pray, let me finish! Arsenic, as you know, is one of the preferred poisons of our times: it is easy to obtain and produces symptoms that the untrained eye can mistake

354

for digestive tract ailments such as cholera or gastric fever – even our forensic man, despite his undeniable skills, failed to spot the subtle differences. I, in particular, became very familiar with arsenic's properties while investigating the case of Good Mary Brown – the woman who poisoned five husbands, if you recall; it was the most famous case I'd worked on before the Ripper . . .'

'Give it a rest; we've all heard that story a million times!'

'All right! Well, arsenic is also poisonous when absorbed through the skin. It is not the preferred method of murderers, as it produces eruptions and hyperpigmentation, and most importantly, it only becomes lethal after prolonged contact . . . and you knew that, Joe.'

'I didnae!'

'Oh, but you did! It was a brilliant way to exclusively kill the violinists who dared play this violin. You did not want to kill everyone who came to hold it – McGray and I have repeatedly touched the violin, but that never gave us any symptoms. No, you only poisoned the chinrest because you wanted to kill violinists, who must hold the instrument with their neck and chin, for hours at a time. My own brother happened to play this violin, and could well have been poisoned, but thank goodness he protects his neck with a cloth.

'That reminds me of another advantage you must have recognized: you knew that the inevitable hyperpigmentation that came with arsenic could easily be mistaken for . . . what do you call it, McGray?'

'Fiddler's hickey.'

'Exactly, and that was what happened with Theodore Wood; the man had such a bad case of fiddler's bruise we could never have related it to poisoning.' I recalled vividly the sight of Wood lying in his coffin: a pale corpse with a bright red mark on his neck. 'We only made the connection after checking the body of Alistair Ardglass, who happened to have the same reddened marks on his skin, and also began to show symptoms of arsenic poisoning moments before being run over.

'I probably should have realized it much sooner, since I had the chance of examining the violin not long after the murder occurred.' I stretched out a hand and seized one of the pictures. 'Now it is clear to me, even obvious, but back then I could not pinpoint it . . . I simply felt like I'd spotted something out of place, and for a while . . .'

'Frey, yer rambling again.'

'All right, all right! But I am still astounded by my omission! I saw the blasted violin closely, I held it with my own hands, yet I did not manage to see what these pictures show us: Fontaine's throat was sliced open while he played, so his blood was splattered all over the instrument . . . *but not on the chinrest*. I even recall thinking that the rosewood looked *pristine*.'

'So someone changed the thingy for the poisoned one *after* slaughtering Fontaine,' McGray added, mocking my inflexions.

'Yes, and I still cannot fathom why you did that. Did you want people to become fearful of the instrument until it eventually fell into your hands? Did you want us all to suspect the cursed violin rather than human agency, and thus draw eyes away from you? Which reminds me of the many other aspects of the murders that you need to explain. How did you manage to climb those chimneys? Where did you learn all that blasted witchcraft? And most importantly, where is your workshop and what are your plans for the catgut you are making? The more I think about it, the more it astounds me that I did not suspect you from the very start; you are obviously a very accomplished luthier, and string making *must* be one of your skills.'

'Catgut? Witchcraft?' He turned to McGray. 'What the Hell's he talking about? Maybe I just cannae get his doddy accent.'

He looked utterly baffled. Not once did he flinch or tremble in the way guilty men do when panic betrays them. He *was* nervous, of course, but in the way anybody about to go to jail would be.

McGray noticed it too; he stroked his stubble and spoke gently. 'What can ye tell us to defend yerself?'

Joe Fiddler breathed anxiously. 'What d'ye want me to tell ye? These are all cock-and-bull stories! Abody uses that bug-killer!' He cast a filthy look at the bottle. 'I'm sure yer maids use it to clean yer shitty linen too! That makes youse murderers? Even my dead wife used the stuff to make her skin all white and pretty!'

'No wonder you are a widower,' I muttered.

'And also, I didnae make that chinrest for Guilleum. He didnae like rosewood; he always used ebony.'

I had to grant him that. 'Rosewood *is* unusual for a chinrest . . .'

'Aye! That's why I recall making this piece perfectly. I hardly ever work with rosewood; it smells vile!'

Nine-Nails let out a loud cackle. 'It surely does!'

'I can tell youse who commissioned that chinrest and even the day I delivered it.'

'I am sure ye can tell us, laddie, but can ye prove it?'

Joe rose immediately. 'Course I can! I got a letter requestin' it. 'Tis even dated and all.' He opened an old chest that was heaving with crumpled documents. After rifling through them he produced a small letter. 'Aye, it was in September, not so long ago . . .'

I snatched the letter and looked at it. The handwriting was beautifully neat and the order did seem genuine; a specific request for a rosewood chinrest. When I realized who'd written it, I gasped.

'So who bought that chinrest?' McGray prompted.

Joe showed a wry smile. 'Tell him, laddie.'

I uttered a name I would have never expected:

'Lorena Caroli.'

32

The hard rain hammered my umbrella as McGray and I stood, staggered, by the Carolis' front door. The mourning wreath still hung there: the yew branches still green and upright, but the laurel leaves, wilted by the elements, lay miserably on the black bow. We saw with sorrow that they'd added a thinner ribbon of white silk, and for a solid minute neither of us could speak. We knew too well that white was the colour of the innocent.

'Are you sure you want to do this right now?' I asked at last, only after feeling the icy rain through my damp trousers. The violin case, which McGray had brought, was now dripping wet.

'Can ye think of a good time?' McGray said, reluctantly knocking at the door, and he was right. Difficult as it was, we had to carry out our duty.

It was the younger maid who received us. Her eyes were red and she pressed a wet handkerchief against her face. She tried to send us away, but McGray walked in nonetheless.

'We've got to see yer mistress, lass. How's she coping?'

The girl shuddered. 'Oh, she hasn't spoken for a while, sir – or eaten. All she does is walk up and down her room. We've been hearing her steps since yesterday, all through the night. I pray to God she stops.'

We could hear them too, echoing from above; thuds that came and went in an anxious rhythm.

'When did it happen?' I murmured. 'The baby, I mean.'

The poor girl tried to utter some answer, but then she choked, burst into tears and ran to the kitchen. For an awkward moment McGray and I stood in the hall, not knowing what to do. Except for the insistent pacing upstairs, the house was in absolute silence.

'C'mon, Frey,' McGray said, making his way to the stairs. My heart was thumping when he knocked at Lorena's door. 'Mrs Caroli?'

No reply, but her steps never stopped. McGray knocked another two times.

'We're coming in,' he said, slowly opening the door.

Shyly, almost fearfully, I followed McGray into the room. The first thing I saw was the empty crib, still beautifully decked with white lace and an embroidered blanket. Then a tall shadow passed in front of it, and my heart sank at the image of Lorena, who now looked like a female embodiment of the Grim Reaper: draped in black, her cheeks sunken and the skin so pale that it almost shone like clean bones.

She paced with such anguish, such uncontainable distress, from one end of the room to the other, sometimes bumping into her little table. With one hand she clutched her rosary beads, pressing her still swollen belly; with the other she rubbed her chest, as if trying to rid herself of an unbearable chill.

'Mrs Caroli,' said McGray, 'we need to ask ye some questions.'

She did not reply, or even seem to notice our presence.

She simply kept pacing, and for a moment I thought she had lost her mind.

McGray placed the violin case on the small round table and opened it.

'I believe this still belongs to ye.'

Lorena paced on for a moment, oblivious to us, but upon reaching the table she caught a glance of the violin.

She immediately halted, her eyes almost falling out of their sockets. After a troubled gulp she tried to speak. Her mouth was dry, so the words came out rough.

'Where did you find it?'

McGray spoke softly. 'Lord Ardglass had it.' Then he pointed at the chinrest. 'And we ken that this piece is poisoned. We've also been told *ye* had it specially made.'

It must have been a mere few seconds, but it felt like hours before Lorena moved or even blinked. There was nothing left of the flawless beauty and the vivacity we'd seen but a few days before. That evening she was nothing but despair.

'It's all my fault,' she whispered, dropping the rosary, then pressing her temples with her knotted, stiff hands.

A shrill sound came out of her throat. It grew slowly into a mad squeal from the darkest depths of her body, worse than the squealing of pigs in the slaughterhouse. I flinched at the howl, wanting to cover my ears, but she held it until she ran out of breath and slowly sank onto the bed.

McGray went closer, held her gently by the shoulders and helped her sit up. 'How can ye say it's yer fault? Ye cannae have done it, missus.'

She was trembling. 'Not myself . . . but Heaven knows

what I have done. I could have held the knives and slashed their throats myself . . . My husband's –'

She rubbed her chest again, this time so desperately I thought she'd tear her dress.

McGray picked up the rosary and put it back into her hands. 'Whatever it is, we need ye to tell us.'

Mrs Caroli only sobbed, wanting to pull her hands away, but McGray would not let go.

'I've felt what yer feeling now,' he whispered. 'It cuts deep. I felt it when I lost my folks; in one day all my kin got shattered and I was left all alone, just like ye. My wee sister's still alive, but some days it feels like she's gone further than my dead ones . . .'

I'd never heard Nine-Nails talk with such intensity. He had clearly wanted to say those words out loud, and I could only wonder for how long he'd repressed them.

'We're almost partners in disgrace,' he added, showing her what was left of his fourth finger; an eerie parallel to her awful arthritis. 'There's nothing ye can say that I won't understand.'

Lorena Caroli shed copious, silent tears, but after a while she managed to nod.

'Good,' McGray said. 'Take yer time, missus. We've got all night.'

McGray somehow persuaded Mrs Caroli to have some tea and a light supper. Amidst her wails and stuttering, it became evident that we'd have to calm her down if we wanted a coherent statement.

The maid soon came in with a tray, her entire body shaking, the cutlery and crockery rattling. Her wary eyes were fixed on the cradle as she poured the tea, and I had to take the pot out of her hands when the cup was full to the brim.

'That will be all,' I told her, and the girl was more than happy to leave.

Mrs Caroli had to use both hands to lift the cup, her fingers pointing at abnormal angles. She swallowed a few short sips, but when she tried to put the cup down she dropped it; the china caught the edge of the table and shattered on the carpet.

She stared at her inflamed joints, her eyes bloodshot. 'This is where it all started,' she said, suddenly focused. '*These damned bones!* The curse of the Zangrando family! My grandmother had them, my mother had them, my sister Lucía and I . . . We thought only us women would have it, but then my poor Lucía married and had a son.'

I looked up so quickly I nearly snapped my neck. McGray was thunderstruck.

'A son, ye said?'

Lorena nodded. 'Yes. Giacomo. I'll never forget the day he was born: the midwife thought that Lucía had given birth to the Devil and I can't blame her.' The tears rolled and rolled. 'The wretched child was hideous . . .'

At once I pictured the horrible figure we had seen in the graveyard.

'He was a big baby,' Lorena continued, 'and his arms and legs never seemed to stop growing. And he could do things with them that nobody else could: he could twist his fingers in all directions, dislocate his shoulders and thighs at will . . . oh, if people had seen him they would have burned him alive! All the family, for that matter!

'So we sent the boy to my uncle. He was a glass blower on this little island near Venice, Murano. People only ever go there to trade glass, so he remained well hidden. My uncle taught Giacomo his craft and the boy learned very quickly. He made the most beautiful things – my rosaries, beautiful vases and figurines . . . Giacomo was the most gifted young boy I'd ever seen. He also liked to carve wood and draw and read and recite the names of the stars.'

For a moment I even thought she was about to smile, but of course things had eventually gone so terribly wrong.

'Then my uncle and sister died, and there was nobody left but me to look after Giacomo . . .' Again she pressed her chest. 'Oh, you have to understand . . . On her death-bed Lucía made me swear on our mother's grave that nobody would ever know about the boy. *I couldn't say no! I –*'

'Don't dwell on that, missus,' McGray said in the most soothing manner. 'Just go on.'

'I was already engaged to Danilo,' she said after a gulp, 'and we had already decided that we would live in London, so Giacomo had to come with us.'

McGray leaned forward. 'What did yer husband think o' the arrangement?'

It was like throwing salt into her wounds. 'Oh, he hated the whole affair. He never wanted Giacomo in our house. He said that he should be in an institution. He was right, of course . . .'

I remembered Danilo glaring at her when she said she wanted to name their child Giacomo.

Mentioning her dead husband made Lorena tremble again, so I changed the subject before she fell apart; we needed her level-headed. 'How did Giacomo cope in London?'

'Badly,' she replied, struggling to stay calm, 'it was then that things went wrong. Giacomo missed my uncle and he abhorred the English weather, but what affected him the most was not being able to work on his glass any more. We couldn't keep a furnace or all the tools and pigments he needed – not without half the neighbourhood noticing.

'I remember him staring at his old pieces, the poor boy. He did a lot of wood carving then, but it was too . . . easy for him; he made some wonderful pieces he liked us to give away, but it bored him very soon. I could see him thinking and thinking when he worked on the wood. He became unruly, started to ask questions. He wanted to go out and a couple of times he did manage to escape. The neighbours gossiped, of course. That's why we had to move here, where nobody knew us.

'One day, almost by accident, Giacomo picked Danilo's violin and began to play. He had heard my husband practising many times and he simply imitated the sounds. He learned so quickly we couldn't believe it.'

'Did you encourage him to learn?' I asked.

'Of course we did. That kept the boy busy. If he found a melody he liked he would practise it all day long. The questions stopped for a short while . . . at least until I met Guilleum.' She sobbed, her face distorted, and her next words were barely intelligible. 'I – I introduced them. It was me who asked Guilleum to teach Giacomo . . .'

She jumped up and started pacing again. It was as if her body could not contain the remorse. I could imagine that quality in her nephew; his restless, brilliant mind locked within walls that surely felt horrendously narrow – and then Katerina's words hit my memory. An encaged genius.

'It was fine at first,' Mrs Caroli was saying, 'but then Giacomo wanted to learn more and more. He escaped at night to meet Guilleum. He could crawl through every crevice – through the chimneys . . .' Lorena shuddered. 'One night, God, one night I woke up and found him perched at the foot of my bed, watching us; just watching Danilo and me sleep. I still see him in my nightmares, perched right there, like a crow!

'The months passed and he became more distant and strange. Even poor Guilleum was frightened, but he managed to keep him appeased with his music. He was so understanding. Then odd things began to happen: some of the vases and figurines disappeared, and the neighbours began to gossip about strangers lurking around our home . . .'

I jumped in, remembering Joan's words. 'Did they talk about a demon walking round your house at night?'

'*Yes!* And I knew it was him, going out at night and not returning until the small hours. Some nights Danilo had to lock him in the hounds' shed. I never knew what he was up to, until I found something in his bedroom . . .' She went to her bedside table, rummaged through a drawer and produced a small shard of glass. It looked like an arrowhead, skilfully pointed and sharpened; the glass had beautiful specks of cobalt blue amidst a cyan base. 'I discovered why the glasswork had gone missing. This was part of a figurine: it came off the skirts of an Andalusian dancer Giacomo made when he was twelve. One of my favourites. When I asked him what this meant he – he –'

She shook from head to toes. I knew we did not have much time before she fell apart.

So did McGray, and he had to cut to the point: 'Did ye ken he was doing the killings?'

Lorena shook her head, once more pressing her temples, ever pacing. 'No! No! *I* . . . Part of me guessed. One can feel these things. The servants told me the bottles of bug killer kept disappearing, but I never thought that my nephew . . .' She hit the table with her hip, lost balance and McGray had to hold her before she fell. '*Why would he do it?*'

McGray gave her the most compassionate look. 'Only he can tell us . . .'

He helped her to the bed and we gave her a moment to grieve. Telling her about the horrors Giacomo had perpetrated – and the even more disturbing deeds we imagined he was up to – was simply out of the question. Later, perhaps.

As she wept I thought how much of her tragedy had always been there, just underneath the surface, waiting to happen. Despite the pity she inspired I perfectly understood her guilt.

'Mrs Caroli,' I said, 'we have reasons to believe that Giacomo may harm more people if we don't act quickly. We need you to help us find him. Do you have any idea where he might be hiding? Any hint at all?'

Mrs Caroli lifted her face and looked at me with grim eyes. 'What will happen to him then?'

I wanted to give her an earnest answer, but McGray and I could only look down. Suddenly the rain outside was deafening.

'I don't have any clues for you,' she mumbled, her eyes fixed on the little blue blade.

McGray and I exchanged frustrated looks. We were about to stand up when she spoke again.

'I know for sure.'

33

It was well past midnight and an icy wind blew hard along the Royal Mile. Nobody would want to go out in such inclement weather, even less after the recent headlines, so the street was as lonely as a grave.

McNair was leading the horses with extreme care, for the snow had turned into dark slush and the wheels of the carriage skidded whenever we took a turn. The ride felt eternal, until I finally saw the outline of Holyrood Palace; the lights from its windows were casting gloomy shadows on the road, and as we turned right we found the imposing outline of Arthur's Seat. The mount looked like a sleeping giant, the woods around it pitch black.

'We are almost there,' Mrs Caroli said, pointing at the darkened fields. 'Right here,' she announced when we reached a jagged wall of rock. McNair stopped the carriage and Mrs Caroli alighted before either of us could offer help.

She walked with faltering steps and pointed at a rather narrow crack at the foot of the mount: the entrance to some sort of cavern. It was barely noticeable; I would have taken it for a simple fracture in the rock had Mrs Caroli not identified it.

'There,' she whispered, her eyes watering.

'Ye don't need to go any further,' McGray said, gently holding her arm.

'I do not *dare* go any further,' she replied, wrapping her shawl tighter around herself.

'McNair, look after the lady,' I told him and the constable nodded. 'We shan't be long . . . I hope.'

As we made to enter the cavern Mrs Caroli grabbed us by the arms and gabbled with a desperate voice: 'Do not harm him, *I beg you!* He's the only family I have left.'

McGray forced a smile as he patted her shoulder, his blue eyes all benevolence. 'We'll do our best not to,' he said, but I knew that he was only trying to comfort her.

I had to squeeze myself through the opening, but McGray had it much worse: he snorted and jerked for some time before his broad shoulders passed through.

Fortunately the narrow entrance gave way to a much wider tunnel. We both lit our respective gas lanterns and pointed the beams forwards, but the passage was too long and winding for its end to be visible.

'Ladies first,' McGray said, but I was too anxious to mind his idiotic humour. My hands were quivering in the cold cave as we descended, and the grim stories Mrs Caroli had told us kept playing tricks in my mind. At any moment I expected to see those five demonic eyes emerging from the darkness, yet there was nothing but silence. Every time I directed my lantern at a new nook in the rocks, the shadows trembled in a macabre dance, making my heart leap once and again. Every crack in the rocks was the claw of a new monster, and every eroded stone was the teasing face of a new fiend. My heart leaped again when we finally heard a soft noise. McGray halted and asked me to listen. We heard it again; the soft echoes of a distant dripping.

We moved on.

After a few yards we reached a bend in the tunnel and McGray unholstered his gun silently. I did the same, and just as we turned we found a most dreadful vision waiting for us: five eyes flashing right in front of us!

I screamed and jumped sideways, crashing against McGray and knocking his lantern from his hand. Out of pure reflex I pointed my gun at the horrendous face, expecting to be attacked there and then, but the eyes did not move; their vertical pupils stared incisively at me, glimmering under the beams of our lanterns.

My heart was still pounding when I realized what I was really looking at.

'It's a mask,' McGray whispered, picking up his lantern and drawing it closer to the object.

Nailed to the rock, it was the most intricate piece of carved rosewood I have ever seen. Grapevine leaves sprouted from the centre of the triangular mask, like those foliate heads sculpted in cathedrals. The borders of the leaves outlined three pairs of eye sockets, one of them purposely left empty. The other five sockets held eyes made of blown glass, each one of a different colour. The work was so detailed that I could even see streaks of coloured glass resembling fine veins around the vertical pupils.

The wooden leaves formed a ferocious frown, and combined with the intense stare of the glass eyes, the mask looked frighteningly alive.

'Wood carver, glass blower and violin player . . .' I murmured, enthralled.

'And murderer,' McGray concluded, resuming his way.

We walked past the mask and from that point on the temperature began to rise. The dripping sound also became clearer.

After a few steps we reached another bend, and as soon as McGray lit it we heard a soft, metallic sound.

McGray speeded up and we found that the bend opened into a large gallery.

By lantern light I first thought that I was looking at a plantation of straight, very thin trees, but McGray's nauseated gasp made me understand. I cannot describe the sheer horror I felt, for before my eyes lay one of the most disturbing spectacles I'd ever see: A jungle of human intestines, all hanging by hooks nailed to the ceiling and swinging like corpses on a gallows. Some of them were still dripping blood that formed ghastly pools on the ground. For a moment neither of us managed to move or utter a word.

McGray was the first one to step ahead.

'They're sorted in three lines,' he said, walking around the place with an inquisitive look. 'From the freshest to the oldest . . .'

I forced myself to take a deep breath. I expected the place to reek like a butcher's shop, but instead I perceived a strong smell of soap and oil, more like a tannery.

I saw McGray leaning over some shiny objects. Four long knives were displayed under the intestines, one in front of each line, and close to each of them there was a piece of paper bearing some scribble.

Like the mask, each knife was a true work of art: the handles were richly carved wood and the blades were made of sharpened glass.

They looked so beautiful yet so deadly, and I could only think of their advantages: a glass blade would remain sharp for much longer than a metal one.

McGray walked closer to the line with the oldest guts, which looked dry and shrunken – almost ready to become violin strings. He leaned over the respective knife, which had a mighty broad blade made of green glass, mottled with tiny yellow spots.

'The paper's just got a letter G on it,' McGray told me.

I looked over his shoulder and the first thing I noticed was that the blade was missing its tip.

'The G must stand for Guilleum Fontaine,' I said, 'and that is the knife he used to kill him. The missing piece of this blade ended up in Larry's foot.'

Nearby there was a stack of paper, soaked in blood. I had a close look and recognized the pages of the Devil's Trill Sonata.

'He used that score to wrap up the guts,' McGray said. 'Like newspaper from the butcher's!'

'Indeed, and I always thought that taking the score of that particular composition had some profound meaning . . .'

I shrugged and went to the next line of bowels. Those ones also looked shrunken, but some of them still had a revolting, slippery look. The note next to the knife showed a D.

'Danilo Caroli,' McGray said, and the hanging guts appeared all the more unsettling.

'Yes. Theodore was never part of Giacomo's plan. Do you think he killed him just so that the violin kept moving from hand to hand?'

'I cannae tell,' McGray said.

We moved on and found the blue knife I'd seen at Calton Hill, shining only inches from my face. As expected, the piece of paper showed an A.

'Alistair,' McGray said, and the very fresh, still bloody intestines proved it.

Next to the blade I saw a pair of tiny, glittering eyes. I first thought it was a rat, but then I realized that it was the wooden lion head that had adorned the Amati violin. McGray lifted it to examine it closely.

'So Ardglass was telling the truth,' I said. 'Giacomo *did* give him the violin! He must have sneaked in through the chimney and left it for him. And the stupid Ardglass thought he was looking at the Devil!'

'What an idiot to just take it!' McGray grunted. 'Typical Ardglass! He knew we were looking for this fiddle; he knew it had been stolen but he simply kept it and played it 'til it made him puke his guts out!'

I sighed. 'I cannot say I am too aggrieved . . .'

It was then chilling to find a fourth knife, lying by itself on the humid soil, no note attached yet. To me it looked like the most menacing one: the unusually long blade was dark red with black, tiger-like stripes. McGray lit the ceiling and we saw a line of empty hooks already nailed to the rock.

'He's prepared for the next one,' McGray gasped. 'I'd say he planned four killings from the very start.'

'Maybe, but then why four?' I whispered. 'Perhaps we can find something here that will tell us.'

We found a cheap violin, most likely an instrument the Carolis had given Giacomo to keep him happy. It lay on top of a pile of damp books, which spanned everything from history, theory of music and astronomy, to – of course – witchcraft and chemistry. There was a small volume made of scrap sheets neatly stitched together by hand. I leafed through it and found it full of childish scribbles. McGray drew his light closer and read aloud.

'*Blood! I hate blood! And how he squealed! Like one o' those slaughtered pigs* . . .' he turned a few pages. '*Scrape off* . . . *scrape off* . . . *scrape off the slimy stuff* . . .' McGray shivered. 'Keep that, Frey. That's evidence.'

I shoved the notebook in my breast pocket and we moved along. Close to the books there was a pile of empty bottles, all labelled as bed-bug killer.

'That explains the strong soapy smell,' I realized. 'It is here where he prepared the poison from common soap.'

In the farthest corner of the gallery we found a bundle of blankets forming an improvised bed. There was a section of intestine lying there. Someone had been scraping the mucous coating from it. There was a slimy mash of scraped tripe piled alongside the clean gut, and we also found a small disc of brass lying right next to it: *that* had been the metallic sound we'd heard but seconds ago.

'He was working here,' McGray whispered, 'using that disc to scrape the guts clean. He heard us coming and dropped it . . . so . . . he still . . .'

'Still must be around,' I mumbled, and then flashed my lantern about in mad movements, searching frantically. Again the shadows played tricks on my eyes and the wavering shapes projected by the intestines became an army of monsters.

'*Frey, stop it!*'

Right then one of the shadows came to life and threw itself onto me. I leaped, Nine-Nails shot twice and after a blurry glimpse of a hooded figure I felt two potent kicks to my arm and stomach. I dropped my gun and lantern, and then saw the black cloak dashing towards McGray.

He did not even have time to scream and I could not see more than a glimpse, for McGray's lantern smashed on the rocks and the cave fell into the thickest shadows. Suddenly all I had before my eyes was blackness. *Blackness!*

I was expecting to hear more turmoil, but all that followed was silence; the three of us had gone still in the pitch black cave.

After a moment of utter confusion I felt McGray's hand seizing my arm, and slowly pulling me to one side. We moved a few inches in utter silence and I understood what he wanted to do; we would move about quietly and pray for the beast not to find us.

Can Giacomo possibly see in the absolute darkness? I thought. *And how well?* Perhaps he could see us perfectly, as in summer daylight, and was only basking in our terrified, slow motions.

We heard a splash in the pools of blood and halted immediately, our hearts pounding.

Then only silence.

No sounds, no vision. For me, the universe had reduced to the pounding of my heart and McGray's hand gripping my arm.

Slowly, a terror began to grow in me. I could almost feel it like a solid mass swelling in my chest; the terror of not knowing when we were going to be attacked, or who would be wounded first, or where in my body I'd feel the first stab . . .

Gently, McGray pulled my arm and we moved another few steps. Not even when dissecting bodies at Oxford had I thought so carefully before moving.

There was another splash and we halted. Again, the deepest silence, and this time it felt like an eternity.

McGray tapped my arm with a finger. I still do not know how I managed to comprehend what he was trying to tell me: Giacomo could not see either!

He was hiding in the darkness, as cautiously as we were. And equally sightless.

He'd been mighty clever, though. He knew that he could not beat the two of us, so he had disarmed and blinded us before we could do anything.

I felt my lighter in my pocket. How tempting it was to ignite it and rush for my gun; or my lantern – I had dropped it but I'd not heard it shatter. However, my lighter would be like a beacon amidst such darkness, revealing our position long before I could reach for weapon.

Just when I thought that we would be waiting for ever, a coarse, venomous voice resounded throughout the cave. The words bounced on the walls in otherworldly echoes: '*I kill four . . .*'

It was an odd voice, its open vowels and the rolling 'r' undoubtedly Mediterranean, yet not entirely.

'*Want to know why?*' The question was asked in a mawkish tone that chilled my blood.

Neither of us replied. With that echo we could not tell where the voice had come from, but our adversary undoubtedly had a much finer ear.

'*Youse don't wanna know? But youse are too interested in me!*'

The voice was wicked indeed, and it had a childlike quality that made it even more terrifying. It was the kind of voice we dread in our infancy; those voices we think we hear in the darkness of our childhood bedrooms.

'*I a creepy crawly . . . everybody say to me . . . lock me away when visits come . . . but 'tis handy to be a creepy crawly . . . I see and hear everything! I go everywhere!*'

I heard the brushing of clothes dancing around us. The sound came and went from every direction.

'*Sure youse don't wanna know? Youse shy!*' The voice became a startling howl. '*Then I show youse!*'

Again the sound of brushing clothes, this time frantically, and then I heard a wooden echo; one I'd heard every time Elgie picked up his violin.

Low notes filled the cave. It was a frantic melody embellished with flashing trills; enthralling yet terrifying, like those tempestuous organ fugues by Bach.

Then silence.

A moment later there was second burst of notes. It was the same melody, but in a higher key and played twice as fast. Again it stopped abruptly, only to be resumed a third time in an even higher key and tempo. Then it stopped.

Just as I thought there could not be a higher pitch or a faster rhythm, the fourth outburst came, shrilling and maddening. It pierced my ears like nails scratching glass, yet part of me wanted to light up the cave and see those fingers pressing the strings in a crazy blur.

Thank goodness it stopped, but then Giacomo's voice resounded again.

'*Youse can't guess? Stupid fools. Then I do it!*'

I saw a tiny flame igniting on the other side of the gallery. It was only a match, but to my eyes it looked as bright as a roaring fire. I caught a glimpse of the five-eyed mask and the red knife. He was standing by the entrance to a narrow passage. *'I take knife. I kill tonight . . .'*

McGray ran towards the light, shooting compulsively, as the creature dropped the match and ran away. Using my lighter I found my gas lantern intact, but as soon as I lit it Nine-Nails snatched it and went after Giacomo.

I shouted, *'It's a trap! McGray!'* but he would not listen; he was already entering the passage. I had no time to think so I yelled the first thing that came to my head: *'Killing yourself won't bring your sister back!'*

McGray halted. I had touched his most sensitive nerve.

He stood still for a moment . . . then panted and grunted in a terrible inner struggle. God knows how many thoughts haunted him in those brief seconds . . . and then he thrust himself forward recklessly.

'Bloody, stubborn Scot!' I yelled, running after him. Two would stand more chance than one.

By then McGray had run a good stretch, carrying our only remaining light. I had to follow him blindly, running hysterically and stumbling among the rocks until I finally found the gleam of the lantern.

'Where is he?' I asked, but McGray was motionless; in front of him the passage branched in three directions.

'I think I lost –'

McGray leaped forwards as soon as he saw a faint gleam in the central tunnel. Again we ran madly, this time along a snaking, claustrophobic tunnel that seemed to stretch for ever.

The terrifying voice was gabbling madly, the echoes bouncing across the cave: '*Come on! I show youse! Youse led me to it, now I lead youse!*'

I do not know how far we ran, but McGray stopped dead all of a sudden. I crashed against him and we almost fell into a wide channel that opened before us.

It was a perfectly round tunnel: lined with bricks, three yards wide, with a gush of stinking water running through it.

'The cave's connected to the sewerage,' McGray spluttered. 'That's how he brought Caroli's –'

By then McGray was already jumping into the murky waters. He'd seen the creature.

'Christ, why when I am wearing fine clothes?' I moaned, jumping right behind him.

I sank in the brown stream up to my thighs, wincing at the foul stench. I tried to run but my overcoat dragged me backwards like an anchor. I saw McGray getting rid of his own coat and I had to do the same (even then, a part of my brain regretted the loss of my fur-trimmed garment).

'I'm losing him!' McGray shouted, lighting the channel ahead of us. The black figure was swimming merrily against the current while we painfully kicked and splashed in the sludge.

'He doesn't want to get away, he wants us to follow him,' I grunted, feeling my legs burning. The stream was a constant onslaught and very soon we were panting.

I will never know how I managed to keep on among the squealing rats and the dreadful stench. I envied McGray: he just clenched his lantern and progressed stoically.

From time to time the hooded head turned back to

catch a glimpse of us, the five eyes gleaming under the lantern's beam. A couple of times McGray was tempted to shoot it, but decided to save the bullets until he had a closer target.

We lost sight of him after he turned a corner in the sewer. We had lagged behind quite a gap so it took us a worryingly long time to reach that point. When we turned we found the wide channel going on indefinitely; even the lantern's white beam could not reach its end. Right next to us we found the mouth of some side pipe that discharged a scanty flow into the main channel.

There was nobody around.

'Did he go that way?' Nine-Nails asked desperately, pointing at the inlet pipe. 'Or did he go straight? *What did he do?*'

'Could have been either,' I said. 'We should separate. You go straight and I —'

'Nae. We need to fight him together. He can take one of us, but not two.'

McGray looked at both channels, waving the lantern in frustration. 'Well, I can play his game too.' Then he hollered, '*Come on!* Come on, Giacomo! Yer aunty told us everything about ye!'

There was no reply. McGray shouted louder. 'She told us how yer mother kept ye locked with the hounds when ye were a wee child! How on her deathbed she made yer aunt swear she'd never show ye to the world!'

We listened intently, but there was nothing besides the dull sound of the waters.

'We ken it's been difficult for ye!' McGray shouted. 'But we can help ye! Even if ye look the way ye —'

'*I can help you to Hell!*'

It was not a yell but a bitter, scornful whisper. We barely heard it and instantly rushed into the side channel. We heard some splashing ahead; frantic steps not too far away.

'Aye, ye betrayed yerself, laddie!' McGray said.

We ran through so many bends and bifurcations that I completely lost track of our way. I remembered the mess of dotted lines I'd seen on the city plans; we were somewhere underneath the Old Town.

Without the current coming against us we gained ground swiftly; we could hear Giacomo's steps ever more clearly, and even his panting breath.

'Come on, laddie! Yer in over yer head!'

It was Giacomo's turn to cackle. '*I think otherwise . . .*'

We made it to another wide channel, and as we entered we saw the edge of Giacomo's cloak hurrying into a very narrow side duct.

McGray pushed me forward. 'Go! I won't fit in there!'

The pipe ascended to the street; the light of a lamp lit Giacomo as he crawled upwards.

I did my best to follow but the duct was wet and slippery, and almost as soon as I jumped upon it I dropped my gun and slid all the way back.

McGray pushed me upwards as if I were a puppet. This time I dug my very nails into the bricks, feeling myself slide down while the dark cloak moved agilely towards the open drain.

Roaring and thrashing my legs, I managed to push myself upwards, but it was too late: I felt sick when I saw Giacomo contorting in an unthinkable way, almost squeezing himself as if he had no bones, and passing through the narrow drain towards the streets.

Out of pure rage I reached the drain and stretched my arm out of the sewers; a feeble attempt to reach the bastard. No normal adult could get through that opening.

Giacomo cackled again. I could see the eyes of his mask and the red knife reflecting the light of the street lamps. He kneeled by the drain and made a stab at me, so I had to retreat.

He whispered as eerily as before: '*Four murders. One for each string . . .*'

'McGray, toss me the gun!'

'*You know what the letters mean? The wee letters on the paper?*'

McGray was throwing both weapons but I could not seize them without falling down.

'The names of the people you have killed,' I snorted.

Again Giacomo laughed: '*You know nothing of music. Four strings on a violin . . . a* quinta *of notes between each string . . .*'

'What the Hell?'

He spoke slowly, as if talking to a retarded man. '*The lowest string, where it all begins. String of G . . . G for Guilleum.*'

'Gui – Guilleum?'

'*Then five notes higher, the string of D, Danilo, my uncle the idiot . . . then string of A, the fat man Alistair . . . then I have problems to find next string. Can you tell me what note follows?*'

My heart went ice cold.

'*Oh, I see you know! And you know well: string of E, which of course is . . .*'

'Elgie.'

I experienced a panic I had never felt before; a wave tearing through my chest, as the memory of a gypsy's whisper rushed into my head: *You're about to lose your most beloved one.*

Giacomo cackled cruelly and again spoke in his terrifying, sly tone. '*I spy youse from the chimneys, I hear him play. I find him fit for me . . . Now I get youse lost down there. No way youse get out in time to stop me . . . I win! I get my fiddle set for Satan!*'

And then I saw him run maniacally down the street.

34

Defeated, I slid down the pipe, my entire body shaking. My legs sank in the murky waters and McGray had to pull me up.

'Yer brother's still in the New Club?'

A fit took hold of me. 'Yes, but how do we get out? *How-do-we-get-out?* We'll never be –'

'Calm down, Frey! We just need to find a manhole –'

'*Oh, do we?*' I shrieked. 'And how are we going to find it in this fucking mess?'

'Yer forgetting I spent hours looking at those plans! I may remember. Now tell me: what did ye see up there? Any landmark ye recognized.'

'N-no, I –'

'Then get up there again and tell me!'

I did so at once, this time clinging with all my strength. 'We are right under the Royal Mile . . .'

'All right. Whereabouts?'

'Erm . . . I see a church. It looks funny . . . curved outline and a tiny portico.'

'Canongate Church,' McGray said at once. 'I think I remember one main pipe running along High Street . . . and . . .'

Then I lost my temper. 'How are you possibly going to remember a single spot you saw days ago on a five-foot-long piece of paper?'

'Och, shut it and let me think!'

McGray then covered his face with both hands, mumbling to himself.

I paced around frenetically, my nerves tumbling down. How could I have been so stupid? Following Nine-Nails into that blasted race had been my worst choice. And while he tried to remember, that murderer – that *monster* – was running entire blocks towards my youngest brother! The dreadful image of those hanging bowels made me shudder again, and I could not repress an anguished roar.

A burning rage followed. I was about to punch McGray in the face but right then he opened his eyes in exhilaration.

'I'm so stupid! *Of course!*'

'Did you remember?'

'Aye, but not from the plans . . . There's a huge manhole right in front o' the Ensign Ewart pub! So if this is the Mile's main pipe and Canongate Church is right there . . . *Follow me!*'

I ran after McGray in an anguished sprint until we found a wider drain that let in the yellow light of the street's lampposts.

We both pushed the manhole plate, grunting and cursing. I did not expect the blasted thing to be so heavy! For a frightening moment it would not move, but then its rusty hinges squeaked and, painfully, we managed to push it aside. The aperture was barely wide enough to let me through.

'I'll have to find another way,' McGray said, pushing me ahead.

I jumped out of the sewer and as I stood up McGray

howled something I could not catch. Only after having run halfway down the street did I realize he'd told me to take a gun, but it was too late to return now. I had no time to ponder my options; I set my mind on getting to the New Club and protecting my brother, trying not to think that it might be already too late.

Suddenly I was running at full speed, my legs about to collapse, ignoring puddles and passing carriages, but the world still seemed to move more slowly than ever. I descended through the closes of Castle Rock, crossed Princes Street Gardens, passing right next to the deserted art gallery, and almost lost my balance when the Georgian façade of the New Club finally emerged in front of me. I was so desperate I crossed Princes Road without even looking – I can only tell that there were no carts passing by because I made it to the entrance in one piece.

I stormed through the lobby, showing my credentials, and shouted at the sleepy clerk to fetch as many guards as he could. Then I darted upstairs and, after what had felt like an eternity, arrived at Elgie's corridor.

My heart skipped a beat when I saw that the door to his room was ajar. I kicked it open, and then . . .

The room was empty, dimly lit by a weak fire and a lonely gas lamp.

It became hard to breathe; a suffocating pressure on my chest . . .

'What is it?'

I cannot describe the relief I felt when Elgie's head peered at me from behind an armchair. I ran towards him, pulled his slender body to me and squeezed him in the tightest embrace.

'Good Lord, Ian, you stink!' I could not expect warmer words from him.

'Oh, shush! I need to get you out of –'

I turned around and a monstrous vision made us both scream.

Giacomo had arrived, the five glassy eyes of his mask gleaming as he slithered out of the fireplace. The edge of his cloak was ablaze but he carelessly extinguished it with his bare hand. He seemed shapeless, and bending like a snake he hurried into the room and stood right before the door. We heard the ghastly crack of bones as he moved his dislocated shoulders back into place.

I stepped in front of my brother and together we retreated to the very back of the room. 'If you want him you will have to get me first!'

Elgie crouched behind me, trembling uncontrollably, and I knew that my words were empty. I had no weapon of any kind and Giacomo knew it. He cackled as he produced the long knife.

I gulped as the terrible truth hit me: we would die there and then. The face of that five-eyed demon would be the last thing I'd ever see . . .

'*Come on!*' I roared in a last act of bravado. 'Come and get this sack of bones! He doesn't have enough gut to give you half a string!'

I saw the shiny blade rising, so sharp it would slice us effortlessly. Giacomo was hissing like an angry bull.

Then a roar and a deafening blast . . . An explosion of blood spilt all over my face and then I saw the shiny blade flying away.

Giacomo's hand had been shot clean through and he

fell sideways, roaring like the beast he'd become. I saw a tall figure by the doorframe and instantly recognized the square shoulders of Nine-Nails McGray, holding a gun in each hand.

The knife fell to the floor and McGray smashed it with his boot, pieces of red glass ejected all around. Giacomo tried to rise and attack him, but McGray hit him in the head with a gun's butt. The misshapen devil fell unconscious onto the floor.

It had all happened so quickly . . . it had been barely a blink. After the thump on the carpet we fell into deep silence, our minds struggling to take in what we'd just seen. The first voice I heard was Elgie's.

'What the Hell is that?'

McGray leaned over Giacomo to pull off the hood and mask. I was astonished by how childlike he looked. Mrs Caroli had implied his young age, but I did not fully realize it until I saw his very sparse beard and thick locks of dark hair.

'He's a fiddler,' McGray told Elgie. 'Around yer age, laddie.'

At last I managed to take a deep breath, and exhaling felt like unloading the weight of the world off my shoulders.

It was all over.

All we had left to do was to face Campbell and explain everything.

35

Campbell's office looked as compulsively neat as always, and the white snow that could be seen through the window made the room appear even brighter. As a result, the mighty bruise McGray had given him right in the eye stuck out like a raw steak on an immaculate china plate.

No wonder he did not want Nine-Nails around for the time being.

'Will you please summarize your report, Frey?' he said, leafing distractedly through the thin file.

'By all means,' I said, thinking that reading a four-page report was evidently beyond the man's attention span – the fact that I'd spent hours questioning Lorena Caroli for the finer details was obviously irrelevant to him. 'Basically, it all began seventeen years ago, when Lucía Zangrando – Mrs Caroli's sister – sadly gave birth to an awfully deformed child, who she named Giacomo. I am not familiar with the young man's condition – it is something I have never seen before – but it appears to be some sort of bone disorder that runs in their family; Mrs Caroli, for instance, has an unusually advanced case of arthritis for a woman of her age, and she told us that her mother and sister showed similar symptoms.

'Lucía Zangrando and her husband were terribly embarrassed by the child – there were already rumours of the family being cursed with this bone condition, and apparently Giacomo was an extreme case. However, they never gathered the courage to get rid of him. It is not rare that such children are abandoned or sent away as circus freaks, so they decided to simply keep him hidden. Giacomo, nevertheless, turned out to be an incredibly intelligent creature, and the boy easily mastered music, mask carving and glass blowing; all those Venetian arts.

'Both of his parents passed away almost simultaneously, Lucía only a few months after her husband. On her deathbed she made her sister swear that she would take care of the boy, regardless of his abnormality, and that she would also keep him hidden . . . In Mrs Caroli's words, her sister dreaded the idea of the world knowing that her womb had produced such a child. Lorena married Danilo Caroli, who eventually was invited to teach in Scotland, so Giacomo was brought along to Edinburgh – locked in a box, along with the hounds.

'Mrs Caroli and her husband kept him hidden, albeit not as strictly as his late parents would have liked: they gave him a proper bedroom, dined with him, and only locked him away with the dogs when they had visitors. Mrs Caroli taught him how to read and write, and she would allow him to wander the town at night, when nobody could see him. She even arranged for her best friend in Edinburgh to teach him classical violin.'

'Fontaine,' Campbell said.

'Yes, and thus he signed his death sentence. Mr Fontaine, being half French himself, understood perfectly the situation of the Carolis: they were new to Scotland, foreign-looking and with unfamiliar habits – not to mention Lorena's illness – so it was hard for them to make close acquaintances. They became so attached to the man that they decided to trust him with their darkest secret. I have come to understand that Fontaine had the most compassionate nature, yet he was childless, so he embraced the boy and agreed to train him in secret. For his playing, Giacomo's deformity became an advantage: as I was unfortunate enough to witness, the boy has remarkably long fingers and he can disjoint them at will, which gives him dexterity unthinkable for a normal person. He can also disjoint his shoulders and pelvis, which enabled him to crawl through the narrowest passages; he would leave the Carolis' home at night and then make his way discreetly through the chimney into Fontaine's study. Giacomo soon mastered the classical pieces.'

'And then something went wrong, I presume.'

'Yes, sir. According to Mrs Caroli, Giacomo became irascible and rebellious. The Carolis never quite understood why, even though the reasons are downright obvious: The boy must, *must* have been conscious of his own talents, so the constant seclusion became a torture, as his own notes testify. The worst that can be done to an eager mind is to keep it locked up; it becomes restless and twisted. In Giacomo's case, I believe it was all worsened by the natural swings of adolescence.

'Even though nobody ever knew about Fontaine's secret student, his presence did not pass entirely unnoticed to the people around him. His housekeeper, an old woman nicknamed Goodwife Hill, declared that during an odd period, around three years ago, Fontaine's playing became rather sloppy and noticeably below his usual standard. What she was hearing was actually Giacomo's first attempts at classical pieces. The woman also told us that Fontaine would lock himself in his studio, even taking all the spare keys with him – which was exactly what he did on the night of his death.

'Fontaine's luthier – one Joe Fiddler – also gave account of Fontaine's strange behaviour: one of his favourite violins suddenly broke from heavy use; something that had never happened to the man's instruments. That was the violin that Giacomo would borrow from Fontaine, and he himself carved the unusual lion head to compensate for his over-zealousness.'

'Oh, yes. That infamous "cursed" violin.'

'I must admit that the little violin has enough history to make one's mind wonder. Poor Giacomo, yearning to get out of his shed and show his talents to the world, fed his fantasies on these stories: the Devil's Trill Sonata, Paganini's dealings with Satan, violin strings made out of human gut . . . He intended to devote his soul to the Devil, most likely to create his own Devil's Sonata and thus become the best composer in history. In order to do that, he fashioned a macabre plan, somewhat detailed in his notes: he would use the bodies – and souls – of four virtuosos, each one giving him a string to play his new piece. And he managed to find players whose Christian names matched with the string that would come from their bodies: Guilleum for the string that would be tuned to G, Danilo for the D string, then Alistair and . . . Elgie . . .'

I gulped and saw that Campbell was nodding, his face showing empathy for once.

'It seems that Giacomo also killed following the musical scale in ascending order, and only killed people who had played the violin in life. Whether this first was coincidence or part of his ritual, we cannot tell; the second, however, was most definitely deliberate.'

'Clever soul . . .' Campbell muttered.

'Indeed. He knew that after Fontaine died the violin would go to Theodore Wood, and that if Wood died the violin would go to the Carolis, his own household, so Wood had to be taken out of the way, even though he was not part of the boy's twisted sequence.'

'And he did that in a very creative way, Frey.'

'Genius, I would say: he *poisoned* the violin after killing Fontaine, and he managed to do it in a way that would only harm someone who played that violin for a very long time, not someone who merely happened to touch it or hold it. Theodore's death really confused us since it completely departed from the pattern.'

'Now tell me about Caroli.'

'The night of Theodore's funeral was also the moment when Giacomo escaped from Mrs Caroli; she went into labour and could not lock him in the shed, so the boy decided to seize the violin – too easy, since it was in his own home – and then he set off to get the *material* for his second string.' I sighed; his was the death I regretted the most. 'I believe that Mr Caroli was a potential victim from the very beginning: an obvious D and also a figure of authority Giacomo did not particularly like. From his notes I gather that he somewhat recognized the power of his relatives, but he saw Caroli as an intruder.'

'And what about the butchery he committed on Calton Hill?'

'Oh, that was Giacomo's great mistake. The death of

394

Ardglass was unexpected for him – and for us all. I believe he intended to murder Ardglass that very night, so he would have been hiding in the chimneys, spying; it must have been then when he heard my brother play. Since Ardglass was killed by the cart, Giacomo risked all to get to his corpse before the bowels decayed. Desecrating his grave was a truly bold crime to commit so close to Calton Jail . . . and then running straight towards the City Chambers!'

'It was very lucky that you and McGray were in the cemetery that very night looking for – will-o'-the-wisps, you mentioned?' Campbell said that in a monotone, his eyes combing those lines in the report.

'Very lucky indeed,' I said shamelessly. I was sure he knew what had really taken us there. 'As you know, it was the red mark on Alistair's neck that led us to the poisoned chinrest . . . and from there to Mrs Caroli, who had commissioned it especially for her nephew. The poor lady told us that she suspected something untoward was going on, but did not fully realize it until we took the evidence to her.'

'Or so she claimed,' said Campbell.

'We will never be able to tell how much Mrs Caroli suspected; however, I would give her the benefit of the doubt. The secrecy in which we kept Fontaine's death played in Giacomo's favour; without knowing the particulars, it *is* possible that she simply did not make the connection.'

Campbell nodded slowly. 'I have one last question, Frey. McGray kept babbling nonsense about the Devil's five eyes and the satanic ritual that Giacomo would practise on his victims.'

'That is correct.'

'Where did Giacomo learn all that gibberish?'

'We can only guess that he had secret friends even the Carolis would not know about. A gloomy, deformed chap wandering at night would be likely to catch the eye of those interested in the occult. At the end of my report I do recommend a further investigation.'

Campbell turned the pages hastily. 'Why, you have a suspect already! Some . . . "Madame Katerina".'

'The evidence is only circumstantial, but yes. That woman knew things nobody else could have known; she referred to the murderer as an "encaged genius"; the cart that killed Ardglass happened to be driven by one of her minions, and later on she foresaw my brother's being in peril. Besides, McGray repeatedly revealed vital information to her.'

'What is Inspector McGray's view on her?'

'Oh, he does not know I included that in the report. He believes the woman is *gifted* and seems to utterly trust her. Personally, I believe that her actual gift is her craftiness.'

Campbell nodded. 'Good. We shall keep a close eye on her.' He closed the file. 'You may go, Frey. Now it is up to us to decide your future.'

It was snowing hard over Edinburgh's castle.

Seated on a sheltered bench, I watched how its roofs and the side of the dead volcano were being slowly painted white. Soon the dark branches of the bare trees were the only hint of colour in Princes Street Gardens.

I recalled that not so long ago those gardens had been under water; North Loch, they used to call it. Looking at the castle, I could only imagine what a staggering view it must have been, the aged brown walls and the craggy rocks of the mount reflected on the quiet waters of a lake.

I wrapped up tighter in my coat before checking the time again. Sir Charles Warren was late for our meeting and I was freezing.

After a rather long wait I saw the man swiftly descending the stairs that led from Princes Street to the sunken gardens. He too was freezing, and was probably having a harder time than me, for his coat seemed quite thin for the time of the year. I instantly recognized his scant hair and broad moustache, as white as the snow around us.

He sat next to me and greeted me with a firm handshake – a decided show of emotion from a man like him.

'You have been very busy, Frey.'

'I take it you read my report.'

'I did, and Lord Salisbury was delighted to have it in his hands. Outstanding piece of work, Frey. Even that incident in the cemetery did you good. Your findings were perfectly timed to refute the papers' stupid theories.'

'Did you hear about our . . . quarrel with Superintendent Campbell?'

'We did! I should not tell you this, but some officers now murmur that he bruises like a peach . . .' He saw I was about to smile. 'Do not take this so humorously, Frey! It was a most dishonourable display. However, all things considered, it proved useful to have an informant over here, and you and McGray seem to complement one another, in your respective skills, quite well. The prime minister spoke to Monro and ordered him to intervene. He sent Campbell a strong letter asking him to overlook his differences with you and McGray. You both shall keep your little subdivision.'

Those words came along with a gust of wind. The snowflakes that hit my face were just as icy as that news.

'Pa– pardon me? *Our* subdivision? Does that mean that I must remain stranded here with the demented Nine-Nails McGray? I thought that Lord Salisbury would have the morals to reinstate me in London!'

Sir Charles sighed. 'I did try to persuade him, but he said that at this time you are more useful to the CID up here than in London. He finds it very convenient to have a pair of good agents he can move around without arousing suspicions. I should not tell you this either, but I doubt that mock Rippers are the only cases the prime minister has in mind for you.'

I felt my face reddening in fury. 'So will I not be reinstated?'

'Well . . . no. Not yet, at least.'

There were so many things I wanted to say but nothing came out; I was too drained to fight back, and I also knew that no argument could help my case. I simply looked away, crestfallen. Sir Charles patted my shoulder as he spoke rather soothingly.

'Don't distress yourself, Frey. I have always believed that this sort of thing happens for the best.' He heard my wry chuckle. 'Besides, I do not see why you wish to return to London so soon, given the very inopportune engagement of your brother.'

I raised my head, frowning. 'I beg your pardon?'

'Come, Frey. Your eldest brother marrying your former fiancée must be far from agreeable . . .'

'*What!*' I shouted, jumping to my feet and yelling in the most barbaric manner. 'Laurence and Eugenia! *Bu-but – How? When?*'

Sir Charles blushed intensely, his old phlegm offended by my coarse exhibition. I cleared my throat and rearranged my collar, trying to appear self-possessed – a pointless effort, given my red face and gushes of steaming breath.

'Had you not been informed?' he said with more incredulity than embarrassment. 'I thought that – well – having your youngest brother in Edinburgh . . . you would know by now.'

I do not recall his precise words after that, but he said that the new engagement had been announced only a few days after my departure. Then he excused himself and walked away as soon as decorum allowed, leaving me in a temper as bitter as the winter cold. I wandered in the gardens for a while, looking for a quiet spot, and an area of frosted wilderness was the unfortunate recipient of my wrath. Once I was sure nobody was looking, I abandoned myself to downright savagery, thrashing and kicking and stamping on leaves, branches and acorns, as I spluttered the foulest profanities in my repertoire.

Lack of breath was the only thing that stopped me, and I rested my hands on my knees, panting and oblivious to the snowflakes fluttering around me. I then realized that I had one spectator: a black cat that stared at me with bewildered green eyes. Somehow, it made me feel more embarrassed than if I had been observed by Queen Victoria herself.

I walked back to McGray's house thinking that

399

Christmas was approaching, and with it my family's annual deer stalking in Gloucestershire. Far from looking forward to it, I could only wonder whether Laurence would have the nerve to invite Eugenia and the Ferrars to my uncle's estate. A Christmas gathering, I knew too well, was a perfect opportunity to celebrate a new engagement.

'At least we will be hunting,' I told myself. 'I could always claim it was a stray bullet . . .'

Epilogue

McGray was up very early that morning – not that he'd been sleeping much, anyway. When I walked into the breakfast parlour I found he had almost finished eating and was chatting merrily with Joan.

She had prepared whisky fudge, toffee and other sweets, and while I had breakfast she arranged them prettily in small pouches that she tied with ribbon. George brought some fresh white roses from the florist, and as soon as he saw Joan's wrappings he remarked how sissy they looked. Joan retorted with her vulgar wit and I shuddered to think how they must bask in their rough love. I still had not told McGray about the horrid sight of our servants in flagrante delicto.

McGray and I left them arguing at ease and went to get our horses. Larry had already prepared the mounts and we found him feeding Rye and Philippa with a bucket of oats. The boy's eye had been healing speedily during the last couple of days, and Joan had scrubbed almost all the soot off his face. I was glad his parents had still not inquired after him; I would hate it to see him go back to that abusive home.

We set off and our first stop was the Caledonian Railway Station. We found Elgie on the first-class platform, watching as his luggage was loaded.

'Why on earth would you buy a bloody bagpipe?' I

cried when I saw the offending instrument protruding from one of the trunks.

'I might give it a try,' Elgie said. 'I will be rehearsing day and night with the orchestra in the coming months, so I'd better let the violin rest until the New Year.'

'Well,' I snorted, 'if you want to play something that sounds like the cry of a cat being castrated –'

'Hey!' McGray protested. 'Say something like that again and I'll make a bagpipe out o' yer Londoner's bowel!' Then McGray noticed that the destination of my brother's train was Bristol. 'Ye not going to London, laddie?'

'No. I have only a short leave,' explained Elgie, 'so I will go directly to my uncle's Gloucestershire estate. It is almost Christmas time and we always hunt with him. I hope you let my brother come . . . for a couple of days, at least.'

'*You hope he lets me!* What do you mean by that?' I grunted.

'Mr McGray is your superior, is he not?'

I stammered for a moment, indignant. 'Just . . . go away!'

Elgie shook hands with McGray and hopped into the carriage. He grinned and waved goodbye, and as the train took him away I envied him a little: young, untroubled and spirited. I shuddered when I thought how close I'd been to losing him. We then set off to the Royal Lunatic Asylum. There was still some paperwork we needed to complete regarding Giacomo, and McGray, as usual, would take the chance to visit Pansy.

Dr Clouston was waiting for us, and as soon as we had dealt with the paperwork he led us to the asylum's wide lawns. He pointed at a teenager guarded by two orderlies, and we instantly recognized Giacomo's odd figure: the boy was seated on a bench with his legs tangled in an impossible lotus position.

We looked at him for a while before saying anything. It was hard to believe that such a young man had committed those gruesome crimes: dressed in a thick robe, curly black hair framing his rounded cheeks, he looked his tender age – seventeen. He was absorbed in a piece of wet clay, his very long fingers shaping it like a five-eyed mask. His right hand – the one McGray had shot – was still bandaged, but it did not seem to bother him at all.

'Givin' the laddie some fresh air?' McGray said.

'Yes,' Clouston replied. 'I still don't know how to approach him, but I definitely won't keep him locked in his room; confinement is precisely what turned him into . . . this.'

'And keeping him occupied,' I added, pointing at the clay.

'I want to keep his mind from wandering, yes. Besides, he has not said a word since you brought him here, and the arts are the clearest form of communication. Of course, we can't give him a violin – that would only reinforce his delusions – and for obvious reasons I will not give him sharp tools to carve wood. I considered allowing him to paint, but God knows what sort of poisons he could prepare with all those chemicals . . . So for now he will have to make do with clay.'

'Ye heard the news about Mrs Caroli?' McGray asked.

'That she is leaving Scotland? Yes. She is going to her father's old house in Venice, I believe. One of her servants came yesterday with a letter from her. The woman will be sending a handsome stipend to keep this fellow well treated.'

I let out a long sigh. 'Poor Mrs Caroli . . .'

Clouston dropped his notepad out of sheer indignation. '*Poor Mrs Caroli!* The worst crime here was committed by that bloody woman! She kept this creature in hiding only because he looks different. Imagine if he'd had the chance to grow like a normal child; the wonders he could have contributed to music, to art, maybe even to science! And that lady cannot even be prosecuted because Giacomo is still underage and thus has no legal rights!' He leaned to pick up the pad, an apologetic look in his face. 'Excuse my outburst. I simply –'

Just then a screeching madman ran past us – I dodged him with a swift movement, for I had lost too many good suits already. Clouston had to join the orderlies in their chase and left us behind without having the chance to say a proper farewell. What a dedicated man, old Dr Clouston.

I shook my head and turned to leave, but then I noticed that McGray was looking at Giacomo with the most melancholic expression He was touching the stump of his fourth finger with the same hand's thumb.

'No demon, just a boy,' he sighed, looking weary. 'Ye must be pleased, laddie.'

In a way I was, but McGray seemed so dispirited that I preferred not to mention it.

'I am sorry you did not find what you expected,' I said . . . and I was honest.

'I ken I was reckless with this case. I mean, I'm always

reckless, but I think I overdid it this time . . . I should've never given the fiddle to the Carolis . . .'

'Listen, I stated it in my report and I am telling you: I do not believe we could have avoided Caroli's death. We practically put the violin in Giacomo's hands, but that was probably our luckiest move; had we not found the violin in Ardglass's hands, we would probably be mourning my brother now, still without clues.' Again I meant every word, but it did not seem to cheer McGray up.

'I'm glad I helped Elgie,' McGray said. Then he let out the most tired sigh I'd heard from him. 'When my folks died, and this . . .' He showed his mutilated hand. 'When this happened, I saw someone . . . someone like him, Frey,' he looked intently at Giacomo. 'I saw someone like him crawling in the room, when my parents' bodies were still lying there and my sister had gone berserk. I always thought that it had been a demon. Until now, I'd never thought it might've been something else . . .'

'Does that mean that you no longer believe in all this "odd and ghostly" absurdity?'

McGray smiled. 'Nae. It means that now I have wider possibilities in mind. Ye should try that too, lassie.'

I clicked my tongue as I saw him walk away, carrying the pouches of fudge.

'Take the day off, dandy. Ye deserve it.'

I shook my head as I saw McGray walking into the asylum. As soon as I lost sight of him I made my way to the entrance. The patient was still running about the gardens and I'd had too many unpleasant surprises in the last weeks.

I looked back and glimpsed Nine-Nails and Pansy

through one of the upper windows. Despite the distance it was a heartbreaking sight: McGray lovingly pulling strands of dark hair off his sister's face, then sitting next to her and narrating the events of the last few days in utter detail. I saw him placing the pouches of sweets next to her and waving his arms excitedly as he spoke, his face lightened with a grin.

There is something peculiar about McGray's face; you look at him from one angle and he seems lively, careless . . . even childlike. Then he shifts his head, or wrinkles his nose, or adopts a weary gesture, and you can see how the strains of life have lined him.

Now I understand him. He needs to hunt the spooks, to go after the odd and ghostly stories and believe they are real . . . He needs something to fight for and to make him feel that his life still has some purpose. Perhaps that is precisely what has kept *him* from madness.

Perhaps that is also why I need the CID.

I shook my head, trying to rid it of such thoughts, and asked the asylum clerks to bring my mount. As I waited I noticed that the weather was dry and sunny, despite being the first days of December.

The bright blue sky and the cool air were like an invitation to live; it seemed a perfect moment to gaze at the castle while having a good cigar in the New Club, or to wander among the Georgian mansions, or to finally climb Calton Hill and have a proper view of Edinburgh with neither the fog nor the ghosts armed with daggers.

'No need to hurry, Ian,' I told myself while riding along the snowy street. 'It looks like you will be stuck in this town for a good while . . .'